PRAISE FOR *ROLA*

"How I rooted for Roland to fin ... he surprised me by becoming est Brothers series. To quote him: *You can't act on your ... just because you love someone.* Therein lie the strength and beauty of the story message. Sometimes, like some of the characters in *Roland West, Outcast*, young people believe that their feelings justify their actions. The results can be harmful to themselves or to the ones they love. Both Roland and Peter prove what pure love can be. And they are put to the test in defending their faith and demonstrating it, in spite of strong criticism, while solving a mystery and righting a wrong committed against a new girl at their school. I highly recommend this novel to young people. Or anyone."

~ **Cynthia T. Toney, author of *The Other Side of Freedom*, 2018 Catholic Press Association Book Award winner**

"In this story, Linden touches upon issues that are prevalent in our society, and she captures them with God's truth and compassion. Struggling as Christians in a world that is so focused on selfish desires, *Outcast* reminds us that we should always stand up for what's right, regardless of what the mass tries to push us to believe. *Outcast* is a fun, emotional roller-coaster, with realistic characters and a lot of suspense."

~ **T. M. Gaouette, author of the *Faith & Kung Fu* series**

"Roland West, Outcast is both entertaining and timely! Theresa Linden is at her best in capturing Roland's shy reluctance and Peter's awkward infatuation. A well-written book for Catholic teens that addresses the social pressure to kowtow to shifting notions of right and wrong (particularly in regard to same-sex attraction) is long overdue. If you've ever been silent when you should've spoken up, if your beliefs have ever been mischaracterized or misunderstood, if you want to get along without compromising your conscience, then *Roland West, Outcast* is for you."

~ **Carolyn Astfalk, author of coming-of-age romance *Rightfully Ours***

"A courageous, compassionate (and, believe it or not, fun!) story about a topic many of us would prefer to ignore: Same-Sex Attraction and our duty as Catholics to stand up for God's immutable laws, even when to do so is painful. If you're a teen facing this situation, or know someone who is, you need to read this newest novel in Theresa Linden's award-winning *West Brothers Series*. This story is difficult to put down and a brilliant handling of a tough subject!"
~ **Susan Peek, author of bestseller *Saint Magnus the Last Viking***

"This book runs parallel to many events in the book *Standing Strong*. But we see different aspects of those events. Roland is stuck in a hard place. He is reserved but is pushed to join a new group trying to counter intolerance. But soon he feels like any view but his is acceptable. Linden handles these elements in a masterful way. And they are questions and attitudes that could be taken from the headlines of almost any paper today. An excellent read for teens, and for us older folks that just love a great read!"
~ **Steven R. McEvoy, Book Reviews & More**

BOOKS BY THERESA LINDEN

CHASING LIBERTY TRILOGY
Chasing Liberty
Testing Liberty
Fight for Liberty

WEST BROTHERS SERIES
Roland West, Loner
Life-Changing Love
Battle for His Soul
Standing Strong
Roland West, Outcast

ADULT FICTION
Anyone but Him
Tortured Soul

SHORT STORIES
"Bound to Find Freedom"
"A Symbol of Hope"
"A Battle for the Faith"
"Made for Love" (in the anthology *Image and Likeness:*
Literary Reflections on the Theology of the Body)
"Full Reversal" (in the anthology *Image and Likeness:*
Literary Reflections on the Theology of the Body)
"The Portrait of the Fire Starters"
(in the anthology *Secrets: Visible and Invisible*)

ROLAND WEST, OUTCAST

Theresa Linden

SILVER FIRE
PUBLISHING

http://theresalinden.com
Library of Congress Control Number: 2018911513

Paperback ISBN-13: 978-0-9976747-6-7
eBook ISBN: xxxx

First Edition, Silver Fire Publishing, November 2018

Cover: Theresa Linden

Editor: Ellen Gable Hrkach

SILVER FIRE
PUBLISHING

DEDICATION

This book is dedicated to everyone who has at one time or another felt like an outcast and to those who have reached out to them.

ACKNOWLEDGMENTS

I am grateful for the encouragement and assistance I received from my editor, Ellen Gable Hrkach, and several talented authors, including Carolyn Astfalk, Corinna Turner, Susan Peek, and T. M. Gaouette.

Additionally, I appreciate the suggestions Steven R. McEvoy offered concerning both the story and the cover design; you can really thank him for the inspiration for the book cover because I almost went with something else.

I am very proud to have had the help of two of my boys. My youngest, Cisco, tolerated a photo shoot, giving me the silhouette I used on the book cover. And Justin did an amazing job gathering information about the martyrs in this story, and many more martyrs that I was not able to use but which inspired me nonetheless.

And I am extremely thankful for the insights and suggestions Tina from Courage International gave me. Her ideas helped me develop the character Brice and strengthen important threads in this story.

Last but not least, I will always be thankful for the love and support of my husband and three boys; I wouldn't be able to write my stories without them.

"For Jesus Christ I am prepared to suffer still more."
~ St. Maximilian Kolbe

"Nothing can happen to me that God doesn't want.
And all that He wants, no matter how bad it may appear to us,
is really for the best."
~ St. Thomas More

"For to me, to live is Christ and to die is gain."
~ St. Paul the Apostle

"I am not afraid . . . I was born to do this."
~ St. Joan of Arc

"It is Jesus that you seek when you dream of happiness; He is
waiting for you when nothing else you find satisfies you; He is the
beauty to which you are so attracted; it is He who provoked you
with that thirst for fullness that will not let you settle for
compromise; it is He who urges you to shed the masks of a false
life; it is He who reads in your hearts your most genuine choices,
the choices that others try to stifle."
~ St. John Paul II

PROLOGUE

BURN

WITH FISTS CLENCHED AND SWINGING, fear clashing with rage and determination, sixteen-year-old Brice fought her way through the shadows of a nightmare to wakefulness. Her eyes fluttered open to a dark room. Window in the wrong place. Door shut and on the wrong wall.

Oh wait . . . this was her new bedroom. She was safe. She had nothing to worry about. Not like *then.*

Drenched in sweat and heart pounding, she threw the covers back and sat up, dropping her feet to the carpeted floor.

Sitting hunched, one arm resting on her thigh, she rubbed her face and sucked in a deep breath. The panic of her nightmare continued to course through her veins.

Inhuman hands latched onto her sister and lifted her up, up, up. Desperate to save her, Brice swung at the hands and tried grasping onto her sister's legs until she could no longer reach her.

"Mom, help!" Brice cried, tearing from one room to another. Not in her bedroom, not in the living room. Strangers lay strewn on the furniture, Mom not among them. "Mom, where are you?" she shrieked in anger.

Brice shoved a hand into her hair and grunted, pushing the thoughts back as far as she could. She wanted to move on. And she was tired of the interrupted sleep. Tired of being tired. She could relax now. That part of her life was over.

Three breaths later, something moved overhead. A patch of yellow light danced on the ceiling. It streamed in through the gap between curtains, making pictures on the ceiling. Dipping, twisting, leaping.

The hairs on her arms stood up and a chill shuddered down her spine.

Brice tore to the window and shoved back the curtain.

Flames licked the branches and engulfed the trunk of the sweetgum tree in the front yard. A trail of flame burned the grass, stretching a few feet, maybe yards, from the tree. Dark smoke swirled above it all, disappearing in the blackness of the night.

The all-too-familiar sense of emergency surged inside her. Brice raced into the dark hallway and pounded on the Escotts' bedroom door. "Fire! Get up!"

A thump came from inside the room. And the rustle of blankets. "What's that? Fire?" scraped Mr. Escott's low voice, and then louder, "Fire!"

Brice flung open the door to the boys' bedroom, then the girls' bedroom. "Get up," she demanded. Then she took off, thumping down the steps and through the living room. Maybe she'd catch the person who'd done it.

On the back of the couch lay the jacket her foster mother had given her last week, on the first day of school. She grabbed it and opened the front door to a burst of cool, smoky air and the pungent odor of burning leaves and wood. Her gaze snapped to the yellow and orange flames as she staggered barefooted out onto the front porch. A distant siren sounded. A neighbor must've called the fire department already. No need to panic. The fire wouldn't reach the house.

Stuffing her arm into her jacket, she crossed the porch and her foot brushed something soft and cold. A plant?

As her gaze shifted, she took in a scene that made her heart sink. Plants and flowers lay uprooted and strewn in the yard, near the flowerbed, some on the porch. Garbage made a trail from the side of the garage where they kept the cans to the end of the driveway.

Anger rippled through her, tensing every muscle in her body and making her need to do something. But do what? Brice stomped down the porch steps and to the cold, gritty driveway.

She stopped between a plastic milk container and a wet pile of junk mail and scanned the two streets that came off the Escotts' corner lot. Why would anyone do this to the Escotts? Brice didn't much like living with a foster family, but these people were nice. They couldn't have kids of their own, so they'd opened their home to foster children. Like the two little boys and the baby girl who had lived with them for the past year or so. And like her, a last-minute emergency placement.

What could anyone have against them?

A smoky breeze ruffled the loose fabric of Brice's basketball shorts and made goosebumps pop out on her legs.

The flames grew higher, totally engulfing the tree now.

The front door squeaked. Footfalls on the porch. A pause. "Brice, are you okay?" Mr. Escott pounded down the steps, his eyebrows slanting, his eyes on her. As he neared, he spread his arms as if ready to pull her into a hug or to safety or something.

Brice stiffened and folded her arms across her chest. "I'm fine."

He stopped four feet away and ran a hand through his salt-and-pepper hair, giving her a sad smile as he likely remembered her request to not be touched or hugged. "Did you see anyone?"

She shook her head.

"Well, I'm glad you're okay. No one was hurt." He made a sweeping gaze of the yard. "Who could've done this?"

"And how?" she mumbled. The leaves on the old tree had only started to turn. Someone would've needed an accelerant to burn it like this.

Staring out at the tree with a hint of sadness in his eyes, he shook his head. "Stay here. I'll grab the hose." He disappeared around the side of the house.

The rest of the family spilled through the front door and drew near, Mrs. Escott holding the little girl on her hip and the youngest boy by the hand, everyone wide awake and staring at the burning tree.

Mr. Escott returned a moment later, dragging the hose. "Not sure the hose is long enough. What a mess, huh?"

3

Mrs. Escott finally snapped out of it and turned to her husband. "I called the fire department, but they already knew. And Mrs. Abelson. She's invited us over for the rest of the night, at least until we make sure the house is safe."

"Oh, good." Mr. Escott reached for Brice again, as if to guide her to the Abelson's house next door.

Brice stepped back, her jaw tensing. "No, thanks. I'm fine here."

Two firetrucks rounded the corner at the end of the street, their lights on but sirens now off. A few neighbors had stepped outside and stood watching from their driveways and porches. Others watched from their windows.

The Escotts stared at Brice for a moment, probably not liking her answer, but she was sixteen and they needed to respect her choices. There was no real danger here.

Mr. Escott glanced at the approaching firetrucks and dropped the hose. "That'll be fine, honey." He gave his wife a reassuring nod. "Take the little ones over. Brice and I will keep an eye on things here and talk to the firemen."

Resignation in her expression, Mrs. Escott turned and started across the driveway. Three steps later, she stopped, and her head swiveled to the garage door. She jerked back but then corralled the children past the garage and into the neighboring yard.

Curious, Brice looked to see what had startled Mrs. Escott. Her breath caught, and a shiver ran through her. Suddenly queasy, she stormed away from the garage and into the cool grass of the front yard, moving toward the tree but not intentionally. She wanted to get away from the garage. Away from the vandalism.

Firetrucks pulled up and firemen swarmed onto the scene, way more than the situation warranted. They probably had nothing better to do.

Brice strode past them, ignoring a few questions thrown her way. Mr. Escott would talk to them. Picking up her pace, thumping through the yard while her pulse beat in her ears, she left the flaming tree behind and plunged into the strip of woods at the end of the Escotts' yard.

Dead leaves crunched under her steps. Twigs poked her bare feet.

Certain no one could see her now, she stopped and flung herself against the rough bark of a thick tree trunk and hid her face with her arm. Deep pain bubbled inside, threatening to erupt. Not ready to release it, Brice turned toward the house and breathed and watched the firemen unwind a hose. And breathed again. Her gaze shifted back to the garage. She could almost read the graffiti from here.

A toxic mix of guilt, anger, disgust, and insecurity assailed her. She allowed one hot tear to escape. But no more.

The vandalism wasn't done because someone had something against the Escotts. It was done against her.

The hard, ugly words spray painted in big black letters on the garage door proved it. Harsh labels, offensive names Brice had hoped to leave behind her. Who would've done it? She now lived over an hour from where she'd grown up. No one knew her here, not really. School had only started a week ago. She'd barely spoken a word to anyone. Who would know anything about her? Or did they simply hate what they thought she was? They judged her based on her appearance. The way she dressed, the way she walked, maybe. They put her into a category. Rejected her. Gave her a label to make sure she knew what she was. What she was and always would be . . .

Brice, the outcast.

1

SPEECH FAIL

ROLAND'S STOMACH SEIZED UP. A fifteen-year-old shouldn't have to go through this, but any minute now it would begin.

Mrs. Kauffman sat at her desk next to the windows, the sunlight framing her smooth, shoulder-length dark hair. Whispers and murmurs traveled around the room. The teacher studied an electronic notepad, probably deciding who would go first. She lifted her head and looked out.

Roland tensed and turned to his friend Peter Brandt, who sat next to him, to see if he showed signs of fear or even mild apprehension.

Peter sat slouched with his legs stretched out, one in the aisle and the other under the chair in front of him. He cleaned a fingernail then bit a hangnail and spit it to the side. Didn't seem to notice Roland's glance. Didn't seem concerned about anything. He could've been sitting in his own backyard on a lazy summer afternoon.

Mrs. Kauffman's chair screeched as she scooted it back. She stood, tugged on her blazer, and flounced to the front of the sunny classroom. Younger than most teachers at River Run High, she always dressed professionally and in the latest styles. Today she wore a dark blazer over a turquoise blue top and tan dress pants. Dangling earrings drew attention to her cheerful face. Confident, approachable, and fearless—at least when it came to speaking to groups—kids identified with her. All the girls loved her, and all the boys tolerated her, probably because of her pretty face.

Her gaze traveled across the room, landing on every student in turn.

Roland shifted his eyes to the folder on his desk. No one could get out of this class, and no one would get out of this assignment.

"Okay, class . . ." Mrs. Kauffman grabbed the projector remote, tapped something on her laptop keypad, and turned to the interactive whiteboard.

Roland sucked in a breath and slumped down in his chair, four rows from the front of the classroom. He should've taken a seat in the back by the door.

Peter looked his way.

He saw it out of the corner of his eye, but he couldn't get himself to meet his stare. Peter knew Roland's terror of this class: speech class.

"In an effort to be fair and impartial, I've put all your names into a random winner generator to see who gets the honor of going first." Mrs. Kauffman smiled, giving the same encouraging look she'd given from day one.

"The honor," Peter mumbled and then chuckled under his breath.

Roland breathed again and finally glanced Peter's way in a show of solidarity.

"Is everybody ready?" Mrs. Kauffman said with an extra note of cheerfulness.

"Yes," half the class said in unison. Groans and muttering came from the other half. Silence from Roland.

No, no, no. The words bounced around Roland's head. He sank down further, the top edge of the chair scraping his sweaty back through his polo shirt.

"Okay, here we go." Mrs. Kauffman pressed a key on her laptop. Everyone looked at the whiteboard.

Roland cut a glance to Peter, who grinned knowingly as if completely aware of Roland's fear. Holding his breath, Roland shifted his gaze to the folder on his desk, the folder that held his double-spaced speech typed in twelve-point font with one-inch margins.

Please, God. Please, God. Please, God. He should've stayed home sick. Why did every tenth-grader have to take speech class anyway? When in his life would he ever use this skill? He had no intention of becoming a teacher, a leader, or entering public life. He'd become a detective or something, a private eye who communicated via email and sneaked through the shadows.

"And our first speaker is . . ."

A hush fell over the class as the name appeared on the whiteboard.

"Brice Maddox." Mrs. Kauffman smiled, her gaze sweeping from one side of the classroom to the other.

Roland exhaled, relief shuddering through him. Then the name registered in his mind. Brice Maddox, a new girl at River Run High, wasn't in class today. Had she even come to school? He'd heard rumors about her this morning, something about her house being vandalized and other things he'd tried to tune out. He knew from first-hand experience that kids could be mean, especially to new students.

Mrs. Kauffman's smile faded and the look in her eyes said she remembered something. Maybe she'd heard the rumors too. "Since Brice isn't here today, we'll pick another name." She turned and tapped a key on her laptop.

Roland squeezed his eyes shut. *Please, God. Please, God. Please . . .*

Gasps of relief sounded from every corner of the room then laughter from a couple of kids and a few whispered comments.

"The voiceless one."

"Does he even know how to talk?"

Ice-cold dread fell over Roland as he lifted his gaze. He knew before reading his name on the whiteboard, before hearing the teacher announce, "Roland West!"

"Oh, man," Peter said with sympathy.

Roland spared him a panicked glance. His body turned to dead weight, his limbs to rubber. His hands trembled like dried leaves fighting to cling to a tree in a hot fall breeze. He couldn't even visualize getting up from his desk, much less walking to the front of the room.

"I'll introduce each speaker before they come up," Mrs. Kauffman said. "Ready, Roland?"

He wanted to say "no" and beg her to pick another winner, but his eyes only flickered to her. He glimpsed her steady smile and hard look that said she knew his fear but he wasn't getting out of this.

"Roland West is one of our quieter students, but you'll soon learn he's lived an incredibly interesting life of adventure. Let's welcome Roland to the front of the room where he'll tell us a bit about himself." She clapped, everyone in the class following suit.

He wiped his sweaty palms on his jeans. In his peripheral vision he saw faces turning toward him, adding a hundred pounds to the dead weight that he couldn't fathom lifting from his seat.

Peter leaned in and grabbed his shoulder. "You got this," he whispered. He was probably the only one who really knew Roland's fear, or who cared.

"Roland?" Mrs. Kauffman said with firmness in her tone as she continued to lead the applause.

Making the most of Peter's vote of confidence, Roland latched onto the desk and forced himself to stand. A sharp pain in his knee made him wince. He'd had a leg cast removed three days ago, so he would need to concentrate on not limping. He slid his speech from the folder with a trembling hand. The applause continued as he strode forward with all the confidence he could muster—*oh, God, I'm limping!*—past three rows of desks to the front of the classroom and to the podium. He made a mental note not to lean on the cheap maple podium, noticing it had wheels.

He set his papers down, and the clapping stopped. The room grew hot and quiet except for a whispered comment by troublemaker Foster Masson in the back row.

Roland stared at his speech until the words blurred. He was back in ninth grade, his first year in a brick-and-mortar school. He hadn't found his name on any of the homeroom lists hanging on the wall. So, he'd had to go to every freshman class and ask if he belonged there, introducing himself over and over in front of every ninth-grader in school. He'd been the subject of gossip from the first day, the new kid who'd lost his voice and croaked out his name. The mute.

And then the spray tan incident a week ago—on the first day of this school year—had renewed all the gossip from last year and added a new dimension. Three kids who didn't like his pale skin had dragged him, despite the leg cast, into an empty classroom. He'd dropped his crutches, trying to get away. He'd never felt more helpless, humiliated, or vulnerable in all his life. They'd pinned him to a wall and assaulted him with spray tan. His older brother Jarret found out and sought retribution, getting suspended on the first day of school.

Something inside Roland changed that day. All the confidence he'd gained over the previous year had left him.

A bead of sweat traced a path down Roland's back, under his black polo shirt, bringing him to the present moment. He lifted his head and looked out at faces, most blank, a few sympathetic, and others smirking. He'd barely spoken two words to any of these kids, other than Peter. Thank God his friend Caitlyn wasn't in his speech class. He'd hate for her to see this.

Roland cleared his throat. He squinted at his speech, trying to bring the first line into focus. He'd memorized the entire thing anyway, practicing it in the mirror every night for a week.

Now that he thought about it, that first line was lame. It was like a noose that would hang him. Was he really going to say it? Would the speech work if he skipped it?

He looked out at his classmates. Fiery yellow light messed with his vision, bright splotches appearing on faces. Too bad it didn't hide them completely. He hated having all eyes on him.

"Roland?" Mrs. Kauffman sat behind her desk, practically invisible with the sunlit window behind her and the yellow spots in front of her. "You may begin," she said, encouraging him to the noose that would soon hang him.

Roland nodded and planted his trembling hands on the podium.

He sucked in a breath and made himself do it, stick his head in the noose, read the first line. "There's gold in them . . . them thar hills."

Someone snorted, the sound a person makes when trying to hold back laughter. Was it Foster? *Yeah.* Then he let loose, throwing his head back and guffawing, and everyone else joined in. Even Peter? Peter sat face down on his desk, one hand sunk in his messy blond hair.

The trembling spread to Roland's entire body. Mouth going dry, he tried to find his place. "In 1849, relatives on my, on my father's side . . ."

He bit his tongue, hoping to activate his spit glands or at least draw a little blood to moisten his mouth.

The laughter subsided, but the fiery splotches increased. He couldn't see the words of his speech, couldn't see his classmates. Instead of comforting him, panic set in. His head grew light, and he couldn't suck in a breath. Someone said something, maybe called his name, but it sounded far off.

Moving as if in a dream, he snatched his speech from the podium and bolted—with a limp—through the moving yellow splotches to the only thing he could see: the door.

~ ~ ~

Several thin streams of water arched into the old sink in the boys' bathroom. Stomping on the foot pedal, Roland held cupped hands under the pathetic streams and tried to get enough water to splash on his clammy face.

He stared at his reflection in the mirror. He looked like an ordinary kid with average height, weight, and short dark hair. Okay, so maybe his skin was a bit paler than the typical white boy. And the overhead lights made it match the off-white walls so that a ghost looked back at him through the mirror. He wished he could disappear like a ghost or at least blend into the shadows.

Roland splashed onto his face the little water he'd managed to collect and rubbed his eyes. Lifting the hem of his polo shirt, he dried his face. Then he leaned on the edge of the curved sink and glared at himself in the mirror.

He sure didn't feel ordinary. He felt like a freak. Couldn't even blurt out the speech he'd spent two days writing and almost a week memorizing. Every kid in the tenth grade would end up giving a speech, several speeches. And his story wasn't boring. His father was an archaeologist who had traveled all over, his grandparents, farmers in southern Arizona, a more distant relative had been a 49er . . .

Maybe he shouldn't have started with that stupid line from Mark Twain's novel The American Claimant. Or maybe he should've made a Power Point presentation to take the attention off himself.

Aggravation mounting, Roland turned and kicked in a stall door, making it bang against the metal partition. He'd kicked it with his good leg, but his bad leg screamed anyway.

An archaeologist, farmer, and gold digger. . . It wasn't in his blood to stand up and talk before a group. It rubbed against every fiber of his being and tore at the threads holding him together, causing those fiery splotches that signaled his downfall. What was that about anyway? Low blood sugar? Panic attack?

He leaned against the wall and ran a hand through his hair, combing the wet strands into place.

Whatever. He wasn't going back to speech class today, but he couldn't really stay in the bathroom for an entire class period. Where could he go?

With a sigh, he strode from the bathroom, turned the corner, and crashed into a boy who must've been cruising down the hall.

The boy cussed and shoved him into the wall. "Watch it," he said, his voice an octave too high. He wore an over-sized white t-shirt under a weathered denim jacket. Messy white-blond hair fell over his eyes, but Roland sensed the bitterness in them.

"Sorry." Heart racing, Roland lifted his hands, palms out. At least he hadn't run into a teacher.

The kid glared for a second then turned and lumbered away with attitude and haste in his steps.

As Roland watched him go, he realized with shock that he was a she. It was the girl everyone was talking about today: Brice Maddox.

2

INSENSITIVE

CHAOS DESCENDED UPON THE GYM. Kids streamed in through two sets of double doors and plowed through groups of other kids, everyone talking over one another. A cacophony of chatter, footfalls on the bleachers, and sneakers squeaking on the polished hardwood floor drowned out the teachers' random commands.

Peter Brandt stood amid the chaos, the sole stationary and silent figure, scanning for a pale kid in black clothes. Not that he remembered what Roland wore today. Peter hadn't seen him since he'd zipped out of Speech. But it had to be black or something close to black. He rarely wore anything else.

Peter's attention kept slipping to kids with short white-blond hair, a strange feeling threatening to take over until he forced himself back to his primary search. He was looking for his friend Roland. Not someone else.

A loud, familiar laugh rose above the chatter. Dominic Miato and Foster Masson sauntered through the wide-open doors, a group of kids around them. Peter liked seeing the two friends back together. They'd reconciled about this time last year, giving Peter a bit of distance from all of Dominic's gossip. Despite the growth spurt in his spiritual life—the result of a miraculous healing—Dominic had maintained his status as chief gossip-monger. Gossiping always rubbed Peter raw, but he hated it even more now. Especially since it often concerned friends or, in one case, a potential friend.

Peter's heart spasmed. He took a deep breath. *Look for dark hair not blond.*

Dominic moved toward the bleachers, but then his head turned, he flipped his shiny black hair out of his eyes, and his gaze caught Peter.

Peter nodded and looked away, not wanting to talk, especially if Dominic had anything to say about the reason for the last-minute assembly.

Dominic said something to Foster and they parted ways, Dominic now swaggering to Peter. Foster and five other kids climbed the bleachers to the top row.

"Eh, *vato*, whassup?" he said in Chicano English and punched Peter's shoulder. Dominic was of Mexican descent and his older family members spoke full-blown Spanish, switching to English only when company came over.

"Hey, Dominic." Peter spared a glance but returned to scanning faces. The influx of students had slowed, and three teachers huddled by the podium on the stage. The podium looked exactly like the one in speech class. Had they rolled it down here?

"Let me guess, you are searching for Roland."

"Yeah, I'm sure he'll slide in just before the bell rings."

"He is probably lying low after his speech fail."

"You heard about that?" Peter glanced over Dominic's shoulder at Foster on the top row. Foster was in their speech class and had probably told Dominic.

"I hear everything."

"Yeah, well, don't say anything to Roland. I'm sure he's still feeling tight."

Dominic laughed. "He has my sympathy." His gaze shifted, and he tilted his chin at one of the open doors. "There he is, sliding in last."

"Please have a seat in the bleachers." Principal Freeman's voice boomed through the speakers. Then he mumbled something about volume control to one of the other teachers in his huddle.

Roland, in a black polo shirt and jeans, skulked along the end of the bleachers. He gave Peter the slightest glance and turned to find a seat as if he hadn't seen him.

"Roland!" Peter shouted. A few kids looked in Roland's direction. Peter cringed. Roland would hate him for drawing attention, but that's what he got for pretending he didn't notice him.

Running a hand through his hair, Roland turned around. Glaring, he shuffled toward Peter and Dominic. He walked stiffly, probably working hard to hide his limp. "Let's sit down," he said to Peter, jabbing a thumb over his shoulder.

Peter smiled. Roland's shyness never ceased to amuse him. He must've been hyper-aware that no other students still stood in the middle of the gym.

"Yeah, I'm over there." Dominic indicated the opposite side of the gym. "You guys coming to Fire Starters tonight?"

"I think so." Peter looked to Roland for confirmation. Roland had said yesterday that he might go to the Catholic youth group's first meeting of the school year.

Never one to commit, Roland shrugged.

"Okay, see ya." Dominic slapped Roland's arm. "Don't be hard on yourself, Roland. First time's always rough." He gave a friendly nod and jogged to the bleachers.

Roland's mouth fell open. "Is he talking about— how would he know?"

"Come on." Peter jabbed his side to get him moving. "I dunno what he's talking about."

They climbed the bleachers, a few kids having to move out of their way.

"Did you get detention for skipping class?" Peter said as they neared the top.

Roland glanced around, no doubt worried who else might've heard Peter. No one seemed to have noticed. "No. Not yet anyway. I'm sure I'll find out tomorrow."

Now alone on the stage, Principal Freeman's voice boomed through the speakers again. "So, we'll get started here. I imagine you're all wondering what this last-minute assembly is about."

"Burn, baby, burn!" a boy shouted. The voice came from a group of juniors, one of whom was Gavin Wheeler, one of the rudest kids in school.

At the top row, Roland found a corner where the wall jutted out a foot. Two girls scooted aside, way farther than necessary, letting Peter sit beside Roland.

"Some of you, no doubt," the principal continued, "have heard about the troubling events that happened in our community over the weekend, what happened to the house of one of our own students."

A sudden burst of heat struck Peter. He glanced to either side with the insane idea that Roland or one of the girls might've noticed him blush. Then he surveyed the bleachers, not looking for pale skin and black clothes this time. Looking for her. She'd come late to Speech, and he hadn't seen her in Woodworking. Had she gone home early?

"We at River Run High are committed to creating a safe and compassionate environment for everyone. And we want to foster an attitude of tolerance and sensitivity that filters out into the larger community. The hateful behavior over the weekend is a sign that we've failed, that we haven't done enough, that we still have work to do."

"What's he talking about?" Roland mumbled.

Peter squinted at him with disbelief. "Are you kidding me? You don't watch the news? You didn't hear the gossip all day?"

Roland's gray eyes shifted to Peter, accusing him. "You listen to gossip?" Last year, the rumors at River Run High had centered around Roland and his older twin brothers. As a result, Roland had grown paranoid and that had almost kept him and Peter from becoming friends. The spray tan incident had Roland back on the rumor radar this year. Bum deal for such a shy kid.

"I didn't say I believed them, but I've got ears." A hint of guilt giving way to self-righteousness, Peter let Roland's accusation bounce back. "You're honestly telling me you've heard nothing?" He smirked and cocked a brow in challenge.

Roland's gaze flickered and he shrugged, his way of admitting he had. He turned his attention back to Principal Freeman on the stage.

"We live in a world of diversity. The way you choose to live your life is not necessarily the way everyone chooses to live their lives. And just because you think something is right, doesn't mean everyone agrees. What's right and true for you might not be right or true for someone else."

Peter bristled, ten years of Catholic catechism racing through his brain. "That's a tub of hogwash."

Roland glanced, looking as unemotional as ever, not even hinting at his opinion. How well did he know his faith?

"There's only one truth," Peter whispered to Roland, compelled to know if he agreed. "Objective truth. God's truth. Am I right?"

Roland nodded but not in a way that convinced Peter of anything.

"We each need to look into our heart," the principal blathered on, "to see if we have become judgmental and condemning of others. That behavior is not acceptable. We need to learn to be more compassionate, more accepting of differences. Again, there is not one right way."

Peter folded his arms, agitation making him tense. "Hm. I beg to differ."

"Yeah, just ignore him," Roland said. "He's just trying to say people shouldn't torch other people's trees."

Peter grinned. He'd caught Roland. "Oh, so you do listen to rumors."

Roland shifted but acted like Peter's remark didn't affect him.

"I am aware," the principal continued, "that some cliques at school and groups in the community embrace ideas that promote biased and intolerant views. In fact, one group even goes by a name that promotes the very vandalism that happened over the weekend . . ."

Indignation shooting through him, Peter straightened. "What's he talking about? He's not referring to the Catholic youth group, is he?"

Roland's scrunched brows and wild eyes said he wondered the same thing. The Catholic youth group had taken the name "Fire Starters" last year, basing it on Luke 12:49: *I came to cast fire upon the earth; and would that it were already kindled!*

19

"In order to bring about change," Principal Freeman bellowed, "we are in the process of developing a sensitivity program for the entire school. And each of you is encouraged to join Empowerment, our diversity club, to help with this initiative."

"Our *what* club?" Peter jerked back.

"The mandatory diversity program will help spread awareness and develop an appreciation of differences."

Peter and Roland exchanged glances, but then Peter glimpsed movement among the students in the bleachers across the way. And short white-blond hair.

"Again, if you'd like to take part in the development of this program, you're welcome to join Empowerment, which meets immediately after school."

Brice Maddox had been sitting near the special needs kids in the lower rows. How had he missed that? He'd been looking that way earlier because one of the kids reminded him of his younger brother, Toby, the way he stared off into space. But there she was, a towhead with a no-nonsense pixie hairstyle he'd venture to say she cut herself. Taking long confident steps with a "don't mess with me" attitude, she strode to the end of the bleachers and around the corner. Then she slammed open a door and left the gym.

Peter's heart thumped like mad, and he'd broken out in a cool sweat. As he took a deep breath and turned back to the principal, he realized Roland was staring at him.

"What?" Peter said, feeling a mix of guilt and hostility. Not ready for anyone to know.

The faintest smile crept onto Roland's pale face, a knowing look in his cool gray eyes. He shrugged and turned toward the stage.

Roland didn't know anything. There was nothing *to* know.

3

NEW RIDE

ROLAND GLARED OVER HIS SHOULDER then slung his backpack over his back and limped to the front of the bus, Peter stomping behind him. A weight lifted as he thumped unevenly down the steps and dropped a boot to the Brandts' driveway. The kids in the back of the bus would have to find someone else to trash talk. Had they all heard what happened in speech class? Didn't seem possible.

Giving a speech didn't seem possible either. Maybe he could talk to Peter about some of the things in his speech and it would get easier.

The bus door squeaked shut, and the bus took off rumbling down the road.

"Hey, I got something to show you." Peter passed Roland and mounted the front stoop.

Roland followed Peter inside. His stomach lurched in expectation of a crowd. The Brandts operated the Forest Gateway Bed & Breakfast and guests often lingered in the over-sized dining room, sitting at one of the three booths against the wall or the long table in the middle.

Finding the dining room empty, Roland breathed and exhaled. A warm pastry aroma hit him, and his mouth watered, reminding him he'd skipped lunch. Not wanting to face anyone after speech class, he'd sat alone behind the big oak tree in the back of the schoolyard.

"Stop rewinding it," Mrs. Brandt shouted. Wearing a white bandanna and an apron over a casual flower-print dress, she stood between the kitchen and living room, looking at Toby over the couch.

Three feet from the television, Peter's nine-year-old brother, Toby, wielded the remote and rewound a cartoon. He made no sign that he'd heard her. But he probably had. He was autistic not deaf.

"Toby, you're driving me mad." Mrs. Brandt propped her hands on her hips. "I don't want to hear that—"

The screen door slammed behind Roland, and Mrs. Brandt's frown lifted to a smile as she turned to them. "Oh hey, boys. Is it that time already?" She twisted and glanced over her shoulder, maybe at a clock in the kitchen. "Are you hungry?"

"Nah, what is that, pie?" Peter dropped his backpack onto the loveseat and motioned for Roland to do the same.

"Your Aunt Lotti and I made cherry, apple, peach, and mincemeat. Go on and have some. I bet Roland's hungry." She smiled at Roland.

Not wanting to admit his weakness, Roland shrugged, but his gaze snapped to the pies cooling on the kitchen bar counter.

"Nah, I'm gonna show Roland my Durango." Peter shuffled toward the front door.

"Your what?" A tinge of jealousy teased him. Peter had just turned sixteen. Roland would have to wait another year. Would Papa help him get a car the way he'd helped Jarret, one of his older twin brothers? Of course, Keefe, the other twin, still didn't have a car and he was seventeen.

"What's the hurry? Have some pie first." Mrs. Brandt paused then gave a sly smile, showing a side of her Roland had never seen before. "Your beater's not going anywhere."

"Ha ha." Peter smirked. "It will soon. You'll see."

She gave Roland a sweet, motherly smile. "What's your favorite kind of pie, Roland?"

"Uh." Roland squirmed, feeling put on the spot. How could he ever give a speech in front of his class when it rattled him to answer a simple question from anyone other than family and close friends? Forget the pie. He needed to talk to Peter about his speech. They wouldn't have the chance later, since they were going to the Fire Starters meeting.

"Oh, and I was thinking," Mrs. Brandt continued. "If you boys want to practice your speeches afterward, Lotti and I would love to be your audience."

Roland's mouth fell open and his temperature spiked. He shot his betrayer with a death glare.

Peter laughed and grabbed him by the sleeve. "Come on, my paranoid friend. Out to the garage."

The cooler air hit him as Peter dragged him back outside. Forget sharing his speech with Peter. Maybe he could find a way out of speech class entirely. His brothers didn't have to take it. Why should he? Of course, they were seniors so it wasn't the same. "So, you called your mom, huh," he said, his tone accusing, "told her about speech class?"

Still laughing, Peter yanked the garage door open. "You're as vain as Jarret. You know that? You think everyone's talking about you. Only difference: it makes Jarret puff up like a peacock, but you want to crawl under a rock."

Roland's jaw twitched, but he couldn't argue that point. He found himself rubbing the thigh of his sore leg.

Peter stepped inside the shady, cluttered garage. Tennis rackets and yard tools hung on the wall just inside the big garage door, and on the opposite wall, boxes bulged with sports balls, plastic sheets, and other junk. "So, you know I've been wanting a four-wheel-drive. Well, my dad helped me locate one. She needs a bit of work, but I'll get her running in no time."

Peter slapped a switch and overhead florescent lights blinked on, illuminating the black Dodge Durango in the middle of the two-car garage. "We towed it here last night."

Jealousy growing, Roland walked around it. "Wow, and you're just now telling me?" He opened the driver-side door and—bending his leg with care—eased into the driver's seat to check out the interior. A bit of cleaning and a deodorizer to hide the stale smell, and it wouldn't be half bad.

"Wanted to tell you earlier, but you made yourself scarce all day." Peter's eyes narrowed with a look that said he wanted to bring up speech class. He rested a hand on the open driver-side door.

"Then we had that assembly. Didn't think about it then." Peter propped his foot on the running board and leaned in. "So, what's your speech about?"

Roland tensed. Then he leaned to get out of the Durango, making Peter back out of the way. "So, you like Brice, huh?" He threw the question like a grenade, knowing the mention of her name would keep Peter from thinking further about speech class. Roland had seen the look on Peter's face when he'd spotted her in the gym. He'd seen Peter watching for her between classes too. Other kids at River Run High may have considered her a bit of an anomaly, but Peter had more than mild curiosity.

"Wow, what?" The grenade having its desired effect, Peter's face blazed red and looked like it might explode. He slammed the car door. "Thought you didn't listen to rumors."

"I don't." Roland smiled to himself, satisfied with his ability to redirect Peter and relieved he was no longer the subject of their conversation. "Didn't hear it from anyone. I've seen you."

Peter turned his back on Roland and made like he needed to find something on a workbench. "You've seen me *what*?"

"Never mind. So it's not true?"

Peter turned around with a beat-up manual in his hand. "So . . . I've got to install a new starter. That's all the guy said was wrong with it, but I'm sure there's more, you know, like . . ." He flipped a few pages then tossed the manual over his shoulder, his gaze sliding back to Roland. "You know the vandalism our dear principal was talking about, that happened to her house. You know that, right?"

"Wasn't her house." Roland cringed, realizing he'd just repeated rumors he'd heard. Brice Maddox lived with a foster family.

"Okay, her foster home. Same thing. It was directed at her."

"You know this, how?"

Peter rubbed his forehead, looking perplexed. "I don't know. You think it was directed at her foster parents? Who's gonna do something like that, burn a tree and spray paint bad words on a garage door?" He paced toward the back of the garage. "Kids at school, that's who." He arranged tools on a disorganized workbench.

"Well, she's new to River Run High and new to town. I doubt anyone knows her well enough to hate her."

Peter walked up to him, his eyes narrowing. "People don't have to know someone to hate them. Remember all the rumors about you and your family when you West boys first showed up at River Run High?"

Trying to avoid showing that Peter's words convicted him, Roland shrugged and stared outside. Sunlight made the driveway glow. The trees across the street had a scattering of orange and yellow leaves. A car drove by. Yeah, he remembered. He'd hated his freshman year, especially the beginning when he hadn't a single friend. People judged and condemned him without even knowing him.

"I think we should find out who did it." Peter rested an arm on Roland's shoulder.

"Us? How are we going to do that?"

"I don't know. You've got some detective in you. You figured out who'd been stealing from your dad's friend in Arizona, didn't you?"

Roland's pride swelled with the compliment, but he stuffed his hands in the front pockets of his jeans and tried to downplay it. He did like investigating and problem-solving. And he had found that thief. But then resistance made Roland squirm. If he started asking questions and really looking into it, he'd draw attention to himself. Probably get labeled and add to the gossip already going around about him.

A grin stretched across Peter's face, as if he sensed Roland's thoughts. "So, I challenge you, my little buddy, to find out who did this to Brice."

"Okay, on one condition."

Peter slid his arm from Roland's shoulder and backed off, his wary look saying he knew the condition. He backed all the way out of the garage then combed a hand through messy hair turned gold from the sunlight. When he met Roland's gaze, resignation showed in his eyes. "Okay, what's your condition?"

"I just want to know." Roland leaned against the Durango, taking pressure off his sore leg, and he smiled. "Am I right that you like Brice?"

Peter stared at Roland for a moment. "Okay, I'll answer that, but we're going to practice our speeches before we go tonight."

"No."

"Yes, and we're practicing in front of an audience: Mom and Aunt Lotti."

"No! What's that got to do with my condition?"

"Nothing. But if you're gonna make me say something I'm not ready to say, then you're gonna say something you're not ready to say."

"Forget it." Roland gave a confident grin and strode—well, with that lousy limp—from the garage. "You've already answered me."

Peter yanked the garage door shut a bit too forcefully. "No, I didn't."

"Yes, you did. You like her."

4

BLAME

"THANKS FOR THE RIDE," Peter blurted to his mom through the open front passenger-side window of her compact car. "See ya around nine." He turned, thinking he might find Roland walking away.

Roland had muttered a thank you and climbed out of the car before it had fully stopped. Now he stood with his back to the school building attached to Saint Michael Church, his hands in the front pockets of his black jeans. His gaze followed Peter's Mom's car. Apprehension showed in the tilt of his head and his posture—one foot poised to make a break for it. He probably wished he hadn't come over to Peter's place after school. He could be home right now, doing therapy for his lame leg.

Granted they'd only met last year, but Peter knew him well enough to guess his thoughts. He was probably picturing every kid in speech class, trying to remember if any of them belonged to the Fire Starters. He'd want to avoid them tonight because of his speech fail.

Or wait . . . he was probably wondering who knew about the spray tan incident from last week. Rotten way to begin the school year. While Roland hadn't spoken much about it, he'd crawled back into his shell since then. Peter would bet that Roland was thinking up an excuse right now as to why he had to go home.

"Let's go." Peter motioned for Roland to go first, making a sweeping gesture toward steps that rose up to the side entrance of the school.

Roland's head dipped down, and he peered up at Peter. "Um, you know, I just remembered—"

"Oh, no, you don't." Peter grabbed him by the upper arm and shoved. He and Roland still had to talk. Roland hadn't actually committed himself to investigating the vandalism of Brice's house. Finding and exposing her enemy might not get Peter closer to Brice, but then again it might. Either way, it ticked Peter off that someone would do that to her because she's different. That's what he liked about her. She was cool, heavy metal, not into glitter and girly things. So this had become mission number one for Peter. He was getting that commitment from Roland tonight.

With a sigh, Roland jerked his arm free. On the upwards swing, he combed a hand through his hair. Then he finally faced the school building.

"What're you worried about anyway?" Peter mounted the steps alongside Roland and yanked open the door.

Roland shook his head, his eyes saying he didn't want his motives found out. "Nothing."

Peter laughed. "Stop being paranoid. These kids are your friends. And with the rest of the scuttlebutt going around today, no one's thinking about vain Roland West."

Roland threw Peter a sulky glare as he walked past. His gaze shifting to the half-open door down the hallway. Light streamed from it onto the shiny and seriously-old dark laminate flooring. Voices and laughter grew louder.

"Come on." Peter led the way. Having a shy friend who liked to keep to himself had its benefits. Roland would never tell Peter's secrets, like the one Peter almost gave up in the garage.

A funny feeling coursed through Peter, as if his body suddenly pixelated and then returned to normal. He shouldn't think about Brice. Roland obviously knew he liked her, but he wouldn't tell anyone. Did anyone else know? Peter shook his head. *Don't pick up Roland's paranoia.*

Peter stopped outside the open door. If they didn't talk now, he might not get the chance. "Hey, before we go in, I just wanna hear you say you agree to it. We should get to work right away."

Roland stared for a full two seconds, his expression giving away nothing. "Agree to what?"

"Really?" Peter smirked. "Back at my house, we were talking about—"

"Hey, *vato*."

A blur of tan arms and shiny black hair appeared in Peter's peripheral vision, Dominic Miato emerging from the meeting room. Then he was right next to Peter, slapping him on the back.

Peter seized up, his heart sailing to his throat as he faced Dominic—the last person he'd trust with a secret. Dominic didn't even need a secret—or a shred of truth—to spread a rumor. You'd think a guy that had received a miraculous healing would have a different attitude toward confidentiality. Okay, maybe he'd changed a little bit, but Peter still didn't trust him.

Roland and Dominic exchanged nods in greeting, Dominic's silky black hair shifting and making his new haircut look like a shiny motorcycle helmet.

"So today we are planning the camping trip, no?" Dominic said.

"Right." Peter relaxed. He loved planning the annual camping trip. Last year he'd devised the most awesome way yet to ignite the bonfire. This year he would come up with something more spectacular. "Might as well get started." Since they had no hope of talking privately now, Peter motioned Roland into the room.

Roland must've steeled himself to his paranoid thoughts. He strode into the room with a cool composure and a blank expression, immediately scanning faces.

A group of boys stood just inside the doorway. Fred Buchanan, the tallest kid at River Run High, said something that had the other guys laughing. He always had a hysterical story to tell. Peter wished he'd heard it. Doug Baxter doubled over with laughter in that effeminate way of his. He'd once admitted his struggles to the whole group during a retreat, assuring the guys they had nothing to worry about. They'd all sort of guessed anyway, but he lived his faith wholeheartedly, probably knew the Bible and Catechism better than anyone. Knew the patron saint for everything. Everyone considered him a friend.

"So, we get to come up with all kinds of loco ideas for fun," Dominic said, shuffling past the group, "and Father gets to shoot them down, no?"

Peter followed Dominic further into the room. "Is that how Father works?" He hadn't planned camping activities with Father and the Fire Starters last year.

Twenty or so kids stood or sat in groups. Two kids set up folding metal chairs between and around the three mismatched couches and four old armchairs in the room, the teachers' lounge by day and youth center by night. End tables and shelves held lamps that made the lounge look homey, though overhead fluorescent lights countered the effect.

Roland scanned the room, and his gaze locked onto Caitlyn Summer, who sat on the couch by the wall lined with tall windows. Kiara sat next to her, dressed in long shorts, her knee resting on the flaring skirt of Caitlyn's turquoise vintage swing dress. Phoebe—who could only be described as an eclectic mess—stood behind them, leaning on the back of the couch, forcing them to twist around to see her. More girls sat on the other couches, and a few on windowsills.

As if sensing Roland's presence in the room, Caitlyn turned her head.

Their eyes met for a split second then Roland pretended he needed to check his phone.

Peter laughed. "Why don't you go talk to her? She's—" Peter froze. While Roland wouldn't divulge secrets to anyone else, he always lost his mind around Caitlyn. He wouldn't tell her Peter liked Brice, would he?

Phone in hand, Roland stared at Peter. "Go talk to who?"

"Never mind." Peter shut his mouth before his foot got stuck in there.

Father Carston—dressed in a long black cassock, his white hair glowing under the artificial light—sat at a laptop, two boys and a girl at the table with him. They were probably going over notes for the camping trip.

Any way Peter could get Brice to go? She probably wouldn't want to go alone. Who could she go with? From what he'd noticed, she didn't get along with many girls. Or guys, for that matter. Still, he could get her to go. He'd just have to make it interesting. He'd convinced Roland to go last year. And his brother Jarret.

"You don't like my idea?" Dominic said.

Peter snapped from his thoughts and focused on the blurry tan face in front of him. He hadn't heard anything Dominic had said. "I, uh . . ."

Roland finally went over to Caitlyn just as Keefe West strode into the room, flushed and breathing hard. Keefe veered toward the group of guys and greeted a few with "Hey" and "What's up?" Then he scanned the room until his gaze found Roland.

"Okay, gather around." Father Carston pushed a couch across the hardwood floor with an awful noise, moving it closer to the rest of the furniture and making a big oval-shaped arrangement.

The chatter lessened. Folding chairs scraped on the floor as everyone took seats.

Dominic merged with the rest of the guys moving toward the furniture. "Hey, Padre," he shouted, "have you heard about the vandalism here in town? Trees burning, yard trashed, graffiti on the garage."

Peter flinched as if it had to do with his own house. Or his girlfriend's house. He sat on a folding chair next to Roland. "They only burned one tree," Peter said, though Roland looked indifferent.

"As a matter of fact, I have heard." Father sat on the arm of a chair, the power of his voice and his authoritative posture immediately commanding everyone's attention.

"You have?" One of Dominic's eyes narrowed. It must've disappointed him that someone else spread the rumor first. "Who told you?"

"The principal of your high school, Mr. Freeman."

"He told you?" Now both eyes narrowed, and his brows climbed up his forehead and disappeared under the black helmet hair.

"Yes, he informed me of the vandalism, stressing that the vandals had set a tree on fire the way the KKK used to burn crosses in yards. Then he wanted to know how you kids got the name for your group." Father gave the slightest grin. "I began to enlighten him with scriptures, but I guess he didn't really want to know." Father glanced down then up, his expression turning grim. "He asked me to talk to you all about a few things. He believes the vandalism was a hate crime, and he's concerned that kids from the Fire Starters might be responsible."

"What?" Peter said, indignation making his voice squeak.

"Additionally"—Father's voice took on an even more serious tone—"A police officer contacted me and will likely be contacting you for questioning."

Objections filled the air, some kids grumbling, others speaking in raised voices.

A peaceful expression on his face, Father motioned with both hands for silence. "Calm down, calm down." When the group quieted, he continued. "I know you kids. I know you had nothing to do with this, and I told them so. But I can guess why you are on the list of suspects."

"They're blaming us because we're Catholics," Phoebe shouted.

"They think the name Fire Starters means we're pyros," someone else shouted.

A jumble of comments followed.

Peter glanced at Roland. "It's because we're so insensitive," he said mockingly.

"Wait!" Caitlyn shouted, jumping up from the couch. "I have an idea." She smoothed her turquoise skirt and looked from kid to kid.

Father—and of course Roland—turned to her, but the chatter and sarcastic comments continued.

Sliding off a window sill, Phoebe stuck her fingers in her mouth and—

Knowing what would come next, Peter jammed his fingers in his ears.

Phoebe's high-pitched whistle overrode all other sound and might've broken an eardrum.

Father winced, one hand lifting to his ear. Everyone quieted.

"Caitlyn has the floor." Phoebe shot angry looks at random kids as she leaned over the back of the couch. Dark eye makeup, spiky purple-streaked hair, eclectic clothes, and sharp features made the girl someone not to mess with.

"Go ahead, Caitlyn," Father said, still perched on the arm of the chair and with hands now folded neatly on one leg.

Caitlyn gave Father a little smile. "I have an idea." Her green eyes lit up like traffic lights as she glanced from face to face. "Why don't we volunteer to repair the damage? We can wash the bad words off the garage door, clean up the trash, and chop down the burnt tree." She bounced on her toes, looking increasingly pleased with her plan. "We could even buy and plant a new tree!"

The group stared in silence for a moment.

"*Un momento*, Caitlyn, I know you mean well," Dominic said, "but do you not think that will make us look guilty?"

"No, it'll show that we care." Phoebe folded her arms. "It'll show the type of people we really are. We don't tear down, we build up."

A few made quiet comments, their tones gradually showing openness to the idea.

Kiara jumped up next to Caitlyn. "I love it!" She grabbed Caitlyn's hands, and the two of them bounced on their toes. "Who cares what people think? It's a good thing to do."

"Oh, brother." Peter rolled his eyes.

"You don't like the idea?" Roland said.

"It's just that Caitlyn and Kiara get so excited; they're like two little girls." He wasn't going to admit it, but he loved the idea. Roland could begin the investigation at the scene of the crime. Peter would find out where Brice lived and maybe get to talk to her. She'd appreciate that he was helping her foster family and showing support, right?

This was perfect!

5

ATTITUDE

ROLAND STEPPED INSIDE a peaceful, quiet house and closed the front door. Peter had talked his ear off all the way from Saint Michael Church. He was determined to have Roland investigate into the vandalism at Brice's house. Should he do it?

The hum of the Brandts' car engine faded.

Whenever Peter's mother dropped Roland at home, she always waited until he got inside before taking off. What did she think could happen in the few seconds it took him to get from her car to the house? Leg sore from walking around school all day, he'd had to climb the porch steps favoring his leg, knowing they watched him.

Rubbing his thigh, Roland glanced down the front hallway. A patch of light stretched across the floor by Papa's study. He had taken a teaching job with an online school, but he usually closed the door when class began. Dim light came from the kitchen down the other hallway too.

Wanting to avoid notice, Roland took off his shoes—more of a process with his sore leg—and tread in his socks toward the kitchen and stairs. He concentrated on pointing his toe straight ahead and walking without the limp, but every other step bothered him, and he kept turning his toe out. Would his leg ever feel normal again?

As he neared the kitchen, he heard the twins' voices. Keefe had gotten a text message—probably from Jarret—and left the Fire Starters meeting early. He hadn't missed anything. They'd already discussed the camping trip and going to Brice's house and anything else of importance. The group spent the rest of the night socializing and eating snacks while a dark sky sucked up the sunset and the windows became mirrors that reflected the chaos in the meeting room.

Caitlyn's face flitted into his mind.

Roland sighed. Peeking up at him through gorgeous green eyes, locks of curly red hair framing her face, Caitlyn had told him she was sorry about speech class. He'd probably turned every shade of red. How had she heard? Peter denied telling her. But Dominic's best friend, Foster Masson, was in his speech class, so the whole school probably knew by now. Too bad he couldn't be homeschooled.

The voices from the kitchen became clearer.

"Come on, man," Jarret begged rather than bossed. "I need you to do this for me."

"I can't. You know what I want to do with my life," Keefe replied. "So I think it'd be wrong."

Roland sighed, his heart sinking with disappointment. When he and Jarret returned from their vacation in Arizona, Jarret had seemed changed. Drastically changed. And for the better. He'd stopped smoking, started going to Mass on Sundays, and caught himself mid-sentence ten times a day before rude comments or bad language slipped out. He and Keefe had reconciled. And he even gave Roland the time of day now and then.

Little more than a month had passed. Was he back to his old self already?

"Why would it be wrong?" Jarret said.

"I don't want to mislead anyone. My heart belongs to God."

"Oh, brother." His tone showed weariness and disgust. "You're not going to mislead anyone. It's not like girls in high school are looking for husbands. Girls just wanna have fun."

"Isn't that a song?" Keefe said, and then the two of them sang the line in high voices.

Roland cracked a smile. He stopped near the doorway but not where they could see him.

"Besides, half the school's probably heard that you want to be a monk anyway. You're ruining my reputation."

Keefe laughed. "You've already done that. If anything, I'm salvaging it. But I really don't think anyone knows about me."

Jarret muttered a reply.

Conscience pricking him for eavesdropping, Roland shuffled from hiding and into the kitchen.

Jarret and Keefe sat at the bar counter, under the glow from the recessed lights, a cookie sheet of French fries and cans of Coke in front of them.

Keefe rested one hand on an old brown book nearby on the marble countertop. He twisted around. "Hey, Roland. Hungry?"

"Nah, just getting a drink." No longer concerned about favoring his sore leg, Roland shuffled around the counter island and took a glass from a cupboard.

"You know you can use my weight bench, right?" Jarret followed him with his eyes. "Get the strength back in your leg."

"Yeah, thanks. I might do that." Roland brought the glass to the sink and ran the cold water. Since he'd had the cast removed last Friday, he'd been reluctant to do his prescribed therapy. Any pressure on it made him worry he'd break it again.

"Probably wanna do leg lifts and leg curls," Jarret said.

"Yeah, okay." After giving Jarret a nod of appreciation, he stuck his glass under the stream of water.

"Did you guys see the warnings hanging all over school right after the assembly?" Keefe looked from Jarret to Roland.

Roland shrugged. He'd seen Mr. Bunker yanking a page ripped from a notebook off the wall outside the boys' bathroom. Glaring both ways down the hallway, the teacher had crumpled the paper in one hand and tossed it.

"Warnings about what?" Jarret asked.

"I don't know. The few I saw said, 'OUTCASTS, BEWARE' in big black letters."

"What's that supposed to mean?" Jarret's eyes narrowed.

Roland shuddered, his skin crawling, and a memory flashed into his mind: C.W., Trent and Konner shoving him into an empty classroom, razzing him about his pale skin. He remembered the helpless feeling of losing his crutches. The rattle of a can of paint. And then—

Roland sucked in a breath. Cool water ran over the lip of his full glass and onto his hand. He shut off the water and dumped some from the glass.

"Heard about your speech," Jarret said matter-of-fact.

The cup slipped in Roland's hand. He tightened his grip and caught it before he lost it, more cool water running over his hand and heat rushing up his neck. Did the whole world know and have to comment on it? Was he the only person to lose it in speech class?

"I'm glad we got out of that," Keefe said to Jarret.

"Yeah, so why did you guys get out of it, anyway?" Drippy glass in hand, Roland turned and leaned against the counter. Life always seemed to rule in their favor.

"Ah, you know." Jarret grinned, his brown eyes glowing as if he remembered something humorous. "We had rhetoric in tenth grade."

"Rhetoric?" Roland remembered the hard time the twins had given various tutors over the years. "Was that when the tutor tried explaining something and you gave smart remarks?"

Still grinning and with a hint of pride in his eyes, Jarret nodded. "Yup. Rhetoric."

Keefe stuffed a fry in his mouth and shook his head, apparently not remembering it with the same fondness. That tutor hadn't lasted longer than one year.

"Why should that count?" Roland set his cup on the counter and grabbed the dishtowel from the oven door handle.

"Don't know. Don't care. I wouldn't even mind having speech class. You got nothing to be afraid of." Sliding his Coke aside, Jarret leaned toward Roland across the bar counter. His eyes turned grim and convicting. "Those kids ain't better than you."

"I know." Roland forced himself to hold Jarret's gaze.

Jarret continued to stare as if wanting more of a response.

Needing a break from Jarret's intense look, Roland took a swig of water, which of course went down the wrong pipe. He turned away and coughed, throat stinging, eyes watering. Jarret waiting.

Finally settling down and regaining the ability to speak, he faced Jarret. "Look, Jarret, not everybody has your confidence and . . . attitude."

His narrowing eyes said he didn't approve of Roland's wimpy answer. He held Roland's gaze for a moment then sat back. "Well, you'd better find your attitude. Find your voice. You might have something to say one day. And you wanna be able to say it." He stuffed a fry in his mouth.

"Hey," Keefe said to Jarret. "Why don't you ask Roland?"

Jarret stopped chewing and his gaze slid to Keefe. "Uh. I don't think so."

"Why not?" Keefe turned to Roland, who was in the middle of gulping down water. "Hey, do you have a girlfriend?"

Water slid down the wrong pipe again, choking Roland. He turned away, hacking and coughing. "No."

"Well, you still like Caitlyn, right?"

Roland shook his head, not that he meant to say "no", but he didn't like the turn in the conversation. He'd rather talk about speech class.

"Forget about it." Jarret still hadn't looked at Roland for the answer to Keefe's question. "I can't imagine double dating with that girl. She's an accident waiting to happen. If you won't help me, I'll just do what I do."

"Yeah, that's smart," Keefe said.

"What's that supposed to mean?" Jarret's jaw twitched.

"You know what it means."

"Whatever. I haven't even decided if I want to ask her out."

Before the conversation turned back to him, Roland strode from the room. He couldn't see himself double-dating with Jarret. Actually, he couldn't see Jarret double-dating with him. Jarret cared too much about his image and Roland was a bit of a . . . well, an outcast.

Heading for his bedroom, Roland froze at the foot of the steps. If someone was going after outcasts, Roland might even be on their list. Especially after speech class today. Could C.W., Trent, and Konner have something to do with the vandalism of Brice's house? Maybe tomorrow, when the Fire Starters went over to Brice's house after school, he'd snoop around a bit.

6

BUST A MOVE

PETER, IN HIGH STEALTH MODE, stood peering around the corner. Kids milled past him in either direction. A few kids stood talking. He'd already dropped his books at his locker and grabbed his Woodworking notebook. He had three minutes before the bell rang, three minutes to spy.

Brice slammed the heel of her palm against her locker, drawing glances from nearby kids. She tried her lock again. She never paid attention to the cold stares of students, as if everyone was irrelevant to her world. Every day—well, since the first day of school—she moved with determination between classes. Okay, so sometimes she took a wrong turn, but she always knew her destination. She didn't waste time hanging out in the hallway, gossiping or blabbering about silly girl stuff with friends. She did hit the bathroom a lot. Maybe she wanted to text without people looking over her shoulder. Or maybe she smoked.

Peter's lip curled. He never saw the sense in smoking. It stunk up your clothes and your breath and sucked up money. He'd rather waste his money on other things. Like electronics and tools. Maybe he and Brice would become friends, and he could help her break the habit.

Brice swung her locker open and her head turned in Peter's direction.

Pulse kicking up, Peter jerked back out of view and bumped into someone behind him.

Books slammed to the ground and a girl said, "Oh."

"Of course, it's you." Letting out a breath, Peter peered down at the skinny redhead at his feet: Caitlyn stooping for her books.

She smiled up at him as she straightened, arranging books in her arms. "Hi."

"Why you gotta sneak up on a guy and get in his space?" Resigned to leave Brice to her business, Peter leaned a shoulder against the wall. And not a moment too soon. Dominic and Foster shuffled down the hallway and would've caught him spying if not for Caitlyn's rude interruption. He'd give Caitlyn thirty seconds to explain what she wanted then he was taking off for Woodworking. Today was the day. He'd finally have a chance to bust a move.

An eighties song popped into his mind, and he started bobbing his head.

Caitlyn focused her doe eyes on him. "We're going over there tonight, right?"

Embarrassed at the thought of her figuring him out, he pushed off the wall. She just said "over there" without being specific. Did she realize he'd been spying on Brice? "Over where?" He braced himself for Caitlyn's response, a glance around the corner or a wide-eyed look that would show she knew.

Before Caitlyn replied, a figure zipped by. Short blond hair and a resolute gait. Peter allowed himself the slightest glimpse of her. *Ah, Brice.*

"Have you forgotten already?"

"Forgotten what?" While Brice's image hovered in his mind, Peter shifted his attention back to Caitlyn.

"We're all going to help clean up the vandalized house." Caitlyn's face lit up the way it had last night at the Fire Starters meeting when she'd first mentioned the idea. "Remember? The meeting last night?"

Peter exhaled. Good. She hadn't noticed him spying, and she hadn't figured him out yet. "Yeah, sure. Why not?" He tried to look as indifferent as possible. "You need a ride?"

"Okay." Now her eyes opened wide. "Is Roland riding with you?"

Peter laughed. "I gotta run." He walked backwards away from her. The crowds in the hallway had lessened. A teacher somewhere shouted, "Get to class," and shoes squeaked on the floor.

"Oh, me too." She glanced up as if noticing a fly or searching for a clock. She was the only girl he knew who didn't have a cell phone to check the time with. "See you at lunch." They hadn't eaten lunch together once this school year, but they did share the same lunch period and they usually acknowledged each other.

He turned and headed for the woodworking class, walking to the beat of that stupid 1980s song that had gotten wedged in his mind. He created his own lyrics as he strutted down the hallway, an occasional phrase coming out audibly.

This here's a jam to psych myself up
Hopin' in shop class I don't mess up
Get shot down 'cuz I'm over-zealous
Talk 'bout tools like with other fellas
This girl's different in her element
She's got skills that other girls haven't
Look at her calculating angles
The girl's at ease with wood or metals
Working on the lathe or band saw mill
That girl has got me at a standstill
Table saw buzzing,
Spindle humming
Watching her moves got my heart drumming
Other guys probably think I'm crazy
Can't deny she makes my mind hazy
Here I go, hope she don't disapprove

Peter pumped his arms to the beat as he crossed the threshold to the shop room. The bell rang at the same moment.

Fred Buchanan stood just inside, talking with two other boys.

Fred and Peter exchanged a fist bump as Peter silently finished his song with, *"Praying for a chance as I bust a move."*

A lathe on the far side of the room hummed. Mr. Hart shouted over the noise, instructing some kid from last period . . . making him

43

late for whatever class he had next. Tall and lanky, Mr. Hart stood an inch or two shorter than the tallest kid in school—yeah, that would be Fred. And his dark hair stuck up everywhere, especially when he wore eye protection. Still, Peter rated him the best shop teacher ever. Even though he seemed scatterbrained when it came to anything else.

"Hey, man, what's up?" Fred walked with Peter to a workbench with two available stools. They'd been sitting next to each other since the first day of school, taking notes and whispering back and forth while Mr. Hart rattled on about machine operation and safety rules. Today they'd finally get their hands dirty. And they'd pair up.

Peter had tried to keep himself from staring outright at Brice, but the thought of working with a partner today had him turning to her.

She sat at the end of a workbench, her usual spot, carving something into the table with a pocketknife that she shouldn't have in school. She wore her t-shirt inside out. It probably had words or an image on the right side—a violation of the dress code. A quiet kid and three other guys—best buddies Liam, Emmett, and King— shared the table with her. She rarely spoke to them. When Mr. Hart made everyone pair up today, they would have one extra person at that table. And that's when Peter would step in. Maybe he should go sit over there now.

"He's gonna be late." Fred stared at Mr. Hart and the kid from the last class.

"Hey, Mr. Hart," Peter hollered. "Bell rang, you know."

Mr. Hart glanced at the wall clock then he mouthed, "Oh," and shut off the lathe. He motioned for the boy to scram, then his round eyes shifted to the kids at the workbenches and his brows lowered. "Let me grab something and we'll get started." He took off for his desk in the corner of the room.

Peter slid off his stool, a thought coming to him. What if Brice and the shy kid paired up? "You know . . ." he said to Fred, who was now staring at him. How was he going to explain this without giving away his real motive?

"You know what?"

"Well . . ." Pulse pounding at the base of his neck, Peter backed up. "We've got an odd number at our table, and so do they." He jabbed his thumb in the direction of Brice's table. "So . . . I think I'll just . . . sit over there." He did an about-face and marched to Brice's table.

"I thought you were working with me, man," Fred shouted. "What gives?"

Everyone at Brice's table jerked their faces to Peter, including Brice.

"Anyone care if I sit here?" Peter scraped the stool out and sat before anyone answered.

"Is this seat taken?" Emmett said, his voice high. "What a lame pickup line."

Peter's gaze snapped to Brice, who was thumbing her artwork on the edge of the table, and back to Emmett. Did Emmett suspect his motives? Nah. He was just a dork like that, always mocking everyone. "Just trying to even out the tables. We've got to pair up, right?"

"So, you wanna pair up with me?" Emmett gave Peter the once-over.

"I uh . . ." Peter's mind went blank. How should he answer that?

Liam flung one hand up. "I thought you and me were gonna work together making Cajun drums for our band."

"Yeah, we are," Emmett said.

Peter exhaled. Chewed dry skin on his bottom lip. Glanced at Brice.

As if sensing his thoughts, she put her knife away and glanced back, her eyes holding an aggressive don't-tread-on-me look.

Something inside Peter flipped. He stopped chewing his lip and gave her a weak smile.

She didn't smile back, but no biggie.

"Okay, class." Mr. Hart thumped toward the workbenches, focusing on the notebook in his hands.

Peter's innards flipped again. Any second now, Mr. Hart would tell them to pick a partner. How was he going to ask her? What if she said no?

Mumbling to himself, Mr. Hart stopped and propped his foot on the rungs of a stool. The class quieted and he looked up. "You'll get to start your projects today. It might help to choose the same project as your partner, but it's not necessary. You'll need to help each other out and kind of work together, double-checking each other's ideas and measurements. Like I've explained already." His voice lowered and he hunched over his notebook, which he'd set on the workbench.

Peter's mouth went dry. As soon as Mr. Hart said it, he would just look at her and say, "Want to? You and me?" No, no, no. That wouldn't sound right. He needed to make it real casual-like. He could scan the room as if not sure whom to pair up with and then turn to her and say, "We could be partners. How about it?" Or no, he should wait until the other dudes at the table paired off, then he could just look at her and shrug. "Looks like it's you and me." She wouldn't pick one of them first, would she? Like maybe the shy dude?

"Right. So today—" Mr. Hart looked up from his notebook.

Peter's heart turned into a rock and shot to his throat. He couldn't help but glance at Brice.

Bored indifference in her eyes, she stared at the teacher.

"I'll assign partners and machines." Mr. Hart turned a page and pointed to a line in his notebook. "Ethan, you're with Daniel. King, you're with Logan . . ."

Kids groaned and muttered.

"You're assigning partners?" Peter slouched, his hope grinding to a halt. "You mean, we don't get to pick?"

Mr. Hart rattled off names. Kids got up and stood by their partners, everyone talking.

"He's probably pairing smart kids with idiots." Brice smirked. "It'll make it easier on him in the long run."

A crooked smile took over Peter's face. He wanted to give a smart reply—they could bond with their sarcasm—but his mind drew a blank.

She turned and stared at him. "Well?"

"Well, what?" Temperature spiking under her gaze, Peter still couldn't think of a reply. Wait! Was she expecting him to say something? She wanted to talk to him? Any chance she liked him? If he could get his brain to work, they could talk and she'd see they had a lot in common.

"Hart paired you with Owen." Humor and a bit of attitude glinted in her eyes, as if she were testing or challenging him.

"What? Oh, I didn't hear him call my name." His heart was doing a strange number in his chest, thumping its own little rap song. He looked around the room. Two kids sat at a table. Everyone else stood with their partner. Where was Owen?

"He's not here today," Brice said. "Neither is Jayden."

"Jayden?" He knew who Jayden was, but his tone of voice said he didn't. *Work, brain. Kick into gear.*

"Are you listening to Mr. Hart at all?" Brice leaned over the table, her biceps flexing as she folded her arms, that look of challenge still in her eyes.

"Uh, yeah."

"He's calling out partners. Jayden's my partner, but he's not here. Looks like we start off flying solo."

"Flying . . . Oh, right." He'd better go find his partner. Peter slid off the stool and turned from the table, but wait— "Did you say your partner's not here?" And neither was his!

Brice laughed. "So, I guess Owen's the smart one, huh?"

Not getting it, Peter shook his head. "Hey, since our partners aren't here, why don't we see if we can work together?"

She shrugged. "You can ask the teacher if you want to. I don't care who I'm working with. I'm making me a gun rack."

"Yeah, okay. Cool." Peter walked backwards, nodding at her, flat out impressed by her project choice. "I-I'll go ask." He turned and slammed into a beefy kid.

"Watch it, homey." King shoved him back, a mocking smile on his face. Then he draped an arm over Peter's shoulders and walked a few steps with him. "You actually hitting on Brice?"

A nearby group of guys caught King's question. They laughed and commented to each other, their tones as mocking as King's. They all must've figured Peter out.

Peter's face burned. Mom always told him he turned red as a tomato when he blushed. He gave the slightest headshake. If Brice was watching and if she heard the question, he didn't want to deny it.

King leaned closer, his lanky arm digging into Peter's shoulder. "You know that girl be into girls, right?"

Yeah, he knew it, but things could change. Maybe she hadn't met the right guy yet. Irritation shooting through him, Peter flung King's arm off his shoulders and got a few feet of distance between them. "Don't you have a project to start, a machine to run? A finger to lop off?"

"You're wasting your time on her." King cut a glance back to where Brice sat, but she paid them no mind. "Better to bust a move on a real girl."

Cuss words and nasty replies filled his mind, but Peter took a breath and kept them all in. Brice was better than a "real" girl. Real girls were fake. And there was that 1980s song back in his head.

7

PRANKED

ROLAND ROUNDED THE CORNER and crashed into a girl, books falling to his feet, red hair sailing to his face, and a squeal sounding in his ear. The girl stumbled back and lifted her eyes to him, gorgeous green eyes that made Roland's heart flip-flop in his chest. *Caitlyn Summer.* If he had to bump into anyone . . .

"This is like the fifth boy you've crashed into this week," Phoebe said.

"Oh. Hi, Roland. Sorry I . . ." Caitlyn exchanged looks with her friends Kiara and Phoebe then the three of them giggled. "Stinks down there." She pointed over her shoulder. Kiara whispered something to Phoebe and giggled again.

"Oh." Roland's mind drew a blank. Unable to process what she'd said, he felt lucky to have gotten the word "Oh" out. He stooped for her books, dropping down without thinking. Pain shot through his knee. His backpack, which he'd been carrying over one shoulder, slid to floor.

Giggling, she dropped to one knee with him and half-knelt in her long skirt. "I think someone's been pranked." She grabbed his backpack and handed it to him.

He tried exchanging her books for the backpack, but she didn't have a free hand. "Pranked?" His brain kicked back into gear and he blinked, thinking over what she'd said. "You mean, like a prank on an outcast?" He glanced over her shoulder at the hallway and inhaled a deep breath to see what she meant by "stinks down there." The odor of dead fish slapped the back of his throat, and he gagged.

"Did you see the posters yesterday?" she said.

Roland coughed, pushing down the urge to retch, then he breathed out of his mouth. "Keefe told me what they said." *Wait!* His attention snapped back to his locker, which wasn't that far away. His heart thudded hard against his ribs. Was he the target today? Him again?

"Yeah, someone's mean, huh?"

"Yeah." He managed to return his gaze to hers, and they stood up together.

"Come on, Caitlyn. I can't breathe." Eyes rolling back and mouth hanging open, Phoebe waved a hand in front of her nose, making her ten million bracelets jangle. "And we have to get to Geometry."

Caitlyn walked backwards, nearing her friends. "See ya tonight, right?"

"Huh?" His brain froze again. Words from his conversation with his twin brothers last night flashed in his mind, and he pictured them double dating with Jarret and— No, that would never happen.

Still inching back, she hugged her books. "With the Fire Starters? To help clean up?"

"Oh, right. Yeah."

She smiled and skipped off with her friends, her wild curls swinging across her back.

Once she disappeared from view, Roland turned and exhaled. Then he took an unguarded breath, gagging this time. What caused the smell? Dead fish or something worse?

Three kids stood at their lockers. No, make that two. The third kid slammed his locker and took off. The few remaining kids in the hallway breathed through their mouths and jog-walked, their faces scrunched.

Mustering an ounce of determination, Roland sucked in a breath and held it as he strode to his locker. He needed his books, so he might as well get it over with. If someone had targeted him, he'd just have to clean out his locker and show up late for his next class.

A bit hesitant, he lowered his backpack to the floor and reached for the combination lock.

A locker slammed nearby.

He jerked his hand back from the lock and glanced to the side.

Five lockers down stood a girl in black pants, a long purple sweater, and a thin cream-colored scarf that covered every trace of her hair. Her palm rested chest-high on her closed locker door. She grunted and slammed her hand to the locker again. Her gaze flickered to Roland and back to her lock. She spun her lock one way and another.

Minding his own business, Roland braced himself, ready for whatever he'd find, and then he spun his lock and eased open the door.

The overhead light removed all shadows, revealing . . . a tidy stack of books and folders on the metal shelf, a black jacket hanging from a hook, and his silver insulated water bottle in a bottom corner. Everything just as he'd left it.

The tension drained from his body. The smell didn't come from his locker.

After he traded books, he slung his backpack over a shoulder, slammed his locker, and turned, ready to bolt to fresher air. Glimpsing the girl five lockers down, he stopped.

She made a fist and looked ready to pound her locker again. She still hadn't gotten it open.

"Can I help?" Adjusting his backpack on his back and breathing through his mouth, he stepped toward her.

With her dark brown eyes narrowed, she gave him the once-over, maybe deciding if she could trust him. "I can't get the lock." She stepped back and handed him a folded piece of paper.

He glanced at her combination, swirly numbers written in pink marker, and grabbed the lock.

"Someone put glue in my last lock." She watched him work. "The janitor had to cut it off."

Roland spun the dial one way and the other then he stepped back so she could open it. His foot brushed a paper on the floor. The words "out of order" had been written in black marker on a piece of paper ripped from a spiral notebook. It reminded him of the warning posters someone had posted all over school. The blood drained from Roland's face.

"Wait!" he blurted, swinging a hand out to stop her.

He was too slow.

She flung the door open, creating a burst of putrid fishy odor, and stood gaping at something in the bottom of her locker. Face contorted with a look of disgust, she staggered back and turned away.

A gazillion tiny fish—maybe sardines—lay scattered on the bottom of the locker. Particles of fish clung to the inside of the door, and one little fish hung on the sleeve of a dark blue jacket. Kids must've pushed them in through the vent slots.

A wave of empathy washing over him and a hint of anger, Roland flicked the fish from the jacket sleeve. "Let's go report this."

She turned enough to glance at him and nodded, her eyes glittering with tears but her jaw set with a show of strength.

They walked side by side into fresher air and clusters of students loitering outside classrooms. When he'd been pranked by C.W., Trent, and Konner on the first day of school, he hadn't wanted to report it. He'd abandoned his books and hobbled straight to the bathroom to wash his face, hoping the smallest number of people had seen him and wishing he could go home. He'd considered skipping the last class of the day, but when the principal had found him, he'd been given a pass anyway.

Why were kids so cruel? What did they gain from making someone else miserable?

Could C.W., Trent, and Konner be responsible for all the pranks? Who could have such a vendetta against outcasts? Did anyone really think they were better than anyone else because of skin color, religion, popularity, or anything else?

The girl stopped a few feet from the office doorway, her eyes now dry and resolve coloring her expression. "Thank you for your help. I've got this."

"Yeah, okay. Want me to wait?"

She shook her head then she turned to the office, lifted her chin, and strode through the open doorway.

Not wanting to pass through the fish odor again, Roland limped down an empty hall, taking the long way to his next class. He stopped at a water fountain to rinse the bad taste from his mouth.

Tension-filled voices came from around the nearest corner, two girls at odds.

"I know you, Brice. How many years?"

"Doesn't matter. You only think you know me." She paused. "How did you end up down here, anyway? Following me? Why?"

"Listen, you think I don't know you but I do. And I see you trying to hide who you are."

The other girl—Brice from his speech class?—called the first girl a bad name.

"Instead of going it alone, you should join us. We're there for each other, and you need someone on your side."

"Oh, I do?" Brice sounded sarcastic and closed to the other's suggestion.

"We all do. That's why Empowerment exists. It's not just to help change the attitudes of others. We're here for support."

"Sorry, Tessia. I'm not interested."

A locker slammed as Roland straightened up from the fountain. He took one step.

Brice rushed from around the corner and came within inches of smacking into Roland, reminding Roland of the first time he crashed into her.

Jaw clenched and eyes dark, she glared as she swerved around him. "You again. Watch where you're going."

Acting as if he'd heard nothing and not looking at her twice, Roland strode on his way. He'd recognized the look in her eyes. It spoke of anger and an intense desire for privacy, things he could relate to.

A list began forming in Roland's mind: names of people he would have to spy on, character traits of victims of the "hate crimes" and pranks, and patterns he would have to note, tactics he could use to uncover the perpetrators. Who would be next on the outcast list? Maybe Roland West, loner.

Unless he uncovered them first.

8

CLEAN UP

"WHERE IS SHE?" A crisp breeze toyed with Peter's hair and rustled the leaves of the young tree beside him. Standing in the back of Dad's full-sized truck parked on the curb, one foot propped up on a wheel well, he visually inspected the front yard and the older split-level house. Brice's house. It sat on a corner lot, separated by a chain link fence from a hillbilly house on the next street over.

He sighed though he had no reason to feel disappointment. It would've been nice, but he hadn't really expected to see her here. She'd probably taken off for a friend's house an hour before the Fire Starters said they'd come over. Did she have friends? She was new to the area. Where'd she move from anyway?

Well, whatever . . . she might not've gone anywhere. In fact, she might've been inside right now, peering out at the Fire Starters milling around the front yard. Maybe even looking at him.

Something inside Peter stirred.

While she probably hated the attention, a part of her might've been thankful to have the Fire Starters' help.

The Fire Starters . . . how many? Two, four, six . . . Peter's gaze latched onto the burnt tree with eerie black limbs that reached like claws toward the clear blue sky, and he stopped counting.

A pensive mood had settled upon all of them when they'd first viewed the unnerving scene. Now playful voices carried. Three boys walked by with shovels, heading for the black tree. Charred grass surrounded it in an uneven circle. The scumbags who'd done all this had even uprooted the mums that had grown near the house and scattered their clumpy yellow flowers everywhere. Bits of trash formed a trail through another part of the yard, leading toward the garage. Another trail, less obvious—little two-inch circles spaced a few feet apart—ran through the grass, but those could've been caused by the kids and one of their toys, like a pogo stick or something. And the garage . . .

Peter's jaw tensed. Angry black letters stretched across the weathered white garage door, spelling hateful words that made anger creep up in Peter. Who would call her those things? What did they know? Just because she was different . . .

"Maybe it'll look even better than before. Most importantly, we want you to know we care." Father Carston's voice and his message of consolation rose above the din. He stood on the front porch with Brice's foster mother, Mrs. Escott, a rounded middle-aged woman in jeans, pullover sweater, and a ponytail. A toddler flopped and flailed around her feet. For the past fifteen minutes, Father and Mrs. Escott had been talking. In the window behind them, images flashed on a big TV in the living room, half-drawn curtains moved, and two little faces popped into and out of view. Yellow light shone in an upstairs window. Blinds covered another bedroom window. And a third window was entirely dark. Hers?

"If you don't have anything to do, you can help pick up trash." Yanking a black garbage bag from a box, Phoebe stomped to two other girls who looked a bit lost. Sounding and acting like a boss, she swung out an arm full of bracelets and pointed to the trail of trash and to a bulging garbage bag at the end of the driveway. The creeps had dumped out the family's garbage cans. It looked like someone had picked up some of it already—Brice had probably even helped— but they'd probably waited until after filing an official police report. Who could blame them? The foster parents had their hands full with three preschool-age foster children.

Peter glanced at the upstairs bedroom windows again, his gaze lingering on the darkest one.

"Oh, careful," a girl said, snagging Peter's attention.

Caitlyn bounced by with Kiara and another girl, Kiara lugging a folded card table, the other girl a case of water. Caitlyn cradled three plates of cookies covered with tinfoil, maybe more than she should try to carry. At the meeting last night, the girls had suggested bringing snacks, thinking it would ensure more people came to help.

"Two, four, six, eight . . ." Peter finished counting this time: about a dozen Fire Starters had come to help. Where was Roland? He hadn't changed his mind, had he? Peter still needed to convince Roland to find the dorkwads who'd done this. Sure, Peter could investigate on his own, but he didn't want Brice to find out. Better for Roland to do it.

"Peter, snap out of it." Dad's low voice and urgent tone unsettled Peter. "You're supposed to be unloading everything. We need that tree." Standing between the trailer with the stump grinder and the open tailgate, Dad waved a hand. Then he dragged a coiled hose off the back of the truck bed and handed it to Dominic. "Everyone's working but you."

Peter slid his foot from the wheel well and turned to the tree Dad had picked up today, a Japanese Tree Lilac. A bunch of stuff blocked it in: wet and smelly bags of mulch and fertilizer, flats of pansies, containers of spring-blooming bulbs, paint remover, and several yard tools. Once Father Carston had told Dad the plan, Dad had stopped by Brice's foster parents' house to see what kind of tree they'd like. Guess they wanted something ornamental to replace whatever ornamental thing that black skeleton of a tree had been.

"Lift the tree on up over the side." A breeze tousling his dirty-blond hair and work gloves hanging from a pocket, Dad walked around the side of the truck to where he could almost reach the tree.

Stepping in the few inches of space he found between things, Peter grabbed each side of the eighteen-inch diameter bucket that held the tree and hoisted it up. With a grunt and a bit of effort, he lugged the fifty-or-so-pound bucket toward Dad's waiting hands.

"Easy now." Dad grabbed the bucket from Peter and swung it to the ground, making it look light. "I'll carry it over," he said to four boys who had come to help. "We'll need to chop off the limbs of the old tree before we dig it up, load 'em in the back of the truck. And, you two . . ." He pointed to Fred and another kid. "Make sure the new hole is twice as wide . . ."

For the next few minutes, Peter handed things to Dad, who handed things to various kids and gave instructions for where to place them and what jobs needed done.

As Peter handed the last items to Dad—a box of scrapers and rags—car doors slammed. Peter turned to see a group of girls exiting a blue sedan two driveways down. The sedan took off.

Where was Roland? He better not have changed his mind about helping. *Wait!* Peter did a double take.

The Wests' silver Lexus rolled down the street, gleaming in the late afternoon sunlight. Finally!

Peter thumped across the empty truck bed, put a hand to the side, and jumped out. Dad continued rattling off instructions to the three boys that walked with him toward the burnt tree in the middle of the front yard. Two kids had started digging around it. Caitlyn squatted by the card table Kiara had set up, picking up things from the grass. Cookies?

Peter shook his head and turned away. Roland and Keefe strolled down the sidewalk. *Wait, if I want Roland to help investigate, all I have to do is—* "Hey, Caitlyn!"

She popped up, grabbed a plate of cookies, and scurried toward Peter, brushing one hand on her denim skirt.

Dumbfounded, Peter squinted at her. "What do you think you're doing?"

A smile on her face, she lifted the plate with both hands and brought the chocolate-chip cookies up to his nose. "Isn't that why you called me over here?"

"No." He pushed the plate back. "I want to ask you something. Besides, I totally saw you pick cookies up off the ground and put 'em back on the plate."

"They only landed on the grass. I'm sure it's clean. It's nature."

"Right." Peter rolled his eyes. "Do dogs and squirrels have bathrooms?"

She tilted her head to one side, apparently not getting it. Then her gaze shifted, her eyes opened wide, and she sucked in a breath.

Still a dozen steps away, Roland and Keefe drew near, walking in step and carrying that calm, cool, and collected West boy air about them. Even though Keefe now seemed supercharged with the faith, he still had something of his twin's pompous demeanor.

Caitlyn whispered something to herself. Then one hand lifted from the plate of cookies—which then tilted—and her hand shot to her hair.

Peter laughed. "Don't worry. He likes you just the way you are."

As if unaware he'd caught her primping, she gave him a funny look and returned her hand to the plate.

Peter shouted to Roland and Keefe, "Hey, there you are. Better late than never, huh?"

Keefe's gaze dropped to his watch. Roland's shifted to Caitlyn. Caitlyn dipped her head and offered the plate of cookies.

"No, thanks." Keefe scanned the yard.

"Looking for Father?" Peter said, just as unsuspecting Roland took a cookie. "He's on the front porch, talking to the family, well, the mom, anyways, and a toddler, but not . . ." Peter breathed. He shouldn't say Brice's name. Keefe might suspect he liked her. They probably wouldn't even see her this evening. She'd probably taken off.

Keefe nodded and strode toward Father. Peter found himself peering past Roland at a strip of trees between houses. Brice could be anywhere.

"So, what did you want me for?" Caitlyn tapped Peter's leg with her sneaker. "You said you wanted to ask me something."

"Oh, yeah. So, it's pretty rotten what someone did here, right?" He wanted to ease into the subject matter, making sure he got Caitlyn on his side. Because if he had her, he'd have Roland. And Roland could crack this case.

Caitlyn glanced over her shoulder, in the direction of the burnt tree. "Right. That's why we're here. Shouldn't you be helping your dad with the tree?"

Wielding pruning shears and gesturing while he spoke, Dad babbled on to three teens about how deep they'd need to dig the hole for the new tree. Always the teacher. A pile of black branches lay on the ground, the tree now almost stripped clean.

"Yeah. I'll help in a minute." Peter glanced at Roland and returned his attention to Caitlyn. "But first, we need to talk. We're gonna clean all this up, make it better than ever, but don't you still wanna know who did this?"

Caitlyn shrugged. "I guess so. Someone should be held responsible and not think they can get away with something so mean."

"Exactly." Peter folded his arms and grinned at Roland.

Roland remained stone-faced, apparently having no clue he was about to fall into Peter's trap.

"So, I think we should investigate." Peter slapped his palms together, showing his readiness.

"Didn't Father say the police were investigating," Caitlyn said, "like, they might even question us?"

"Well, yeah, but I'm sure they've got other priorities. And you know we're on their suspect list, right? So, I think we should solve it first, before they even consider laying the blame on us."

Roland bobbed his head—nodding in agreement?—and he made a sweeping gaze of their surroundings—planning the investigation? When he stopped nodding and looking around, he turned to Peter. "What's your plan?"

"Gotcha. Now you'll do it because of—"

Roland shot a hostile glare, and Peter shut up. They both knew the reason he agreed to help now. Caitlyn.

"I was already going to help." He gave a sulky look.

"Yeah, right."

"Right."

"What do we do first?" Caitlyn whispered, leaning toward Peter.

"I don't know. Ask Roland. He's our chief investigator."

"Me?" His eyebrows climbed up his forehead.

"You know you're the most qualified."

"Yeah," Caitlyn whispered, looking a bit awestruck. "You found that thief in Arizona, right?"

Roland and Caitlyn looked into each other's eyes, Roland with his mouth hanging open as if he'd forgotten how to speak.

"That's right." Peter shoved Roland to snap him out of it. "So, what's our plan?"

Stuffing his hands into his jacket pockets, Roland scanned their surroundings again. Then he looked at Caitlyn. "We should thoroughly investigate the yard, check every inch of grass—"

Peter slapped Caitlyn's arm, jarring the plate of cookies. "Caitlyn can do that. In fact, didn't I see you checking the grass already?"

She glared and tried to kick him, but he hopped back. "Well, I did see something in the grass that you probably didn't even notice."

"Oh yeah, what's that? Cookie crumbs?"

"No, circles. They're here and there, in little double rows." No longer appearing fazed by Peter's mocking, she pointed toward a section of grass.

Roland looked where she pointed.

"I saw 'em," Peter said. "The kids probably made them."

"We'll make a note of it anyway. It's a good observation." Roland turned to Peter. "Now you figure out how they started the fire. They didn't just take a lighter to that tree."

The thrill of adventure making him a bit giddy, Peter nodded. "Right! Like for the annual camping trip, when we ignite our massive tepee of branches, we always use some kind of fuel."

"Okay, let's do it." Roland turned to go.

"Wait a sec." Peter grabbed his arm. "And what are you going to do?"

"Someone needs to poke around the backyard and stuff."

"And stuff?" Red flags popped up in Peter's mind. What would Brice think of them digging around? Maybe she already knew who'd done it, and she didn't want the world to know. "I mean, we want to investigate, but we don't want anyone to know we're trying to, you know, investigate. We've gotta use cloak-and-dagger tactics. Understand?"

The hint of a smile played on Roland's lips. "Don't worry. I can move around unseen."

"Yeah, if anybody can . . ." Peter glanced at Roland's leg. Before he'd broken it, he could sneak up on anyone, but now with his limp, Peter always heard him coming. "You sure you're able to resume stealth mode?"

The slant of Roland's eyebrows showed he took offense. "I got it."

"We should probably try to help clean up while we're at it," Caitlyn said.

"Or at least look like we're helping, right?" Peter grinned at her. "Put the cookies down and you can dig through the mums, pretend you're replanting them."

Caitlyn smacked his arm and turned away with the plate of cookies. Roland took off too, his limp less obvious.

Peter shuffled toward the tree, assessing the growing stack of black branches and the charred tree trunk two boys dug around.

A few feet away, Dad crouched by the hole for the new tree. "It's helpful to prune off dead roots," he said to the two kids with him. Then he said something about slicing through the root ball, and he jerked his face to Peter. "Hey, Peter!"

Before Peter could reply, he glimpsed the scorched grass and the pattern he hadn't noticed before. A strip of burnt grass stretched out from the rest of the singed grass. Which probably meant—

"Peter, we're going to need that stump grinder unloaded."

"What?" Anxious to investigate and share his thoughts with Roland, Peter ran a hand through his hair. "But I've got to—" He flung a hand out, pointing anywhere but here.

Dad threw a "do it now" look.

Peter sighed. "Yeah, all right."

Half an hour or so later, they'd ground the stump down and filled the hole. Keefe and two others had planted the Japanese Tree Lilac a few feet away and created a three-inch ring of soil around the edges of the root zone. Now Keefe watered it with the hose while Fred ripped open the mulch bags.

"Hey, Peter." Dad wiped down the stump grinder. He'd sprayed it with the hose before giving the hose to Keefe.

"Yeah?" Feeling grimy from head to toe, Peter brushed sawdust off his hands. How much more would Dad have him do? He needed to talk to Roland and Caitlyn and see if they discovered anything.

"Take that fertilizer." Dad pointed. "And go see where Mrs. Escott wants you to put it. They won't need it for a month."

"Yeah, okay." Peter hoisted the bag up and lugged it under one arm toward the house.

Caitlyn and Kiara, both on their knees, arranged pansies in the flowerbed along the front of the house. They'd raked smooth the dirt between the rhododendron bushes. Another girl bagged up damaged plants and the plastic containers that had held the flowers. A kid with a bulging black bag picked up something, probably the last traces of garbage. Everything was coming together. They'd probably be done in half an hour.

Peter climbed the steps to the empty front porch. The TV still flickered in the living room and a figure moved past. Might've been Mrs. Escott. Might've been . . .

Heartbeat kicking up, he set the mulch at his feet and pounded on the door.

A second later, the door creaked open. Mrs. Escott pushed open the storm door and smiled. "Peter, right?"

"Uh, yeah." How did she know his name? Dad might've mentioned it. Any chance Brice did? Peter forced his thoughts back to business. "Hey, so, my dad says you'll need to fertilize the tree in a month. So, he got this." He lifted the bag to show her. "Where do you want me to put it?"

"Anywhere in the garage is fine, somewhere off to the side. Oh, wait." She peeked outside in the direction of the garage. Phoebe and another girl, both wearing yellow rubber gloves, scrubbed the last of the graffiti off the garage door. "There's a gate along the side." She pointed. "Go around to the back door of the garage."

"Okey dokey. I mean, yes, ma'am."

Mrs. Escott smiled. "Okey dokey."

Peter followed the sidewalk to the driveway, a sharp odor of mineral-spirits filling the air. A can of paint remover sat at the edge of the driveway. He'd drop off the fertilizer and find Roland.

"Hey, Peter!"

Peter jumped and turned, giving Caitlyn an irritated glare. "Don't sneak up behind me like that."

"Did I scare you?" With hands behind her back and an elfish grin, she looked pleased with the idea.

Standing slouched so he could rest the bag on the ground, Peter exhaled and rolled his eyes. "What's up?"

"Look what I found." She brought one hand forward and dangled a beaded bracelet up at eye level.

"Hey." A whispered voice came from behind Peter, making the hair on his neck stand on end.

He spun around, the bag of fertilizer slipping from his grip.

Roland stood behind him, sporting the hint of a grin.

"Hey, yourself. So where've you been?" Peter glanced around but saw no one near enough to overhear them. "Find anything?"

"Yeah, I did. You?"

"I did too," Caitlyn said, again lifting the bracelet.

Looking mesmerized, Roland stared at the bracelet. Or maybe at her. The setting sun created long shadows from houses and trees, but she stood between shadows and a beam of golden sunlight made her green eyes sparkle and her hair glow like orange flames.

"Okay, lemme see." Peter snatched the bracelet and nudged Caitlyn into a shadow. The bracelet was made of glass starbursts and polished wood beads in different colors: birch-like yellow, orangish maple or oak, cherry red, some kind of black wood, bluish gray, and chocolate brown . . . maybe walnut.

"It's pretty in the sunlight." She snatched it back and stepped into the light again. "So, what do we do next? We should talk to the neighbors. Someone might've seen something. And maybe we can learn something from kids at school."

Roland stared at her again, his mouth half open.

"Caitlyn, you're distracting someone, and we don't want to draw attention." Peter grabbed her arm and yanked her back into the shadows. "So where'd you find it?"

"Over there." She twisted around and pointed toward the porch. "It was hanging from the lattice around the porch, like maybe it had fallen from the railing or something."

"On the garage side?" Roland asked, back in detective mode.

She nodded.

"Ah, it's probably one of the foster kids." Peter reached for it.

Caitlyn turned so he couldn't get it and slid it over her hand. "This isn't a little kid's bracelet." She admired it on her skinny wrist. Roland admired it too.

"Well, anyway, you told me to figure out how they started the fire." Peter shifted to block Roland's view of Caitlyn and get him back on track. "And I'd say they used gasoline. A trail of scorched grass comes off the bigger circle of black grass, and it's pretty wide. So, unless I had a flaming arrow or something to throw at it from a distance, I'd make a little trail of gasoline that led away from the gasoline-soaked tree. Then I'd toss a burning stick onto the end of the trail. And I'd run like heck. They could've used kerosene or lighter fluid or something but gasoline's so fumy, you know, with its vapor density and low flash point, so it would really burst in every direction. And like I said, the burned trail is pretty wide . . ."

"Who cares?" Caitlyn sighed. "Is this a chemistry lesson?"

"No, he's right," Roland said. "I mean, not about vapor density and all that, but he's right about them using gas."

"And how do you know?" Peter folded his arms and lifted a brow.

"Found a gas can in the woods over there." Roland threw a glance over his shoulder, without indicating anywhere in particular.

"Where is it?"

"I tossed it in the trunk of the Lexus."

"Why?" Caitlyn said.

Roland shrugged. "Maybe we'll find out whose it is. The Escotts didn't mention anyone taking anything, so one of the punks probably brought it."

"Hmm, yeah." Peter grinned, glad to have Roland on the case. They had something to go on now. Maybe two somethings. "Let me have the bracelet. I'll see if it's Brice's."

"Okay, well, I have to get back to work." Caitlyn handed him the bracelet and drew flowered gardening gloves from the pocket of her denim skirt. "We're planting flowers. Either of you want to help?"

"Not me." Peter lifted the fertilizer bag. "I need to get this in the garage." He opened the gate and left Roland and Caitlyn staring at each other.

A sidewalk ran along the garage, leading to a cement slab with a grill and white wicker patio furniture. Plastic green and yellow toys lay scattered in a well-manicured fenced-in lawn, most of them near a swing set, slide, tree-house combo.

Peter found the back door of the garage and turned the knob. A crack of light ran along the bottom of the big garage door, and a bit of light came from the door he'd just opened. Unable to make out much inside the garage, he found a light switch.

Florescent lights flickered on, revealing one car in a two-car garage, a worn yellow BMX bike with a low seat and high handle bars, and organized clutter all along the walls: a pile of shoes, metal shelves with ratty cardboard boxes, a can of WD-40 and spray bottles of cleaners, stacks of green plastic planters, an old wooden toy box with a crooked lid, and a long metal toolbox in an otherwise empty corner.

Maybe he could shove the toolbox further down and make room for the fertilizer. A combination lock hung from the front of the toolbox and someone had scraped initials on the lid. B.A.M.

Peter's heart shimmied in his chest. Was it Brice's toolbox?

A sound came from outside, snagging his attention. The rattle of a chain-link fence. Quick footfalls. Then a flash of blond hair and a figure appeared in the doorway: Brice Maddox in over-sized jeans and a sweatshirt with an image of a coiled rattlesnake, her hair tousled, her face flushed . . .

Peter forgot how to breathe.

Two steps in, Brice stopped in her tracks and her eyes narrowed at Peter. "Whatdya doing in here?"

"Uh, I'm . . ." Peter lifted the bag of fertilizer. "Fertilizer."

Still with an unfriendly look, she gave him a crooked grin. "You're fertilizer?"

"Uh, no. I'm not." Heat spreading from head to toe, he shook his head. He was such a dork around her. "I'm not fertilizer. But you'll need to fertilize the new tree in a month so we . . ." His mouth hung open for one full second while he debated what to say next. "And I wanted to put it somewhere, so I asked your . . . uh . . ."

"Foster mother?"

"Right." He breathed. Cool sweat gathered on his neck. "She said to put it in here, out of the way."

"Lean it against the corner." She flicked her index finger at the corner nearest him. Then she seemed to study him for a second. "So, you're with the Catholic youth group, huh?"

"Um . . ." If he said yes, would that impact his chances with her? What was he thinking? All his friends, and especially Keefe West, would probably walk on coals rather than deny their faith for a girl. "Yeah, I am. We all felt pretty bad about, you know, what happened—"

"You guys about done here?"

"Uh, yeah. Probably half an hour. Got the old tree out, new tree in. Just gotta paint the garage door and spread some mulch." Was she asking because she wanted to help? Or was she annoyed to find them still here? Was he improving his chances with her? Or blowing it?

Without another word, Brice stomped up three cement steps to the side door of the house. She yanked it open, slipped inside, and slammed it behind her.

Peter blew out a breath, his body relaxing. He wiped the sweat from his neck and combed a hand through his hair. Okay, he'd have to see where he stood with her tomorrow. Maybe he'd ask her about the bracelet. He wasn't giving up.

9

SNOOP

ROLAND SAT NEXT TO PETER and across from Caitlyn and her friends Kiara and Phoebe, the chatter and electricity in the school cafeteria disrupting his thoughts about the investigation. Or maybe something else distracted him more. A swirling pattern of royal blue leaves, stems, and flowers edged the neckline and sleeves of Caitlyn's crinkled white dress. Elegant and homey, it reminded him of their live-in maid's heirloom china.

Nanny had served her husband, Mr. Digby, cherry streusel on those plates just last night while they'd had a one-sided conversation. Mr. Digby never shared his feelings or opinions about anything. Not that Roland blamed him. He preferred to keep things to himself too. Maybe it was a guy thing.

A slight breeze and movement in his peripheral vision snapped Roland from his thoughts and alerted him to something whizzing by overhead.

Peter laughed and jumped up, planting one foot on the bench seat and standing like a lumberjack as he peered across the cafeteria. "Was that a meat patty?"

"It's like a zoo in here. We should've met outside." Caitlyn dipped a potato stick into a chocolate pudding cup. Her peanut butter and jelly sandwich lay untouched. She peered over her shoulder for the fourth time in five minutes. "I wonder what they've been whispering about."

Roland looked.

A group of River Run High's most popular junior and senior girls sat together, filling an entire table. One whispered to another, who turned . . . possibly looking at the table of outcasts. The outcasts tended to sit at the table by the garbage cans, each in their own world for the most part. The girl with the headscarf walked past the outcasts, not making eye contact. She carried a water bottle and a flowered lunch bag to the far cafeteria doors. Did she have friends? Would her house be next?

Roland took a deep breath, forcing his mind to task. They needed to move on their investigations. He couldn't organize the ideas in his mind, at the moment, but maybe if they talked about it . . .

"So, hey." Roland tossed a grape from his lunch and hit Peter on the forehead.

"Oh, you want in on the food fight?" With a look of challenge, Peter sat down and stabbed a bowtie pasta with his plastic fork. He'd brought leftover pasta salad, cold kielbasa, and a slice of cake.

"Don't be a zoo animal," Caitlyn said to Peter, just before turning toward the popular girls again.

"There's no food fight," Roland said to Peter. "It was just one meat patty."

"But it could be the beginning." Peter waggled his brows and grinned.

"You act like you're six years old," Phoebe said with a condescending tilt of her head.

"You have room to talk," Peter retorted, imitating her head tilt while his gaze roved over her spiky purple-streaked hair and the black plaid jacket she wore over her lemon-yellow tie-die shirt. Then he faced Caitlyn and flung the bowtie pasta at her. "I can't believe you already told people. It was supposed to be the three of us, cloak-and-dagger style."

The pasta got stuck in a tangle of curls on the side of Caitlyn's head. She felt around for it, missing it by inches. "I didn't tell anyone but them. And they're not going to tell anyone. They can help." She still couldn't locate the pasta.

Roland resisted the urge to help her. "Yeah, maybe having more people is a good thing."

"Huh. We'll see." Peter reached across the table and flicked the pasta from Caitlyn's hair. "But everyone needs to promise to be discreet. I don't want anyone knowing we're doing this. Got it?" He eyed everyone in turn, everyone nodding in reply. Then he slammed his palm on the table near Roland. "Okay, Sherlock, let's get started."

"Okay, we'll start with what we know from last night." He'd made a list at home of all the damage, from the most obvious thing—the burnt tree—to the least obvious thing—the trail of two-inch circles in the yard.

Caitlyn leaned across the table, her eyes on Peter. "Did you ask Brice?"

Peter's face flushed. He gave Roland a wary glance, maybe thinking Roland had told her about Peter's infatuation. "Ask her what?"

Knowing where Peter's mind had gone, Roland laughed. "She's talking about the bracelet." It could've belonged to Brice or one of the other foster kids. Then again, one of the vandals could've dropped it by accident.

"Oh." Peter hunched over his lunch. "Not yet. So . . . we know they used gasoline to torch the tree."

"Right. And they tossed the gas can in the nearest wooded area," Roland added. "It wasn't a new can either, so they hadn't bought it for the occasion. It was probably one of theirs, and they might even plan to come back for it."

"If it belonged to one of them, why would they have left it?" Kiara asked.

"Eh." His complexion returning to normal, Peter gestured with his fork. "Maybe a car came down the road, they got scared, tossed the gas can, and bolted. Maybe they took off through the woods."

"Or the gas can didn't belong to them," Roland said.

"Oh, like they stole it?" Caitlyn said, her eyes round. And green, like two shiny emeralds. And surrounded by pale whispery lashes. . .

Roland averted his gaze and shrugged. "And . . . and as far as time-frame, they had to have set the fire last."

"Oh, right." Peter nodded. "Time frame. So, like, they probably did less obvious things first: destroy the flower bed, paint the graffiti—"

"Spray cans rattle," Phoebe interrupted. "So, they probably did that just before igniting the tree or at the same time."

"Right." Peter rubbed his chin. "Then they took off. Think one of 'em had a car for a quick getaway?"

"Nah, they wouldn't want to risk anyone seeing their license plate." Roland thought about it a second longer. "But they could've parked on another street."

"Right." Peter's index finger shot up. "Maybe cut through the wooded area where you found the gas can."

"Why do we care about the order of things?" Caitlyn said, then she gave the popular girls another glance and grabbed her purse.

"I don't know," Roland said. "We have to gather all the information we can and see how it all looks together."

"Oh," she whispered, her gaze lingering as if thinking through what he'd said. Then she dug through her purse.

"So, what now?" Peter spoke with a mouthful of food.

"We should eavesdrop." Caitlyn glanced up, still digging through her purse.

"No, we should talk to people." Phoebe craned her neck and peered around the cafeteria.

"Oh, right." Peter gave Roland a look to show his disapproval. "Like, hey, what'd you do last weekend? Vandalize Brice's house?"

Phoebe curled her lip, making a childish face at Peter. "No. Questions like 'What do you think about the vandalism?' and 'Who do you think would do something like that?'"

"Oh," Kiara said, "and maybe we can ask if anyone thinks they're targeting specific kids."

Caitlyn pulled something from her purse and set her purse on the bench seat, next to Kiara.

"Good idea," Peter said to Kiara with a sarcastic tone. "Then we'll have everyone pointing the finger at everyone else, and we'll start something worse than a food fight at River Run High."

"No, I think she's right," Roland said just as Caitlyn swung her leg over the bench seat and stood.

"Will you watch my purse?" Caitlyn asked Kiara, who nodded in reply.

"Wait. Where you going?" Peter's face twisted with worry.

"That table of girls." She nodded to indicate it. "They've been whispering to each other and glancing around for the past ten minutes."

Peter laughed. "You think they vandalized Brice's house? No way. They're too prissy. They're all about hair, clothes, and makeup. No way they'd set a tree on fire or spread trash in the lawn."

"Why not?" Caitlyn shook her head. "Girls can be mean."

"And risk damaging an acrylic nail?" Peter gave Roland a cheesy grin.

"So, you think guys did it? Why would they?" Caitlyn said. "What could they have against a new girl?"

Peter scrunched his face up at Caitlyn. "How can you not know—?" Not finishing his sentence—probably something about the rumors about Brice—he turned to Roland. "So, what do you think? Guys or girls?"

"Well, they did a lot of damage," Roland said. "So, we know it was more than one person. Could've been both girls and boys. Probably not those girls, tougher girls."

"Wish me luck." Caitlyn smiled at Roland and turned away, her red curls swishing across the back of her white dress. The royal blue pattern circled around the bottom edge of the skirt too. And what was that in her hand? A flip phone?

"She's got the right idea," Phoebe said. "Come on."

"You're staring." Peter nudged Roland's arm.

"I-I didn't know she had a phone." Roland turned back, trying to look nonchalant.

Phoebe and Kiara had gotten up and headed toward the opposite side of the cafeteria.

"Disappointed she didn't give you her number?" Peter said, glimpsing Phoebe and Kiara as they neared a table of freshman. "What are they—"

Before Roland could think of a response to Peter's comment, his cell phone vibrated in his back pocket, so he settled with shooting Peter a glare. He yanked the phone out and accepted the call, vaguely aware that he didn't recognize the number. Suddenly, a warning flashed inside, and he turned just in time.

Drawing near the table of popular girls, Caitlyn somehow tripped on . . . her own feet? A tray she must've picked up along the way sailed through the air and slammed to the floor with a bang. "Oh," she shouted, losing balance, one hand landing on the popular girls' table, the other near a big purse on the bench seat.

The popular girls drew back, their mouths falling open and eyes narrowing, as if they all blamed Caitlyn for tripping. Then cruel laughter came from one girl and spread to the others.

"Sorry." Caitlyn raised her hands, backed away, and smiled sweetly. Then she took off toward Roland and Peter, speed-walking. As she drew near, she glanced at Roland's hand.

"Oh, yeah." Embarrassed that he'd left the caller hanging, he lifted his phone to his ear. "Hello?"

Eyes popping open wide, Caitlyn snatched the phone from him and put it to her ear as she sat across from him at the table.

He opened his mouth to ask why she did that, but she shushed him with a finger to her mouth.

Peter laughed. "So that's your plan, huh, Caitlyn? Brilliant."

She glared at him, held up her index finger, and mouthed, "Wait."

"So, to put you at ease," Peter said, elbowing Roland's arm, "I picked up that generic phone yesterday because we need to be able to get a hold of each other during the investigations. I didn't think she'd be planting her new phone in girls' bags."

"Oh." Finally understanding what Caitlyn had done, Roland glanced at the table of girls. Could she really hear their conversation with her flip phone in the bottom of a purse?

"Plus, she's wasting minutes, yours and hers." Peter glanced from Roland to Caitlyn. "Hear that, Caitlyn? You're wasting Roland's minutes."

Roland shrugged. "I don't care." To prove he didn't care, he turned away and found Phoebe and Kiara still at the freshman table, Phoebe doing all the talking . . . Kiara taking notes?

"Yeah, your father probably pays for yours. And even if he didn't, you'd go along with whatever she wanted."

Roland shot a glance at Caitlyn. Had she heard that? "No, I wouldn't. I wouldn't kill anyone."

"Ha. Like she'd ask you to do that." His crooked grin faded. Then he groaned impatiently and leaned toward Caitlyn. "So, what are they saying?"

With a sigh, Caitlyn handed the phone to Peter. "Nothing interesting. They're talking about boys and stupid reality shows."

Peter pressed the phone to his ear for two seconds, made a face, and ended the connection. "Take your phone back, Roland."

"Forget eavesdropping." Caitlyn jumped up again. "I'll just do what Phoebe and Kiara are doing and go talk to people."

"Wait!" Peter jumped up too and lunged for her, but she skipped around a passing student and got away. Face beet red again, Peter sat down. "This is a bad idea, isn't it? She shouldn't have told Kiara and Phoebe. I shouldn't have told Caitlyn. Everyone's gonna know we're investigating."

"Everyone's going to know *they're* investigating. So distance yourself from them."

"Yeah, and we should only meet in private, not during school hours. I don't want it getting back to . . ." He threw Roland a panicked glance.

Feeling merciful, Roland decided to rescue Peter. "I know you like Brice. Don't worry about it. And you don't want her to know you're doing all this in case she wouldn't like it."

Peter didn't move. Didn't even seem to breathe. Staring at Roland, he sat frozen with his jaw slack for two seconds. Then he sucked in a breath and exhaled. "Okay, good. But don't tell anyone. Especially not Caitlyn or the other two. And we've gotta watch them. They're so obvious." His gaze shifted to some distant point, and his eyebrows scrunched up. "Is she crazy?"

Roland turned. He blinked twice, not believing what he saw. He would never do what she was doing.

Caitlyn stood in the corner of the cafeteria, in the midst of a group of varsity football players. She folded her arms but otherwise appeared unfazed as she looked up at them and asked them questions. One of the jocks said something and gave her a crooked smile. He'd probably said something lewd. The other jocks laughed.

Caitlyn either didn't get it or didn't care. She asked another question. When they responded in the same way, her shoulders lifted and sagged. Then she marched away, heading toward the table by the garbage cans.

"Wow, she's so brave." Roland hadn't meant to comment aloud. Caitlyn, Kiara, Phoebe . . . they had no problem going up to anyone.

"That or stupid. She's not gonna find anything out. Of course, she did suggest talking to the neighbors. That might be a good idea. Maybe you and her can do that."

"Me?" As much as he liked the idea of hanging out with her, he couldn't see himself knocking on doors and asking strangers questions. He should probably get used to that though. Maybe it would help him overcome his fear of speaking before groups. Maybe even help him get the courage to give his lousy speech.

"Or maybe she can do it with Phoebe and Kiara. Everyone knows you're my friend."

"Yeah, good idea." A wave of relief rushed over him.

After a few minutes, Phoebe and Kiara moved to a table of seniors and Caitlyn disappeared.

"What is she doing now?" Peter stared through the windows that overlooked the hallway. "Man, she can't just go up to anybody. I mean some people are just too . . ."

Arms folded across her chest, Caitlyn stood in the hallway talking to a dark-haired kid who leaned against the wall with a somewhat arrogant posture.

Wait. Roland's mouth went dry. Was that . . . Was she actually talking to . . . Jarret?

Peter was still babbling, but Roland couldn't focus on what he said. Switching into high-alert mode and not comfortable with the idea of Caitlyn talking to his brother, he shifted so he could glimpse Jarret's face. What was she saying to him? How would he respond? He could get rude with people. Would he be rude to her?

Stomach flipping, Roland jumped up. "Hey, I'll be back." He glanced at Peter, who was still saying something, then he walked—forcing himself not to run—through the cafeteria and into the hall.

Caitlyn unfolded her arms and gestured as she spoke.

Jarret raised his eyebrows and peered down at her, looking a bit perplexed as to why she would ask him whatever she had asked him.

Roland had seen the look countless times before. It usually preceded a litany of rude remarks. Jarret and Caitlyn were black and white. Not just because Jarret was accustomed to a life of maid-service and expensive shirts and she a life of penny-pinching and second-hand clothes, but because she was simplicity and purity itself and he . . . well, he still seemed to struggle, though he'd turned away from the wide and dangerous path he'd been on.

Jarret's eyes narrowed even more, and he opened his mouth. In a matter of seconds, something snide would come out.

"Caitlyn." Roland zipped toward her but didn't want to stop. He didn't want to join the conversation and risk further provoking Jarret.

She turned toward him, flipping her long red mane over one shoulder.

At the sight, Roland's heart did something funny in his chest. Jarret's somewhat cold look shoved Roland's heart back into place. Three steps from her, he gave a nod for her to walk with him.

Her wide eyes showed confusion and a hint of irritation, whether from something Jarret had already said or from Roland's interruption, he couldn't guess. But she didn't look ready to comply.

One step from her, not slowing down, he reached for her arm. She lifted her arm as though she thought he was pointing out a bug or something, and his hand slid down it and right into her hand. Heart pounding from unintentionally holding her hand, he made a split-second decision to roll with it and tightened his grip to drag her down the hall, away from Jarret.

"What's wrong?" Caitlyn said.

Out of the corner of his eye, Roland caught Jarret's confused glare. Whatever Caitlyn had said to him, he didn't seem to understand.

Roland led Caitlyn down the hall to the farther cafeteria entrance, ignoring her puzzled glances as he took the long way back to Peter. Hotly aware of several kids dropping their gazes to their handhold, he weaved around a group of girls. They had to go single-file through a group of boys, so Roland released her hand and breathed.

Caitlyn mumbled something Roland didn't hear over the chatter. Then she darted back toward the table of popular girls, probably to retrieve her phone. Roland continued back to the table.

"Where'd ya go?" Peter wrinkled his forehead, looking a bit peeved. "I'm talking to you and you take off."

Taking his seat, Roland shrugged and searched for Phoebe and Kiara. They were getting up from another table.

"Were you two holding hands?" Peter gave Roland a crooked grin. "'Cuz when I saw you—"

"Drop it." Roland gave a warning look.

Caitlyn returned to the table at the same time as Phoebe and Kiara, who both had proud grins on their faces.

"Okay, so what'd you find out?" Peter leaned across the table toward them.

"Well . . ." Kiara tucked her short stringy hair behind her ear and peered at the pocket notebook in her hand. "The only ones who really answered our questions were the outcasts."

"I didn't get much either, but I have a few ideas." The gleam in Caitlyn's eyes showed she loved detective work.

"One kid said he didn't agree with vandalism," Kiara said, "and he would never do something like that, but he said people have different ways of expressing themselves."

"What?" Peter burst out. "So, he thinks it's fine?"

"No, that's not what he said." Phoebe pushed her half-eaten lunch aside and hunched over the table. "He said that type of expression shows profound bigotry. Which he thought was the reason for the talk on tolerance and all that."

"Oh, yeah. Hey . . ." Peter looked at Roland. "One of us should talk to the kids in the diversity group, Empowerment, you know, in the spirit of democracy. Maybe . . ." He slid his folded arms across the table, lowering himself over his half-eaten lunch. ". . . one of us should attend the Empowerment meetings."

Caitlyn sucked in a breath. "Yes, they're probably still talking about what happened. I bet they have a ton of ideas about who might've done it."

"Okay, so who's going to go to the meeting?" Phoebe said. "'Cuz I'm not. Kids already label me. I don't need more labels."

"Oh, I can't go either. I have something else . . ." Kiara's voice trailed off with her possibly made-up excuse.

"I would but . . ." Caitlyn bit into her peanut butter and jelly sandwich. ". . . they meet on a bad day for me," she said over her mouthful, reminding Roland of Peter.

Peter straightened. "Well, I can't." He shot Roland an accusatory glare.

"I didn't say you could." Roland didn't need Peter to tell him again how he wanted to remain anonymous.

"You'll have to do it." Peter stared, a half-crazed look in his brown eyes.

Roland shook his head in disbelief. He couldn't picture himself attending even one meeting, but someone had to. They'd likely get their best leads from that group. What would people think? Only the strangest kids belonged to that group. He exhaled long and hard. "Okay, I'll do it."

10

GUARDED

"SO, WHO'S READY to set and tune the band saw?" Mr. Hart stood with his lanky arms bent and his hands on his hips, glancing from face to face. The students stood in a semi-circle around him, no one making eye contact. Everyone would have to take a turn over the next two weeks.

Peter averted his gaze, not because he didn't know how—he could do it blindfolded . . . probably—but because he wanted to talk to Brice, and setting and tuning the band saw would take time. They could measure their wood together at a workbench instead. He could ask her about the bracelet.

Just outside the circle of guys, Brice leaned back against the corner of the nearest workbench, worrying a hangnail or something.

"What about you, Fred?" Mr. Hart bounced on his heels and flung a hand out, palm up. "You know what you're doing, right?"

Hunching as if to camouflage his height, Fred ran a hand through his dark blond hair. "Um, I wanted to watch one more time. Maybe I'll do it tomorrow."

"Okay, so . . . anyone?" Mr. Hart pivoted, scanning the circle of students, all boys except for Brice.

A kid cleared his throat. Someone else sniffed. And another guy whispered something and stifled a nervous laugh.

Mr. Hart played with a tuft of his wild hair while he waited a few seconds more. "Well, someone's got to go first."

Brice pushed off from the workbench, flicked her safety glasses open, and stomped through the circle of boys. Then she yanked the plug of the Delta 14-inch band saw, flung open the wheel guard, and set to work.

A few guys sighed in relief. And over half walked away, mumbling to each other. They could start measuring the wood for their projects.

"If you're not sure what you're doing, better stick around," Mr. Hart hollered after them. But a few more kids walked off, leaving Peter and three other guys to watch Brice work.

Admiration brought a grin to Peter's face. The bravest kid in class was the only girl.

"Okay, so Brice is adjusting the blade so that the deepest part of the gullet—that's the curved area at the base of the tooth—is lined up with the center of the wheel, which is always smart . . ." Mr. Hart started giving the remaining observers his play-by-play commentary.

Brice moved like no one was watching, spinning the wheel, her eye on the blade as it crept into position. Then she stepped to the side of the machine and reached up, the sleeve of her t-shirt riding up her solid arm. She checked the tension of the blade from the point just inside the wheel door—which was not how Mr. Hart had taught them to do it.

Peter tensed, hoping Mr. Hart didn't notice or didn't care.

"Okay, so that's another way to check the tension," Mr. Hart said, hands on hips and leaning to watch her.

Brice, acting like she hadn't heard him, stepped back around the band saw and rotated the wheel again.

Next, she pulled a wallet from the back pocket of her loose-fitting faded jeans and removed a business card. Then with efficient, confident moves and no wasted steps, she set up the upper and lower side guides—using an Allen wrench and a business card. How cool was that? Brice was a mechanical wizard.

"A business card, huh?" Mr. Hart folded his arms and twisted his lips to one side. "I guess that works."

Brice spared a glance. "It gets the right distance for the guides every time."

"Yeah, yeah, I can see that." Mr. Hart bobbed his head, looking impressed.

Within a few minutes, Brice completed the job and stepped back so Mr. Hart could check her work. She stuffed her thumbs in her belt loops and slouched, waiting as the teacher checked each part. Then Mr. Hart flipped the band saw on and it made a contended, easy humming noise. Finally, he ran a scrap of a two-by-four through and mumbled something to her about leveling the table—which Peter thought sure she'd done. The rest of the observers moseyed away, but Peter didn't budge.

"Okay, good job." The teacher scribbled something into his notebook and shuffled to the drill press. He'd want another victim to set that one up.

Brice turned and her gaze fell on Peter. Looking a tad suspicious, she gave him the once-over before blowing past him.

Peter warmed under her attention, even though it lasted a split second and didn't seem entirely friendly. Then he followed her to their workbench. At the beginning of class, while everyone else had been talking, they'd grabbed the boards and the measuring instruments they would need for their projects and set them on the table. They were both building wall-mounted three-rifle gun racks.

"So, you totally owned that." Peter propped his foot on the rung of a stool.

"Thanks." Brice pulled a folded white paper from her back pocket and straddled a stool. "I don't get what everyone's afraid of, why no one wants to go first. Go first, get it over with, I say."

"Yeah, I'll get it over with tomorrow." He glanced at the drill press. Mr. Hart motioned Fred over.

Back to her own business, Brice unfolded the pattern for the side of her gun rack and clicked a mechanical pencil. She placed the pattern on a board and smoothed it out. Unlike girls obsessed with fancy fingernails, Brice had chewed hers to the quick.

She glanced up.

Peter's stomach did a strange squirrelly thing. He yanked his backpack off the floor and found the folder that held his gun rack pattern. He'd used Dad's wall-mounted gun rack as a guide.

For the next several minutes they passed the mechanical pencil, a ruler, and a try square back and forth. And in a few minutes more, they'd have their curvy patterns transferred to the boards and they'd move to a machine. And he'd have blown his chance to talk to her.

Two machines hummed now, creating a comfortable white noise. The oil and sawdust smell in the air intensified. One kid spoke loudly to another, but everyone else worked in relative silence.

Peter stuffed his hand into a front pocket of his jeans and pushed past his keys to the wooden beads of the bracelet. What was he going to say to her? She didn't seem the type to wear jewelry. Hand still in his pocket, he wriggled the bracelet onto his fingers and then up past his thumb. The bracelet probably belonged to her foster mom. Maybe she was shaking out a rug and it slipped off and sailed over the porch rail.

The bracelet popped up past his thumb knuckle and slid to his wrist.

"Are you done?" Brice's stool squeaked. She stood next to it, two boards in her hands.

"Huh?" Snapping from thought, Peter grabbed the mechanical pencil and looked to see where he'd left off. She was already done? He still had the backboard to trace, but he wanted to go to the band saw with her. In fact, she *had* to wait for him. That was Mr. Hart's policy. They could only go to the machines two by two, like animals on Noah's ark or like Jesus's disciples. Or Jehovah's Witnesses.

"Where'd you get that?"

Peter snapped his head up. "Huh?"

She glared at the bracelet—now on his wrist. Then she looked him in the eyes. "I said, 'Where'd you get that?'"

"Get what?" Why had he pretended not to know what she meant?

"That. Thing on your wrist."

"Oh yeah, I was gonna ask." Dropping the mechanical pencil, he peeled the bracelet over his knuckles and held it out to her. "So, I found it at your house last night. You know, when we—"

"I know." She snatched up the mechanical pencil and traced a line she'd already made on one of her boards, getting down to business with quick movements. "Where'd you find it, exactly?"

"Oh, on the porch." Was that what Caitlyn had said? "Er, not on it, really, but hanging off the lattice. Like maybe it fell. Is it yours?"

She shot a hard glare. He could almost see her guard going up. "No."

"Well, do you know whose it is? Someone in your house? Or a friend who came over?" He offered it to her again. "Want to take it and see?"

Jaw clenched, she shook her head, grabbed her pile of wood, and stalked away.

Peter shoved the bracelet into his pocket, grabbed the board he'd finished marking, and followed her. Why would she respond with cold anger? . . . unless she knew something about the bracelet. It couldn't have simply belonged to her foster mom or someone else in the house. Everyone else was too little anyways. So, she must've recognized it.

Peter stood by while Brice cut every one of her pieces at the band saw. He even helped, holding the boards she wasn't working on. Her adept movements had him spellbound. How could anyone be so quick and accurate on a band saw? He could watch her work all day. Better yet, he could work *with* her all day.

She made her last cut and grabbed her pieces back from Peter without a word.

His own board in hand, Peter stepped up to the machine. Though he loved and felt at home in every kind of workshop, his heart raced and his hands were all sweaty now. Transferring the board to one hand, he wiped the other on his jeans and a thought occurred to him. Directly asking about the bracelet had been the wrong tactic, but she'd probably talk shop with him.

"So, are you as good with cars as you are on a band saw?" After adjusting his safety glasses, Peter lined his board up with the humming blade.

"I dunno. Why?" She stood nearby, looking cool and relaxed now, her cut pieces all held to one side.

Peter guided the wood to the blade, turning it one way and the other as he followed the curves of the pattern. "Well, I've got this twelve-year-old Dodge Durango." He wanted to check out her reaction, but he needed to focus on his work. He couldn't have her outdo him completely. "It was pretty cheap, 'cuz it needs a bit of work. But I like doing that, working on things."

"Oh, yeah?" She sounded either amused or skeptical.

"Yeah, I've been working on projects all my life," he said, his tone defensive. "I mean, granted, working on a car's new to me, but I'm mechanically inclined so . . ."

"Yeah, I bet."

The urge to glance almost overpowered him, but he had a few inches left to cut. *Do not mess this up.* He could wait. "The Durango wouldn't start. And it was all filthy when we got it. Came from a farmer and he must've used the heck out of it, so I scrubbed the dirt off it, inside and out." He finished his cut and shut off the band saw. They walked side by side back to the table. They'd need to see how their cuts turned out and sand the pieces down.

"So what was the problem? New starter?" She placed her boards on the table and took a stool.

Peter smiled to himself. He had her. She couldn't resist car talk. "Yeah, it just needed a new starter. And I ran new wires, but it still sounded rough so I changed—"

"Spark plugs and wires. I'd have changed those first. Any older car. It'll run ten times better."

"Now I need to work on the brakes. I took a look at them but not sure."

She fidgeted with a piece of sandpaper but hadn't touched it to the wood yet. "Not sure about what? If it's that old and beat down, you'll need new brakes."

"Yeah, I figured." Flipping the mechanical pencil between two fingers over a piece of wood he had yet to mark, Peter considered the best way to word his next statement. He'd hooked her, but he needed to reel her in. "I, uh, watched some online videos, so I'm sure I know what I'm doing."

"Ha!" A big smile appeared but her eyes showed sarcasm. "You've never helped your father or anyone with brakes?"

"You have?" he challenged.

"I've done brakes." She took his challenge.

He posed a new challenge. "Oh, well, I'm sure it's not that hard."

"You'll need someone to help you," she corrected him.

He'd expected it. "You don't think I'm competent?"

"Even if you were, it's a two-man job."

Peter smiled, impressed by her sexist wording. "Well, my dad never has time, and my only brother's autistic. My mom and aunt are always busy with the Bed-n-Breakfast, so I guess I'll have to manage. Why is it a two-man job anyway?" He cringed, fearing she would see right through him. Everyone knew it took two people to bleed brakes. Unless you made a contraption. But he'd already watched online videos about that too. He'd need a plastic bottle, drill and drill bit, zip tie, and clear plastic tubing. While it was not how he wanted to do it, he'd have no problem going it alone.

"If you don't even know how to bleed brakes, don't attempt the brakes on your own." As if she'd just dropped the final word, she set to work sanding a side panel.

He grabbed a sheet of sandpaper too. They'd need to drill a few pocket holes in the top and bottom brackets. "So what else am I gonna do? Just leave 'em all rusty and gross? I'll watch more online videos. I'm sure I can figure it out."

She stopped sanding and looked at him a long second. "Where do you live?"

Peter met her gaze, smiling inside and trying not to show it. Had he won? "Forest Gateway B & B. Heard of it?"

"Out on Forest Road?"

Both hope and fear spiked inside him. Straining to maintain his equilibrium, he nodded. "That's the one."

"I know where that is. You got all the parts you need?"

"Uh, yeah."

"I can help you around six." She stared for a moment.

Peter's mind swirled with a strange mix of emotions that kept his mouth from working.

"That time good for you?"

Peter sucked in a breath. "Uh, yeah. Perfect."

Without another word, she went back to sanding.

Peter did too, but inside he pumped a fist in the air. Victory!

11

DISCOMFORT ZONE

ROLAND SLUNG HIS BACKPACK over his shoulder and closed his locker. Waves of apprehension washed over him. The diversity group met in twenty minutes and while he didn't want to show up early, he didn't want to stroll in late either. Actually, he didn't want to go at all. Maybe he'd go hide in the library for a few minutes and then lurk in the hallway outside the room where they met.

Attentive to the way his body moved with his healing leg, he strode to the end of the hallway and turned a corner.

"Roland!" a girl shrieked from somewhere down the hall behind him.

Recognizing the voice, Roland turned.

A group of kids passed by and Caitlyn—in her crinkled white dress with the royal blue pattern around the edges—came into view, her green eyes locked on him, her wild red hair framing her sweet face . . .

His heart rate kicked up a notch, and a tingle of excitement replaced the waves of apprehension. "Hi, Caitlyn, I, uh . . ." he stammered. His backpack slid half off his shoulder, but he grabbed it before it fell.

"I was hoping to catch you before you left." She smiled.

"I'm not leaving for a while."

"Oh, that's right." She glanced in four directions, then turned back to him with eyes open wide and whispered, "You're joining the diversity group."

"Yeah." The apprehension returned with the sensation of thick moth wings flapping in his chest. He appreciated that she'd whispered it, but everyone would know soon enough. He could only imagine the rumors that would come from this impulsive decision. *Way to keep a low profile.*

"I just wanted to tell you who else I talked to today. I don't know his name. He's a junior." She grabbed the top of her head. "He's got spiky red hair. Not red like mine . . ."

Roland's gaze drifted to Caitlyn's wild mane of red curls.

". . . but more crayon red."

"Oh." Roland couldn't remember what she was talking about. Something about hair. He glimpsed movement out of the corner of his eye. Turning, he couldn't believe what he saw and the moth wings in his chest flapped harder.

Jarret jogged toward him, somehow making the hasty action look cool. Kids moved out of his way, a few of them turning to watch. A blond girl—a cheerleader?—stood back near Jarret's locker, probably where he came from. Keefe walked up to her. She said something to him, tossed her hair, and sauntered away. Jarret kept coming, looking uncharacteristically anxious. He had been acting weird lately. Maybe he had something to say about whatever Caitlyn had said to him in the hallway on lunch break. Roland never did ask how that went.

"Anyway," Caitlyn said, "I asked what he thought about the vandalism to Brice's house, and he said he knew who did it."

Acutely aware that he had seconds before Jarret reached him, Roland shifted his attention back to her. "Who are you talking about? Who knows?"

"The junior. The one with spiky red hair." Frustration flitted across her pale face, making her reddish-brown eyebrows twitch.

"Oh, okay, so who's he think did it?"

Her eyes opened wide and she leaned toward Roland. "A subgroup of jocks, the mean ones with the super short hair. He knows it was them."

Not one for labeling kids and even less interested in gossip, Roland didn't know the kids. Granted, he knew "jocks" referred to the kids that lived for sports, but . . . "Why do you call them the mean jocks?"

"Oh." She gazed into his eyes for a second, probably thinking of how to word her answer or maybe confused as to why he didn't understand in the first place. "You know, the ones who've been thrown off the teams, they pick on younger kids, make fun of outcasts . . ."

He shifted, feeling a bit self-conscious at her last remark. "Right. Okay. So how does he *know* it was them?" Overwhelmed by her fresh-air and candy scent, Roland stepped back and his gaze slid to Jarret again.

Jarret slowed his pace and stopped two feet away. "Hey, Roland, we need to talk." He shoved his thumbs in his belt loops and gave Caitlyn a sullen glance, looking like he wished she'd leave.

She hugged her books and angled her body away from him and toward Roland, straightening with that air of confidence that she showed around arrogant kids. "Well, I asked him that, but he didn't have an answer. I'm sure it's just his opinion. I don't think he has any proof." She leaned and whispered in Roland's ear, "He might be in the diversity club. It's called Empowerment, right? Look for a junior with crayon red hair."

Her breath on his ear made the moths leave his chest and zip from his head to his toes.

A smirk flashed on Jarret's face. "You need to come with me."

"Okay, well . . ." Caitlyn shifted her gaze to Jarret and stumbled back a few steps. "I'll talk to you tomorrow."

"See ya." Roland watched until she turned around. A bit hesitant, he faced Jarret. "What's up?"

Jarret tilted his chin, indicating that he wanted to walk while he talked. They headed toward Keefe. "We need to talk about something, you, me, and Keefe. But not here and not at home."

"Now?" Roland whined. The opportunity to get out of going to Empowerment tempted him, but he couldn't let Caitlyn and Peter down.

"Now," Jarret commanded.

They neared Keefe, who busied himself in his locker.

"But I just joined a group," Roland said, "and they meet right after school."

Keefe slammed his locker shut and turned as Roland and Jarret walked up to him.

"You did what? What group?" Jarret sneered, looking both incredulous and disgusted. "Never mind. I'll take you right back up here. Okay? We won't be that long. We just need to talk."

~ ~ ~

Almost half an hour later, Roland jogged down the empty hallway, every other step sending daggers through his healing leg. Jarret had dropped him off at the door after their "meeting" in the park. What a waste of time. Apparently, Jarret found Papa's recent behavior troubling. Just because he'd taken the online teaching job and was around the house more. Why shouldn't Jarret be thankful instead? And, really, why didn't he just talk to Papa about it? Roland remembered distinctly Jarret's advice about finding his attitude in case he had something to say one day. Maybe Jarret needed to take his own advice.

Turning the corner, Roland's stomach churned. He hated being late, walking into a room right in the middle of things, interrupting someone's talk, all eyes on him. It always made his temperature spike to around 200 degrees. And it took him forever to cool down. Maybe he could slip into the room and no one would notice.

Voices and laughter traveled through the open door to the art room. A handmade sign with the word "Empowerment" surrounded by construction-paper people in every shape and color, hung on the wall next to the open door. They'd probably started the meeting already.

Roland glimpsed a boy at the front of the classroom and a girl sitting on an art table. Taking the plunge, he darted into the room and, without making eye contact, strode along the wall toward the back of the room.

Everyone stopped talking. Roland felt their eyes on him before he turned his head. Five kids sat on the tops of the art tables, and four sat on stools. No boy with crayon red hair. Some kids shot daggers with their eyes, but most looks held questions. *What's*

Roland West, loner, doing here? Looking for someone? Delivering a message? Forget something in art class? Is he lost?

The teacher, Mrs. Addie Lowrey, one of the twelfth-grade literature teachers, leaned her backside against the art teacher's tall desk. A boy with bubblegum-pink streaks in his tufted brown hair stood by a whiteboard covered with doodling, a marker in his hand. His eyes narrowed with suspicion, then he moved his head from side to side and arched his brows.

"Are you here to join Empowerment?" Mrs. Lowrey pushed off the desk and tugged on her shirt, removing the crease over her ample midriff.

Roland's Adam's apple bobbed before he could speak. He cleared his throat and found an empty stretch of wall to lean against. "Um. Yeah. The sign by the door said, um, Empowerment."

"Yes, that's right. Just making sure you were in the right place." She flashed a smile and adjusted the silky scarf around her neck.

The boy with the pink-streaked hair set the marker down and approached Roland, offering his hand. "Marshall Pierce." His big smile brought dimples to his cheeks. "Welcome. I'd always hoped we'd see you here."

Heat slid up Roland's neck as he shook Marshall's cold hand. What'd the boy mean by that?

"So why are you here . . ." Mrs. Lowrey said, smoothing her hair now, "I'm sorry, what's your name?"

"Roland West," two girls and Marshall answered for him.

Another wave of heat washed over him, bringing the smell of sweat and deodorant to his nose. Still leaning his back against the wall, he stuffed his hands in the front pockets of his jeans and shifted his weight off his sore leg. Why did everyone know his name? "I'm here, uh . . ." What reason could he give without admitting the truth—that he was investigating the vandalism of Brice's house—but also without lying? "The principal suggested it, right? So, we could help, uh, I don't know." He swallowed his Adam's apple again, wishing the attention were off him, but all the staring seemed to imply they wanted more of an answer. "I hate what happened to that girl's house." There. That was true.

"Brice Maddox," several kids said in unison. Then a few long-haired girls exchanged glances and giggled.

"Okay, that's admirable. You saw an injustice and you want to do something about it. You could say that's what Empowerment is all about." She made a sweeping gesture. "Why don't you find a seat, Roland? Actually, why don't we *all* find seats? Off the tabletops."

A few groans and mutters followed the suggestion.

Marshall took a seat at the table nearest Roland and pushed the chair next to him out. "Sit here." He beamed a smile.

Wishing he could keep his spot against the wall, Roland shuffled to the offered chair and sat down, all under Marshall's attentive gaze.

Indicating each student with her upturned hand, the teacher introduced everyone. Then she sat on the edge of an art table and clasped her hands on one leg. "Principal Freeman has commissioned our group to develop a program to help educate the entire school." She paused. "I suppose I should first explain the purpose of our group, of Empowerment, for Roland here and anyone else who may have lost focus."

Two girls moaned in an exaggerated way, one dropping her face to her arm on the table.

"So, Empowerment's first concern is for the individual student. We are here to offer support to students who've been discriminated against because of their differences. This goes beyond racial or ethnic identities. This includes people with disabilities, those from different socioeconomic backgrounds, or people who embrace different ideas and beliefs or practices, and even those who feel different in other ways."

Marshall shifted in his seat, kicking the leg of Roland's chair in the process. Intentionally or accidentally?

"Sorry," Marshall mouthed and put a hand to his mouth.

"Basically," Mrs. Lowrey said, "we don't want anyone to feel bad or left out because of their differences."

The girls in Empowerment outnumbered the boys eight to three. Two tables away, a heavyset girl with jet black hair, a long-sleeved black plaid shirt, and dark lipstick sat hunched with her arms crossed over her abdomen and her head down. With a shy glance, she leaned and whispered to the dark-skinned girl with the purplish hair next to her.

A girl with sunglasses, a white shirt buttoned up to her neck, and stringy light brown hair slouched across from them, her legs stretched out on another chair. At the next table, sat a chubby black kid in a t-shirt worn inside out and a black fedora. He sat with another boy and two girls. Three other girls sat at the table nearest the teacher, one dressed in eclectic style—like Caitlyn's friend Phoebe—and another with a super short haircut. The third wore her hood up. None of them fit into the "popular kids" category. Were these kids all considered outcasts? Would one of them end up the next victim?

Even though a bunch of misfits made up the group, Roland liked what he heard. No one should be made to feel like less of a person. No matter what. Maybe this group could help all outcasts to feel less like outcasts—not that every outcast would want to fall into another category and get a new label, but maybe the pranks against outcasts would stop.

Mrs. Lowrey was still talking. ". . . we also try to understand each other and build bridges—relationships—across differences. We want to find ways to develop an appreciation for and celebrate our differences."

"Right, so how do we do that?" The girl with the hoodie flung her hand out, and her sleeve slid back to reveal a brown bracelet.

"Well, Tessia, we need to come up with ideas. That's our mission, your mission too. We want to find ways to celebrate differences, but I think it's also necessary to find ways to educate our student body about unconscious bias and hurtful stereotypes."

"Unconscious bias?" Roland mumbled, the words slipping out inadvertently.

"So, like . . ." Marshall leaned into his space, gesturing dramatically with one hand while he spoke.

Everyone else turned to Roland and Marshall.

Roland shifted in his seat, angling his body toward Marshall while inching away from him, hoping to gain a more comfortable distance between them.

". . . you put people into boxes, stereotypes based on gender, appearance, mannerisms . . . and you treat them differently because of that. Subconsciously." He tapped his head and winked at Roland.

Roland jerked back. "Treat them differently, like what?" He always thought he treated people the way he wanted them to treat him, with respect for their privacy and a healthy distance.

"Well, you see someone fat and you think they're lazy," Marshall said. "So maybe you don't invite them with everyone else on a hike."

"Or you don't make accommodations for the kid in the wheelchair or the autistic kid to come on the hike," the girl in the eclectic outfit said.

Roland thought of Peter's younger brother, Toby, who had autism. Did he feel left out of things at his school? Roland had never really thought about it before. Maybe he did have subconscious bias, or unconscious . . . or whatever she'd said.

"Or someone's black, so you think he's a criminal," the black boy said, gesturing with gang hand signs.

"Or you avoid relationships with people because they're different." Marshall gave him a long, unblinking gaze.

A girl at the table near the front of the room, the girl with the hoodie, looked directly at Roland. The teacher had called her Tessia. With elbows planted on the table and hands raised, she played with her bracelet. Dark wood beads in different colors . . .

It reminded Roland of the bracelet they'd found at Brice's house, except Tessia's didn't have glass beads between the wood ones.

"Let me guess?" Tessia said, her voice sounding familiar though her face was not. "All your friends are straight, white, and privileged. You come from similar backgrounds. You all like the same things, believe the same things, and do the same things."

A few comments came from around the room, the word "privileged" standing out.

Roland opened his mouth to reply but didn't know how to respond. All his friends? He considered two people to be close friends: Peter and Caitlyn. The rest of the Fire Starters were friends too, just not as close. He had a hard time making friends. And so what? It didn't mean he hated everyone else.

"I hope there's more to you than that." Marshall smiled, his dimples popping out. "Is that who you are?"

"Well, I-I don't have a ton of friends. And yeah, they're white, but one's a girl." Why did he feel like everyone was judging him?

Tessia stopped playing with her bracelet and leaned toward him, her eyes accusing. "All your friends are Catholics, right? And

Catholics have a rigid belief system. They're always condemning people and telling them what to believe."

"Well, I . . ." How should he answer that? It wasn't rigid. What did that even mean?

"You think everyone who doesn't agree with you is wrong. You're not open to people who are different." She flung her hand up and slouched back in her chair. "Why are you even here?"

"That's not who I am." Roland tugged at the neckline of his shirt to avoid overheating. He felt like he'd been stuffed in an oven and he wanted out.

"Phew." Marshall wiped his forehead with the back of his hand. "That's a relief."

"Tessia, don't be so hard on Roland." Mrs. Lowrey slid her leg off the table and pushed her fists onto it instead. "If Roland does have a few wrong beliefs, you can't blame him. I'm sure we all have, at one point in our lives. And that's why we have Empowerment." She stared intently at Roland. "If we want to understand one another and build bridges, we need to fight judgmental and discriminatory belief systems. We need to take a close look at ourselves. Are we blindly following old-fashioned ways of thinking that condemn others for their choices? We aren't living in the Dark Ages."

She smiled, her toothy grin at odds with the pointed look in her eyes. "In looking closer, we might find we need to change. We don't want to be haters, hiding behind outdated religious beliefs." She made air quotes around the last two words, her gaze still pointed. "Right, Roland?"

All eyes focused on him, most kids looking curious or interested in his response, one looking a bit hostile.

Was Mrs. Lowrey expecting him to answer? Overheating from the attention, Roland wiped his sweaty forehead and dried his hand on his jeans. His conscience nudged him. Or maybe his guardian angel. Or God. He should try to explain himself, let everyone know what Catholics believed. But what could he say? He sure didn't want to get into a lengthy debate about religion and morality. He wasn't a "hater" because he believed in right and wrong. Should he have to change his beliefs or keep them to himself because someone else disagreed with them? No, he should speak up.

Marshall elbowed him in the arm, as if he too expected an answer.

"Well, I . . ." His mouth had gone dry but he tried to swallow anyway.

After an uncomfortable pause, Mrs. Lowrey straightened, triumph in her posture now. "No need to answer, Roland. Your silence is enough. It's never too late for us to open our minds, embrace our differences, and be more tolerant. *That* is what Empowerment is all about."

12

MECHANICS

STANDING JUST INSIDE the open garage door, Peter toyed with the keys in his pocket and peered each way down Forest Road. A few puffy white clouds hung in the pale blue sky. It would start getting dark in an hour or so and probably chilly and maybe even buggy. A car drove past. Then another. Neither one slowed. *Oh well.* Brice would get here in her own time. He should stop watching for her and get something done. He could at least clean up a bit. How did she feel about a messy garage?

Peter assessed the two-car garage. Boxes of sports equipment and junk sat just inside the door. A neat row of yard tools hung from nails high on the opposite wall, his kendo swords balancing atop the nails. He should probably bring those in the house before the weather got cold. Did cold affect bamboo?

Wanting to know what she'd think of the place, he pretended he'd never seen the garage before in his life and continued scanning. Toolboxes of various sizes lay everywhere with no obvious rhyme or reason. Tools that no one had bothered putting away, old and new parts, chemicals, cleaners, and scrap wood covered every inch of the work benches and shelves along the back and another wall. Not looking maintained in the least. Did Brice take care of her stuff? Would a cluttered garage prove he used it and impress her? Or would she be more impressed with organization that showed he cared about his tools? Well, his dad's tools anyway. Except for the few he'd gotten for Christmas gifts the past several years. But those were all jumbled up with Dad's.

Brice kept her garage clean, he noticed when he'd carried the fertilizer into it. Of course, that wasn't really her garage. But the toolbox was. Did she work on things out in the garage? What would she work on?

His mind had pulled up an image of the long metal toolbox he'd seen and the initials B.A.M. scratched on the lid. Was it really hers? She kept it locked. What was in it? What did the "A" in her initials stand for?

Forcing himself into action and trying to ignore the strange pitter-pattering of his heart, Peter tossed a scraper and pliers into a toolbox and hung cutters on the wall. Within a few minutes, he'd cleared a surface on the back workbench. Then he grabbed a big flat screwdriver, deciding to lay out the tools they'd need. He paused and ran two fingers up and down the screwdriver. In Woodworking Class, he'd acted like he needed help. And that's why she offered to come over. Should he pretend he wasn't sure what all they'd need?

Nah. He shook his head. That'd be lame. They couldn't build a relationship on lies.

He set the screwdriver down and gathered a socket and ratchet set, a hammer, torque wrench . . . What else would they need? Oh, his keys.

He stuffed a hand into the front pocket of his jeans and pulled out his keys on his new Jedi symbol keyring and . . . the bracelet of wood and glass beads. Was it really not hers? She'd given him a strange look when she'd seen it, hostile even.

With a shrug, he tossed the keys and the bracelet onto the workbench. What else would they need? Would they have enough light when the sun went down?

The overhead florescent bulbs might not cut it. He dug out the portable halogen work light, plugged it in, and set it up near the front right tire. Then he grabbed the scissor jack. He'd parked the Durango in the middle of the garage so they could get around it easily. He'd had to beg Dad to park his truck over in the guests' parking lot so Peter could use the driveway if he needed it. It probably wouldn't have mattered, but he wanted everything to be just right.

Peter glanced outside again and then at his watch, which told him it was sixty-seven degrees outside, he faced northeast, his altitude was 1,520 meters above sea level, the barometric pressure remained stable, and—the only reason he'd looked at his watch— Brice was four minutes late.

He'd better at least get the car jacked up and take the tire off, or he'd look like a loser who didn't know the first thing about cars and was waiting for a girl to show him what to do. Peter grabbed triangular scraps of wood and shoved one in front of and the other behind the back left tire. Then he crouched by the front right tire, dropping a knee to the cold cement, and loosened the lug nuts with a lug wrench. He positioned the scissors jack under the Durango, on the body flange just behind the front tire, then he set to work turning the jack screw.

A minute later, a scuffing sound came from outside. And a voice. Her voice.

"How high you gonna jack 'er up?"

Peter straightened, still gripping the jack handle and accidentally jerking it from the jack . . . then nearly losing it as it slipped from his hand. With a hasty movement and totally dorking out, he caught it before it got completely away from him. Then his gaze found her.

Dressed in grungy jeans, black boots, and a button-front blue shirt with the sleeves rolled up to the elbows, stood the coolest girl in school: Brice Maddox. Her windblown white-blond hair lay in unkempt tufts resembling a cat's fur after a forced bath. Behind her and off to the side of the driveway stood the worn yellow BMX bike Peter had seen in Brice's foster family's garage.

"Hey, you're here," he said.

"Didn't think I'd show?"

Peter set the jack handle on a pile of tools on the workbench. "Nah, I knew you'd show. You seem like, uh, a woman of her word." He jutted his chin to indicate her bike. "Nice ride. Do you race? Do stunts?"

Brice snorted and strutted further into the garage. "No, it gets me around," she said, eyes on the car and not on him. "Thought you'd have a tire off by now."

"Yeah, give me two minutes." He glanced at the Durango and back at her. They didn't need to rush. In fact, it wouldn't kill him if she came over to help on another day too. Maybe he could stretch things out. "Hey, you hungry? 'Cuz we got like a ton of food, you know, with the B&B." Not wanting to risk missing her, he'd rushed his own dinner of Fettuccine Alfredo with chicken, a side of broccoli, and some kind of weird Italian dessert that Aunt Lotti had made for the first time . . . and that he'd introduced to the garbage disposal. He'd been in a hurry and not in the mood for strange new things. For some reason, he doubted Brice would come to the door, so he'd wanted to get the garage open and make a presence.

"Nah, I ate something after school." She grabbed a lug wrench, went to the tire, and tested a lug nut. Peter had loosened them already, so she removed them by hand.

"I can do that," Peter said, though he liked watching her work, the way she held the lug wrench at her side, the way her fingers twisted off the lug nuts. Quick, precise, not a single wasted movement.

"So can I. Why don't you get the new brakes out or grab the socket wrench or something?"

"Yeah, okay." He darted to the bench where he'd laid everything out and grabbed the box of front brake pads.

As he turned back, she heaved the tire off and laid it flat on the floor.

"So, hey," she said, sitting on the tire. "I gotta question for you." With a hand on each side of the steel wheel and leaning into it, the muscles in her forearms flexing, she turned the wheel at an angle, making the caliper easier to reach.

"Yeah, sure." Peter handed her a screwdriver so she could pry the brake pads open, then he returned to the workbench. "What's your question?" He grabbed a ratchet and a couple of different sockets, not sure what size they'd need to loosen the bolts on the caliper.

"Why do you stalk me?" She didn't look up from her work.

Peter's stomach leaped. "What? I don't stalk you."

"Yes, you do." She glanced, her eyes saying she'd have her answer. "So, is it curiosity? Fuel for rumors? I know you're friends with that gossipy kid. What's his name . . . Dominic?"

Forcing himself to act cool and collected, Peter drew near her, crouched, and reached behind the caliper to try a socket on one of the bolts. "Yeah, his name's Dominic. And he's my friend, but I hate how he gossips." Finding the socket too large, he tried the next one in his hand. "And I never say anything to add to it. I sure don't talk to him about you."

He found the correct socket, stuck it on the ratchet, and twisted to shove the others into a pocket of his jeans.

"Oh, yeah? Then why do I see you—"

"Peter!" Mom shouted, her high, strong voice probably carrying to the far corners of town.

Mortified, the blood draining from his face, Peter straightened up. "What?" he shouted back.

Brice grabbed the socket wrench from him.

Not wanting Mom to come into the garage—he hadn't told her a girl was coming over—he stomped toward the open garage door.

Mom appeared in front of him, probably coming from the front porch.

Just outside the garage, he staggered back to avoid crashing into her. "What?" he repeated, irritation heavy in his tone, though a voice in his head told him rudeness would make a bad impression.

"Oh, there you are." Mom smiled and glanced into the garage.

Peter put his hands on his hips and his elbows way out, hoping to make his body into a screen that she wouldn't look behind. Hoping the clank of metal and click and rattle of the socket wrench didn't pique her curiosity. "I told you I'd be working in the garage." And he told her he'd be working with a friend. He just never gave a name. Or a gender.

"Caitlyn's on the phone. She sounds urgent." Mom lifted a hand and produced the old cordless phone.

Peter rolled his eyes. "She always sounds urgent." He raised his hands palms out to reject the phone. "Tell her I'll call back."

Mom pursed her lips and twisted them to one side, showing her disapproval. "I don't know why that girl puts up with you." She turned away, heading for the house. "Keep an eye on the time. You still have homework, don't you? And I expect you to clean your room for real this time. It's becoming a fire hazard."

"Yeah, okay." Exhaling, Peter turned toward Brice. She wouldn't think Caitlyn was his girlfriend, would she?

Brice lifted the caliper, set it aside with a clank, and pried off a brake pad with a big screwdriver. "Your mom, huh?"

"Uh, yeah. Guess I should've introduced you." Peter stood over her, glancing from the brake pad in her hands to her windblown white-blond locks. Her roots, a darker shade of blond, and the pale little hairs on her arms said she was a hundred percent natural.

Brice glanced up from the brake pad and gave him a funny look. Her eyes were pale too, golden brown near the pupil and fanning out to smoky green.

"Uh." Peter took a breath. "Brakes are pretty thin, huh?"

"Yeah but . . ." She ran a fingernail—chewed to the quick—over the rotor. "Guess these aren't too bad."

"Whatdya mean?" It occurred to him that he should've picked up rotors too. Now he was gonna look dumb. Way to impress a girl.

"When the rotors get deep grooves, you need to change 'em. But these don't look bad."

"Oh. Good. 'Cuz I didn't buy rotors."

"Eh, no biggie." She continued studying parts as if she totally knew what she was doing. "Got a wire brush to clean the caliper bracket?"

Peter returned to the workbench and dug for it. He'd seen it earlier, hadn't he? He shoved rags and a roll of duct tape aside, opened a small tool box, and peered under a few blocks of wood. *Wait,* hadn't he'd put it with the other things they'd need?

"So, Caitlyn's your girlfriend, huh? She that redhead who doesn't know how to match her socks?" Brice stepped to the other workbench and picked up the wire brush.

A defensive, sinking sensation started in his chest. "Caitlyn? No, she is *not* my girlfriend. She's more like the annoying sister I never had. We've known each since . . . well, since I was born."

Brice made no reply. Didn't even look, just scrubbed the slides on the caliper bracket with the wire brush. The girl was totally unreadable. She believed him, right? Should he confess that he liked her?

His chest tingled. No, not yet. Maybe that could come out naturally. Without words. They'd spend all their time together and she'd just know.

Once she replaced the bracket and tightened the bolts, she got up and let Peter finish the job. He installed the new brake pads and put the caliper back in place, with a few welcome but unnecessary suggestions from her. Wanting to impress her, he tried moving as methodically as she had, but his moves felt choppy and rough.

One set of brakes complete, they remounted the tire and lowered the car. Then he jacked up the other side and removed the front left tire.

Just as Peter shoved the socket over the bolt on the caliper, Mom's voice came from out of nowhere. "How are you two doing out here?"

Peter's heart leaped two feet and the socket wrench slipped. It clanked against the jack and hit the cement floor. And somehow, he banged his head on the edge of the wheel well.

Brice, who'd been sitting on a box of junk and watching him, let out a hearty laugh.

He liked her smile, but humiliation made blood shoot through his vessels, racing to his face, which then threatened to explode. Rubbing his head, Peter straightened and whined, "Mom, are you kidding me?"

Mom stepped into the garage with a tray of muffins, mugs, and a thermos. Blocking her view earlier must not have worked. Did she care that he had a girl out here with him? Maybe she liked the idea. He'd never made a big deal about girls before. She could've been wondering when or if he would ever get interested in them. "I thought you might want a snack." Mom trotted around the back of the car and stood where Brice could see her.

"So . . . that's my mom." Standing sideways to her and resigning himself to fate, Peter flung his hand toward Mom and then toward Brice. "Mom, Brice."

"Nice to meet you, Mrs. Brandt." Brice stepped forward, wiping her hands on a rag.

"I'll just set this here." Mom shoved tools and junk aside on the workbench nearest her. She set the tray down and reached past Peter for Brice's hand. Then her eyebrows shot up. "Oh, that's some grip."

"Sorry, I . . ." Brice withdrew her hand and wiped it again, as if wanting Mom's touch off her hand.

"Nothing to be sorry about. A firm handshake shows a strong, confident personality." Mom smiled, clasping her hands. "Or something like that."

Brice let out another laugh, a hint of sarcasm in this one. "Yeah, that's me. Miss Confidence." She rolled her eyes then stooped to retrieve the socket wrench Peter had dropped.

Certain Brice couldn't see his face, Peter bugged his eyes at Mom, signaling for her to go. "Well, thanks, Mom. We're trying to get the brake pads changed before . . . I don't know. Before the cows come home." He hated that he'd just used a stupid cliché, but he couldn't think of anything else. And he needed Mom to scram before his younger brother, Toby, came looking for her. Once Toby realized Peter had company, he'd hang around forever, talking to himself and getting in the way. Then Peter would have to explain that his brother had autism and blah, blah, blah. She'd end up thinking his family was too out there.

Mom laughed and walked to the open garage door. The sky had darkened a few shades. "Okay, fine, but don't forget your homework and your room. And, Brice, you're welcome to come inside and have something else to eat when you're done."

"Sure, thanks." Brice glanced, looking and sounding totally casual. She knelt with one knee on the tire they'd removed from the front wheel and reached behind the caliper, back to work.

A few minutes later, she got up, wiped her hands on her jeans and went to the tray Mom had brought out. "Your mom seems nice." She grabbed a muffin.

"Uh, yeah, Mom's nice. I know I probably sounded like a jerk but . . ." Having no idea what to give for an excuse, he shut his mouth and slid a brake pad from its box.

Brice stuffed half a muffin in her mouth and came back with the other half, cheek bulging while she chewed. She took the brake pad from Peter. "Back brakes will be harder," she said over her mouthful.

"Yeah." He stared until she stuffed the other half of the muffin in her mouth, a part of him wishing she would've offered it to him. Not that he couldn't get his own muffin, but it would've been nice to share . . . Shaking the thought away, Peter went to the tray and poured hot tea into two mugs. Too bad it wasn't iced tea instead. The temperature had dropped a bit, at least according to his watch, but working made him sweat. "Where'd you learn to fix brakes anyways?"

"Why do you need to know?"

"Well, I . . ." Her distrustful tone threw him. "I-I don't need to know. You're just good at it, so I wondered."

They worked in silence for a few minutes, him handing her tools and watching. Then Brice gave him a long look, seeming to size him up with her golden, smoky eyes. "One of my mother's ex-boyfriends was a mechanic. He was always working on cars for extra money. I picked up a few things."

"Oh." Her decision to trust him lifted a weight he hadn't known was there, but it also threw his brain for a loop and made a reply impossible. So he just focused on the brake job.

Working like a well-oiled machine, they finished the front and started on the back. The sky darkened and the garage threw a rectangle of light on the driveway, but no bugs came around.

Peter worked on loosening the bolts on the back left caliper. "So, I'm glad Mr. Hart let us work together after all."

Brice sat on the tire, eating another muffin and resting one arm on her raised knee. "Oh, yeah?"

"Aren't you?"

"I don't really care. I just want to make my gun rack."

With a careful grip, Peter lifted the dirty caliper off the wheel but realized he didn't know where to set it. The brake line didn't give him much leeway. And she sat on the tire so he couldn't use that. Besides it wasn't close enough.

Using her foot, Brice slid a closed packing box to him. She'd finished the mug of tea he'd handed her and now drank directly from the thermos.

"Thanks." He set the heavy caliper on the box and brushed the grit off his hands. "Well, don't you think some of those guys in Woodworking are jerks?"

"*Some* of them?"

Struck dumb, he stared. Was she saying that all guys were jerks? Was she including him in that judgment? "Well, I'm not a jerk."

She gave him a look. Was it a smirk? A teasing look? "Some people think you are."

"What? Who?"

Rolling forward onto her knees, she grabbed the socket wrench and fitted it onto a bolt on the caliper. "Grab the new pads."

Peter jumped up. "Aren't you gonna tell me who thinks I'm a jerk?"

She laughed, the same short sarcastic type of laugh that flew out of her often. "That list might be kinda long, don't you think?"

Returning to her with two new brake pads, he gave her a glare, though he liked that she felt comfortable teasing him. "What about you? Do you think I'm a jerk?"

She shrugged. "I don't worry over what people think about me. You shouldn't worry about it either." Shifting her position, moving closer to him, she pulled the caliper apart and wiggled the old pads out.

While thinking up a response, he chewed the dry skin on his bottom lip. What direction did he want the conversation to go in now? "I guess I don't care what most people think about me. But I do care what you think." He took the new pads from the box and worked one of them into place.

She grabbed the other. "Why?"

Heat rushed to his face again and the truth flew out without him giving it permission. "Because I like you."

Showing no sign she'd heard him, she worked the second brake pad into place. Then she looked him in the eye. "You know I don't like guys, right?"

"Uh . . ." He gulped. Yeah, he knew it but he still had hope. These things weren't set in stone, were they? "Well, you just insinuated all guys are jerks, so I guess so. But that doesn't mean we can't be, uh, can't be friends, right? I mean, you like me enough to come over here." And maybe she'd get to know him and he could change her mind about guys, or at least about him.

"You seemed desperate. And I like to work on cars."

"Oh. So . . ."

"I'll help you with your car." She wiped her hands on a dirty rag and stood up. "You got a C-clamp?" Not waiting for his answer, she

108

strode directly to the bench where he'd laid out tools earlier. "Uh . .
. What's this doing here?"

"Huh?" He approached her at the workbench.

The bracelet dangled off her index finger, the glass starbursts
glinting under the florescent light. Her narrowed eyes shifted from
the bracelet to him. "Why do you still have this?"

"Uh. You said it wasn't yours, right?" He stood directly beside
her. The bracelet meant something to her. Any chance she'd explain
why?

"Yeah. It's not mine." She flipped her hand over, dropping the
bracelet into her palm and gazing at it. Her expression softened and
her eyes grew distant.

"So, you know whose it is?"

"I know who made it."

"Oh?" He debated whether he should or shouldn't push for
more. "So, who made it?"

A bit of silence stretched out, her mouth and chin twitching.
Then she answered, "My sister. She made several with these kinds of
beads."

"Okay, then take it." Risking physical contact, he touched her
cupped hand and folded her fingers over the bracelet the way
Aragorn had done with Frodo in *The Lord of the Rings*. "Give it back
to her."

Her eyes lifted to his, one of them squinting. "Don't be a dork."
Then she pulled away and tossed the bracelet to the workbench. Her
jaw tensed and she shook her head. "Can't exactly do that. She's
dead."

Brice grabbed the C-clamp and stomped away, leaving Peter
staring into space, stunned.

Her sister was dead? Since she lived in foster care without
biological siblings, he'd assumed she'd had none. How long ago had
her sister died? How old could her sister have been? How'd she die?
Why did Brice end up in foster care, anyway? Her cold attitude
must've resulted from something that had happened in her past.
Something bad.

A pain of sympathy stabbed Peter's heart.

13

CONFIDENCE

A LESS-TRAVELED HALLWAY STRETCHED OUT before Roland, a shortcut to his last class of the day. The straps of his backpack hung unevenly, the right side digging into his shoulder and the left side threatening to slip down his arm. A bead of sweat traced a path down his back. He didn't like this shirt Nanny had bought for him. The dark green color wasn't so bad, but the satiny material didn't breathe.

Roland planted his crutches, took a step with his good leg, and swung his crutches forward again. Step, swing, step, swing, step . . .

Footfalls and whispers came from somewhere behind him. Senses heightening and skin crawling, he resisted the urge to glance over his shoulder, though he couldn't shake the feeling that whoever had been following him all day was near.

"Hey, white boy," came a low voice from behind him.

Peter joking around? Roland stopped, leaned his weight on one crutch, and started to turn around.

He'd turned no more than an inch when chaos struck, everything happening too quickly.

Someone from behind ripped the crutches from him, the pads raking his underarms and one arm twisting when he didn't release

111

the hand grip right away. The aluminum crutches clattered to the floor.

Roland's heart leaped to his throat. Losing balance, he flung his arms out.

Hands latched onto his upper arms, keeping him from falling and forcing him to move. A boy in an open doorway—Roland glimpsed him while turning to one of his captors—shouted, "In here."

One of the kids shoving him along laughed in his ear. The three kids looked familiar. Seniors? Jarret's friends? What did they want with him? They dragged him into an empty classroom and tossed his backpack. One of them held him from behind, locking his arms behind his back, and another ripped open his shirt.

"We're just here to help you out, white boy." With a twisted grin on his face and trouble in his eyes, the third boy shook an orange spray bottle.

"What are you—?"

The boy aimed the bottle at Roland's chest and sprayed.

Panic stealing his breath and making him lightheaded—what was the kid doing?—Roland jerked back and twisted to get away.

The other two held him tighter, their grips pinching his skin. "Might want to close your eyes."

The kid sprayed haphazardly, covering Roland's chest, collarbone, neck, chin—

Roland sucked in a breath and squeezed his eyes shut. He tried turning his face away as the spray went higher and higher.

One of the kids yanked him by the hair, forcing his face forward. Cold droplets pelted his forehead, eyes, nose, cheeks . . . every inch of his face, it seemed.

Commotion . . . voices in the hallway, maybe other kids wanting to see the spectacle.

Then it was done. Laughing and saying stupid things that barely registered in Roland's mind, his attackers released him and took off.

Roland jerked forward, losing his balance, and staggered to the nearest wall.

With a gasp, Roland sat bolt upright in bed and opened his eyes wide. Air cooled his sweaty neck as the blanket fell. Heart racing, he glanced around. A dark door on the wall across from him. A dark rectangular-shaped piece of furniture. A sliver of dark blue between heavy drapes.

Relief shuddered through him and he took a breath. This was his bedroom and that was just a dream. He hadn't thought about the spray tan incident in such detail for days. Why was he dreaming about it now?

~ ~ ~

With a hint of reservation, Roland selected the "workout" playlist on Jarret's mp3 player. Then he stuffed a hand into the front pocket of his sweatpants and pulled out a folded piece of paper. His physical therapist had given him a list of exercises he should've been doing ever since the cast came off. As he studied it, he shuffled past Jarret's deluxe gym set to the thick red mat he'd laid out on the hard cement floor of the basement. He should've been doing these exercises all along, but simply walking through the school halls had left him aching—

Thump, thump, thump, thump . . . A hard beat blasted through the speakers of the docking system.

Roland's heart leaped, and his attention snapped to the door shrouded in darkness at the top of the basement steps. He didn't want anyone to hear it. Anyone . . . meaning Jarret. His momentary panic was unfounded, residual fear of Jarret's wrath over any little thing. But Jarret had told him to use whatever he wanted down here, whenever he wanted. And Jarret wouldn't hear the music from all the way down here anyways. He wouldn't even wake up for another hour. Roland had made sure to set his alarm clock extra early so he could work out without interfering with Jarret's routine.

Dropping the crinkled paper of exercises, Roland snatched the mp3 player and turned the volume down. Jarret always listened to bouncy tunes, super loud, when working out. A female singer belted out a song Roland didn't recognize. It did have a good workout beat.

With a yawn from having woken earlier than comfortable, he stooped for the paper and plopped down on the mat. Cold seeped through his sweatpants. Knowing how chilly the basement always got, he should've worn a jacket over his t-shirt. Eh, maybe he'd warm up from the exercise.

Tilting the paper toward the only light he'd turned on—the lamp near the weight equipment—Roland studied the first exercise on the sheet. Twenty reps, huh? He leaned back and planted his hands behind him. Following the instructions, he lifted his foot, the sneaker making it feel extra heavy to his weak leg, then bent his ankle up and down. One, two, three . . .

His ankle didn't look swollen this morning, but it had every day after school.

Five, six, seven . . .

As he counted, he caught the words of the lyrics. You make me brave. You make me brave. You call me out beyond the shore into the waves.

Still bending his foot at the ankle, he stopped counting and focused on the song. When had Jarret started listening to Christian music?

You make me brave. You make me brave . . .

Roland felt a stab of self-reproach. He wasn't brave. He'd practically denied his faith in the Empowerment group. Tessia had said things about Christians, and he'd said nothing in defense. Should he have? What difference would it have made? It's not like anyone would've listened to him or changed their mind. He'd just have drawn more attention.

He spoke up when he had to, right? Last winter he'd confronted Jarret to keep him from making a big mistake. That had been hard. He almost hadn't done it, but then that Scripture verse had come to mind, and the Word of God had spoken to his heart. *Go and tell him his fault between you and him alone.*

One to one. He could do that. But in front of an entire class? No, thanks. Besides, he'd only joined the group as part of their investigations. He wasn't there to convert anyone.

Twenty or so reps later, he switched to the second exercise, bending his foot from side to side now. Every movement came with a bit of stiffness and pain. He did not want to do this. Maybe all the walking he had to do between classes would be enough. Maybe too much. The physical therapist had told him to take it easy for a couple of weeks . . . but he'd also told him to do the exercises. He could do this.

Another Christian song came on, with more encouraging words that helped him ignore the soreness of his leg and keep exercising. Since getting the cast removed—almost a week ago—he'd never completed in one day all the exercises the therapist had prescribed. And he walked with that lousy limp that often made people look twice. The exercises would help with that. He wanted his stealthy stride back. He would make himself do it today. And every day from now on.

The next exercise required a towel or resistance band, so he climbed to his feet to find one. Another Christian song came on, this one by King & Country, a band Roland recognized.

. . . my strength comes from God who made heaven, and earth, and the mountains . . .

If he wanted the strength in his leg back, he had to work for it.

A red resistance band hung over a bar on the gym set. He grabbed it and returned to the mat, thinking of the song lyrics as he started the next exercise.

My help comes from You. You're right here, pulling me through.

He believed that. Why didn't he feel it in speech class? He'd asked the teacher for an "F" to get out of the first speech. She said he could give his speech last, so he had another week or so to worry about it. But he still had to do it.

Speech class . . . Empowerment group . . . Why did it terrify him to stand up in front of everyone and talk? He'd never liked attention. Maybe he didn't want people to see the real him. Afraid of rejection. Of standing out.

His calf complained as he stretched it, but he didn't give up. He needed to push past the discomfort to get his leg back in shape.

The cast had made him stand out. The limp did too. If he exercised every day, he'd strengthen his leg in no time. Maybe he needed a similar plan for overcoming his fear of speaking. What could he do to prepare for the speech, besides practicing in front of a mirror?

The investigations . . . instead of asking Caitlyn and her girlfriends to prospect for clues in Brice's neighborhood, he could go instead. Or maybe he could go with them. He could force himself to knock on doors and ask the neighbors questions. He could force himself outside of his comfort zone, and maybe it would help him for the bigger moment, for speech class.

Roland counted his twenty reps and stood for the next exercise, feeling it in his leg. After he finished the therapist's exercises, he'd take Jarret's suggestions and do a few leg curls. He was getting his strength back. And he'd get over his fear of talking to people too.

Maybe they could go around the neighborhood tonight. But not if Brice was home. She might see them. And since Peter didn't want her knowing about their investigations, they'd have to wait until she went somewhere.

~ ~ ~

Sitting in the back of speech class at the desk nearest the door, Roland rubbed his sore leg and tried paying attention to the kid at the front of the classroom. Marshall Pierce. The eleventh kid to give his speech this week. Twenty-six kids in the class, four speeches a day . . .

Roland's gut tensed and he shifted in his seat. Mrs. Kauffman had said he could give his last, so he'd be giving his speech next Tuesday.

An image of Cary Grant appeared on the white board, replacing an image of Lucille Ball. ". . . making him my all-time favorite movie actor . . ." Marshall paused and smiled. His dimples and the happy gleam in his eyes gave him a childish air. He glanced up and shifted from side to side, for the tenth time. Maybe it was a habit, but it made him seem pleased to have all eyes on him. "So, like . . . *Bringing up Baby, His Girl Friday,* and the *Philadelphia Story* with Audrey Hepburn and John Howard . . . those are, like, total must-see, essential Cary Grant movies . . ."

For the first speech, everyone was supposed to talk about themselves, but Marshall had spent the past four minutes going over his favorite black-and-white movies, actors, and actresses. Granted, he did mention that he had two older sisters, eight and ten years older, and that his parents hadn't expected to have another child so many years later, and they seemed tired with the idea of parenthood, so they were really laid back with him. And he'd told everyone that he collected old movie memorabilia, and that he was in the drama club and Empowerment. "So the thing I get from Empowerment, the message I get: everybody is different and that's okay. It's okay to be different. You don't have to change. You don't have to hide it. We can accept each other for who we are, but let's focus on what we have in common." He'd used that line to transition to the bulk of his speech content: "Everybody loves movies."

Roland's thoughts didn't transition as quickly. Did Marshall mean no one should focus on differences of opinion? Wouldn't that keep people from really getting to know each other? The diversity club, of all groups, should welcome diversity in belief.

Peter, who sat at the desk beside Roland, sunk his hand in his messy hair and turned to Roland, his arm blocking his face from the teacher's view. "Leg hurt?" he whispered.

Roland stopped rubbing his leg and folded his arms on his desk. "I'm fine," he mouthed.

"Really?" Peter gave a knowing grin. "You're limping worse than ever today."

Shifting and uncomfortable, instinctual defense mechanisms kicked in and he change the subject. "I have a plan for after school," he whispered, glancing in Brice's direction. She sat on the far side of the classroom, also in the back row, slouching back in her seat and with her legs stretched out in the aisle.

A serious expression replaced Peter's grin. "What's the plan?"

"Questioning the neighbors."

"Tonight?"

Roland nodded, though he would only do it if they knew Brice wouldn't be home.

Peter sneaked a glance at Brice and turned back with ruddy cheeks. "Wait until after six."

"Why?"

"She'll be at my house." His mouth twitched and he pressed his lips together, making it seem like he struggled to keep from smiling. "She's helping me with the brakes."

Applause broke out. Beaming from ear to ear, Marshall swaggered to his seat, the one in front of Roland. He set his note cards on his desk. "How'd I do?" he asked Roland and smiled, one dimple popping out.

"Uh." Roland straightened and cleared his throat. "Great."

"Thank you," he mouthed before swinging into his seat.

"And our final speaker of the day is . . ." Mrs. Kauffman said, her voice loud and clear, "Peter Brandt." She gave Peter a confident nod. "If you're ready, I'll introduce you."

"Ready as I'll ever be." Peter flipped open a folder, grabbed note cards from the pocket, and stood. "Hope you guys like to hear about cars and electronics." He looked at Roland and stuck out a fist. "Wish me luck."

Roland bumped his fist and nodded, but Peter didn't need luck.

The ruddy color had left his cheeks. He didn't seem the least bit nervous as he strode to the podium in the front of the classroom. After his introduction, he flipped through his cards for a second, as if putting them in order, then he looked out at everyone with a confident grin and said, "I was born to build things. And I'll build things 'til I die."

A hint of jealousy teasing him, Roland exhaled. Why couldn't he have that confidence?

Brice sat up, a crooked but somewhat proud grin on her face. She hadn't given her speech yet, but with her self-possessed attitude, she'd probably have no problem. Besides, while the boys tended to stare at their notes, blush, and say "um" fifty times, the girls so far seemed to have an easier time.

Maybe Roland would "find his attitude" after knocking on a dozen doors tonight.

Half listening to Peter ramble on about an award he'd won for a science project, Roland's gaze settled on a kid two rows up who wore a South Dakota Coyotes t-shirt. Gavin Wheeler, who used to be wide receiver on River Run High's football team. And one of the meanest of the subcategory of mean jocks. A single notebook lay on his desk, a bunch of thin scraps hanging out by the spiral binding, as if he'd ripped out several pages.

The gears in Roland's mind turned.

The "Outcasts Beware" posters had come from a spiral-bound notebook . . .

14

FALSE ACCUSATIONS

GIVING LITTLE THOUGHT to the glances and outright stares of the kids he passed, Peter gripped the straps of his backpack at the chest and raced down the hallway like a madman. He could see it in his mind: walking side by side with Brice Maddox to their woodworking class. Unfortunately, he just got out of a class clear across the building from her last one. Having memorized Brice's schedule, he knew exactly which route to take to intercept her.

Unless . . . she stopped at her locker first.

Did she ever carry extra books to Woodworking? No, just one worn composition book with doodling on the cover. Of course, she stopped at her locker first!

He had to recalculate. Different routes flashed in his mind until he realized which hall he needed to take for the most direct route to her locker. He neared that hall now.

Sneakers squeaking, he rounded the corner.

Roadblocks stood in the way, a huddle of girls on one side and Caitlyn juggling her books directly in his path. One book almost slipping from her hand, catching it, another almost slipping . . .

Desperate to avoid crashing, Peter put on the brakes, sneakers squeaking again. He came within a foot of Caitlyn.

As if he'd just emitted an invisible force, her books tumbled to the floor and she groaned. "What'd you do that for?" She stooped for her books.

"What were you doing? You looked like a clown." He snatched a folder from the floor, glanced at the big-eyed owl on the cover, and handed it to her.

"I was trying to organize my books, but they kept shifting." She regrouped her books and folders on the floor and stood up hugging them, strands of red hair hanging over one eye. "What's your hurry?"

"I, uh, gotta . . ." No way was he gonna tell her, not unless Brice officially became his girlfriend. Then he'd tell the world. He'd shout it from the rooftops. But for now . . . "Never mind." Anxious to get going, he adjusted his backpack and squeezed between her and the wall of lockers.

"See you at lunch," she said as he passed.

"Yeah." They could share what they've each discovered and hope no one overheard them. Or maybe— He turned to her, walking backwards as he spoke. "Hey, let's all meet outside for lunch."

"Oh, okay."

He bolted. As he rounded the next corner, he saw her.

Dressed in camouflage joggers and an olive-green t-shirt, she slammed her locker with her combat boot and strode away, her single composition book at her hip, don't-mess-with-me in her step.

Picking up his pace, Peter came within a few yards of her. "Hey," he said too loudly, drawing the attention of a group of kids and another guy at a locker, but not Brice's attention.

She strode along like a girl with purpose. Nothing bothered her. She had her destination in mind and nothing would stand in her way.

Peter jogged again, closing the distance between them. He was about to slap her arm with the back of his hand in greeting. Not sure she'd like that, he looped his thumbs in the straps of his backpack and simply said, "Hey, what's up?"

She looked him up and down, let out that cocky laugh, and— wouldn't you know?—she punched him in the arm in greeting! "Worried you're gonna be late to Woodworking?"

"What? No." He rubbed his arm where she'd punched it and forced himself to stop breathing hard as he walked alongside her.

"So why were you running?"

"Uh . . ." *I wanted to walk you to class*. No, he couldn't say that. She'd run from anything that hinted of a typical boy-girl relationship. "Getting some exercise."

Facing forward now, she laughed again, her smile lingering. "Right."

His insides leaped. The sight of her smile . . . the sound of her laugh . . . he needed more of that. "So, you're coming over tonight, right? To help bleed the brakes?"

"I guess so. Unless you've rigged something up so you can do it yourself."

"Yeah, I saw a video on the Internet, explained how to go it alone. I'm sure I totally could. But for my first time, I'd rather have someone who knows what they're doing. And that's you."

As they walked along, Peter became vaguely aware of heads turning toward them. A girl at her locker watched them as they passed. She whispered to the girl next to her, who also turned and looked. Two guys glimpsed them too, one doing a double-take.

Peter puffed up inside. Brice never walked through the halls with anyone. But right here, right now, she was walking with him.

"Hey, whatdya think you're doing?" A petite, lanky girl in a hoodie shot from a locker and stood superwoman style directly in their path. Black eye makeup surrounded dark, angry eyes. She tilted her head to one side.

Brice turned to stone, her mouth becoming a grim line. She gripped her composition book, the muscles in her arm rippling. "Get outta my way."

"You know who he is, right?" The girl threw Peter a cold glance.

A wave of heat smacked Peter. "Wait? Me? You're talking about me?"

"Yeah, I know who he is. He's my partner in Woodworking. Which is where I'm headed. So move." Chin lifting, Brice stepped toward her.

The other girl held her ground. "He's one of the Fire Starters, you know, that *Catholic* group, the ones who probably did that to your house."

"Wait, what?" Every muscle in Peter's body tensed. "You're blaming us? We would never do something like that. In fact, we're the ones—" He slammed his mouth shut before more words flew out. *We're the ones trying to find out who did it.*

"Drop it, Tessia." With a hand to the girl's shoulder, Brice shoved her out of the way. "I don't care who did it." She moved past her, Tessia flattening herself to the lockers so Brice could get by.

Peter stood stunned for a moment, his gaze connecting with Tessia's. They glared at each other, communicating nonverbal threats. *Don't even go there*, Peter said in his mind. Then Peter doubled his steps to catch up with Brice. "Hey, you don't believe the Fire Starters had anything to do with it, do you? 'Cuz we would never—"

Walking double-time, Brice flung her hand up, palm towards him. "Chill, brother."

"Well, I don't want you to think—"

She stopped outside the woodworking shop and faced him, the hum of machines traveling through the open door. "I don't think that."

"Okay. Good."

She pivoted, turning toward the open door.

Needing to know one more thing, he reached out—doubting that he should've, even as he did it—and he grabbed her arm . . . warm, smooth, muscular. "Wait."

She looked at his hand and then at his eyes, the golden brown around her pupils flaring into smoky green irises. "What?" she asked in a cold, low voice as she tugged free of his grip.

"So, who do you think did it?" His heart hammered erratically.

One eye narrowed and one side of her lip curled up. "You, maybe. To get my attention."

"Wha . . ." Peter shrunk back. "I-I would never."

A genuine smile replaced the crooked grin and she laughed. "I'm joking. But it doesn't matter who did it." She swung into the classroom.

He followed. "Yes, it does. Just because someone doesn't like you, doesn't give them the right to tear up your yard. Besides, they don't even know the real you. Probably judging you based on rumors."

"And do you know the real me?" She slapped her composition book onto a workbench and folded her arms across her chest.

"I . . ." A smile forced its way to his face. "I'm trying."

~ ~ ~

He'd asked Mom to pack a Baby Ruth candy bar in his lunch. Where was it?

Peter dug through his insulated lunch bag as he headed to the back doors of the school. With a hip to the crash bar, he opened the door. A pleasant 77-degree breeze ruffled his hair as he strode across the schoolyard. Kids played basketball off to the left, racing with cloud shadows across the court. Kids sat at picnic tables to his right. And more kids, mostly girls, walked by twos and threes along the perimeter of the paved area.

He pushed aside a plastic bag of celery sticks and a wrapped slice of Italian bread and maneuvered a plastic container of lasagna onto its side. There!

As he glimpsed the Baby Ruth, someone bumped his shoulder from behind, and the lasagna fell back in place, hiding the candy bar.

"All right, who—" Feigning anger, he turned around. But then he swallowed the rest of his words.

That lanky girl in the hoodie stood behind him, shooting hate through her black-rimmed eyes. She looked angrier than when she'd stopped him and Brice on the way to Woodworking. Brice had called her Tessia, right?

"You." She shoved her hands in her jacket pockets as if trying to keep herself from shoving him again—or worse.

"Uh, yeah?" Peter swung his lunch bag to his side and shifted his weight to one leg with attitude. "What about me?"

Her eyes narrowed even more. "Whatever game you're playing with Brice, it's over."

"What game? I-I'm not playing a game." On impulse, his hand flew up in a gesture of innocence.

"Right." Tessia took two steps back. "I'm watching you." She turned and stomped off toward the back doors of the school.

Dazed, Peter stared until she disappeared inside the building. Then he ran a hand through his hair and resumed walking out to his friends.

Everyone had beat him outside. Roland leaned against the sole tree in a big stretch of grass that ended at a farmer's field. Caitlyn faced Roland, holding onto a branch overhead and twisting from side to side as she spoke. Whatever she said had Roland dipping his head like a shy nerd. Kiara and Phoebe sat in the grass, eating their lunches and scanning the schoolyard. Phoebe's gaze connected with Peter's and he gave a nod. They were far enough away from the rest of the students that they could hold a private meeting. Although people would see them. Fortunately, Tessia had gone back inside. He definitely didn't want her realizing Brice was the subject of their investigations.

What was her deal anyway? Judging by Brice's cold attitude earlier, Brice didn't like her. Maybe they were friends once and had a falling out, but Tessia still cared about her.

"About time." Phoebe tossed something at Peter as he drew near.

He caught it: a fancy chocolate wrapped in orange foil, probably leftover from Trick-or-Treat last year. "Great. You're all here." Peter plopped down in the grass, at an angle from Kiara, and unwrapped the chocolate. After a few generic greetings, he got down to business. "Anybody discover the guilty party?"

"No, but we're working on it." Caitlyn let go of the tree branch and sat in the grass in her long flowing skirt, near Phoebe and opposite Peter.

Roland remained leaning against the tree, hands stuffed in the front pockets of his dark jeans.

"What'd anybody find out?" Peter popped the chocolate into his mouth, dumped his lunch in the grass, and grabbed the Baby Ruth.

"Well . . ." Kiara leaned forward, resting her arms on her crossed legs. "I asked about ten people today. And most of them think the pranksters are responsible, not just for Brice's house but for the stinky locker and the warning to outcasts too. And everyone expects more to come."

The pranksters, often led by Doug Baxter, a member of the Fire Starters, were notorious at River Run High. They once taped a bunch of balloons inside the window of the principal's office to give the impression the room was filled with balloons. They'd rearranged classrooms, putting the teacher's desk on the opposite wall. They'd used crime-scene tape to make body outlines and to block off classrooms. And a dozen other harmless pranks.

"I don't think so." Peter grabbed the bread from his lunch. "They don't do anything I wouldn't do." In fact, he'd helped with more than a few pranks last year.

"Right," Phoebe said. "They're just having fun. They've never done anything dangerous or mean."

"And they don't target specific people." Still leaning against the tree, Roland shifted his position and stood with his feet apart.

"So, you're in charge of investigations," Peter said to Roland. "What've you got?"

Roland shrugged.

"How was the Empowerment meeting?"

He glanced upward and shook his head, shadows of leaves playing on his pale face.

"Something go badly?"

"No. But we wanted a list of possible outcasts—er, targets, right?" Roland pulled his phone from a pocket of his jeans. "Got it."

"Good. But who's on our list of suspects?"

"What do we know about Gavin Wheeler?"

"That jerk? He's in our speech class, right? Why?"

Roland shrugged again. "Just a hunch. Might be nothing."

"Okay, so who else is on the list?" Peter said.

"I discovered just how much the stuck-up girls don't like Brice." Phoebe pushed her blue-streaked hair off her forehead.

"What'd they say about her?" Caitlyn said.

"The ones in gym class with her seemed jealous over how many pull-ups and stuff she can do." Phoebe laughed. "Guess it makes them look bad when they struggle to do just one."

"Okay," Peter said, "who else is on our suspect list?"

"The mean jocks," Caitlyn said. "We know for a fact they attacked . . ." She froze, her eyes popping open, then she glanced over her shoulder at Roland, probably wishing she hadn't brought it up.

Roland sucked in a breath and shifted his position again, taking the weight off his healing leg.

"Right." Phoebe tossed her lunch bag and leaned back on her arms. "C.W., Trent, and Konner fall under that category. A few people told me they suspect them. Only one thing doesn't make sense."

"What's that?" Peter pried open the plastic container and stabbed a fork in his cold lasagna.

"When they attacked Roland, they didn't care who knew."

"Oh, right." Peter studied a forkful of lasagna, not sure he wanted to eat it cold. "So why are they now attacking secretly?" He shoved the lasagna into his mouth, the cold flavors making his mouth water and not tasting too bad.

Kiara rocked forward. "Maybe they meant to attack Roland secretly, too. They did pick a quiet hallway."

"So, what'd you find out, Peter?" Roland blurted, no doubt anxious to turn the subject away from his mortifying experience. "You were going to talk to Brice, right? See what enemies she has?"

"Oh, and ask her about the bracelet?" Caitlyn added.

"Right. I did that. Well, I didn't ask about enemies. She's new here. How would she have any? But I did ask about the bracelet." Peter paused, deciding how much to reveal. Brice had told him in confidence. Did he really want to tell everyone?

Peter motioned Roland over.

Roland pushed off the tree, weaved past Caitlyn without the hint of a limp, and sat next to Peter in the grass. "What'cha got?"

"I . . ." Peter glanced at everyone in turn. "I can't share this yet. It's kind of personal to Brice. Don't get peeved." Then he leaned toward Roland and cupped a hand to his mouth to block anyone from reading his lips. "Brice's sister made the bracelet, but she's . . . she's dead now. So I figure Brice must've left it on the porch and the wind probably blew it to where Caitlyn found it. Or something. But it's probably not a clue."

Roland shifted his gray eyes to Peter, the gears in his mind almost visible. "Someone in Empowerment has one like it," he said to Peter but loud enough for the group to hear.

"Really? Who?" Peter said.

"Her name's Tessia. Thin girl, wears a hoodie."

"Oh, I know exactly who you mean. She confronted Brice on the way to Woodworking, told her she shouldn't be hanging out with me. And she just now threatened me."

"You?"

126

"Yeah." Peter glanced at the back doors of the school. "She said whatever game I was playing with Brice, it's over."

"What game?"

Peter shrugged. "She probably sees me talking to Brice now and then, maybe thinks I'm out to get her or something."

"You could always tell her the truth."

Peter locked eyes with Roland for a second. Was he serious? He didn't want anyone to know how he felt about Brice until the day Brice agreed to be his girlfriend. "She can't handle the truth," he said, imitating Jack Nicholson in *A Few Good Men*.

Roland looked away, laughing.

"Anyway, I gather she and Brice used to be friends."

"Brice is new here," Phoebe said. "How can they have been friends?"

"Maybe Tessia's new here too," Caitlyn said. "Does anyone know her?"

Peter shrugged. "Okay, so let's find out where Tessia came from. I'll see if Brice will tell me how they know each other. Maybe one of you can get to know Tessia."

"Why would she care if Brice hangs out with you?" Kiara asked.

"Maybe because he's a Fire Starter." Phoebe said, irritation in her tone. "And Fire Starters get the blame, even though we were the only ones out there trying to repair the damage."

"Right. Which is why we're going to find out who really did it." Peter turned to Roland.

"Before the police turn to us," Roland said.

"Right." Peter nodded. If the police didn't find the true criminals, would they believe the rumors and blame the Fire Starters too? "So what's our next step? I mean besides finding out about Tessia."

"Well, we can't just decide someone from school did it. We need to consider other options, so I think we should question the neighbors. Anybody with me?" Roland's gaze shifted to Caitlyn.

Her face lit up. "I am. When are we doing it?"

"Tonight."

15

GENERATING LEADS

"WHO'S GOING WITH WHO?" Phoebe stood with her hands on her hips, the sunlight reflecting off her silver bracelets and illuminating the purple streaks in her hair. They'd agreed to go around by twos so they could hit more houses but always have backup.

Kiara shielded her eyes from sunlight and peered in the direction of the houses down the street from Brice's split-level on an inner corner lot. Kiara's mother had picked up everyone—Phoebe, Caitlyn, and Roland—dropped them a few houses away from Brice's house, and given them two hours to "play" before she would return and take everyone home. Kiara never liked to make waves, so Roland wondered what she'd told her mom. Certainly not that they planned to investigate into the vandalism of Brice's house.

"Oh, I thought you two . . ." Caitlyn glanced at Phoebe and Kiara and then at Roland, her reddish eyebrows slanting over gorgeous green eyes that glittered in the sunlight.

Roland held her gaze. He'd thought the same thing: Phoebe and Kiara would pair up, and he and Caitlyn could go around together. He'd been looking forward to it more than he cared to admit. But who would do the talking when they knocked at doors? No, that wasn't a question. He would. He would take the lead, and he'd get comfortable talking to strangers. Wasn't that one reason he'd decided to go? *Hi, mind if we ask you a few questions?* Roland started rehearsing in his mind. *Did you happen to see who set fire to your neighbors' tree?*

"I want to go with you," Kiara said to Caitlyn. "You'll know just what to say."

"Oh." Caitlyn's eyes opened wide. "Maybe we should all say the same things. We can practice before we split up. Then it won't matter who's with who."

"Practice? It's not that complicated." Phoebe shifted her weight to one leg and folded her arms over her quilted brown vest. "We'll just ask if anyone saw anything that night or if they've heard any neighborhood gossip about the Escott family and their foster children."

Hi, mind if we ask you a few . . . Roland stopped rehearsing in his mind.

"Right." Caitlyn nodded, looking relieved. "See? Phoebe knows just what to say. And we have our phones, right?" Caitlyn opened the purse that hung from her shoulder and dug inside, probably looking for the phone Peter had given her. "We can call each other if there's anything . . ." She pulled a candy bar, rosary, and brush out of her purse. "I know it's in here." A pocket notebook jumped out and landed at her feet.

Acting on impulse, Roland stooped for it. Unfortunately, so did she and they bumped heads before either of them touched the notebook. Then they both straightened. "Sorry," he said.

Head dipped, she gave him a shy smile and ran a hand through her hair. "Me too," she said softly, her pupils dilating as she gazed at him.

"Okay, then," Phoebe said.

Her voice snapped Roland from his trance. He snatched the notebook off the sidewalk and handed it to Caitlyn.

"You can look for your phone when you actually need it," Phoebe said, bossy as ever. "Besides, Kiara has a phone too. Let's get going." She directed her last words to Roland.

"Oh, I thought . . ." He stood with his mouth hanging open, not actually admitting what he'd thought.

"You're with me." Phoebe stomped off, not giving him a chance to contest her decision.

Or did he have a chance? Of course, he did. He only had to say something. *I'm with Caitlyn.* He should say that. Why didn't he just say it?

"Okay, come on." Bouncing on her feet and looking as happy as a kid about to go trick-or-treating, Kiara grabbed Caitlyn's arm.

Caitlyn stood motionless, her chin tilted down and her eyes looking up at him. A frown on her face. "Bye," she whispered, stepping back.

"Yeah, see you in a few." Guilt needling him, Roland watched until she turned away and looped arms with Kiara. She wouldn't have looped arms with him, but it would've been nice hanging out with her for two hours. Why hadn't he spoken up?

"Come on!" Phoebe shouted. She had almost reached the driveway of the nearest house.

Afraid to jog, Roland speed-limped to catch up to her and they strode up an empty driveway together. How was he going to take the lead with her? She'd probably do all the talking. Maybe they could switch partners in an hour.

Reaching the door first, Phoebe pressed the glowing doorbell button and turned eyes surrounded in black to Roland. "We didn't get much from the kids at school, so I hope we get something tonight."

Not sure how to talk to her, Roland stuffed his hands into the front pockets of his jeans and nodded. "Yeah." She was wrong, though. They did have a few things to go on. A gas can and bracelet found at the crime scene, even though Peter didn't think the bracelet mattered anymore. And Caitlyn had said that some redheaded boy thought the mean jocks had done it. Roland had seen one of them in his speech class, the kid in the Coyotes shirt with the scraps hanging out of his spiral notebook.

No one answered, so Phoebe opened the storm door and pounded on the door with her fist.

Roland would've never done that. He'd have taken off for the next house, assuming no one was at home or that they wanted privacy.

A few seconds later, the doorknob jiggled and the door creaked open to a stale-smelling, dimly-lit house and an old man with silver whiskers and a tan button-front shirt. "Whatever you're selling, I don't want any." He started to close the door.

"Wait, sir." Phoebe held the storm door open. "We just wanted to ask you a question. We're worried about what's going on in the neighborhood."

The door creaked back open. "Don't know what you mean."

A few minutes later, they left with nothing more to go on. The man heard the firetrucks that night but thought he'd been dreaming until he saw the burnt tree the next day. He figured neighborhood kids had done it, but he didn't have names. "Kids today got no respect. Think they can go around and do anything they want."

"Thank you for your time," Phoebe had said. "We appreciate it."

"Not saying all kids are bad," the man replied. "You two seem mighty respectful."

As Roland limped alongside Phoebe to the next house, he realized he'd get absolutely no practice talking to strangers with her as a partner. But she made him uncomfortable too, so he could still get practice by talking to her. "So . . ." he forced himself to say, "did Caitlyn tell you about the kid at school she talked to, the junior?"

"No, what? Who?"

"She didn't give a name." And Caitlyn hadn't mentioned it at lunch, but it could be important so they ought to think more about it. "The kid said he knew who vandalized Brice's house."

"Oh, I know what you're talking about. Yeah, he thinks the football players did it. But that's not likely. I mean, they go out and party, but they've got to be careful or they'll get thrown off the team."

"No, she said it wasn't the jocks but a subgroup of jocks, the mean ones."

"The mean ones?" She gave him a skeptical look. "Oh, right, the mean jocks. The boys who love sports but are too undisciplined to join organized sports."

"Right."

"Could've been them. Some of them are mean. And they pick on people. And I've caught a few rumors about the stupid things they've done over the weekends."

"So, who knows all their names?" He would add it to the list of people he wanted to spy on and learn more about.

"I bet between the four of us, we can make a list."

He debated telling her about the notebook, since it could be nothing, but he wanted to conquer his fears so he made himself say it. "One of them's in my speech class. And he's got a spiral notebook with a bunch of pages missing."

"Oh?" They climbed the porch steps of the next house. "You mean, he could've been responsible for those posters all over school."

Roland shrugged. "It's not really proof, but yeah. Could've been him." Too bad he hadn't thought about grabbing one of the posters for comparison.

"That would make sense. The posters came directly after the school assembly, the diversity talk. And some of the mean jocks have been vocal about Empowerment's goals. But they aren't the only ones who don't like the Empowerment group."

"What do you mean?" Roland hadn't heard this before.

"Some people think the Empowerment group is pushy. They insist that everyone agree with them." Phoebe pressed the doorbell and, without hesitation, yanked open the storm door to knock. "But they don't speak up because they don't want to be labeled."

"Labeled what?"

"Haters."

Almost an hour later, Roland stood beside Phoebe on yet another front porch, the last on this side of the street. Canvassing the neighborhood no longer seemed like such a good idea. His leg begged for a break and they'd discovered little to nothing. They knocked on doors that no one answered. The few that did answer saw nothing. Apparently, the perpetrators worked so quietly that even the couple of people who'd been up at that hour hadn't heard them. And no one had heard any negative talk about Brice's foster family either. Those that knew the family, liked and admired them.

And as far as getting practice talking to strangers, the only practice Roland got was talking to Phoebe.

"Let's turn around after this house." Phoebe pressed the doorbell, pounded on the door, and glanced at her watch. "We'll see what Kiara and Caitlyn found out."

The door swung open. A gray-haired woman in a thick bathrobe eyed them suspiciously. "May I help you?"

"Oh, hey." Phoebe kicked into action with a smile and hand gestures as she rolled out her spiel.

When she finished, the woman scratched her neck and glanced across the street. "You're talking about last Saturday, right?"

"Right." Phoebe glanced at her watch again and gave Roland a look that said they were wasting their time. "Or more like early Sunday morning."

"Seems no one in the neighborhood saw anything," Roland said, just to make himself speak at least once before going home. So far, he'd only nodded a few times and said *yeah* or *don't think so* at the appropriate times.

"Well, I can't see the house from any of my windows, too far down." She turned her head in the direction of the Escotts' house. "But the firetrucks woke me, and I did see a boy in the middle of the road."

Phoebe jerked back. "A boy?"

Roland sucked in a breath. "How old was he?"

"About your age. Standing in the middle of the road in shorts and bare feet, watching the firetrucks, I suppose." She looked across the street again and pointed. "I think he lives over there."

"Thank you for your time," Phoebe said, then she led their retreat down the porch steps. "At least we got something." Eyes on the house across the street, Phoebe stopped on the sidewalk and stood hands on hips, evening sunlight glinting off her armful of bracelets. "But the boy was probably doing what she was doing, trying to see what the commotion was about."

"Probably." Roland studied the house, an ordinary tan two-story with green shutters, five steps leading up to a wraparound porch, and a white cat and red South Dakota Coyotes decal in the window. They'd been visiting houses on both sides of the street, skipping only the few that seemed empty. They hadn't gone to the last three houses across the street though.

"I wonder what Caitlyn and Kiara found out." Phoebe took her phone out.

"We should at least knock on that door." Rather than ask her the time, Roland pulled his own phone from his back pocket. As he tapped it, the display lit up and played his ringtone. His heart skipped a beat. Caitlyn was calling.

He tapped to answer the call, brought the phone to his ear, and said, "Hey."

"Hi, Roland."

Even over the phone, her voice rippled through him, disturbing every cell in his body. "You guys done?"

"Um, no. But we have a lead."

Phoebe must've heard Caitlyn because her eyes popped open and snapped to the phone.

Roland held the phone out so they could both hear. "Okay, Phoebe can hear too. Tell us what you got."

"Well, someone told us that the neighbor over the fence—he lives on another street—he doesn't like the Escott family because of that tree."

Phoebe gasped, her gaze connecting with Roland's. "Do you know why?"

"I guess it was a gumball tree—"

"No, not gumball." Kiara's voice came over the phone, cutting off Caitlyn. "It was a sweetgum tree. They're kind of pretty, especially in the fall, but they drop all those brown, spiky balls."

Phoebe nodded. Roland knew the type of tree too. He'd almost twisted his ankle, walking under one of them.

"Right," Caitlyn said. "And apparently, the neighbor was always complaining because the gumballs fall over the fence and into his yard. And they're impossible to rake up."

"And"—Kiara jumped in—"he was always complaining that you can't even mow them up because they're like grenades."

"And to make things worse," Caitlyn said, "he recently slipped on one and broke his ankle."

Phoebe and Roland's gazes connected again, giving Roland a feeling of solidarity.

"Wow," Phoebe said. "He definitely had a motive for burning down that tree."

"Yeah," Caitlyn and Kiara said at the same time.

"Let's go talk to him." Phoebe snatched Roland's phone and turned away, peering down the street. "Where are you?" She paused but Roland could no longer hear the other side of the conversation. "Well, wait for me."

Phoebe turned back and handed Roland his phone. "You can get that last house on your own, right?"

"Yeah, sure," he said, though he would've rather gone with the rest of them. Maybe no one would answer, and he could jog to catch up. No, his aching leg said that wasn't an option. "Go check it out. Then let's meet where Kiara's mother dropped us off."

"Great." Phoebe took off running, her bracelets making a soft clinking sound with every step.

With a sigh, Roland turned to the house across the street, the one with the wraparound porch and the five steps he'd need to climb. He took a breath, steeling himself and, favoring his leg without inhibition, hobbled across the street. Grabbing the handrail for support, barely caring who saw how pathetic he looked, he mounted the steps.

Another South Dakota Coyotes decal hung in the little decorative window high on the door.

Roland reached for the doorbell but stopped two inches away. He'd have to do this one alone. What was he going to say? Phoebe's spiel was too long. *Hi, mind if we ask you a few questions?* Roland's rehearsed words came to mind. *Did you happen to see who set fire to your neighbors' tree?*

Forcing his finger the last two inches, he pressed the doorbell and knocked on the door for good measure. Then he shifted to alleviate pressure on his leg.

A few seconds later, the door swung open to a familiar face, and a lump formed in Roland's throat.

"Hey, hey, it's one of the West boys." Gavin Wheeler, the jock with the suspicious notebook, pushed the storm door open and leaned against the door frame. "Your name's on the tip of my tongue. You're in my speech class, right?"

"Uh, yeah." Roland fought with himself to keep from shrinking away. He couldn't possibly ask about the vandalism now, could he? Gavin would realize he was investigating. But Gavin had been there, standing outside and watching it happen. Had he been involved? How could Roland find out anything if he didn't ask. Should he? Shouldn't he?

"You gave that memorable speech on Monday." He toyed with the scruffy hair growing on his chin. "Your name's Roman? Romulus? Romeo?"

"Romeo? No, I'm Roland." He couldn't help glaring.

Still holding the screen door with one hand, Gavin slapped his leg with the other. "Oh, that's it. What brings you to my neighborhood? You out slumming?"

"Huh?"

"You live in a castle, don't you? Somewhere off Forest Road? I didn't get invited to your Halloween party last year. You having one this year?"

"Uh, no." Roland glanced over his shoulder, wishing he had back-up. "And we don't live in a castle. It just sort of looks like one."

"Oh, well, that's cool anyway." While his words could've sounded friendly, his tone came across condescending. "What's up, Roland?" One side of his mouth turned up and stretched into a smirk as he looked Roland over.

What should he say? *Hi, mind if I ask you a few questions?* No, no, no, not that. Come up with something else. "So, I, uh—"

"Wait." Gavin lifted his index finger. "Don't tell me. You're selling cookies to raise money for the diversity club. What's it called, Empowerment?" He raised his brows and tilted his head as if waiting for an answer.

Face burning under Gavin's cocky glare, Roland gritted his teeth. "No, not selling cookies."

Gavin shifted his gaze and peered over Roland's shoulder, making a show of looking around. "Where's your mom? Shouldn't she have a wagon loaded with boxes of cookies for me to choose from?"

Every fiber of his being tensed like a rubber band being pulled taught, and he envisioned himself slugging Gavin across his scruffy chin. But his leg ached and wouldn't tolerate the forceful step he'd have to take to do it. Besides, Gavin probably didn't know his mother had died. He was just being annoying.

"You know which ones I really like? Those gooey chewy ones with the chocolate stripes. Mmmm." Eyes rolling back in his head, he rubbed his belly and moaned. "Those are to die for."

"Look, you know I'm not selling cookies."

Gavin's eyes turned hard. "Right, so whatdya want?"

And then, whether or not it was a mistake, the words just came out. "You live near the house that was vandalized."

"Yeah, so?"

"So, we're just trying to see if any neighbors saw anything that night."

"Who's 'we'?" He leaned out of the house again and looked in both directions. "You seem to be alone, Roland."

Roland took a breath and forced it back out. Okay, so he'd messed up his line. Probably should've come up with something else to say. Judging by the attitude, Gavin wasn't going to give him anything useful anyway. He could almost hear himself saying "forget it" and see himself taking off, but he'd come out here for two reasons: one to gain information and the other to speak to people regardless of how uncomfortable it made him feel.

Taking another breath, he said, "So did you? Did you see anything?"

Mouth hanging open, Gavin rubbed his chin. "See anything like what? Firetrucks screaming down the street in the middle of the night? Tree burning in an outcast's yard? That's the only reason I'd be looking in the direction of that girl's house. She's of no interest to me . . . or any dude. Let the entire house burn, I say."

Irritated by the comments, Roland gritted his teeth but he forced a cool reply. "All right. Thanks for the help." And he turned to go, hating that Gavin would watch his every pathetic step as he hobbled off the porch.

"Hey, Romeo," Gavin called as Roland reached the first step. "You'd better watch out. All your snooping could get you in some deep trouble. And you saw the signs at school, right? So you've been warned. Don't want to wake up to a tree burning in the front yard of your castle."

Hand to the rail, heart hammering in his chest, and praying he didn't stumble while Gavin was watching, Roland descended the steps.

Then Gavin spoke again, his voice dark and dramatic.

"Outcast, beware."

16

STEPPING IT UP

SATISFIED WITH HIS JOB jacking up the right rear wheel of the Durango, Peter straightened and wiped his hands on his jeans. His gaze snapped to Brice, and something inside his chest did a happy dance. Man, he loved working with her . . . in Woodworking, on his car . . . anything. She shared his interests. She had skills and confidence in executing them. And she didn't have all the trappings other girls had, all the boring girly things. And there was something else about her, but he couldn't put his finger on it. *Whatever.* He'd have to come up with more things she could help him with or maybe get her to like his friends and family. This just couldn't be the last day they did stuff together.

Brice stood with her back to him, looking at home as she rifled through a pile of used sandpaper and miscellaneous tools on the back workbench. A few seconds later, she turned and folded her arms in resignation. "Don't you have an old pickle jar or something?"

Toby shuffled toward her, his eyes on the wall over the workbench adjacent to the one she leaned against, then he shuffled back the way he came. He'd been leisurely pacing for the past ten minutes. Ever since he'd come out to the garage. Peter had tried like heck to get him to say what he wanted, thinking maybe Mom had sent him with a message. Guess he just wanted to meet Peter's new friend.

Peter walked to Brice and stopped two feet away. "Pickle jar? What size pickle?"

She threw him a glance and her lip curled up into a saucy smile. "Just your ordinary pickle."

"Well, there's your ordinary gherkin in a wee jar like this." He held his hands up to indicate a small jar. "And there's your big dill pickle in jars like this." Stretching the distance between his hands, he indicated a much larger jar.

"Just your ordinary pickle, you dope." Still with the crooked grin, she smacked the side of his head, mostly just brushing her fingertips through his unruly hair.

He laughed and grabbed her wrist on the downswing, his hand drawn to her like metal to a magnet.

Not having it, she twisted her arm free and punched his shoulder. Her eyes held a playful warning. Maybe a challenge.

On impulse Peter drew back his fist, but he probably shouldn't play-hit a girl he liked. Not that she was your ordinary girl. She probably wouldn't care. Anyway . . . *Straighten up or you'll blow it.*

He turned to the shelf behind him to find a jar. The shelf held a row of jars, cans, and small boxes holding various hardware and junk. They should have something the right size for the job of bleeding the brakes.

"Here." He dumped dried palm branches out of a—could've been an ordinary pickle jar. He blew in it and palm particles flew up into his face.

"What'd you just pull out of that jar?"

"Huh? Oh, palm branches. You know, from Palm Sunday Mass."

She shook her head, her look saying she didn't know. So she probably wasn't Catholic or Episcopal. Was she any of the gazillion Protestant denominations? *Eh, who cares?* If they became good friends, he could share his faith with her. Jesus did say to take the Gospel to everyone. Maybe God wanted Peter to be His instrument. Yeah . . . he was on a mission from God.

"Well, they've been blessed," Peter explained, momentarily picturing himself in a suit and shades, like one of the characters from the 1980s Blues Brothers movie, "so you can't just throw them away.

We'll take them back to church before Lent, so Father can burn them and use them on Ash Wednesday."

"So he can burn them?"

"Yeah. That's what he's supposed to do with them . . . I think anyways. Dust to dust and all that."

"So now your blessed palm branches are dumped out on a messy workbench."

"Oh." He hadn't thought about that. Was that sacrilegious?

"Put them back in." Toby squeezed between them and gathered palm branches into his hands with uncoordinated movements.

"Yeah, sure. We'll put 'em back when we're done." He ruffled Toby's hair.

Palm branches in hand, Toby turned to Brice and cocked his head to one side. "I'm Toby."

Brice gave the hint of a smile. "I know. You told me already, like, three times today. Don't you remember?"

"What's your name?"

"I already told you my name, also, like, three times today."

"You're Brice."

"Oh, you do remember." Her grin grew. "So now you can't ask me again 'cuz you already know. And you can't tell me your name again 'cuz I already know."

As if not satisfied with that, Toby mouthed, "My name is Toby" as he resumed pacing.

"Yeah, he just likes to ask questions." Peter had yet to explain that Toby had autism, but Brice probably figured it out. And—Peter's heart tapped out another dance—she seemed to like him, even though he could be a pest.

"I can see that." Brice grabbed a long clear tube from a workbench and snatched the pickle jar from Peter. She dropped to one knee by the jacked-up wheel. "There's a bleed valve on the back of the brake caliper."

"Yeah, I know." Peter squatted beside her.

"You know, huh?" She glanced. "Why am I here? Why don't you do it yourself?" She let the old brake fluid drain from the brake lines.

"Because bleeding the brakes is a—"

"Two-man job," she said along with him. "You keep saying."

"Yeah, well, and besides . . ." His neck and chest got hot as a full confession of his feelings for her came to his mind. He'd sort of told her once. He shouldn't press his luck. Stopping the words from spilling out of his mouth, he simply said, "It's more fun working with someone who likes to work on cars."

She stared for a long second then gave a dry laugh. "Okay, well, if we actually plan on bleeding the brakes, one of us needs to get in the car."

"Oh. Right." Still feeling the joy, Peter went around to the driver side to pump the brakes.

An hour later, Brice stood back, wiping her hands on a rag while Peter dragged the jack out from under the Durango. "Let's take 'er for a spin, make sure the brakes are all seated."

"Yeah, okay." Loving the idea of taking the Durango out—with her—for a spin—Peter turned to Toby. "Hey, go tell Mom we're going for a little drive."

Seeming oblivious to anyone around him, Toby cast a fishing line down the driveway and reeled it back in with vigor. Bored of pacing and messing around in the garage, he'd been casting and reeling for the past twenty minutes.

"Toby!" Peter came up to him. "Listen. Go tell Mom we're going for a drive." He pointed to the sidewalk that led to the front stoop.

Toby turned and cocked his head. "Go for a drive?" He handed the fishing rod to Peter and galloped—his way of running—around to the front door.

Peter laughed and hung the rod on the wall. "Okay, let's go. I'm sure he'll tell Mom something. She'll figure it out when she finds the Durango gone."

"Aren't we gonna wait for him?" Brice stood with one hand on the open driver-side door, as if expecting to drive. She did have her license while Peter only had temps.

Peter went to the passenger side, thrilled to ride shotgun to her. "Yeah, I don't think so. If something goes wrong—"

The front storm door squeaked and slammed. Toby barged into the garage and yanked open a back door of the Durango. He climbed into the seat and closed the door before Peter's senses returned.

Brice laughed. "Looks like he's going with us." She slid into the driver's seat and as she buckled up, she smiled at Peter through the open passenger-side door. "Don't worry. We're just gonna roll down the road and back."

"Yeah, okay. And we'll put the hazards on." Peter twisted in his seat to see Toby. "Put your—"

Toby's seatbelt clicked and he gave the strap a good tug. "Seatbelt on," he whispered, staring out his window.

"Okay. Good." Peter buckled up too.

One hand resting on the steering wheel, Brice cranked the key in the ignition. On the second try the engine turned over. The battery and check engine lights came on and stayed on. "Does it always start like that?"

"I don't know. Just been working on it so far. Probably needs a new battery." A glimmer of hope sparked and a smile stretched across his face. "Maybe you can help me with that."

"You need help changing a battery?" As she twisted to peer out the back window, she tossed him a look that said she knew better. Then she backed down the driveway, swung out onto the road, and shifted into drive, handling the car with crude confidence.

While the engine grumbled a bit and something under the hood squeaked, the brakes made no strange noises. Brice punched it, squealing the tires as she went from zero to forty-five down the two-lane road, a pink sky on the horizon, the setting sun sending blazing sunbeams through trees, and not a car in sight.

She and Peter exchanged glances, her expression showing she got the same rush he did.

Toby laughed. "Faster!"

Peter snapped from the euphoria. "No, better not go faster. In fact, when you get to the next driveway, let's turn around. I want to show you something."

"Yeah? Show me what?" On this end of Forest Road, the houses sat well-spaced, wide yards and clusters of trees between them. But they neared the next long driveway and Brice stepped on the brakes, slowing down smoothly, proving their work a success.

"You'll see." Peter grinned, liking his idea.

Brice swung into a driveway, going a little too fast and running over a bit of grass. With a few cautious glances, she shifted into reverse and zipped back out onto the road. They drove past Peter's house, the neon pink "Forest Gateway B & B" sign looking cool in the dwindling light.

"Slow down. There's a gravel driveway on the right."

Brice eased on the brakes and gripped the wheel for the turn.

"And take it easy," Peter teased.

"What's the fun in that?" She took the turn at a moderate pace and the Durango crunched down the long gravel driveway under a canopy of trees, a few of which had sprinkles of orange and yellow leaves. "So, what's down here?"

"The West castle. Heard of it?"

She laughed. "You mean your friend's house?

"Yeah, but it looks like a castle."

The gravel drive twisted and turned, and before long the stables and then the house came into view. Pink sunbeams fell on a few of the battlements and on the right turret, creating a blinding starburst for a second. Lights glowed inside most of the first-floor windows and on the porch, on either side of the heavy front door.

"Yeah, I guess I've heard about it. Wow, huh?" Leaning forward, Brice stopped the car where the gravel ended and a paved driveway began, and she peered out the windshield. "Hey, is that him? What, is that a four-car garage?"

"Is *what* him?"

A stone's throw away, Roland stood on the paved driveway, blending in with the shadows by an open garage door. He withdrew a hand from the pocket of his dark gray hoodie and motioned as he said something to someone inside the garage. Then, favoring one leg, he strode toward the Durango. As he neared, his gaze caught Brice and his dark eyebrows twitched. He was probably surprised to see her in the driver seat. Then he veered over to the front passenger side.

Peter lowered his window. "Hey, man, what'cha doing?"

"Are you picking me up?" Roland gave Brice a cautious glance. Brice looked indifferent.

"Sure." Peter draped an arm on the window opening, a bit of pride welling up over being seen with Brice. "You need a ride? We were testing out the brakes. Where you going?"

"Uh . . ." Roland glanced at Toby then at Brice again. "Your house. Caitlyn's over there, right?"

"I don't think so." Something turned to stone inside Peter. He didn't want Brice thinking he and Caitlyn were more than friends. "Why would she be over my house?" *Ugh. Shouldn't have asked that. Don't answer, Roland.* Peter knew Caitlyn would want to share whatever she found out today from scouring Brice's neighborhood.

"She said for me to meet her over there. I figured she told you we were coming."

"Uh. No. Maybe she called when we were out. But get in."

Roland walked around the Durango, going behind it instead of in front, and opened the door behind Brice, since Toby sat behind Peter.

Peter glanced at Brice to gauge her reaction to the turn of events. "He's a good friend. You'd like him."

She shrugged, still looking indifferent.

As Roland slid into the backseat, Toby greeted him. "My name's Toby."

"Yeah, hi, Toby. I'm Roland." Roland had long since accepted having to re-introduce himself every time he saw Toby.

They rode back to Peter's house in awkward silence. How could he get his friends to be her friend too? Of course, Roland wasn't the most talkative kid. What did he expect? And maybe it wasn't a good idea anyway. Brice might somehow discover Roland and Caitlyn's efforts to find out who vandalized her house. She might not like them nosing around on her behalf.

As they pulled into the driveway next to the Summers' van, a twinge of guilt over not telling her and fear of her finding out rattled Peter. He pushed those feelings down. This was an opportunity for her to get to know his friends. They wouldn't be stupid enough to let anything slip.

"Caitlyn here," Toby said and then rattled off the names of her brothers and sisters.

"Oh, so you know their names"—Brice twisted around to look at him—"but you can't remember mine?"

"And mine," Roland said. "I've got to tell him every time I see him."

"You're Roland and you're Brice," Toby said.

Everyone laughed. Even Brice. Maybe they could become friends.

Toby and Roland headed for the house. Peter walked around the Durango to Brice, his mouth wrapped around an invitation to come inside.

"See you tomorrow." She plowed past him with barely a glance, heading for her little BMX bike, which she'd parked in the grass next to the garage.

"Hey, wait." He followed. "Why don't you come inside for a while? Have something to eat."

"Nah, I got stuff to do." She grabbed the handlebars and walked the bike onto the driveway.

"Right. Like what?" Disappointment weighed heavy.

"Like, none of your business." Eyes on him, as if testing or teasing him, she swung a leg over the seat and stood straddling the bike.

"All right. Fine." He stepped out of the way, hands raised in surrender. "You're so cold," he added, teasing back.

"Whatever. Tell your mom thanks for the egg rolls." She flashed a smile. "Those were awesome."

Her smile shot a spark through Peter. "Yeah, you should come over for dinner some time. You don't need an invite. They always cook for an army." He meant for it to sound like a casual invitation, but if she wanted to take it as a date, he had no problem with that either.

"Maybe. I gotta go write my speech."

He smiled. Rather than leave with no explanation, she'd given him the reason she had to go. "Wait, you haven't even written it yet? Mrs. Kauffman could've called your name any day so far."

Brice shrugged. "But she didn't."

"Yeah, but you couldn't have known that."

"I have a feeling I'm up next. I guess I can't talk about cars now. You stole my subject."

Peter laughed. "So talk about them anyways. Who cares if we bore the class. Or the teacher."

"Everyone will think we wrote them together."

"I don't care."

"I do."

"All right. Whatever. See ya tomorrow. We can drill the pocket holes for our gun racks, start putting 'em together."

Without a second glance, she gripped the handlebars, put a foot to a pedal, and rode off standing over the low seat.

Impressed by everything about her, Peter watched until she disappeared from view, the evening playing over in his mind. He probably shouldn't have told her she was cold. She must've had a reason for her cold attitude. Somehow her sister had died. And for whatever reason, she didn't live with her parents. Bad things must've happened in her life. And maybe now it was hard for her to let anyone in.

He sighed. He wasn't giving up. Everyone needed a friend. And if that's all she wanted from him, he was cool with that. For now. Maybe next time she'd come inside. Get to know his family. Maybe his friends. *Oh, that's right—*

Peter turned toward the house. Roland and Caitlyn might have found some clues.

~ ~ ~

"Okay, what've you guys got?" On his way through his bedroom, Peter shoved a pile of boxes draped with clothes into the closet. He should've cleaned his room like Mom had been nagging him to do, but Caitlyn was used to it and Roland wouldn't care.

"Well, we've got two things." Roland took measured steps down the path in Peter's bedroom, boxes of projects on the floor to one side, clothes and junk on the other. He stopped in the dormer, glanced out the dark window, and gripped the back of the desk chair. Of course, then his gaze attached to Caitlyn.

Always the mother hen, Caitlyn straightened the sheet on Peter's bed and pulled up the comforter, a mess of red curls hanging in her face. Then she plopped down on the bed and grabbed Peter's red-and-black plaid blanket. "Was Brice really over at your house?"

Peter blinked, his entire body going rigid. Fearing Roland had outed him, he shot Roland a glance.

Roland gave the slightest headshake, communicating that he hadn't.

"Your mom said you two were working in the garage." Caitlyn brought the wrong corners of the blanket together.

"Oh. Right." Peter exhaled and slouched, the tension draining from his body. "Yeah, she was helping me with a brake job. It's a two-man job, you know. She said she'd help me."

"I knew she was in your woodworking class, but I didn't realize you two were becoming friends." Caitlyn gave him a naïve look as she continued trying to fold the blanket with the wrong corners together.

"Wha . . ." Peter's ears burned.

Roland gave a sympathetic look but didn't offer any help.

"Well, we are. Friends. Sort of." The burning sensation spread to his neck and cheeks. "I like to think we're friends, anyway. She's nice. Well, no, not really nice. More like interesting."

"So . . ." Caitlyn gave up on folding the blanket and tossed it to the foot of the bed. ". . . there's a deeper reason for us finding the vandals, huh?"

"A deeper reason?" Panic threatened to overtake him. He didn't want Caitlyn knowing. She might tell someone. It would get back to Brice. Brice wouldn't want anything to do with him.

Mouth twitching, Roland turned away from Peter—abandoning him—and looked out the dark window again. What could he even see out there? A silhouette of a tree and a purple sky?

"You like Brice," Caitlyn said, matter-of-fact.

Her words seemed to take physical form and slam into his chest. Peter jerked back. "Wow, I—"

Caitlyn giggled and exchanged glances with Roland, who was now hiding his mouth with his hand. "How cute. I can't remember you ever really liking a girl before. I mean you've picked on girls, and I kind of thought—"

"Argh!" Peter shoved his hands in his hair and stomped toward the bed. "Stop it!" He grabbed the messy blanket and whipped it at her. "I don't need you telling people who you think I like."

Laughing and almost toppling over, Caitlyn whipped the blanket back. "Peter likes Brice," she taunted, "Peter likes Brice."

"Knock it off." He caught the blanket and threw it again.

Roland strode up to him, without the limp, and stood with his back to Caitlyn. "Hey," he whispered, "why don't you just admit it, so we can get to work?"

Peter couldn't respond for a full second. "You did not just say . . ." He leaned to glance at Caitlyn then gave Roland a look of challenge. "Okay. I'm not the only one who likes someone. Why don't we all just come clean, huh?"

Before Peter even finished his question, Roland's head was shaking and a hint of panic flashed in his gray eyes.

"Right." Peter grinned, giving Roland a gotcha look. "So you get it, then."

"It's different." Roland dipped his head.

"It's not different."

"Is there a reason you don't want anyone to know?"

"Is there a reason you don't?" Peter folded his arms. Roland couldn't throw anything at him that he couldn't throw back.

They stood eye to eye for a minute, neither blinking. Then Roland said, "Whatever," and trekked back to the desk.

Peter sighed, resignation overtaking him. "Oh, all right." He staggered to the bed, sat next to Caitlyn, and flopped onto his back. "Yes, I like Brice. And I don't want anyone to know because I'm afraid if she finds out, she'll avoid me like the plague. I mean, if she's cool with it, I don't care who knows."

Caitlyn hovered over him, smiling from ear to ear, her curly red locks tickling his face. "Wow, Peter has a crush on a girl."

"Would you stop it?" He swatted her curls from his face, sat up, and scooted back to the wall. "Even if I didn't like Brice, it irks me that someone did this to a person just because they're different. Or for whatever reason. It's wrong. And we gotta stick up for people."

"Agreed." Roland finally sat in the desk chair. His leg had to be killing him from all the walking today. "Let's get down to business."

"Okay." Caitlyn straightened and lifted a corner of the red-and-black plaid blanket they'd been throwing back and forth. "And don't worry, Peter, I won't tell your secret." She pressed her lips together as if trying not to smile or maybe trying to keep from teasing him again.

"What'd you guys find out?" Peter glanced from Caitlyn to Roland.

Roland shifted in the chair. "Well, I discovered that Gavin Wheeler lives at the end of Brice's street. You know who he is?"

"He's one of the mean jocks, right?" Caitlyn continued folding, matching the right corners this time.

"Yeah, and from our conversation, I know he definitely has a negative attitude toward Brice."

"Maybe he liked her, too," Caitlyn said in a whispery voice. "He would've seen her move into the neighborhood. Maybe they talked over the summer. Maybe he asked her out or something, and she rejected him."

Not wanting to picture it, Peter scrunched his brows and twisted his mouth to one side. "Well, that's a lot of *maybes*. But we should keep our eyes on him and his buddies."

"The mean jocks," Caitlyn said.

"Right." Peter shook his head, not on board with the label.

"We also discovered," Caitlyn continued, "that the neighbor over the fence was angry about the tree in Brice's yard, I mean, in her foster family's yard. He hated the sweetgum tree because it dropped all those spiky balls."

Interested, Peter straightened. "Oh, yeah?"

"And the neighbor—we met him." Caitlyn glanced at Roland. "Me, Kiara, and Phoebe met him. He's maybe forty years old, grumpy, and jobless. One of his neighbors claim they've seen him wandering around the neighborhood drunk. And somehow he tripped on one of those spiky balls and broke his ankle."

"Ouch." Peter rubbed his chin. "That sounds like a reasonable motive. And he definitely had the means to do it."

Roland nodded. "Motive, means, and opportunity . . . unless he has an alibi."

"We asked him about that night," Caitlyn said, "and he said he was in bed until he heard the firetrucks. Since it happened so late at night, or early morning, I don't think anyone will have a solid alibi. Anyone can claim they were in bed."

"What's the neighbor's name?" Roland asked.

"Oh." Caitlyn glanced down and smoothed her hands over the plaid blanket, which she'd finally folded into a neat square. "We didn't get his name."

"What? What kind of detective work is that?" Peter said, flinging his hands up.

"Well, he wouldn't tell us." Caitlyn folded her arms. "I wanted to peek in the mailbox but Phoebe told me—"

"That's a Federal crime," Roland and Peter said together.

"Right. That's what Phoebe said."

"So what do we do now?" Peter looked at Roland.

"I think we need to spy on people. The truth will come out."

"I think so too." Caitlyn scooted off the bed. "If high school kids did this, they are probably proud of it, and they'll end up saying something to someone."

Peter leaned back, bumping his head on the wall. "So we gotta spy on the neighbor and on kids at school. How?"

"Well, I thought about it. And maybe we can research online." Caitlyn approached Roland at the desk.

Eyebrows climbing up his forehead with a look of confusion, Roland peered up at her.

"Can I?" She pointed to the laptop on the desk.

"Oh. Yeah." He jumped up and offered her the chair. She stepped toward the chair, but Roland bumped a box on the floor, and they did an awkward little dance as they maneuvered out of each other's way.

"So you think you're gonna find Brice online?" Peter came up behind Caitlyn.

"I bet you've already looked her up, huh?" Roland sat on the end of the bed, his eyes on the laptop.

Peter grinned. "You know it. The girl has no online presence that I could find."

"Where'd she move from?" Caitlyn glanced at Peter over her shoulder.

"I dunno."

"What about Tessia?" Roland said. "Maybe she and Brice know each other from before River Run High. Let's try to find something about her."

"Tessia . . ." Caitlyn tapped her chin. "Holbrook, right?" Caitlyn typed Tessia's full name into a search engine. "I think Tessia is a recruiter for Empowerment, so I'm going to talk to her tomorrow."

"What are you going to find out that Roland couldn't?" Peter said. "He was right there in the middle of the hornets' next."

"Well, maybe because I'm a girl—"

"Don't give me that sexist stuff." Peter flicked her hair.

After a fruitless online search, Caitlyn clicked on a social networking site.

"Hey, what are you doing?" Not sure what she'd see in his feed, Peter hunched over her and snagged the mouse. He logged himself off of the site and gave her the mouse back. "You're not on social media, are you?"

"I am now," she said, typing something on the login page. "When I got home from our visit to Brice's neighborhood, I asked Mom if I could open an account for our investigation."

"She let you?" Peter said.

Caitlyn nodded, smiling. "But I didn't use my name. I used the school mascot, the Thunderhawk, and then I sent a friend request to all of the mean jocks and the stuck-up girls and a few other kids." She leaned forward and pointed. "Look! I have friends already! Now I can see their social media pages, right?"

"Wait." Face turning an even paler shade of white, Roland got up from the end of the bed, his eyes on the laptop monitor.

"What?" Peter looked over the website page for trouble but failed to see what had drained Roland of all color.

Eyes wide, Roland pointed. "Audrey Summer . . . is that your mother's name?"

"Yes, that was one of the stipulations. I had to *friend* her first."

Peter smacked his forehead and turned away, his stomach sinking. "We're compromised!"

"What?" Caitlyn said.

"With your mother as your first social media friend," Roland explained calmly, "everyone will know that you're Thunderhawk."

Peter grabbed a handful of his hair and yanked, the pain distracting him from his anger. "And anyone with half a brain might realize Caitlyn—and her friends—are investigating the vandalism of Brice's house. Brice is gonna find out."

"No, they won't," Roland said. "Not unless Caitlyn posted revealing questions."

Feeling sunk, Peter turned toward the window and gazed out at the silhouette of the tree and the purple sky. "Brice is gonna hate me."

17

FIRE STARTERS

ROLAND STOOD APART from the other Fire Starters in the youth center, AKA the teachers' lounge. He leaned in the corner between a curio shelf and the wall, his eyes on the open door. When would Caitlyn get here? He wanted to swap notes with her before the meeting began.

He stuffed his hand into the pocket that held his phone. Maybe he should type up some notes while he waited for her. The visit to Brice's neighborhood after school yesterday had given him several ideas about their investigation, and he didn't want to forget them. He hadn't had time to write anything down after he got home.

Papa had met him in the kitchen, wanting to talk about school, his grades, and what sort of things he did after school. Not sure where Papa was coming from, Roland had replied with a bunch of "ums" and vague answers. He especially didn't want to explain the "new club" Papa had heard he'd joined. Papa would likely jump to conclusions about the members and their agenda and start rattling off his raw, unfiltered opinions. Maybe he'd be right about a few things but . . . a person didn't have to agree with someone to treat them with human dignity.

Fortunately, Caitlyn had called right about then, asking him to meet her at Peter's house. Papa had offered to drive him, probably thinking they could carry on their conversation in the car. Another bit of luck or Divine Providence: Peter showed up to give Roland a ride. He sure hadn't expected to see Brice behind the wheel.

He was glad to see Caitlyn at Peter's house, but something about her made him lose his concentration. The Thunderhawk social media mistake hadn't blown their cover, had it? He hadn't had the chance to ask her at school today.

Not wanting to generate suspicion, the "investigators" agreed not to sit together at lunchtime. Roland had taken his lunch outside and eaten by the tree. Later, he'd seen Caitlyn in the halls, but he was running late for a class. The second time he saw her, she was talking to Tessia. *Wonder how that conversation went.*

Phoebe's voice rose above the rest of the chatter and laughter. She sat on the windowsill, a group of girls surrounding her. Dominic, Peter, Keefe, and Fred huddled together on the opposite side of the room, talking. Father directed two other boys in setting up the folding metal chairs between the couches and armchairs. Some kids started taking seats. Everyone seemed to be here. Except for Caitlyn.

"Okay." Standing in the middle of the seating arrangement, Father clapped his hands together. "What do you say we get started?"

More kids found seats.

Roland pushed off the wall and headed toward Peter, who sat in one of the metal chairs. As he weaved around kids and furniture, he and Keefe crossed paths and exchanged nods. Then Keefe approached Father. Roland set his sights on the empty metal chair next to Peter, but Dominic slid past him and sat down. Finding nothing else free, Roland sat on one end of an old plaid couch. On the bright side, Caitlyn would have nowhere else to sit either. So she'd end up with him on the couch.

"Hey, mind if I sit here?" Phoebe appeared before him, her clothes a gaudy mix of yellow, purple, and black in mismatched patterns.

"Uh . . ." Roland glanced at the door, hoping to see Caitlyn slip into the room. "Sure." Pushing aside his disappointment, he scooted toward the arm of the couch to give Phoebe room.

She sat down with a thwump, her bracelets jangling and her leg bumping his. "So I probably should've stayed with you yesterday, instead going with Caitlyn and Kiara."

Roland's eyes bugged and he glanced around to see if anyone had heard her. They had all agreed not to discuss the investigation in public. "Why?" he finally said. "I handled it."

"Well . . ." Her eyebrows twitched and she blinked a few times. "You're kind of shy. I think I could've gotten more out of Gavin."

Trying not to take offense, Roland took a breath. "He's on our watch list. Even if he is guilty, I'm sure he wouldn't have confessed to it."

"Okay, everyone." Father stood in front of the armchair he typically sat in and waited a moment while everyone stopped talking. "First order of business: prayer." He bowed his head and led them in the Sign of the Cross, a prayer to the Holy Spirit, and a Hail Mary. "Oh, and"—he looked out a window—"we've got a storm headed our way."

A few groans and murmurs filled the air.

"So let's all pray that it comes and goes before our camping weekend." He bowed his head again. "Lord, we pray for Your will and Your blessings."

Everyone said, "Amen," and made the Sign of the Cross again.

"Next order of business . . ." Father rubbed his hands together. "Let's talk about the camping trip."

"Yeah," Peter said with gusto. A few other kids added their enthusiastic grunts and comments too.

"I was thinking we ought to have a theme this year, and I came up with a few ideas." Father sat on the arm of the chair and lifted his index finger. "First idea, one to counter all the selfies: *selfless*. We could use this theme to challenge ourselves to change our ways of thinking, to focus less on ourselves and more on others. I could prepare a few meditations. We could come up with some games."

"That might be fun." Kiara smiled at the two other girls beside her on another couch. "We can find ways to do nice things for other people at the campground, even strangers." The girls with her nodded, and one of them whispered to Kiara behind her hand.

"Next theme idea," Father said, "Fruit of the Spirit. We could focus on one fruit at a time, faithfulness, patience, joy, peace. Another theme could be true love."

"Oh, my true love," a girl in drama club said, striking a dramatic pose. "Where art thou?"

Sneakers squeaked in the hallway.

Roland's heart skipped a beat, and his eyes riveted to the open doorway.

A second later, Caitlyn burst into the room and stopped a few feet in. Her hair hung in messy curls around her face and over her shoulders. The strap of her big gray purse slid down her arm. She swept the hair from her face and pushed up one sleeve of her hunter green dress, keeping the purse from falling. Her gaze connected with Roland's.

He gave her a little smile, wishing he could offer her the seat next to him.

"Come find a seat, Caitlyn." Father motioned toward the empty space on the other side of Phoebe.

"Sorry I'm late. Mom had to . . . well, I . . . never mind." With her next step, her purse escaped her arm, thudded to the floor, and its contents clattered on the linoleum. "Oh, whoops."

On impulse, Roland jerked forward. Thinking better of it, he slouched back. A girl probably wouldn't want help picking up whatever had fallen out of her purse.

"I've got two more theme ideas," Father said.

Caitlyn dropped onto one knee and gathered her things. Everyone redirected their attention to the priest, except for Roland. He couldn't take his eyes off Caitlyn. As soon as the official part of the Fire Starter meeting ended, he'd talk to her.

"That sounds like a good one." Phoebe elbowed Roland in the side.

"What?" Roland turned to listen to Father. He'd missed his last idea.

"Survivors. Overcoming your fears and facing challenges," Phoebe said. "That could be fun."

"Oh, yeah." Roland shifted his gaze back to Caitlyn.

Tucking her hair behind her ear and throwing shy glances, Caitlyn stepped into the oval arrangement of chairs and couches. She glanced at Roland before she sat next to Phoebe.

"And my last idea," Father said, "*crossroads*."

"Crossroads?" Keefe sat next to Father in a folding metal chair.

"Right. So we face crossroads every day," Father explained, "whenever we need to make a choice. But we come to bigger crossroads too, and it's hard to know which way to turn."

Keefe, Fred, and Father talked about that one for a few minutes, all three seeming to like the idea.

Roland bounced one leg. Questions for Caitlyn filled his mind, and he struggled to keep from leaning forward to see her on the other side of Phoebe.

"I have an idea," Phoebe blurted.

"Sure." Father nodded. "Let's hear it."

"Well, we are the Fire Starters. Our theme could be the saints, or maybe not just the saints but the martyrs."

Roland's attention shifted to her. The martyrs? Images popped into his mind: Christians huddled together in the Coliseum, surrounded by hungry lions; Christians tied to stakes, fire at their feet; Christians before firing squads; a Christian standing before a noose—

A noose? His mind flitted to speech class and the noose he'd seen in his mind before beginning his speech.

A clanking noise snapped him back to Phoebe.

As she spoke, she gestured with her armful of metal bracelets. "Yeah, so we can focus on those who've gone before us, you know, the ones who were on fire for the Lord, like so on fire that the threat of death couldn't put out the flame of their love."

A few kids around the room made agreeable sounds, some nodding, others turning toward Father as if anxious to see what he thought.

"That's a great idea." Caitlyn leaned and looked past Phoebe to Roland. "I love the martyrs. And some were even burned with fire."

"Wow." Peter shook his head and let out a laugh, his lip curling on one side. "You make death by fire sound exciting." He laughed and mumbled something to Dominic.

Dominic shrugged. "Mexico gave us a lot of martyrs not too many years ago in the Mexican Cristero War. Most were priests, but there were regular people too. Kids even, you know, like Jose Sanchez del Rio."

"Who's that?" Phoebe asked.

"Wait." Father lifted a hand. "Before you tell us, Dominic, let's vote. I think this is a fantastic idea, and if we choose this theme, you can tell that story on our camping trip."

So they took a vote and everyone but Keefe and another boy chose the martyrs. Not caring what theme they chose, Roland voted with Caitlyn.

"Okay, the martyrs it is." Father clapped his hands together.

"Si, so what do we do?" Dominic said. "Camping is supposed to be fun. We don't want to make more martyrs on that weekend."

Father laughed. Then he glanced at the ceiling as if thinking it over. "To start with, why don't each of you pick a martyr to research. Then find a way to share what you've learned with our group."

"Oh, saint stories by the campfire." Kiara looked at Caitlyn, who nodded vigorously.

"Sure. You can tell your chosen saint's story. Or create a game. Perform a skit. Gather or draw pictures of the saint. Find out their symbols and give clues until you finally reveal the martyr you've chosen. Anything. Be creative. Oh, and invite your friends. If you belong to any groups, why not invite the entire group and their families? Let's make this the best camping weekend ever." Father glanced at Keefe, who sat in the chair next to him.

Keefe gazed out a window, obviously distracted by his thoughts. He'd seemed distracted since the opening prayer. And he'd really seemed to want the "crossroads" theme for their camping trip. Maybe he was facing his own crossroads right now.

"I'm in band," a girl said.

"I'm in theater," a boy said.

"Hey, Roland's in Empowerment." Everyone fell silent at Dominic's loud proclamation.

Roland's stomach leaped and seemed to land upside down.

"Empowerment?" Father turned his gaze to Roland. "What's that group about, Roland?"

Roland heard Father's voice as if from underwater. Then he snapped back to reality. "Uh . . ." With everyone staring at him and waiting for his answer, his mind drew a complete blank. Heat radiated from his body; Phoebe probably noticed. Roland glanced at Peter for help.

Peter slapped Roland's arm and leaned to whisper, "Take one for the team, man." He wouldn't want Roland to say anything that gave away their secret mission.

"It, uh . . ." Roland's mouth went dry, the way it had in speech class. "Empowerment is a group for . . . uh . . ."

"They just try to be a voice for the little guy," Peter blurted. "Right, Roland?"

Roland exhaled, relief washing over him as everyone looked at Peter. "Uh, yeah. They . . . they work to overcome discrimination."

Father gave an approving nod. "So how do they do that?"

"I . . ." Roland looked at Peter again.

Peter flung his hands up. "I don't know. You're the one going to the meetings."

"I only went to one. I thought they'd have ideas for how to stop the pranks against, um, outcasts."

"Well, you'll have to let me know when you find out," Father said. "Maybe we can join in their efforts."

"Yeah, right." Roland hadn't meant to sound sarcastic. He didn't want to share his experience.

Father gave him a look.

Knowing he had to explain, Roland took a breath. "I don't know how open they'd be to having the Fire Starters help."

"Oh, yeah? Why not?"

"I don't know. I guess I'm privileged so I don't count."

"Because your family has money?" Father said.

"Because he's straight, white, and a Christian," Phoebe said before Roland could reply. "And he's a guy, so he's part of the ruling class and, therefore"—she looked at him—"your opinion doesn't count."

"I'm not part of the ruling class," Roland mumbled. "I'm just an ordinary kid trying to get through high school."

"Well, most of the politicians share all those qualities." Phoebe folded her arms.

"So?" Peter said. "People vote 'em in."

"Well, anyways." Father slapped his thighs. "We've got our theme. What else do we need to talk about?"

While the rest of the Fire Starters discussed music, sound systems, food, and everything else they needed for the camping trip, Roland thought of his speech. His experience with Empowerment had given him an idea. Would he have enough courage to talk about it?

18

GOSSIP

LEANING AGAINST THE COLD HOOD of the Durango, Peter slid a screwdriver into the slot on one of the windshield wiper mechanisms. The old blade popped off just as Toby let out a whine.

Hands to his ears, Toby paced back and forth along one of the workbenches. His whining almost ruined the song blaring from the Durango's radio. But not quite. A person would be hard pressed to ruin Sammy Hagar's "I Can't Drive 55."

Peter set the screwdriver down and tossed the old blade over his shoulder, in the general direction of the fiber drum garbage can. It clanked against something metal and scraped against something else, obviously not making it to the can. He grabbed the package with the new blades and slid his torso off the hood, straightening as he tried to figure out how to open it.

If Brice were here, she would have yanked it from his hands by now and ripped it open. If Brice were here . . . Peter smiled, thinking of her. The way she strode with confidence, not caring what anyone thought about her. The way she hunched over her notebook in Woodworking or sat slouched in speech class but could answer any question a teacher threw at her. The way she handled any machine or tool . . .

In Woodworking yesterday, he'd invited her to come over. She must've had better things to do on a Saturday morning. Or maybe he'd turned her off with the way he'd stammered, "Hey, so, like, if you're not doing anything, you know . . . Saturday, uh, tomorrow . . ."

Still fidgeting with the wiper packaging, Peter sighed and his gaze shifted to the view outside the open garage door. A black car drove by as Sammy Hagar sang, "Take my license, all that jive." A woodchuck scuffled through the dew-laden grass across Forest Road. And a fishing pole lay in the yard near the driveway.

"Too loud for Toby." Toby came up beside Peter and stared into the open driver-side window, irritation showing in his big brown eyes. "Too loud for Toby," he said again.

"Yeah, so you said. What're you doing out here, anyway?" Using his thumbnail, he separated the plastic from the paper backing, and a swift yank freed the blades. "Why don't you go see what Mom's doing in the house?"

"Daddy come home, take me bowling." Toby took one hand from his ear and reached through the open window.

"Oh, no, you don't." On impulse, Peter's hand shot out. He grabbed Toby's chubby wrist and yanked his hand out of the car. "Hands off the radio. Hands off the SUV, for that matter."

His face twisting into a babyish pout, Toby wriggled his wrist from Peter's grip. He never like being touched without warning.

A hint of remorse teased Peter.

"Sorry, bud." Still clutching the wipers in one hand, Peter lifted his free hand, palm out, in an apologetic gesture. "Why don't you wait for Daddy inside? Or, you know what? Go play with your fishing pole. You left it in the yard. Then you'll see Daddy coming down the road."

"No. Toby go bowling." Toby covered his ears and shuffled to the workbench.

Taking a breath to stave off frustration, Peter set one wiper on the hood and leaned to install the other. He couldn't wait to get this thing on the road. Maybe he could practice driving today, not that he needed the experience. After all the time he'd spent on the riding lawn mower and racing off-road vehicles, driving came natural to him. But he had nothing better to do, and he needed the hours to get his license.

Hey, maybe he could drive past Brice's house. Of course, with only a temporary license, he'd need Mom in the passenger seat. Not cool.

One brand new wiper installed, he snatched the other and headed for the passenger side. As he rounded the front of the Durango, his foot bumped the bucket he'd gotten out earlier. He wanted to wash the thing inside and out and hopefully get the funky used-car smell out of it, make it something he wouldn't be embarrassed to drive Brice around in.

Oh, wait . . . she'd have to drive him around since he only had his temps. He wouldn't mind that. Maybe he'd ask her over on Monday. She could come for dinner. Not like a date. She'd never agree to that. Just like friends.

Peter leaned across the hood and reached for the screwdriver.

Hopefully, she had no clue that he and his friends had been snooping around to find out who vandalized her house. If she knew and it bothered her, she'd bring it up, right? Or would she just stop talking to him?

What was she doing today? As the old wiper blade popped off, his gaze shifted to his bike. Tempted to stalk Brice for real, he'd pulled it out of the shed this morning.

Peter tossed the old blade into the fiber drum, making a basket as Hagar sang, "Go on and write me up for 125. Post my face—"

The radio shut off.

Peter peered through the windshield of the Durango.

Toby sat behind the steering wheel. "Toby drive," came his voice through the open windows.

"Oh, no, you don't." Peter dropped the new blade onto the hood and yanked open the passenger-side door.

Sitting bolt upright, Toby clutched the steering wheel with both hands. He was tall for a nine-year-old and could've passed for a teenager with his temps. His right hand slid off the steering wheel and dropped to the key in the ignition.

Peter leaned over the shifter and into Toby's space. He rammed a shoulder into him and grabbed his hand. "Get out or you're not going bowling."

"Yes, Toby go bowling," he whined, jerking away.

"Okay, then"—he took a breath to keep from shouting—"you have to get outta my car."

Toby humphed and scooted back out, mumbling to himself.

Peter turned the radio back on, but his song had ended and one with crappy lyrics now played. He shut the radio off and got back to work, installing the last blade.

With his gaze on the road and talking to himself, Toby paced just outside the garage.

Satisfied with his installation of the new wipers, Peter leaned against the Durango and watched Toby for a moment. "I'm such a jerk," he mumbled to himself. Toby couldn't help how the loud music affected him or how physical contact made him cringe or how he interpreted the world. Still . . . Mom always held him responsible for whatever he could control, even when some of it challenged him.

Maybe Brice couldn't help how she felt about guys, any more than he could help feeling attracted to her, or any more than Toby could with his obsessions. But, then again, maybe she just hadn't met the right guy. Maybe he was the right guy, and she just couldn't see it yet.

"Pee-ter." Mom's sing-song voice came from outside. A second later, she stepped into the garage with the cordless phone. "Telephone."

"Thanks, Mom." Glad for a break before he started another project—washing the Durango or something from the list Dad had given him—he took the phone, opened the front passenger-side door, and dropped into the seat. Maybe Caitlyn had news for him. Hopefully not something bad concerning her social media account. "Hey, Caitlyn. So, did you close your social media account already?"

"Oh, so I am right in thinking you were in on it."

Peter tensed like a rubber band ready to snap at the sound of Dominic's voice, and his grip tightened around the phone. *Argh, no!* No one but Caitlyn ever called the landline! "What?"

"Why you no answer your cell phone, *vato*?"

"Huh?" Peter slapped his pockets, finding them empty. "It's probably in my room. So what's up?"

"I heard about Caitlyn's social media account, her pretending to be the school mascot. Doesn't want anyone to know it's her, huh? Why so secretive?"

"What? I don't know." Peter's legs bounced all on its own. Dominic was the last person he'd want to know about all this. "Is that the reason you called? To pump me for information?"

"I am certain you know. Bad idea sending a friend request to *su madre*. Audrey Summer, that is her mother's name, no? Kids have been asking if Caitlyn has an older sister."

Deny, deny, deny, Peter's mind screamed. Throw Caitlyn under the bus if you must. Dominic could not know.

"Look, I don't know what Caitlyn's up to. She's weird, that's all. And I'm sure she's new to all this social media stuff. So she's *friending* a few popular kids. Who cares? Give her a break. And don't assume it has anything to do with me."

"So you know the kids she's friending, huh? Of course, you do. You were probably sitting next to her while she did it. And what's with Roland going door-to-door. Is that all part of it?"

"What? Part of what?" Peter slapped his forehead. He was sunk. Dominic knew what they were up to. He was just toying with Peter, dragging it out of him slowly. Soon everyone would know. Brice would know. What could Peter possibly say to save himself?

"Scouring Brice's neighborhood, that could only mean one thing."

"Forget about it, Dominic. If you're my friend at all, just drop it. Find someone else to gossip about."

"If we are any kind of *amigos*, you would tell me. So, tell me, *vato*. What are you up to?"

"Listen, Dominic—"

"No, you listen, Peter. I think you are trying to find out who trashed Brice's house and burned their tree. Why does it matter to you? And why you did not come to me first? You know I know things."

Feeling vulnerable and exposed, Peter shoved a hand into his hair and considered what to say next. He could hear his heart thumping in his chest. One beat. Two. Three. Four. "Okay, so . . . what do you know, Dominic? Do you know who did it?"

"I have my suspicions. Give me a day or two. I will talk to you at school. Oh, and you know the police have started questioning Fire Starters, right?"

"What? No, I didn't know." That could only be a good thing, right? They'd see that the Fire Starters had nothing to do with it. Did all the Fire Starters have alibis?

"They did not talk to me, yet, but to three others from our group. They are barking up the wrong tree and I will tell them so."

"Okay, but let's not talk to anyone at school about things. I don't want anyone knowing I'm looking into this. Okay?"

"Sure thing, *vato*. You know me. But I know you, too, and I think I know why you want to know so badly. You'll have to tell me in exchange for the information." Dominic ended the call.

Holding the phone to his ear in a death grip, Peter sat staring at streaks of dirt and dust on the dashboard. Snapping out of it, he tapped the button to end the call and dropped the phone to the seat. He was sunk. Dominic may have had good intentions, but he could not keep a secret any more than a punctured tire could hold air.

A sense of urgency ripped through him. Peter's gaze snapped to his bicycle and he jumped out of the car. On the way to the bike, his foot bumped the bucket again, but the car wash and Dad's list would have to wait.

He needed to talk to Roland.

19

HEREDITARY

THE HAIR ON THE BACK OF ROLAND'S NECK stood up, making him aware that someone watched him from a distance.

No one else on the front porch seemed to notice.

Their live-in maid, Nanny, stood talking with Papa's friend Miss Meadows about the full-body scanners and expensive food in airports. Papa and Keefe watched the women talk, occasionally shrugging or nodding in agreement. Mr. Digby—Nanny's husband and their live-in groundskeeper, who occasionally served as their chauffeur—waited by the front door, a suitcase in each hand and a leg bouncing, his eyes on a hedge or something in the yard. He typically spent Saturdays doing yardwork, so the trip to the airport to get Miss Meadows had probably thrown a wrench in his plans.

It had thrown a wrench in Roland's plans too. Papa had warned them only last night about her visit.

And Jarret—

Roland's gaze connected with Jarret's.

He sat on the arm of one of the teak patio chairs and rolled his eyes, communicating his boredom. He used to communicate in this nonverbal way exclusively with Keefe.

A bit honored that Jarret gave him the look instead, Roland shrugged, meaning to communicate back: How long could she stay?

How long would Papa expect them to hang around the house? Couldn't be that long.

Jarret sighed. As the adults laughed, he redirected his gaze to the group.

Still aware that someone watched him, other than Jarret, Roland turned in a circle, scanning the driveway where it curved toward the side of the house, the gravel road that emerged from the woods, and the tree line that edged their deep front lawn.

There. A figure on a bike half-hidden behind brush.

What was Peter doing here? He usually called before coming over. Maybe something was wrong. Or maybe he found out something about the vandals.

Roland's phone buzzed in his pocket, alerting him of a text message. Hoping no one would notice, he slid his phone out and glanced at it.

Peter: Hey, we need to talk.

Roland tapped out a quick reply. *Can't. Got company.*

Peter: C'mon. Give me 5 minutes.

"Well, let's take it inside," Papa said, his voice rising above the others.

As Roland slipped his phone into his pocket, he edged toward a post on the front porch, moving closer to the stairs and further from the front door. He could sneak off and return before anyone noticed.

Miss Meadows stepped inside first, followed by Nanny, Papa, Keefe, Mr. Digby . . .

Jarret shifted into Roland's peripheral vision and stood with his thumbs stuffed in the front pockets of his jeans and his head tilted to one side. "You think you're getting outta this?"

Roland met his gaze but didn't answer. Yeah, he was getting out of this. At least for a few minutes, so he could see what Peter wanted. "I have to check on something." He jabbed a thumb over his shoulder, in Peter's general direction.

Jarret's gaze shifted to the point Roland indicated then his eyelids fluttered and face twitched. "You heard what Papa said yesterday. No one's going anywhere. So we're all stuck at home for a few days." He nodded for Roland to go before him into the house.

Roland stood his ground, a bit weirded out with Jarret's law-enforcement attitude when he only recently started following the rules. "I just need a minute."

"No, you don't. Miss Meadows just got here. Take a minute later." He squinted in the direction of the tree line. "Is that Peter? He can wait."

Sighing in resignation, Roland signaled to Peter, turning his palm out and then jabbing his thumb at the house.

Peter, sitting on his bike, rolled back a few feet. Hopefully, he'd caught and understood Roland's message. Unlike the twins, Roland had never been good at nonverbal communications. He should've just messaged him.

Jarret again nodded for Roland to go in first, his indifferent expression saying he didn't realize what Roland's signal had meant. "How long you think she's staying?" Shuffling through the foyer, he stared down the front hallway to where Mr. Digby lugged Miss Meadows' two big suitcases and a duffel bag toward a guest room.

Papa escorted Miss Meadows down the other hall, toward the Great Room. Keefe trailed behind them. Nanny dodged into the kitchen.

Roland shrugged in answer. "She sure brought a lot of stuff." He now walked alongside Jarret down the long hall, heading toward Great Room.

"Eh, I'm sure it's not all clothes. She's probably like Papa, got rocks or archaeological finds packed away."

Roland laughed. "Maybe a pick-axe." They'd first met Miss Meadows on a dig site in Mississippi. She seemed to love archaeology—the excavating, the tools, and the mud—almost as much as Papa did.

"Exactly." Jarret gave Roland a crooked smile and genuine look of camaraderie.

They continued toward the Great Room. While typically a cold, dark room that they passed on their way to other parts of the house, it now had life. Lamps glowed, their light reflecting off vases and carved walnut end tables, and hazy sunlight streamed in through big windows that heavy dark red drapes usually hid.

Miss Meadows sat in the wingchair visible from the hallway, one leg folded under her and her white hat dangling from her hand.

Keefe and Mr. Digby sat on opposite ends of the long ornate couch that stretched out before the windows along the back wall. Standing in front of the wingchair that matched the one Miss Meadows sat in, Papa studied his watch. Then he gazed out the window and said something about having a campfire in the backyard.

Having in mind to step out and text Peter the moment he could get away with it, Roland took the seat just inside the room. Jarret strode to the far side of the furniture arrangement and sat in the one chair that didn't seem to fit the medieval theme, and the only comfortable chair in the room, an overstuffed gold armchair. He rested a foot on the matching footstool and glanced from one person to the next while the conversation went from campfires to Keefe's chemistry class.

Roland's phone buzzed again. Not wanting to draw attention, he eased it from his pocket and glanced at the message.

Peter: Did you know police started interviewing Fire Starters?

Roland typed out a message with his thumb. *No.*

Peter: We need to talk.

Roland started typing a reply when movement through a window caught his attention, and his breath caught. Blond hair flashed in the sunlight! Peter rode his bike into view, a mere ten or so feet away from the house. He stopped. Jumped off the bike.

What was he doing?

If Papa shifted his gaze, he'd see him. He'd assume Roland had invited Peter over to the house even after Papa had made it clear they were entertaining company this weekend. Jarret would likely share Papa's irritation, since he'd reminded Roland what Papa had said.

Peter stooped, maybe looking at something on his bike, his head no longer visible from Roland's seat. Papa walked around the wingback chair, moving closer to the window. If he glanced outside . . .

"My leg!" Roland blurted, desperate to draw everyone's attention.

Jarret dropped his boot to the floor and jumped up, his eyes wide. "What's wrong?"

Everyone looked at Roland, glancing back and forth from his face to his leg.

"I, uh . . ." A tingly heatwave rolled over him. He cleared his throat. "I was just going to tell you that I-I got the cast off. Papa probably told you, uh, that I'd broken it."

Peter straightened. He walked his bike past the windows, disappearing. He must've thought Roland's signal meant to wait for him in the backyard. He'd probably go to the veranda. Hopefully, he wouldn't knock on the door.

"Yes, he did." Miss Meadows smiled. "How does it feel?"

"Huh?" Roland snapped his attention back to her.

"I imagine it feels sore every now and then." She pointed to his leg.

"Oh, yeah, it's not so bad." He wiped his sweaty hands on his jeans and averted his gaze, glimpsing Jarret's strange sneer, his look of concern having changed to one of annoyance. He must've realized Roland had cried wolf. Maybe he'd also seen Peter out the window.

"Here we are." Nanny bustled into the room with a tray of cookies, teacups, and a stainless-steel carafe. Everyone watched as she set it on the coffee table in the middle of the room.

Roland exhaled, relieved to have their eyes off him. Jarret grabbed a handful of spiced cookie bars and sat back down. Keefe and Mr. Digby sipped tea or coffee or whatever was in the carafe. Finally sitting, Papa started talking about Miss Meadows' recent excavation work. No one looked at Roland now. And Peter had moved out of view. Nothing to worry about. Maybe he could excuse himself and send that text.

Not calling first, riding straight over here . . . Peter must've had something urgent to discuss. Something about the police interviews? Had they spoken with Peter? Was Roland next? No big deal, right? They'd ask if he was involved. He'd say, "No."

Then maybe they'd ask, "Where were you the night of the incident?"

And he'd say . . .

Roland searched his memory. A week ago today, right? He'd just gotten his cast off the day before. His leg had been stiff all day. And he couldn't sleep that night, so he'd stuffed a crutch under his arm and hobbled out to the stables to visit Bueno, his jet-black quarter horse. Not feeling like limping back to the house right away, he'd settled in a camp chair and stretched his leg out on a bale of hay. The night sounds soon lulled him to sleep. Hours later, the snorts and grunts of the horses talking to each other woke him. He inhaled a deep breath of morning air heavy with dew, horse sweat, and hay. Then he opened his eyes to see sunbeams stealing in through the half-open stable door. He'd been out there all night. Alone. No one even knowing he'd gone out there.

So basically, he had no alibi.

But police detectives wouldn't suspect him of anything. He'd just gotten a cast off his leg the day before. He was still using his crutches off and on.

With his next thought, his blood ran cold. The trail of little circles in the yard . . . Those could've been made by crutches!

"About another month," Miss Meadows said, responding to whatever Papa had said to her.

Heart now thumping hard, Roland snapped from his thoughts and glanced out the window. No sign of Peter. But they had to talk. Now.

"Hmmm." Papa nodded and glanced at his watch again. "You think you'll—"

"So, hey, I gotta question." Jarret leaned forward, one hand full of cookie bars.

Papa's eyes narrowed at the interruption, but he closed his mouth and looked at Jarret.

Roland waited expectantly, hoping Jarret would say something that would provide an out for Roland. But Jarret only asked why Miss Meadows had come for a visit. He'd been worried about Papa's recent behavior: hanging around the house more and taking that online teaching job. No one had had the nerve to ask Papa about it directly, and Miss Meadows' visit had no doubt amplified Jarret's concern.

Miss Meadows stared at Jarret for a moment. Then her face broke into a big smile and she turned to Papa. "Well, if I want to see my cowboy, apparently I have to come to him. He doesn't visit me anymore."

Keefe and Jarret exchanged one of their knowing looks.

Papa adjusted his weathered Stetson and shifted in his seat. "Well, Anna, we speak on the phone all the time and you rightly know I've got that teaching job." Another glance at his watch.

"Uh huh." She gave him a playful grin. "But you hardly talk when I call."

The hint of a blush colored Papa's tan face, and he shifted again. "Now, that's not true. We talk all the time."

"*I* talk all the time. You give one-word responses, or one-liners if I'm lucky."

Roland shifted in his seat. He knew how Papa felt. His conversations with Caitlyn went the same way. She did all the talking. He gave one-word responses. Or a headshake. Sometimes just a shrug. Maybe women had more to say. Maybe if Mama had still been alive, things would've been different. She'd have trained them how to talk, whereas Papa trained them how to dig for artifacts. Maybe that's where Roland got his drive to solve mysteries.

Papa shook his head and got to his feet. "Now, Anna, that's not true. We've talked about all sorts of things." He turned to Jarret. "She's here because I've wanted her to see the place. Thought it'd be nice for her to visit." Scuffing toward her, he glanced at his watch again.

She stood as he approached. "Where you off to, cowboy? Leaving me already?"

"I've got a conference call for that teaching job. Shouldn't be that long. Make yourself at home here. The boys can entertain you for a bit." Tipping his hat, he left the room.

Roland's spirits lifted. Maybe he could make a break for it too.

"Let me know when you'd like to see your room." Nanny had taken a seat beside her husband but now she stood and clasped her hands, looking eager to serve. "I've fixed up the nicest guest room, fresh sheets and towels, even some flowers. You're probably tired from the flight."

Mr. Digby got up too and shuffled from the room, mumbling something about hedges.

Roland found himself nodding. If Miss Meadows went to her room to rest, he could go see what Peter wanted.

"Actually . . ." Miss Meadows stretched her arms and looked from Keefe to Jarret to Roland. "I'd like to take a little walk, maybe check out your stables. Your father's told me all about your horses. I'd love to take a ride later."

Roland jerked back. If they went out there, they'd run right into Peter.

"Yeah." Jarret jumped to his feet, his boots clomping on the floor. "We'll show you the stables."

"Uh, no, hey . . ." Roland got up just as Nanny turned to leave the room. He sidestepped to get out of her way, but she sidestepped too. They both sidestepped the opposite way, blocking each other again and increasing Roland's sense of urgency.

"Silly boy." Looking up at him through laughing eyes, Nanny grabbed his arms and moved him out of her way.

"Why don't we play a game of pool or . . . or watch TV?" Roland turned back to Miss Meadows, who had drawn near.

The twins approached Roland, too, Keefe tilting his head, Jarret narrowing one eye and his lip curling up.

"Nooo," Jarret said, his tone heavy with irritation. "Showing her the stables is a perfect idea. Isn't it, Roland?" He must've planned on talking to Miss Meadows outside about Papa.

A pleasant smile on her face, Miss Meadows touched Roland's arm. "You don't have to come if you don't want to, Roland. I bet walking bothers your leg a bit, huh?"

"Huh?" Roland sneaked a peek out the window—no Peter—then returned his eyes to her. "Uh, okay. I'll just stay here." He backed a few steps toward the hallway. "In fact, I'll . . ." Not skilled at lying or making excuses, his mind drew a blank. Plus, Jarret was glaring at him. "I got something . . ." Forget the excuses.

Roland turned and bolted to the kitchen.

"Oh, hello there, Roland." Nanny came around the kitchen island, a tray of something in her hands. "Did you need . . ."

"No, thanks," he called as he sprinted to the door off the laundry room. If he hurried . . .

Adrenaline surging—and for what? Just so no one caught Peter at the house. Did it really matter?—Roland flung open the door and jogged around to the backyard.

Peter crouched at the opposite end of the house, messing with something on his bike, not seeing Roland at all.

Roland swiped a smooth, round rock from the landscaping and thumped toward him, glancing at the Great Room windows as he passed them. Had everyone left that room, or could they see Roland now?

Still too far for Roland to talk to him without hollering, Peter straightened and grabbed the handlebars. He turned away from Roland and toward the stables. Miss Meadows and the twins would be stepping outside any minute now, if they hadn't already.

Roland whipped the rock at Peter's bike and shouted, "Hey!" in a low voice.

Peter turned and saw him.

Roland motioned him over with quick, jerky movements then glanced behind Peter to see if anyone was coming.

Grinning now, Peter hopped on his bike and pedaled toward Roland. "What's your deal?" he shouted.

A woman's voice traveled through the air and three figures came into view, Miss Meadows, Keefe, and Jarret, strolling toward the stables. They didn't appear to have heard or noticed Peter.

Roland motioned harder, though it only served to make Peter's smile grow. He glanced about for a good hiding place. They wouldn't stay in the stables forever.

Coming within two feet of Roland, Peter hopped off his bike. "So my strange, secretive friend, what's your deal—"

Unwilling to have anyone spot him, Roland grabbed Peter's bike from him and dragged it around the corner. "Over here."

As soon as he shoved the bike behind a bush, the door off the laundry room creaked open. On impulse, Roland's hand shot out. He yanked Peter down with him behind the bush.

Peter laughed and looked him in the eye, their faces a few inches apart. "Man, what's your problem today?"

"Nothing." He put a finger to his mouth to shush him.

"What'cha doing there, Roland?" Mr. Digby's face appeared over the bush, a weary look in his heavy-lidded eyes.

With a sigh and the warmth of embarrassment, Roland stood. "Nothing."

"We were just looking for something." Peter stood too. "I think I found it." He tossed a coin in the air and caught it. "My lucky penny." He waggled his brows and stepped out from behind the bush.

Shaking his head and muttering something about kids today, Mr. Digby shuffled off toward the tool shed. Gardening gloves hung from his back pocket, flapping as he walked.

"So, what's your deal, buddy?" Peter stood with folded arms. "You playing hide-and-seek with your family?"

"What's my deal? What's *your* deal? You're the one who came over here unannounced."

"We live across Forest Road from each other. I mean, granted, your house sits waaaay back, but can't I just show up now and then?"

Leaning on the handlebars, Roland pushed Peter's bike in the shade along the house, heading for the front yard. "Okay, fine. So why are you here? Did the police interview you?"

"Me? No. But they interviewed a few other Fire Starters, so I'm sure they'll get to us soon. Dominic told me. And he's why I'm here." His eyes turned hard. "I need your help. Dominic knows we're investigating. Well, he suspects anyway. I mean, I didn't admit anything, not really, or maybe I did. He said he knows what we're up to."

"What can I do about it? If Dominic knows what we're doing, the entire school will know tomorrow."

"Well, he might not know everything, and I told him not to tell. And he said he wouldn't." Peter's wince said he didn't believe Dominic.

"Hey, what do you think made those little holes in the front yard of Brice's house?"

"What?" Peter scrunched up his face. "I'm sure the little kids did that. Why?"

"Do you think someone might believe a crutch made them?"

His face scrunched up again for a split second, and then comprehension dawned on him. "You . . . think someone wanted it to look like you were involved?"

Roland shrugged. He didn't know what to think, but everyone in school knew he belonged to the Fire Starters. What better way to implicate them?

"Oh." Peter's expression fell even more. "Now you've got more incentive to say yes to what I have to ask you."

"Which is?"

"I need to distance myself from the investigations, so you need to take over. Just you. Leave the girls out of it."

Not sure how he felt about Peter's request, Roland didn't answer. He slowed as he neared the corner of the house. If the twins took Miss Meadows to see the grounds, they might run into them. Risking it, Roland pushed the bike forward and peered around the house. Seeing no one, he picked up his pace.

"You've got to, man, for me and for you." Peter jogged alongside him. "And you know Phoebe doesn't care about anyone knowing. And Caitlyn's one slip-up away from drawing the attention of the entire school. So it's gotta be you. Just you."

Roland had yet to talk to Caitlyn about things, what she'd learned from Tessia and if anyone had confronted her about her Thunderhawk identity. And he really wanted to work with her. Maybe he'd run over to her house one day. Or he could call her.

Eh, who was he kidding? He wasn't going to do either of those things. He'd inherited Papa's communication skills, or lack of. He couldn't hold up his end of the conversation, like Papa. He wasn't even efficient at nonverbal communication, unlike the twins.

They neared the woods at the front edge of the yard. No clomping of horse hooves. No voices. No signs of anyone anywhere.

With a sigh of resignation, Roland handed the bike back to Peter. "Yeah, sure. I'll take over."

"Good. I knew I could count on you. We've got a list of suspects now, so you just need to go through them, pin one of them down."

"Yeah, right. And how do I do that?"

"Get some proof."

20

AN OUNCE OF HOPE

WHERE IS SHE? Peter stood outside speech class with his hands on his hips, staring down the hallway he figured Brice would soon come down, getting his courage up. He was gonna ask her over. Before he chickened out. He had nothing to lure her over this time. The Durango was clean inside and out and everything working properly, as far as he knew. Maybe she'd like to see it all cleaned up. Take it for a drive. Stay for dinner.

"Hey," Roland said over Peter's shoulder.

A shiver ran down Peter's neck, making him shudder. He turned and punched Roland's shoulder with the side of his fist. "Don't sneak up on me."

Roland's eyebrows went in opposite directions, one lifting, the other dropping over puzzled gray eyes. "I'm not sneaking up on you. Just coming to class, like everyone else." He gestured to indicate three other kids who strolled through the door. "What're you doing? Looking for someone?" His slight grin showed he knew exactly what Peter was doing.

"Don't worry about it," Peter said. "Why don't you go claim the desk behind Marshall before someone else takes it?"

Roland glanced at the ceiling and shook his head before stepping into the classroom. Four more kids cruised through the door behind him.

Peter checked his watch. Shoot. Ten seconds till the bell rang. And no sign of Brice. Nine, eight, seven . . .

Two stragglers rounded the corner and speed-walked to the classroom. And behind those two—Brice.

The bell rang as Peter glimpsed her. A wave of electricity came from her and shot through him, the earsplitting bell amplifying it. Dressed in a rustic brown vest over a long-sleeved t-shirt, she came within twelve inches of him but made no show of having seen him.

Something inside Peter sank. But with his next breath, and as he followed her into the room, he made a new resolution. He'd ask her in their woodworking class.

Peter took the seat behind Roland—who sat behind Marshall—and he casually turned toward Brice while he stretched.

She also sat in the back, three rows away, in the very corner of the room, gnawing on a fingernail.

"Okay, class." Mrs. Kauffman clapped her hands together and began class in her ever-cheerful way. "I've been so pleased with your speeches so far. And we're over halfway through everyone's first speech. Can you believe it?" Then she bored the class with a general critique of the good and bad points from last week's speeches. After a long pause, she looked up from her pocket computer. "Our first speaker today . . . Brice Maddox."

Peter's breath caught, his attention shifting to Brice.

Again, she didn't look at him. She was still sitting slouched, chewing a fingernail. After spitting the nail to one side, she took a deep breath and straightened up.

As she stood, Peter clapped, everyone else soon joining him. He couldn't wait to hear her speech. Maybe he'd find out more about her.

Looking at no one, she strode with confidence to the front of the room. Two steps from the maple podium, she pulled a folded paper from a back pocket and shook it open. Then she spread her paper on the podium, ran a hand through her shock of blond hair, and unbuttoned her vest, the fleece lining peeking out. Eyes down and the hint of a tremble in her right hand, she cleared her throat and leaned her forearms on the podium. Glancing up, she shot a glare at three or four kids, looking like she stood before her enemies.

Look at me, Peter tried to communicate telepathically. I'm not your enemy. I'm your friend. More than that, if you want. Anything you want—

"Whenever you're ready, Brice," the teacher said cheerfully.

Brice glanced at the teacher, the corner of her mouth twitching as if a snide remark sat on the tip of her tongue. Then she dropped her gaze to her paper, pressed her lips together, and . . . spoke.

"So I know we're supposed to talk about ourselves in this first speech . . ." she said in a voice a bit higher and tighter than usual. Then she paused, fidgeted with her papers for a full two seconds, and finally glanced up. ". . . so we can learn something about each other." She paused again. Fidgeting with her papers. "And over half of you have given speeches . . ." She sort of nodded her head, but it turned into a headshake.

". . . but does anyone in this class know you any better than before? We know what you want people to know about you . . . from your talk, how many sisters and brothers you have, where you were born, what you *think* you're good at, or what you *say* you like to do." Then she looked up, licking her lips. "Do any of us really know anyone else?"

Slouching in his seat with his legs extended in the aisle, Gavin huffed, muttered something to himself, and shook his head.

A little spark of anger had Peter glaring at Gavin and clenching a fist. He'd better not think of mocking Brice while she gave her speech. If he even tried it—

"And I could tell you who I am, where I come from, where I want to go, what I like to do . . . but I think most of you have decided who I am already. And no matter what I told you, you'd never really know me. You'd know whatever *I* wanted you to know, and you'd believe whatever *you* wanted to believe. It could all be lies."

Peter found himself nodding in agreement. And grinning. She'd taken an assignment that made shy kids dread school and everyone else sweaty, and she'd turned it around, making everyone equally uncomfortable. But she was right. Every kid in high school worked on personal image, from the clothes they wore to the friends they made and even the way they sat in class. Peter glared at Gavin's leg stretched out in the aisle between desks. But a kid's image didn't tell a person anything, really.

". . . so for the rest of my speech, I'll tell you about a hobby of mine."

Peter's ears perked at the plot twist in her talk.

"I'm gonna talk about cars."

Several girls groaned and slumped in their seats.

An uncontrollable grin stretched across Peter's face. She was going to talk about the same subject he'd spoken on.

And then—Peter's heart flipped and a tingling sensation washed over him—Brice lifted her gaze.

To him.

And her lips curled up in that crooked grin. Sharing an inside joke . . . just with him. Then she dove into everything everyone didn't want to know about working on a car.

Everyone except for him.

~ ~ ~

Peter sat across from Brice in Woodworking, the happy buzz and hum of machinery mostly drowning the chatter of their classmates, a satisfying smoky wood scent filling the air, and his hands sweating at as he worked himself up to asking her.

"You know we're way ahead of everyone else," Peter boasted as he watched her driving in a pocket hole screw with a drill.

An indifferent look on her face, Brice peered over her shoulder as Fred walked by with a new board. He must've messed up another cut. "Yeah, so?"

"I'm just sayin'." Peter fidgeted with the bottom and one side of his unassembled gun rack, waiting for his turn with the drill but content to watch Brice work. "We work well together, don't you think?"

Brice glanced without turning her head, looking at him sideways, one side of her lip curling up, and she let out a huff. "You don't give up."

"Give up what?" Heat crept up his neck. Not sure what she meant, he decided to change the subject. "So your speech today was totally cool."

"Yeah?" She drove another screw into a pocket hole, her moves smooth and precise, then she glanced at him. "Thanks."

Encouraged by the eye contact, he continued. "You had everyone squirming in their seats with that first part."

"Yeah, and bored to tears with the rest." She grinned, a devious glint in her hazel and green eyes.

Peter laughed. "Not me. I thought the whole thing was great."

"You would."

He stared for a moment, his hands sweating. "So . . ." He was going to do it. He was going to ask her. "What'd you do this weekend?" Okay, wrong question. His mind took him to this past Friday and how he'd stammered his invitation. *Hey, so, like, if you're not doing anything, you know . . . Saturday, uh, tomorrow . . .*

He would not do that this time.

"Not much." She set the drill on the table, midway to him, and grabbed the wood glue.

Peter picked up the drill and a screw and lined up two boards with his sweaty hands. He was gonna say it. Now. Right now. Despite the strange tingly feeling in his head, he forced the words out.

"You doing anything tonight?"

"Why?" Brice kept her eyes on her work.

He'd keep it simple. "Why don't you come over?"

"Why?"

"I cleaned up the Durango, washed it inside and out. If you don't count the scrapes and smells that don't wash out, it's good as new."

She laughed. "I'm sure."

"Come see. We'll take her for a spin."

After staring at him for two seconds, she shrugged a shoulder and turned her attention back to her project.

Not giving a guy an ounce of hope.

21

OUSTED

THE FINAL BELL OF THE DAY rang and Roland headed for his locker. Jarret insisted on giving him and Keefe a ride home from school so they could all talk. Papa had said they weren't to make plans and that they were all to have dinner together. Afterward, maybe Roland could go to the Fire Starters meeting and talk to Caitlyn. And get a break from all the family stuff.

If not, maybe he'd get time to do more martyr research. He'd looked up a few saints between classes. Every one of the Apostles had died a martyr's death, not counting Judas Iscariot, who hung himself, or Saint John, who lived on an island to a ripe old age. But Roland wanted a lesser-known saint, someone the other Fire Starters might not have heard about already. He'd never realized how many hundreds upon hundreds of people had been martyred for refusing to deny their faith, many in groups. Still. None of the ones he'd read about had clicked with him yet. But he was running out of time. Then, once he'd found the right saint, what would he do? Father said they could present what they'd found in any way they wanted. Two boys planned to make up a song. A few girls wanted to do a skit. Peter would probably have everyone laughing, regardless of his method of presentation. Could you present a martyr humorously?

Nearing his locker, Roland walked around a group of girls and glimpsed a boy with pink hair. Marshall leaned one arm and his forehead on the wall and held his phone to his ear.

As Roland lifted the latch on his locker, Marshall spun toward him, stuffed his phone away, and sprang over to Roland. "Hey, Roland West, newest member of Empowerment, you're not out the door, are you?"

"Uh, yeah."

"No, you can't!" came his desperate plea. "We need you to stay. We're having an emergency meeting tonight. You really need to be there."

"What's the emergency?" Roland dropped off two books and picked up one then slammed his locker shut.

"We want to go on that big camping trip that your friends are hosting. Everyone in school's talking about it."

"Oh, that's great." Pushing aside feelings of discomfort, he faked enthusiasm. Everyone in school? "But why is that an emergency?"

"Empowerment never *just goes* anywhere. We'll need to get ready for this." He waggled his brows and smirked. Then he gave Roland's arm a slight tap. "You've got to be there. We need your help. You went last year, right?"

"Uh, yeah." He ran a hand through his hair as he tried to come up with an excuse. If he stayed after school for this, he stood less of a chance of getting out later for the Fire Starters meeting. "I don't think I can."

Marshall sighed, glancing up at the ceiling. "Of course, you can. Just call and get permission." He whipped a phone from his pocket and offered it to Roland with a flick of his wrist.

Roland pulled his own phone out and turned away, not sure why he was even asking. He didn't want to do this. But then again, maybe he should talk to them. They said in the last meeting that they wanted to "build bridges across differences." So maybe they'd be willing to listen to the Fire Starters' saint stories. They could learn something about what made Catholics tick and maybe even change their negative view of them.

A few minutes later, Roland turned down the hall to the room where Empowerment met. Papa had given permission and said he'd pick him up, but he couldn't go to the Fire Starters meeting. It didn't matter. Peter would keep him informed. And he could talk to Caitlyn on another day. Did she still have that phone? He could call her.

"Hey, there you are. We were just getting started." Marshall stood in the doorway, playing with a tuft of his pink-streaked hair and watching Roland walk. Rather than move out of the way, he flattened himself against the doorframe to let Roland pass.

A dozen kids sat at art tables that had been pushed together in the middle of the room. No one sat on the tables this time. Mrs. Lowrey hunched over the art desk nearest the front of the room. She straightened as Roland strode into the room.

"Hi," said the heavyset girl with jet black hair. And another kid nodded at Roland, but the rest simply looked. Except for Tessia. She narrowed her eyes and tilted her chin with a suspicious and challenging air about her.

"Glad you could make it, Roland." Mrs. Lowrey grabbed a paper from the tall teacher's desk in the front corner of the room. "Will you be going camping? I just handed out a signup form."

Marshall took the page from her and brought it to Roland, then he sat on one of the two empty stools left.

Roland took the page and sat on the other empty stool, finding himself on the opposite end of the tables from the teacher, next to Marshall, and two seats from Tessia. He never cared for close seating arrangements.

"Before we talk about camping, I wanted to bring up a mean prank that happened last week. I'm sure you've all heard. Someone put a bunch of smelly fish in a girl's locker. Now this particular student is Muslim, and unless you go through life with blinders on, you know that a lot people are suspicious of Muslims. So I think this is another area that we can focus on."

"I've already met with the drama club, as some of you know." Mrs. Lowrey exchanged smiles with a few of the kids. "The drama club wants to create skits and short videos of different kids in school. Someone even approached this girl for an interview, but she won't do it."

"What will the skits and videos be about?" a girl asked.

"We'll do an interview that shows she's just a regular person, just like anyone else," Mrs. Lowrey said. "We'll ask what she likes to eat and do. Then people won't see her as so different from themselves, and they can stop hating her."

"And we can show that her religious book—what's it called?" an enthusiastic girl said.

"The Koran," Mrs. Lowrey answered.

"Right, well, and it's just the same as the Christians with their Bible," the enthusiastic girl said.

Roland squirmed, disagreeing. It wasn't at all the same as the Bible—which was inspired by God.

"Hey, maybe we can make skits to perform at the camping trip," said a kid with orange hair.

Roland did a double-take. Was he the kid Caitlyn had told him about? So this kid thought he knew who trashed Brice's house?

"Right! Awesome idea!" an enthusiastic girl said, bouncing in her seat. "And we can bring freebies for everyone, like our bookmarks and pins and things that promote our group."

Roland squirmed even more. This was getting out of control. The Fire Starters had their own plans for the camping trip. Would this interfere with them?

"I've heard that there's a big bonfire every year," another girl said. "And that groups get together for activities, so we can participate in that."

"Roland goes every year, right, Roland?" Marshall said, everyone turning to look.

"Um. No. I went last year."

"And what type of activities did they have?" Mrs. Lowrey said.

"Flying kites, paddleboats, hikes, a big bonfire. That kind of stuff."

"Okay, so in the evenings, around the bonfire, we'll have skits that encourage people to accept one another for who they are, you know, without judging or trying to change them."

"I don't think that's a good idea," Roland forced himself to say.

"What's not a good idea?" Tessia said.

He didn't want to answer. Why couldn't they just go camping and have fun? "The Fire Starters already have plans for activities that everyone can participate in and skits that everyone can watch." There. He said it.

Mrs. Lowrey gave him a tight smile and a look he didn't understand. "If I'm not mistaken, the Fire Starters have some rigid ideas about right and wrong."

"Yeah, they're right and everyone else is wrong," Tessia said with hostility.

"Is that what you believe?" Marshall whispered.

Outnumbered and not wanting to discuss it, Roland shrugged. "I don't think everyone's wrong. I mean, I believe in right and wrong, but doesn't everybody?"

"Well, from what I understand, the Fire Starters is one of the groups that could benefit from change." Mrs. Lowrey stared across the tables at him.

"I-I thought you wanted to build bridges." He couldn't believe he'd said that. Now he'd captured everyone's attention.

"We can't build bridges with people who aren't open to change, with people who don't respect others."

He hesitated but only for a second. "Okay, well, respect each other, sure, but we don't have to agree, do we?"

"I'm not sure you belong here, Roland."

"What?" Not sure how to take her, Roland glanced at the others around the table. Cold eyes stared back. "Are you throwing me out?"

"This group is to promote an appreciation for differences, not to say I'm right and you're wrong."

"I didn't say that. *You* were talking about people having to change."

"You didn't say it in so many words, but it doesn't matter what you're saying." Tessia acted as though she hadn't heard the rest of his comment, leaning over the table and glaring past the girl who sat between them. "You don't really understand the purpose of our group, and maybe you never will. Like I pointed out last week, you're white, straight, male, with no handicaps, and you're rich. You can't possibly relate to the struggles of minorities or people with special needs."

Mrs. Lowrey put a hand up. "Tessia has a point, but we aren't here to argue. And . . . maybe this isn't a group for you, Roland."

~ ~ ~

Roland stood outside River Run High, the toes of his boots hanging over the curb and his backpack slung over one shoulder as he peered down the road, looking for Papa's silver Lexus. Leaves on the trees across the street rustled in a gentle breeze. A cloudy sky hung above, reminding Roland that Father had asked them to pray for good weather for the weekend.

Footfalls sounded behind Roland, but he decided not to look.

Then a voice over his shoulder. "Hi, Roland."

Realizing how close someone stood to him, Roland shivered. Then he shrugged to hide it as he turned around to face Marshall. "Hi."

Marshall hugged a single notebook to his chest. Wind blew pink strands over his forehead and revealed dark roots. "Sorry you got thrown out of Empowerment. I've never seen that happen before."

Roland shrugged again. "Doesn't matter."

"It does to me. The group's supposed to be for everyone. And just because you're straight and all that, doesn't mean you don't care." He gave Roland a quirky grin.

"Yeah, thanks."

"Waiting for your ride?"

Roland nodded and turned to look for the Lexus again.

"Could you possibly give me a ride? I just found out I'm stranded. My mom said she can't come get me."

"Where do you live?"

Marshall pointed down the road, opposite the way Roland would go. "Just ten minutes or so that way. I guess I could walk but I wanted to get home before my Dad. I'm s'posed to do some stuff before he gets home."

Roland recognized the sound of the Lexus approaching. He turned toward it and his stomach clenched. Asking if Marshall could have a ride home meant admitting that he had a friend with pink hair. Papa would not understand. And he might jump to conclusions and think he'd need to have a talk with Roland. Which he wouldn't do for a long time, since he didn't talk about difficult subjects easily.

Papa pulled up to the curb and the door locks clicked. He did a double take at Roland. Or maybe at the boy with the pink hair who stood beside him.

Roland opened a back door and stuck his head in.

Miss Meadows turned around in the front passenger seat and smiled.

"Hey, can we give, uh . . ." He couldn't get himself to say *my friend*. "Marshall needs a ride home."

Papa glanced at Roland in the rearview mirror. "Sure. So long as he's not too far. We've got dinner reservations."

Roland nodded to Marshall, who then jogged around the car and got in.

"Thanks," he said, breathless, "I appreciate it. My mom usually picks me up, but she called and said she couldn't. And my dad . . ." Marshall babbled on without pause for the next five minutes, that strange lilt in his voice. Papa nodded every now and then. Miss Meadows responded with polite questions and comments.

Roland added nothing to the conversation and couldn't help exhaling when Marshall stopped talking.

Then Miss Meadows said something to Papa and they mumbled to each other for the rest of the ride, no longer seeming to notice Roland or Marshall.

"Turn down this next street," Marshall said five minutes later.

The house on the corner looked familiar. Roland studied it as they drove past, then he realized what neighborhood Marshall lived in. "You live near Brice?"

Marshall's gaze flitted down the road and then to Roland. "Oh, yeah, I guess I do."

"Which is your house?" Papa said, glancing over his shoulder.

"Oh." Marshall leaned forward and pointed. "Yellow one with the open garage . . . Oh, no. Dad's home already." He pursed his lips and stared as they pulled into the driveway. A heavy middle-aged man in denim shorts and a short-sleeved button-front shirt pushed a lawnmower into the yard. He peered at the car for a moment. As Marshall opened the car door, the man shouted, "'Bout time you got home. What'd you do with the gas can? Leave it out again? One day someone's going to walk off with it."

"Looks like you've got chores to do." Miss Meadows twisted around and smiled at Marshall.

"Yeah, s'posed to cut the grass." One hand on the door handle, he turned to Papa. "I appreciate the ride, Mr. West."

Papa nodded.

Still turned around in her seat, Miss Meadows shook his hand. "I'm glad I got a chance to meet one of Roland's friends."

Roland felt the burn of a blush, but something Marshall's father said bothered him even more, so as Marshall opened the car door, he blurted, "Something happen to your gas can?"

One foot outside, Marshall gave Roland a dumbstruck look. "Uh, I don't know. It's just missing. Misplaced, I guess."

"I found a gas can around here." Roland decided against admitting that the same can was probably still in the trunk of this very car.

"Really?" Marshall scooted from the car, glanced at his father, and then at Roland. "Where?"

"Woods." Roland pointed in the general direction of the woods where he'd found it, though they couldn't see it from here.

"What were you doing in the woods?"

"Marshall, say goodbye and get over here." His father loped back to the garage.

Marshall gave Roland one last look and closed the car door.

22

BROKEN

"TO BE WITH YOU" by Mr. Big blared from the car radio. ". . . so come on over, come on over . . ." Peter belted out, singing into a high-torque ratchet wrench. "Let me be the one to show you."

His own personal music video playing in his mind, he flung himself dramatically onto the Durango's hood and squeezed his eyes shut as he sang, "I'm the one who wants to be with you."

"You're gonna run your battery down."

Heart skyrocketing out of his chest, Peter swallowed his Adam's apple and jerked himself upright. The ratchet wrench slipped from his hand, clanked against the hood, and landed on the cement floor as his eyes found her. "Brice," he whispered, unable to master his voice.

She stood in the driveway a few steps from the open garage door, holding the high handlebars of her BMX bike. Her windblown hair stood up in places like pale flames, her blue jacket hung half off one shoulder, and her eyes held a look of mirth—yeah, she'd totally caught him singing.

"Hey, you came over." Peter kicked himself for stating the obvious. He was glad for the bit of breeze that made it into the garage and reached his burning neck, but his heart raced like mad.

Brice moved her bike to the grass just off the driveway, dropped the kickstand, and sauntered into the garage inspecting the Durango. "Looks nice."

Peter took a deep breath, calming a bit. Proud of his work, he stood with his hands on his hips. "Cleaned the inside too."

"What about the engine?"

"Huh?" Peter glanced at the hood. "Didn't think about that."

"Why not?" She rested a hand on the door frame of the open driver-side window and peered inside as the last bars of "To Be With You" played. "And I'm serious about running the battery down. Do you know how old it is?"

"Uh, no." Eager for any excuse to get close to her, Peter took two steps and reached for the driver-side door handle.

Brice backed out of the way, but as Peter swung the door open, she leaned inside and yanked the hood release.

Finding a strange sort of satisfaction in this turn-taking, Peter strutted to the front of the SUV and lifted the hood. As he reached for the hood prop rod, he half-expected Brice to beat him to it. But she didn't.

"You got a multimeter?" She came up next to him and stood with her thumbs in the back pockets of her jeans.

Peter lifted his gaze from the dirty battery to her. He stared for a second, thrilled by her question. "Words cannot express how exciting it is to hear a girl ask that question."

Brice's lip curled. Then she punched his arm. "You're such a dork."

"I know." He caressed his arm, a bit sore from where she'd punched him but happy for the physical contact, and he turned to a workbench to find the analog multimeter. "The good one's up in my room."

"Nice place for it."

"Hey, I need it for my projects. I've got a bunch of electronic things I'm working on. You wanna see them?"

"No, thanks." She leaned over the engine, resting a hand on the top of a fender. "Battery looks old anyway. You know they don't last forever."

"Yeah, I'm sure it could use a new one." He gave up searching for the old multimeter and stood beside her, studying the engine and hoping she didn't take his invitation the wrong way. "And, you're right, the engine's filthy. We should take a drive to the auto parts store. Get some engine cleaner, degreaser stuff."

"And a battery."

"Yeah." Joy sparked inside, and he couldn't help smiling. Man, oh man, this was great! She was gonna go with him to the auto parts store. They were gonna take his Durango. Of course, . . . she'd have to drive. "You got your license on you?"

She slapped her back pocket, her gaze connecting with his. "Let's go."

"Okay." He reached for the hood prop rod.

She grabbed the hood and together they closed it.

"I just gotta tell . . ." Thumb up, pointing in the direction of the house, Peter froze. Would it seem childish to say he had to tell—?

"Your mom?" She yanked open the driver-side door. "So, go tell her. And hurry up."

Concentrating on his style, Peter strode from the garage. Out of Brice's view, he raced into the house, gave Mom the lowdown, and raced back. Just before reaching the garage, he slowed, ran a hand through his hair, and tucked in his old button-front mustard yellow shirt. If he'd known she was coming over, he'd have put on something nicer. But they were *working* in the garage. And she probably didn't care. Or even notice. Any chance she was starting to like him as more than just a friend?

Uncomfortable with the button-front tucked in, Peter tugged it back out of his jeans and stepped into the garage.

Brice sat behind the steering wheel, adjusting the rearview mirror. As Peter opened the passenger-side door and jumped in, she glanced and revved the engine. With the slightest grin, she shifted into reverse and twisted around, peering over her shoulder as she backed out.

Another good song came on the radio. With a sideways glance at Brice to see if she minded, Peter cranked the volume.

With the windows rolled down and music blaring, they drove down Forest Road and into town. At some point, Brice had lowered her guard. They strolled through the aisles of the auto parts store, taking turns making snide remarks and lame jokes, and spending an incredible amount of time picking out an air-freshener. Over half an hour later, they emerged with a new battery, engine degreaser, and a Star Wars Yoda vanilla air freshener two-pack. On the ride home, "We Will Rock You" came on the radio and they both belted out the refrain because—well, who could resist singing along to that song? As they neared the house, Peter even talked Brice into coming inside for something to eat before they cleaned the engine.

Peter followed Brice into the house, and his heart skidded to a halt, the amazing rush ending and dread replacing it.

Dominic sat on the couch in the living room, his tan lanky arms stretched out along the back and his jet-black hair hanging over his forehead.

Toby paced in front of the living room window, holding a pocket notebook and talking to himself. He'd probably been trying to talk to Dominic, saying his standard questions and comments over and over. "Today is Saturday." "I'm going bowling." "Do you like bowling?"

Rather than say, "Hola, *vato*," as Dominic always did, he stared at Brice through wide eyes, his lips forming a perfect letter "o," the gears of his gossip-hungry brain obviously turning.

Stopping by the coat hooks on the wall, just inside the door, Brice visibly tensed. Rather than take off and hang her jacket, she zipped it up. Then she looked toward the kitchen, where Mom and Aunt Lotti talked over a steaming casserole dish on the counter.

A sudden rush of irrational anger rose up in Peter. He took a breath, fighting like mad to push it back down. "What'cha doing here, Dominic?"

"Oh, I . . ." Dominic's gaze shifted from Brice to Peter. ". . . need a ride to Fire Starters."

"Yeah?" Peter took another breath and moved to the back of the loveseat that separated the foyer from the living room. "No ride today, huh?"

"No. Six people with driver's licenses in my house and three cars, you think I'd always have a ride." Dominic smiled. "I had to get dropped over here a bit early. Your *madre* invited me to have dinner. Smells good, no?"

Peter took another breath, this time recognizing the tomato, garlic, and basil of whatever Italian food Mom had made. But he'd only taken the breath to calm himself. What was Dominic thinking now? What would he say at school tomorrow? What was Brice thinking?

"Come sit down." Dominic swung an arm off the back of the couch. "Dinner won't be ready for ten minutes, your Aunt Lotti said."

Peter looked at Brice to see what she wanted to do, and he read her answer in her eyes. She no longer wanted to be here.

"Ten minutes," Peter said, his voice low. "We'll talk about cars."

She almost smiled. Then she stiffened. "Yeah, whatever." She strode around the loveseat and slumped down in the rocker recliner.

Toby stopped pacing and cocked his head to one side, looking at Brice sideways. He lifted his notebook and crayon.

Peter swung a leg over the back of the loveseat and flumped down into it. He had to control the conversation before Dominic—

"So how are you liking River Run High?" Dominic said to Brice.

Brice shrugged then slouched into the recliner, crossing one ankle over her knee.

"You are probably too new to form an opinion, huh? It's not a bad school," Dominic said. "You will see after you are here a while. Where did you move from?"

"So, Dominic," Peter interrupted to keep Brice from having to answer, "you think we're ready for camping?"

Dominic jerked his face to Peter. "Camping? I am always ready for camping." He spun his head back to Brice. "What about you? You like camping? You should come too."

"No, thanks." She gave him a cursory glance and turned toward the kitchen.

"Why not?" Peter blurted, wishing he'd asked her in private. But he wanted her to go.

"Are you coming to Fire Starters tonight?" Dominic said.

Still watching the activity in the kitchen, Brice huffed. "Yeah, I don't think so."

Dominic titled his head the way Toby had when Brice had first stepped into the living room. "I hope you do not believe the rumors around school."

"Oh, Dominic . . ." Peter flopped his head back. "Don't."

"No, I am serious." Dominic scooted forward on the couch and angled his body toward Brice, who now peered at him through narrowed eyes. "I know some are blaming the Fire Starters for what happened to your house. But you have to know it wasn't us."

"I have to know that, huh?"

"We came out to help. And we are still helping."

"Oh, no." *Please, God, just make him shut his mouth.* A rush of panic forcing him to his feet, Peter raised his voice. "Dominic, would you just quit?"

"Why wouldn't you want her to know, man?"

"Wow." Peter shoved a hand in his hair and turned in a circle, stopping to face Brice. "Brice, let's skip dinner and go hose down the engine."

Brice stood, her jaw clenched. "What's he talking about?"

Dominic stood too. "People care about you, muchacha. We weren't the ones who did that to your house, but we cleaned it up. And we're trying to find out, especially Peter here."

"Find out what?" she spit, shooting Peter with a glare. "*What* are you doing?"

Unable to believe that his worst nightmare was coming to life, Peter shook his head. "Nothing. Dominic just says things." Facing Dominic, he added in a harsh tone, "He talks too much."

Brice crossed the room to Peter and folded her arms, her eyes narrowing to slits.

While he loved standing close to her, this time he squirmed. He did not want that hostile gaze directed at him.

"Is that what this has been about?"

"What—no!" His neck and cheeks burned.

"You wanted help with your SUV, huh?"

"Yes, I did. I totally did. This has nothing to do with whatever happened to your house."

"You're snooping around, trying to figure out who did that to my foster family's house? Why? I didn't ask you to. I don't want you to." One hand shot out. She jabbed a finger at his chest. "You. Need to stop. If I cared, I'd find out myself." She stomped around the loveseat and to the door. As she tore from the house, the screen door slammed in her wake.

"Man, Dominic." A firestorm of angry words ripped through his mind, and he could picture himself punching Dominic in the face.

"Way to ruin a guy's life." Peter went after Brice, storming out onto the porch.

Brice whipped her bike onto the road and pedaled standing up.

Peter's heart dropped to his feet, watching her race away. Then a mess of emotions welled up. He wanted to hop on his bike and take off after her, make things right. And he wanted to punch something, preferably Dominic. Instead, he jumped into the Durango and pulled it into the garage to be alone. The radio blasted a song by the Goo Goo Dolls. "When everything's made to be broken . . . I just want you to know who I am . . ."

Peter shut off the engine, reclined the seat, and let the music play.

23

MESSAGE

HEART THUMPING HARD IN HIS CHEST, leg aching from having walked so far and so fast, Roland slowed his steps as Caitlyn's little yellow ranch house on the next corner came into view. A washed-out gray sky hung overhead, sunbeams piercing through here and there. Was he just going to go up and knock on the door? What would she think? What if she was in the middle of dinner or something? Or she had friends over? He should've called.

But he hadn't meant to come all the way over here. After dinner—they'd eaten at home tonight—he'd gotten permission from Papa to take a walk before he did his homework, using the need to exercise his leg as an excuse. Thoughts about the investigation had hounded his every step along Forest Road and past the downtown square, and next thing he knew . . . there was her house. If his leg didn't hurt so badly, he might keep on walking. But it wouldn't kill him to visit. He'd wanted to talk to her and still hadn't found the opportunity at school. He hadn't even talked with Peter today. But then, Peter had seemed uncharacteristically sullen and distant.

Roland stopped on the sidewalk on the corner opposite Caitlyn's house, in front of a rundown two-story with a missing window shutter. He fished his phone from the front pocket of his jeans, brought up her number, and then froze with his thumb hovering over the phone icon. He swiped the message icon instead and tapped out a text.

Hey. What are you doing right now?

He glanced up at her house and then turned toward the street. In case she looked out a window, he didn't want to seem like a stalker.

A silly shriek came from the direction of Caitlyn's house. Then a little girl called out, "There's that cute boy you like." Giggling followed.

Temperature rising, Roland stuffed his phone away and turned toward the house.

The screen door squeaked open, and Caitlyn stumbled out running a hand through her long red locks. She wore a casual dress that reminded him of an artist's palette, with splashes of blue, orange and yellow.

Roland tried to suppress the ridiculously huge smile that threatened to stretch across his face as he crossed the street.

"Oh, hi, what are you doing here?" She descended the porch steps in her bare feet, stepped on a squashed juice box, and hopped on one foot.

"Taking a walk." He cut across a lawn strewn with red and yellow plastic climbing and riding toys.

She stopped four feet from him, twisted her arms in front of her, and slid one foot back and forth in the grass—probably wiping off juice from the box she'd stepped on.

He stuffed his hands into his pockets, though her clumsy awkwardness made him feel more at ease than when around other girls.

"I'm glad you stopped because I've been wanting to talk to you," she said.

"Yeah, me too."

"Really?"

"Really."

She stared at him for a moment. A sunbeam found her, turning her green eyes to crystals and her flyaway curls into burnished copper. In the next moment, she grabbed his arm.

His heart leaped, and his thoughts scattered.

"I want to show you something." She tugged him toward the house, releasing his arm once they reached the porch steps. Then she thumped up the stairs first and yanked open the screen door. "Mom, can Roland come over?" she shouted over a TV show as she tugged him through the doorway.

Her mother stood over a sinkful of dishes in their little kitchen. "How about after we get these dishes done?" She turned and glanced over the open kitchen bar counter toward the living room.

"Hi, Mrs. Summer." Roland stood just inside the door, unsure of himself. He didn't want to block the TV from the two on the couch: eight-year-old Stacey and three-year-old David. And he didn't want to come too far in if she was going to tell him to leave.

"Oh, hi, Roland." Offering a pleasant smile, she grabbed a dishtowel and stepped away from the sink. Strands of hair hung loose from a sloppy ponytail, red like Caitlyn's hair. "Did you get a ride here?"

"No, walked."

"I thought that would be your answer. You do a lot of walking, don't you? How's your leg?"

Not wanting her to realize he was favoring his healing leg, he shifted his weight, but a sharp pain shot through his calf and he winced. "Better. But kind of hurts right now. Probably from walking."

She smiled. "I'm sure exercise is good, but you don't want to overdo it. I'll see if Mr. Summer will give you a ride home when you're done visiting."

"Mom." Standing on the opposite side of the kitchen bar counter, Caitlyn stretched her arms across toward her mother in pleading fashion. "I have to show him something in my room. Okay?"

"Why don't you bring whatever you have to show him out to the living room?"

Caitlyn exhaled, twisting her mouth to one side as she turned toward Roland. The second they made eye contact, her smile was back. "Okay. Wait here." And she bounced down the little hallway off the kitchen.

"Why don't you sit down, Roland?" Mrs. Summer gestured toward the living room. "Rest your leg."

"Yeah, come sit by me." Stacey dragged a dirty toy tow truck from beside her and set it on her lap, making room for him.

He would've preferred to sit alone on the loveseat or in a chair, but he sat down between her and little David, who was spooning puzzle pieces from a big plastic bowl to the mouth of a twelve-inch T-Rex.

Roland's leg appreciated the rest anyway. He glanced at the cartoon on the TV. As he turned away, he realized what they were watching, and his gaze jerked back to the show.

"That's Saint Maximilian Kolbe," Stacey said, probably having noticed his reaction.

"Oh, cool." He vaguely remembered the saint's story. He was born in Poland, became a Franciscan priest, and did a lot of missionary work. During World War II, Nazis arrested him and he eventually died—a martyr—having offered his life in exchange for another prisoner.

Maybe Caitlyn had chosen him for her martyr.

A minute later, Caitlyn came into the living room carrying a shoe box tucked under her arm and a big corkboard. "Stacey, why don't you take David and go play outside?" She set the corkboard on the carpet and leaned it against the coffee table.

David shoved the bowl of puzzle pieces at Roland and climbed off the couch, his T-Rex tumbling to the floor.

Stacey folded her arms and stuck out her lips. "Why?"

With a groan, Caitlyn snatched the TV remote from an end table and shut off the TV. "Because you've been watching TV for over an hour."

"So? You're not Mom."

Still holding the shoebox, Caitlyn flung the remote to the loveseat, smiled at Roland, and turned wide eyes to Stacey. "I could call Mom."

They held each other's gazes, both looking stubborn. Dishes clanked in the kitchen. A baby fussed somewhere in the house.

"Look, David wants to play with you." Caitlyn begged with her eyes. "You're the only one who really knows how to play and get dirty in the backyard."

Stacey's expression softened.

"Now go." She pointed toward the back of the house.

"Fine." She scooted off the couch. "But I think he's cute too."

Roland blinked. Did she mean him?

Caitlyn's eyes opened wide and she sucked in a breath. Once Stacey bolted from the living room, she exhaled. "Sorry about that."

Roland glanced away and back, not sure how to respond. "No problem."

All business now, Caitlyn set the shoebox on the coffee table, sat beside Roland, and angled the corkboard toward them. Pencil drawings of faces lined the top of the board, under the label "suspects." Names and notecards were underneath, and another row of people at the bottom of the board. "So, I made an evidence board."

Roland nodded, looking it over. "Nice."

She gave him a shy smile. "Like in detective shows."

"Yeah, exactly." He smiled back, impressed with her zeal. Peter wanted him to work alone but Caitlyn would make the perfect detective partner. "You drew those?"

"Yeah." She sighed. "My phone doesn't take good pictures. And I don't know how to get them off my phone anyway."

Her answer amused him, but he tried not to show it. She'd never had her own phone before. He drew his phone out and snapped a picture of her evidence board. The top pictures included Gavin Wheeler, a few other mean jocks, CW, Trent, and Konner, and the neighbor. The lower pictures included Tessia, the kid with orange hair, the Muslim girl, and a few others from the Empowerment group.

"Did I tell you that I spoke with Tessia?" she said.

"What'd she say?"

"She's convinced that we did it or else some other intolerant group of kids."

"So, how'd you word your questions?" He liked that she'd approached Tessia, but he hoped she'd used caution. "I mean, you didn't give away that we're investigating, right?"

"I tried not to. She's in one of my classes, so I sat next to her and told her I was upset by all the mean things going on lately. Which I am, so it wasn't a lie."

Gazing at the evidence board, Roland realized she'd put a name down for Brice's neighbor: Norris Stanton.

He pointed to it. "Hey, how did you—"

She pushed his hand down. "I peeked at his mail."

"But that's a—"

"No, it's only a crime when someone is trying to intercept the mail. I wasn't. I didn't want to take or open anything. I just needed a peek." She bit her lip and seemed to hold her breath for his reply.

"Well, good work. You'd make an awesome detective."

She smiled, looking pleased.

"And I'm glad he didn't catch you. You still could've gotten into trouble."

"I'm stealthy." She pulled the shoebox toward herself, but the lid stayed in her hand while the rest of it crashed at their feet. Notecards, pens, a notebook, and a ball of yarn tumbled out. With a groan, she scooted to the edge of the couch and threw everything back into the box.

"What about you?" She sat back again, put the box on her lap, and pulled out the notebook. "What have you learned from the Empowerment group? They had a special meeting yesterday, right? I heard kids talking about it."

"Yeah, they want to go camping."

"Oh, that's good, isn't it? Maybe all the suspects and possible targets will be in one place and we can set a trap." She opened her eyes so wide that the whites showed all around her irises.

He had to suppress another laugh. "I guess it's good. But I'm not welcome in their group anymore."

"Oh. Why?"

"I had a few questions, and then I was thrown out."

"You were rejected . . . by a club for people who feel rejected?"

He shrugged. "Outcast among outcasts, I guess. It doesn't matter. I wanted to get a list of possible targets, and I've got that." He tapped his phone, which he'd used to make the list.

"I wonder if Peter has anything more—Oh!" She gave him a wide-eyed look. "I forgot to tell you the biggest thing."

"Which is?"

"The police interviewed me."

A strange tingling sensation ran through him from head to toe. "How'd that go?"

"I told them everything I noticed that day we helped clean up. And I told them everyone I thought could be a suspect. They can't possibly suspect the Fire Starters now."

"So, what'd they say?" Despite her positive attitude, worry grew inside him.

"They asked a lot of questions and wrote everything down. Oh, and they wanted to know what happened to the gas can you found."

Another wave of dread passed through him. "You told them I found it?"

Her eyes opened wide again. "Should I not have?"

"Uh . . ." Trying to convey a calm attitude, he forced a smile. "No, that's fine." What would the police think about him tossing the gas can into the back of his father's car? No one was with him when he'd found it. One thing for sure, they'd be calling him for an interview soon. Any chance he could discover the culprits before then?

Then he remembered. He had to tell her Peter wanted everyone else to stop investigating. But how? She wasn't going to like it any more than he liked it. And she really was good at it. "Hey, uh—"

In his peripheral vision he glimpsed movement outside the living room window. Something flew through the air—toward the house. And bam! It crashed against the window. Glass rained down onto the back of the loveseat. A fist-sized stone cracked into the coffee table and thudded to the floor amid glass shards.

Heart leaping to his throat, Roland grabbed Caitlyn and shoved her aside. Then he ran to the screen door. The street and sidewalks were empty. No car. Nobody. Nothing.

Mr. and Mrs. Summer appeared in the living room at once.

"What happened?" Mr. Summer rushed to Roland's side at the door. "Is everyone okay?"

Mr. Summer stepped outside, muttering to himself about who would do such a thing. Mrs. Summer ushered the rest of the family—who had all come to see what had happened—to another room and went to call the police. Caitlyn returned to the living room and stooped by the rock.

"There's a note tied to it." She stood unfolding a white paper.

Roland shot to her side and read over her shoulder.

Tell your boyfriend to stop snooping.

No longer doubting what he had to do, he snatched the note from her, grabbed her shoulders, and turned her to face him. "Okay, we're done here. No more investigating. Leave the rest to me."

"What?" Her eyebrows slanted upward, and trouble showed in her pretty green eyes. "But wait. Do you know which martyr I chose?"

Failing to see the relevance, he threw out a random guess. "Uh . . . Maximilian Kolbe?"

"No. Joan of Arc. And do you know what she said?"

He shrugged, having no clue where she was going with this.

"*I am not afraid. I was born to do this.*" She folded her arms, grim determination coloring her expression. "They're trying to scare us. But they've caused enough trouble and I'm not giving up. I will find out who burned the tree in Brice's yard. I will find out who put fish in the Muslim girl's locker. And who hung those warning signs all over school. And who threw that rock in my window. I am not afraid. And I'm not giving up."

While he had no intention of giving up now, he would never do anything to put her in jeopardy. He wouldn't visit her again, not for a while. And he wouldn't talk to her at school either. He had to keep her out of this. He'd go totally dark and uncover these attackers before they struck again.

24

URGENT

THE STUBBORN TARP UNFOLDED yet again, spilling out of a big plastic storage container of camping supplies. Peter snatched it up and flung it across the garage. It flopped onto the hood of the Durango and slid to the cement floor. A breeze kicked up and pushed the tarp a few inches. Any minute now, it would probably start raining and get the back half of the Durango wet.

He'd pulled it halfway into the garage so he could listen to music while he worked, but for the past ten minutes one stupid commercial followed another. He should probably just back it into the driveway and close the garage so nothing else got wet.

Peter dropped a box of matches, a baggie of tablecloth clips, and an old skillet into the container. The skillet clanked against something metal. He'd wanted to use the tarp like packing material to keep everything from banging and rattling around while they drove to the campground.

He glimpsed the red-and-white checkered tablecloths on a shelf of camping gear. That would work. As he turned back to the box, his conscience pricked him. He'd tossed everything into the container in a big, disorganized heap. Dad wouldn't approve of his sloppy work. Maybe he should've run errands with Dad instead of staying home.

Peter shoved tools aside on the workbench, set the tablecloths down, and started unloading the container.

Dad would probably be out all night running errands for the camping trip and then stopping at the Summers to help them get their stuff together. Ordinarily, Peter would've gone with him. He loved everything to do with camping, including all the running around beforehand—not the putting things away afterward, but whatever. But he couldn't go along because he hadn't done anything from the list Dad had given him days ago.

Didn't matter. Nothing could lift his mood today. This would be the first camping trip he went on where his heart wasn't in it.

After pulling out the last item, Peter kicked the container and sent it scraping three feet along the cold cement floor.

Why'd Dominic have to ruin things for him with Brice, telling her about their investigations?

Peter grabbed the skillet, his hand brushing the jar of palm branches and knocking over a little box next to them. A dozen old medals and a few chains spilled out. After placing the skillet in the bottom of the container, he scooped the medals up and thumbed through them, his attention latching onto a girl in armor. Saint Joan of Arc.

Unable to tear his gaze from the medal of Saint Joan, he dumped the other medals back into the box. After giving Saint Joan a long look, he sighed and lifted the chain on over his head.

Brice wasn't like other girls. She didn't want a guy coming to her rescue. She didn't want to be a damsel in distress. She could handle herself. And he liked that about her. He really liked that about her, but he still couldn't control the urge to protect her and to defend her honor. Regardless of how she felt about it, he had to find out who'd gone after her. He couldn't let it happen again, and he wanted to teach—whoever it was—a lesson. You just didn't treat people like that, whether you agreed with their lifestyle or their ideas or anything else. But he wasn't going to let her know he still wanted to uncover who'd done it. He'd let Roland handle it discreetly. And Roland could be discreet.

Peter stuffed a roll of garbage bags into one corner of the tightly-packed container and the tablecloths between citronella candles. He set the box of matches on top.

Would she ever forgive him? She hadn't given him the time of day in Woodworking all week. They'd worked on their projects silently. Well, she was silent. He kept trying to talk to her and say stupid things to make her laugh. She'd barely given him a glance. Whenever she'd had something to say, she talked to other guys and even the teacher. And since she'd learned to handle all the machines like nobody's business, the other guys had developed a certain level of respect for her.

Peter snatched four black-and-yellow waterproof flashlights from the shelf.

Meanwhile, Brice had lost all respect for him. Just because he wanted to find out—

"You're gonna run the battery down."

Hope stabbed Peter's heart and traveled through his veins at the sound of Brice's voice. He spun to face her.

She stood over her little yellow BMX bike under the open garage door, dressed in an olive canvas jacket and faded jeans, a pale gray evening behind her. An image of coolness and self-reliance. White-blond windblown hair, damp skin, ruddy cheeks, and the slightest smile on her face.

The gears in his brain froze. He released his grip on the flashlights and they tumbled into the box, one of them bouncing out and landing on the concrete floor.

"Brice," he half-whispered.

"Yeah, hey. What'cha doing?"

"Uh . . . right . . .uh . . ." The gears in his brain fit together and started turning again. "I'm getting ready for the camping trip. It's tomorrow, you know." The gears cranked faster now. She'd come over to his house. She didn't hate him! "Wish you'd change your mind and go. It's a lot of fun."

"Eh. I don't know. Probably too late now." She rolled her bike into the garage and dropped the kickstand. A few sprinkles dotted the yellow paint.

"Nah, it's not too late. We've got plenty of camping gear. You could even have your own pup tent."

When she looked at Peter again, her eyes held a strange intensity that rattled him. "I need to borrow your car."

Peter glanced at her bike and then at the Durango. She must've needed to go someplace far; otherwise, she'd take her bike. "Uh, sure, anything you want. When?"

"Now."

"Now? Why?"

She inhaled, her nostrils flaring. "I have to check on something. I'll have it back in two hours."

Unable to imagine what could take that long, a grin forced its way to his face. "Two hours?"

"About that long."

Not sure how to reply, he stared at her. He'd let her borrow the car, sure, but he was going along.

She dipped her head, a hint of vulnerability showing in her eyes. "It's kind of an emergency."

"Okay, the Durango's yours for the night." He pulled his keys from his jacket pocket and dangled them before her. "But I'm coming too."

Without hesitation, she snatched the keys. "I need to go alone."

"No way, sister, that's the deal. You get the keys, but I ride along. And I'll need your number." He'd wanted her number since he'd met her, but now he had a reason to ask for it. "If we're going to be out that long, Mom will want to talk to your foster mom first."

Her mouth became a grim line and her eyes narrowed, but then she sighed and pulled out her phone. She tapped the screen a few times and pressed it to her ear. "Yeah, hey . . ." She stepped outside the garage and mumbled so low that Peter couldn't hear a word she said no matter how hard he strained his ears. A few seconds later, she strode back into the garage and handed him her phone. "I got my foster mom on the phone so she can talk to your mom."

"Oh, smooth. Really don't want me to have your number, huh?" He took the phone, gave her a playful grin, and traipsed through the cool, humid air to the house. He might not get her number, but they were going out. Two hours alone. Heaven.

Less than three minutes later, Peter bounded from the house with the good news. Mom said they could go. He wasn't sure what Brice had told her foster mom or what her foster mom told Mom, but he had permission. They were going for a ride. And—bonus—

Mom had jotted down Mrs. Escott's number, so now he had Brice's foster family's number.

The Durango sat in the middle of the driveway, engine humming and the garage door closed. She must've been in a hurry. He wished he knew why, but he'd find out soon enough.

A thrill shooting through him, he jumped into the passenger seat and handed over her phone. No music played and a heavy water vapor odor permeated the air, but this was going to be the best ride of his life.

Brice twisted around, propping a hand on his seatback—her thumb ending up two inches from his shoulder—and she backed out of the drive.

They drove in silence for a few minutes, down a few busy streets, the sun struggling to peek through threatening storm clouds. Before long, they left the city behind and traveled down a curvy two-lane state road. The northbound traffic lessened, and houses came fewer and farther apart.

Brice didn't seem mad at him, but she wasn't exactly bubbling with friendliness. Should he bring up the investigation, apologize again? What would he say? Maybe she just wanted to pick up where they left off. Or maybe she was just using him for his car.

He admired her calm expression and confident air for a few seconds, then he said, "So where are we going? All my mom said was drive safe when the rain starts."

She leaned forward and peered up at the sky. "Yeah, it's supposed to pour. But maybe we'll get there first."

"Get where first?"

She flipped the windshield wiper on for two wipes, clearing away a few sprinkles, and shut it back off.

Peter counted to three, hoping she'd answer. "Look, maybe you don't think of me as a friend, maybe you think I'm doing a social experiment or something, but I *am* your friend. I'm letting you take my car, and I don't even know where we're going. So, spill it."

A car pulled onto the road in front of them.

She tapped the brakes. Then gripping the steering wheel and glaring at the road, she moved her mouth as if wrestling with the first word of her answer. But she closed her mouth before that word found its way out.

Peter sighed and gazed out the passenger side window. "Forget it. You need my car, and that's good enough for me." Emotion gripped his insides but soon passed. "And yes, I like you, like a lot. And I know you're not attracted to guys, but if you'll let me be your friend, that's good enough for me." Was it good enough for him? He wanted her to like him too. Maybe one day she would.

She sighed. "All right. Drop the guilt trip."

"What?" Emotion tightening its grip on his insides, he spun to face her, ready to say something in his defense.

She flashed him a smile. "Joking."

His insides relaxed, and he whacked her arm.

"My mom texted me." She glanced at him but then stared out at the gray sky, the sprinkle of rain drops, and the dark road. "Said she was in trouble. Asked me to come out 'cause she thinks I can help her. I don't know what she expects me to do."

"What kind of trouble?"

"Not sure. She didn't reply to my text. But she's drawn to jerks and always in a crappy relationship."

"Does your foster mom know that's where we're going? Are you even allowed to see your mom?"

"I told her I needed to see a friend who needed help, which led to a ton of questions, but I said I'd be back in two hours and she needed to trust me. She said okay." She glanced again, her look saying she felt a bit guilty about it. "What else can I do? My mom makes bad choices with men. Gets herself in dangerous situations. I don't want anything to happen to her."

"So . . . what about your dad?"

"I don't know." Eyes on the road, she didn't even blink. "I don't remember him, but I've heard he wasn't nice."

"Oh, that's rough. Sorry. Is that the reason you don't . . . um?" He wished he'd thought before he asked. What did his question mean exactly?

"The reason I don't like *guys*? Why do I have to have a reason? Maybe I just don't like guys. Guys can be real jerks in a relationship. Or maybe I just don't want to be like my mom. And maybe I don't like anyone, right now anyways. People hurt you." Her tone hardened. "But I won't be hurt again."

While the lyrics of a song by The Who started playing in his head, a part of him wanted to defend himself. All guys weren't jerks. He wasn't like that, and neither were most of the guys he knew. But realizing her pain, he kept his mouth shut. Peter had no intention of asking for details, but her extreme toughness and independent spirit sort of made sense now.

"You're wondering if I think you're like that?" She took her eyes off the road and gave him another hard look.

He shrugged and shook his head. *Okay, she asked.* "I'm *not* like that. So you can't say *all* guys."

Her lips curled into a sneaky smile. "You're just waiting for your chance."

Her words cut, even if she didn't really mean them. "I resent that. I've only ever been your friend." He lifted his hands. "See? I'm letting you take my car to Timbuktu, no questions asked."

"You asked."

"Only after I said yes."

"Okay, but you still want to change me."

"Well . . ." Peter squirmed, not sure what to admit. "Yeah, I wish you liked guys. I wish you liked me. But I'll take what I can get."

"See? You sound just like every other guy."

Peter jerked back, realizing how she'd interpreted him. "That's not what I—"

She laughed and threw him a friendly look. Joking. Good.

Before long, they got on the highway. The engine and the hum of the wheels on the pavement made the only sounds for the longest time. Then she spoke again. "My mom lives north of Rapid City."

Rapid City. Okay, about an hour away. "Home, huh? Miss it?"

She let out a sharp breath. "No. I'm glad to be away from there. A lot of bad memories."

While Peter hungered to know more about her, he sensed he should tread lightly. She'd probably lost her sister while living back home. And a person didn't go into foster care for no reason.

"Well, I hope your mom's okay, hope we get there in time." A few disturbing thoughts crept into his mind. "Should we, like, call the police?"

She glanced. "No. It might be nothing." A pause. "Mom can get emotional."

He felt like he stood on the edge of a cliff. Her mellow mood and the way she'd started answering his questions . . .

She was trusting him, and he wanted to keep the rapport going. But if he said the wrong thing . . . "Does she call you often?"

"No." Her eyes narrowed. "First time she's called since I went into foster care. Not sure how she got my number."

The need to understand her, to know her, to show that he cared, pushed him to ask, "Why did you go into foster care?"

Brice made no show of having heard him. She didn't flinch, blink, or glance. Just stared at the road. Finally, she answered. "My mother couldn't hold it together."

He took a breath before asking his next question. "Can I ask how your sister died?"

This time she looked. Teeth clenched and a scowl on her face, she looked at him.

25

BRAINSTORM

DARK DRAPES BILLOWED in the humid breeze that blew through Roland's bedroom window, and the draw cord tapped against the wall. Angry gray clouds shifted in the sky, giving a sickly greenish tint to the world outside.

Taking a deep breath of the heavy air, Roland turned his attention back to the open saint book on his desk. He needed to pick a saint tonight. He wouldn't have time tomorrow. But none of the martyrs he'd read about clicked with him.

Roland studied a pen-and-ink picture in the old saint book he'd borrowed from Papa's study. In the image, a soldier's sword rested on the neck of a decapitated body. The soldier's eyes had fallen out of his head, judging by the lines drawn from his eye sockets to two eye-sized balls in his hand. A few other soldiers looked on.

The decapitated body belonged to Saint Alban, the first recorded British martyr. He'd sheltered a Catholic priest in his house during the Christian persecutions in the fourth century. The faith and piety of that priest impressed Alban so much that he soon converted to Christianity. When soldiers came to search the house for the priest, Alban put on the priest's clothing. The soldiers took him to the judge, who ordered Alban to sacrifice to pagan gods. "I worship and adore the true and living God who created all things,"

Alban said. For standing on the side of truth, Alban was scourged. And beheaded. And, apparently, the soldier who beheaded him went blind.

Roland rubbed his eyes and flipped a few pages. He stopped on a random page and dropped his finger to a saint's name. *Saint Paul of Cyprus.* This eighth-century martyr opposed the decree of the Byzantine Emperors who forbade the venerating of icons. He refused to desecrate a crucifix and so was tortured and burned alive.

Flames shot up in Roland's mind, turning his thoughts to the tree in Brice's yard.

Who would've done that?

The graffiti on the garage showed that whoever had done it wanted to make Brice feel bad. The others who came along for the fun probably thought up trashing the yard. Burning the tree seemed like overkill. Of course, if they'd just been out in the neighborhood "kicking up a row," maybe they came across the gas can outside Marshall's house and decided spontaneously to do it. So that would mean they lived nearby. Gavin lived down the road. He wouldn't pass Marshall's house, but he'd pass his street to get to Brice's house.

Roland's phone rang, jerking him from his thoughts. He picked it up from the back of his desk and glimpsed Caitlyn's number—not the number from the phone Peter had given her, her home phone.

His heart leaped. Then worry pushed the elation down as he tapped the icon to answer her call. Could she have received another threat since he'd seen her last?

"Hey, Caitlyn."

"Hi, Roland," she whispered, then in a louder voice, "I know you wanted me to stop investigating. But . . ."

A little bell went off inside him and he braced himself for what she'd say next. Had something else happened? He'd blame himself for involving her to begin with.

"I was just going over the evidence board and I had a few thoughts. Plus, I wanted to know if you or Peter found out more."

He exhaled. She had some ideas. That was all. "Not really. With the camping trip coming up, and I still haven't picked a martyr . . . but I've been thinking about everything."

"Like what?"

"Like about the burned tree . . . I was thinking it could've been an afterthought." The words poured out, as if he'd been waiting for a sounding board. "The names on the garage were definitely personal, so whoever did it knew Brice pretty well and knew where she lived. Maybe someone in the neighborhood. And I think the gas can came from Marshall's house, not that he did it, but the kids probably stole it from there."

"Marshall? What makes you think it was his?"

"He doesn't live too far from Brice. And his gas can is missing."

"How do you know?"

Roland flipped a few pages of the book absentmindedly, not sure he wanted Caitlyn to think he and Marshall were friends. Then his conscience nudged him. So what if he and Marshall were friends? It didn't mean he'd be coloring his hair pink, too, or that he agreed with Marshall's beliefs or lifestyle. Then again, a person should choose their friends wisely and he didn't have to be friends just because—

"He needed a ride home the other day," Roland blurted. "His father couldn't find the gas can and was complaining about him leaving it out all the time."

"You think one of the vandals lives nearby, his friends were over and they were out late that night, wandering the streets, probably looking for trouble, stole the can from outside his house, and decided to burn the tree?"

He smiled, liking the way she'd summarized his thoughts. "Maybe."

"And the reason they picked her house? They could've picked Marshall's for the same reason."

"That's true. But maybe"—other ideas came to him—"the one who instigated it had seen her move in and tried to get to know her. Maybe she rejected him, and this was payback."

"Hmm . . . didn't you say Gavin lives down the road from her?"

"Yeah, and the woods where I found the gas can run behind houses all the way down the street, down past Gavin's house."

"So that makes Gavin a pretty strong suspect. Who else?"

Roland focused his gaze and realized a picture of Saint Stephen lay open before him. A crowd threw stones at him. Oddly, the stones in the picture made him think of the sweetgum tree and the neighbor who hated it. "I don't think the neighbor is a suspect anymore."

"Norris Stanton? Why not?"

"He hated the tree, not Brice. He wouldn't have spray painted all those insults on the garage. That's something kids would do."

"Well, I found something out yesterday."

His stomach clenched. He couldn't shake the feeling that she was going to put herself in danger to find answers. "What'd you find out?"

"Don't get mad, but . . ."

"Caitlyn." Worry and annoyance put an edge in his tone.

"Don't worry. I was only taking a walk. Down Mr. Stanton's street."

With every pause she made, Roland tensed more.

"And I saw a group of teenage boys on the front porch and a few beer cans peeking out of the recycle bin. At least one of the boys was probably his son, the rest his son's friends." She spoke faster as she went on. "And maybe they saw Brice move in and one of them tried to get to know her, like you were thinking maybe Gavin did, but it could've been one of those boys instead, and she probably wanted nothing to do with them, so they would have a reason for the graffiti *and* for burning the tree down. They would know how Mr. Stanton hated it. Right?"

"Uh, I guess so." Disturbed to hear she'd gone over there, he struggled to analyze her theory. Maybe she hadn't gone alone. Kiara and Phoebe could've gone with her.

"What about the other suspects on the list? And does this mean someone different hung up the 'Outcasts Beware' posters and put fish in that girl's locker at school? It all happened around the same time so . . ."

Roland couldn't transition his thoughts. "Did you go over there alone?"

One second, two seconds passed. "Um. Yes. I was just taking a walk."

"Right but . . ." Roland slouched back and shoved a hand in his hair. "You didn't try talking to them, did you? And if they're the guilty ones, they just threatened us with a rock through your window. Who knows what they'll do next?"

"Oh. Well. I didn't talk to them. I was just taking a walk."

"I know. But let me handle the investigations." He envisioned going over to Norris Stanton's house and accusing his son and his son's friends the way a TV show detective would. *So, you know how your father hates that tree in the Escotts' yard. The spiky gumballs drop over the fence into his backyard, and one day he twisted his ankle on them, didn't he? And over the summer you saw a new girl move in with the Escotts, and you wanted to get to know her better. When she rejected you, it made you mad, so when your friends came over one night . . .*

By the time he would finish with them, they'd know they were caught.

"Well, I want to help too." Caitlyn sounded pouty. "I'm sure no one even noticed me."

"I doubt that." Her long red mane and gorgeous green eyes popped into his mind, preventing him from explaining what he meant. If her looks didn't draw their attention, her clumsiness would've.

"But they didn't look familiar. I don't think they go to our school. So, if the vandals also hung the posters and trashed that girl's locker, it wasn't them. And I didn't get any more threats— Oh! You know what we should do?"

"What?" He leaned forward at the sound of her enthusiasm, and he glimpsed another saint in the book: a king with an arrow sticking out of his chest.

"We should go to Brice's neighborhood after school, get there before the buses drop kids off. Maybe some of the others on our list live in the neighborhood. Like maybe C.W., Trent, or Konner live nearby."

He shuddered and glanced at his pale arm, remembering the "tan job" they'd forced on him.

"Do you think one of your brothers would give us a ride?"

"No, bad idea. If the vandals do live in the neighborhood, they'll see us for sure and they'll know we didn't heed their warning. And I don't want you taking more chances."

She sighed. "I am not afraid. I was born to do this."

"You're not Joan of Arc."

"But I'm still not afraid."

"I know." *But I don't want anything to happen to you,* he thought but couldn't get the words out.

"We do have to consider the possibility that it wasn't the neighbor or Gavin. It might've been someone we don't suspect and for a reason we don't suspect."

He nodded, even though she couldn't see it through the phone. She was right. They could be overlooking the guilty party and the true motive. Would they ever find conclusive evidence or actually get someone to confess? "Okay, well, I gotta work on finding my saint. Call me if you get any other ideas."

"Okay," she whispered the way she had when she first said hello.

Roland set the phone aside and studied the picture in the saint book of the king with the arrow sticking out of his chest.

Edmund the Martyr. The crown had passed to him at age fifteen. A model ruler, he prayed often and even memorized the whole Psalter. Invaders captured him and tried forcing him to accept terms at the expense of the Christian religion. Declaring his religion dearer to him than his life, he refused. Then they beat him with cudgels, tied him to a tree, and whipped him. Unable to break his faith, his enemies shot him with arrows until he looked like a porcupine.

Skin crawling, Roland rubbed his chest. *Hmm* . . . Saint Sebastian was shot with arrows too. It didn't kill him though. He died after they clubbed him. Roland remembered what Jarret had said after learning Saint Sebastian's story. "I don't see the point in all these people dying, all these martyrs. Why didn't they fight? Why didn't Sebastian have his own bow and arrows? Ain't nobody gonna bring me down without a fight."

Roland smiled. While he preferred to remain behind the scenes unnoticed, he admired Jarret's fearless determination. Caitlyn had it too. And, apparently, so did Edmund the Martyr.

He turned a few more pages. Then a picture made him stop. An angry mob in colorful robes and leggings stood around a kneeling man in a long brown robe. One man climbed a ladder that reached to the rafters of a barn, and another man handed him a noose.

Roland's mind took him back to speech class. His classmates were the mob . . . and his speech was the noose. He'd rather do anything other than speak before a group, but this saint devoted himself to speaking before others. He preached against heresy until they swung the noose over his head.

26

TRUTH

"MY SISTER GOT IN A CAR WRECK." Brice gazed stone-faced at the dark road before them. Raindrops sprinkled the windshield, and slow wipers brushed them away. Visible through the driver-side window, a sliver of orange ran along the horizon under heavy storm clouds that stretched across the rest of the sky. "She had a concussion, internal injuries, whiplash . . . two days later, still in the hospital, she died."

"Oh, man, I'm sorry." Peter wished he knew what to say. They'd traveled the past half hour or so with barely a word spoken between them. After the hard look she'd given him, he assumed she wasn't going to answer his question. Maybe he shouldn't have asked her.

"Her girlfriend, the driver, got away with a few scrapes."

"When you say girlfriend . . . ?"

"Yeah, I mean girlfriend. My sister didn't like boys either. And you probably know her girlfriend because she's also new to River Run High. I guess she felt compelled to follow me when I had to move, and she's got an aunt who lives nearby so . . ."

"Wait, who are talking about?"

"Tessia."

"Oh." Peter jerked back in the seat. Tessia's cold attitude toward him made a little more sense. She cared about Brice.

"My sister was messed up before the wreck. Emotionally. She'd been through a lot. Things a girl shouldn't have to go through. And maybe that's why she lived on the edge. I kind of did too. But not like her. It always made me sad." She paused and ground her teeth. "My mom's boyfriend at the time could've helped her, but he didn't."

"He was a doctor?"

"No." She threw him an accusing glance. "He was a Christian."

Peter shook his head, not understanding. A person couldn't expect miracles from prayer. Just because you believed in God . . . "So, you don't think he prayed for her?"

She shrugged. "Oh, he probably prayed for her." After a stretch of silence, she gave him sulky look. "You belong to that Christian group, so . . ."

"So what? You mean the Fire Starters? It's a Catholic group. I mean, of course we're Christians, you know, the original Christians." He gave a confident grin. "But what's your point?"

"They teach you that things are wrong."

"Well, yeah. Lots of things are wrong. Who doesn't know that?"

"Certain things . . . like who you can love."

"Oh, those things. Well . . ." Peter stared at her for a moment, as her eyes turned back to the road and light from the dash cast a pale glow on her solemn features.

He found himself playing with the edge of the seat cushion, his thumb rubbing a rip in the fabric that he hadn't noticed before. *Lord, help me. What do I say?* Would she think he was judging her? If he didn't tell the truth, he'd be lying to her. What would be the point in that? Nobody liked a liar.

Peter took a breath, rubbed his hands down his thighs, and readied himself. *Please, Lord Jesus, don't let my words push her away.* "Okay, here it is. Catholic teaching. You can love whoever you want, but . . . some things belong in marriage. Only." Realizing that the world had become a bit confused lately, he added, "Marriage, meaning a guy and a girl for life. Is that what you're talking about?"

"Does that seem fair? A person can't help who they fall in love with."

"You're telling me."

Her gaze shifted to him and her mouth fell open, turning into a crooked grin. She sort of laughed.

He couldn't have her affection, but it still satisfied him to make her laugh. "Well, love's more than *that*, right? Do you just wanna have what you want, or do you want what's best for the person you love?"

"What does that mean?"

"I mean . . ." His thumb found the rip in the seat cushion again. *Lord, give him the words.* "Y-you don't get to act on your impulses just because you love someone. You gotta do the right thing even if it means you don't get that someone. Otherwise it's selfish. And that's the opposite of love." He exhaled, glad he'd gotten it out.

With her mouth in a grim line, she shook her head. "What you're saying seems hard to live with. Who could do it?"

"I don't know. There's a kid in the Fire Starters who struggles. I don't think he likes girls, but he's getting by. Maybe you could ask him. But life is hard. Most of the time we don't get what we want. We each get what we need to become the person we should be."

For a long moment his gaze rested on the road ahead, and he thought over what he'd said and what she'd asked. Something inside him stirred, making him think he should say something more, but what?

His hand went to his chest, and he felt the Saint Joan of Arc medal through his shirt. The moment he'd found it, he'd hoped to give it to her. Maybe that gesture would open a door for her, lead her to the only one who could really help her understand, help her heal . . . somehow lead her to faith. Would she think he was weird if he gave it to her?

The tires hummed along the road, hotels and fast food restaurants sprang up, rain sprinkled the windshield with growing intensity, and windshield wipers swiped a slow beat. Brice navigated through traffic with a cool confidence.

He'd missed the signs that said they'd entered Rapid City. But he guessed they did ten minutes ago.

She finally spoke. "The only Christian in my sister's life didn't talk to her about the one thing that mattered. Not even as she lay dying in the hospital. Did she die in her sin?"

Washed through with a wave of remorse—had he said too much?—he lifted his hands and shrugged. "Gosh, I-I don't know."

"I'm not asking you. I'm just saying." She gave him a little smile, her eyes sad. "Thank you."

"For what?"

She turned down a two-lane road that led out of town. Little houses sat back further from the road, long stretches of grass between them. "For not lying, not holding back because you want to be my friend."

"Wanna be? You mean we're not friends?" He suppressed a grin.

She shook her head, but she smiled too. When she returned her gaze to the road, the lights dimmed, the defogger fan slowed, and trouble flickered on her face.

"What the—" She glared at the dashboard, which glowed much dimmer now, and then cursed. "Battery warning light just came on. You didn't install the new battery?"

"Uh . . ." Peter's stomach slid down to his feet and an uncomfortable prickling sensation spread across his arms. "I meant to get to that. I didn't think it was urgent."

With a groan, she rubbed her forehead. All the lights on the dashboard lit up like a pinball machine, and the engine started chugging. Brice glanced in the rearview mirror and out the side windows. "I thought it turned over too slow when I'd started it." She shifted into neutral.

Peter leaned forward and peered into the night. Any chance they were near a gas station or service garage? Raindrops glowed in the dimmer-than-usual light from the headlights as they zipped to the ground. A field stretched out on the right, a weathered wooden fence on the left. Of course, there was no gas station in sight. They'd passed a few of them not too long ago. "How close are we to your mom's house?"

As the car died and a sickening silence ensued, Brice eased the Durango onto a wide, muddy berm of the road. She shifted into park, shut off the headlights, slouched back, and sighed. "We're not that far. We can walk the rest of the way."

"Think your mom can help us out?"

The wind kicked up and a branch blew across the road with a few fat raindrops.

Brice lifted an eyebrow and gave him a look that he could interpret even in the dark. They wouldn't find help from her mom;

she needed help. "It's not like we can just get a jump. Your battery's dead. Maybe ruined the alternator."

"Nah, it'll be fine. We just need the battery. So, before we head out, let me call a buddy for help."

"Better hurry. The sky's about to open up."

27

CALL FOR HELP

THE DRAW CORD CONTINUED WHIPPING THE WALL with an annoying tap-tap-tap, but the bursts of cool air that came through Roland's bedroom window refreshed him. Inspired him. Leg bouncing, he sat hunched over the saint book and jotted down notes.

Saint Nicholas Pieck. This was the martyr for him. For whatever reason, this one spoke to him.

He was born in Holland. Where is that? West of Germany, right?

While images of windmills and tulips and wooden shoes popped into his mind, Roland glanced up at the world map he'd pinned to the wall next to his desk. He found the Netherlands, not Holland, west of Germany. Maybe it was renamed like Sri Lanka and Cambodia and Iran.

Back to the biography. Nicholas's parents, both strong in their faith, sent him to some famous college in some unpronounceable town. There he received the habit of the Friars Minor. Wait—

Running a finger down the page, Roland skimmed the biography. He was a Franciscan Friar?

He lived about three hundred years before Saint Conrad of Parzham, Roland's favorite saint, who was also a Franciscan.

Nicholas lived during the time of the upheaval of the Protestant Reformation. Passionate about his faith and undaunted by those who opposed it, he spoke out with humility and clarity, combating heresy everywhere. And when the threat came close to home, he exhorted the townspeople to cling to their Catholic faith no matter the cost.

The upheaval and rebellion against the Faith in Holland grew intense. Calvinists sent mercenary sailors called the "Sea Beggars" to ravage the coast. Aware of the threat, Father Nicholas delivered several speeches to his fellow townsmen, warning against the errors of Calvinism.

Then Calvinist pirates took over the town of Gorkum, where Nicholas lived. They rounded up the local Catholic clergy—nineteen priests and brothers—and threw them into a foul dungeon. During the night, the Calvinists vented their rage against them, singling out Father Nicholas for the cruelest treatment. They choked him with his own cord that he wore around his waist and then touched a burning torch to his face, ears, and tongue. Then the marauders forced the priests and brothers to parade through town reciting litanies to make people laugh.

Roland huffed, disgusted.

Once Father Pieck's family learned of the kidnapping, they tried to get him released, but he refused unless the others would be released with him.

The Calvinists said they would release them all if only they would deny their Catholic faith. All nineteen swiftly rejected the offer and instead confirmed their belief in the Real Presence of Christ in the Eucharist and the authority of the Pope. Father Pieck spoke for them all when he said, "I would rather endure death for the honor of God than swerve even a hair's breadth from the Catholic faith."

By this time, the townspeople and local magistrates, even the Calvinist Prince William, had taken the side of the prisoners. Still, their captors wouldn't let them go. By cover of night, they led them to an abandoned monastery and made nineteen nooses. They strung up the nineteen priests and brothers. And left them to hang until dead.

Roland shuddered. Disturbed at some deep level but also impressed by the courage of these men, he slouched back and rubbed his neck.

Why did the people of that generation care what others believed? Why use violence to try to change someone's mind or to silence them? *Why can't people disagree and still respect each other?*

Something nudged his thoughts, trying to move to the front of his mind. Something Caitlyn said? Something about the vandals?

"It might have been someone we don't suspect and for a reason we don't suspect."

Wait . . .

What made the kids who threw the rock into Caitlyn's house think he was her boyfriend? It must've been someone who saw them together at school, maybe the day he'd grabbed her hand to drag her away from Jarret on lunch break. If so, the culprits shared their lunch break. The neighbors wouldn't have known.

Then again . . . if the neighbor's son had seen Caitlyn peeking in their mailbox, he and his friends could've followed and spied on her. When Roland stopped over two days ago, they might've assumed he was her boyfriend. They could've seen him knocking on doors in the neighborhood too. But he hadn't done that alone. Why would the message attached to the rock have been directed only at him?

Tell your boyfriend to stop snooping.

Maybe the person who threw the rock didn't know about all their investigative work. They only knew his part—

Seized with realization, he looked up from his desk. His gaze fell on the window, but his mind took him somewhere else. He knew who the vandals were. But what was their motive? No, it couldn't be them.

The curtain billowed out just then, the draw cord tapping the wall, and his phone rang. A burst of air cooled his face as he lifted his phone to his ear, increasing his excitement to share his theory with Caitlyn.

"Hey, Caitlyn."

"Uh, no. Don't you check your caller ID?" Peter said with snark in his tone.

"Oh." Peter's voice grounded him. But then he picked up background noises, maybe rain tapping on glass.

"Hey, man, I need your help," Peter shouted over the noise.

"What's wrong? Where are you?"

"The battery in the Durango died, and I need you to find a way to get the new battery out to me."

"Out where?"

"Uh . . . just a bit north of Rapid City."

Roland stood and went to the window. Storm clouds hung over the shadowy woods that edged their deep front lawn. Branches swayed and leaves fluttered in the wind. It might've been sprinkling, but he couldn't tell from his window. Then a tiny drop sailed through the screen and landed on his cheek.

"Rapid City is an hour away," Roland said, not sure how he could possibly help Peter no matter where his car had broken down. "What're you doing out there?"

A pause. "Brice needed a ride. So, look, are you gonna try? My dad's out for the night or I'd ask him, and Mom can't leave the B & B for that long."

"Who am I going to ask? My father's out, too, and Keefe's on that retreat."

"Yeah, I know. But what about . . . I almost hate to even say his name."

"You mean Jarret? He's on a date." Roland bristled at the thought of asking Jarret to do a favor for Peter.

"Come on, man, I need your help. He'll do anything for you, lately, it seems."

"All right. I'll figure something out." Roland grabbed his black hiking boots from his walk-in closet and sat on the end of his bed.

"Great. Thanks, man. The battery's on the back workbench. And grab the blue toolbox next to it. And call me if you don't find a way, but I'm countin' on you."

Roland ended the call and shoved his foot into a boot. Would Jarret do this for him? Peter was right: he'd been helping Roland in every possible way ever since Roland broke his leg.

He pulled up Jarret's number and stared at it for a second. Then he called Keefe. The phone rang a few times while Roland tied the laces on his hiking boots. Keefe finally answered the call.

"Hey, Keefe, it's Roland." Roland grabbed his black waterproof jacket from the closet and stepped into the hallway.

"Roland, what's up?" Keefe spoke fast, sounding a bit anxious. The hum in the background said he was still on the road. Shouldn't he have made it to the Franciscans' place by now?

"I need a favor. I need you to talk Jarret into helping me. It's kind of an emergency." He hurried down the stairs.

"I'm in Minnesota. You should probably ask him yourself. You know he'd do anything for you."

Roland explained the situation on his way through the house. Jarret would probably help Roland, but Peter was the last person on earth he would do a favor for. And Keefe had always stood the greatest chance of convincing him to do anything.

"Okay, let me pull over and I'll call him."

"Thanks, Keefe."

Roland stuffed his phone into a pocket and stepped into the dimly-lit garage. Gray light seeped in through narrow windows in the garage door, showing an empty four-car garage. Jarret had gone out in his red Chrysler. Keefe had taken Papa's truck. Papa had the Lexus and even Mr. Digby had gone somewhere.

If Jarret said no, who else could he call? He grabbed his bike from where it hung on the wall and rolled it out the side door of the garage. A cool breeze greeted him, feeling good on his neck and face, despite the humidity in the air. Intensely aware that he hadn't ridden his bike since he'd broken his leg, he mounted it and took off.

Dropping from the paved driveway to the gravel, a jolt of pain shot through his leg but it passed quickly. He tightened his grip on the handlebars and pressed onward. He could do this. It'd be good exercise. Besides, Peter had no one else to help him.

Raindrops sprinkled his face as he rode toward the path that ran parallel to the long gravel driveway. Under the canopy of leaves, the light rainfall could no longer reach him.

If Jarret said no, he'd ask Leo, a kid from school who had given him a ride in the past. He'd have to pay him. But no big deal. He had a few bucks in his wallet.

Halfway to the Brandts' house, Roland's phone rang. He stopped his bike and yanked out his phone.

"Hey, Roland," Keefe said, "I think you ought to call Jarret yourself. He didn't really answer me, and I gotta get back on the road."

"Okay, well, thanks for trying." He'd half-expected Jarret to say no. Heart racing from having pedaled so hard, Roland ended the call and flipped through names in his phone. None of his friends had their license, much less a car.

He stopped on Leo's number. *Might as well try.*

After a resounding "no" from Leo—he'd temporarily lost his driving privilege for reasons he chose not to disclose—Roland pulled up Jarret's number.

He took a few deep breaths and braced himself.

"Hey, Roland." Jarret's low confident voice came over the phone. "Can't talk. I'm on a date right now."

"Yeah, hi, Jarret. I know." He paused to take another breath. "And if I could think of any other way, I wouldn't bother you." Guilt teased him. He didn't want to take advantage of Jarret's recent streak of kindness, but he didn't know what else to do and this was important.

So Roland begged.

And after a few simple exchanges, Jarret actually said, "So what exactly do you need me to do?"

"Really? You'll help?" Roland couldn't believe it.

"I don't know. Tell me what you need."

"I'm on my way to Peter's." Roland glanced up to see if he could see the pink neon B & B sign between leaves. *No, not close enough.* "His car broke down an hour north of here, and he just needs the battery in his garage."

"Wait. Peter has a car? He's not even sixteen."

"Yes, he is. He turned sixteen last month."

"Okay, so I'm supposed to drive you and a battery out to Peter? Then I leave?" Jarret actually seemed to be considering it.

"Yeah, then you can leave." Roland felt a glimmer of hope. "Peter can get his car going, no problem. I'll ride home with him."

Jarret gave no reply, but he must've been thinking about it.

"Okay, well, I'm gonna get going," Roland said. "I'm five minutes from Peter's. I'll wait there for ten minutes, but then I'll ask Peter's aunt if she can do it. Or someone. I'll find someone. I shouldn't have bothered you. I knew you were on a date. Bye."

With a prayer that Jarret would help him and that the rain would hold up for a little longer, Roland pushed forward.

28

DARK WELCOME

PETER PUMPED HIS ARMS AND LEGS, bolting through the dark night alongside Brice, while cold raindrops pelted them. They crossed the road and a stretch of drenched grass, racing out onto another street. Peter glanced to each side, squinting against the rain. A few cars lined the shiny street a bit further down, barely visible, but no headlights, nothing heading their way.

Water seeped into his sneakers as he splashed through puddles too big to jump over. Water in his eyes, dripping off his nose, saturating his senses. The feeling transported him back in time. He was a kid splashing in puddles with little Toby, playing in the rain until their clothes were drenched and their hair stuck to their heads. He could almost hear Toby's laughter ringing in his ears and see his half-moon eyes.

"This way!" Brice peeped at him from under the hood of her olive-green jacket, then she leaped over a four-foot-wide ditch and pushed between two evergreens.

Not breaking his stride, Peter leaped over the ditch too. As he landed, one foot slipped a few inches down the grassy side of the ditch. His hands flew out, helping him regain his balance, but his knee brushed wet grass anyway. Bushes and evergreen trees formed a wall on the other side of the ditch. As he pushed through them, dripping branches sprayed his face.

Brice cut diagonally across an overgrown lawn, heading for the little covered stoop of a dark ranch house. Like, totally dark. Two-foot high weeds grew among ornamental bushes along the house, beneath black windows.

As soon as Brice leaped onto the stoop, she let out a hoot and shook herself, her hood falling back.

Peter thumped up onto the stoop with her and let out his own howl of excitement. Panting hard and exhilarated, he turned back to see what they'd just run through. A gust of wind created sheets of black raindrops that moved across a black backdrop. Raindrops glowed around a street light visible between branches.

"Is this your mom's house?" He hollered to be heard over the drumming of the rain on the aluminum awning overhead. "Place looks abandoned."

Sparing Peter a single glance, shadows hiding her expression, Brice opened the storm door and jiggled the doorknob. Then she pounded on the door with a fist and muttered under her breath before turning to Peter again. "D'ya notice all those cars parked along the street?"

"Huh?" Peter glanced over his shoulder, again seeing only raindrops before a black backdrop, the bushes and trees hiding the view of the road. But he did remember seeing a few cars. "Is that strange?"

She shrugged. "Wait here." She leaped off the stoop and dashed around the corner of the house, her white blond hair looking bluish in the dark, the rest of her invisible.

"Where else am I gonna go?" he said, the rain stealing his voice. Peter shoved his hood back and wiped rain from his face and damp hair off his forehead. His shoes and the legs of his jeans were soaked. What if Roland couldn't get a ride up here with the battery? He'd have to wait for Dad to get home and come rescue him. Who knew how late that would be?

Within a minute, the front door scraped open and Brice—now inside the house—swung the storm door outward. "Okay, we're in." The instant Peter grabbed the storm door, she turned and disappeared in the dark house.

Peter stepped inside and closed both doors, muffling the sound of the rain. He stepped from a gritty tile floor to soft carpet and peered into the darkness around him. Gray light streamed in through windows without drapes, a big one next to him on the front wall and a smaller one on the opposite wall, probably in the dining area.

A yellowish glow suddenly appeared off to the left, toward the back of the little house, outlining both sides of a kitchen island. Then Brice stepped into view with a blazing lighter and a nearly-spent mason jar candle. "There're a ton of old candles in the cupboard over the range. Let's get some light in this place."

"Yeah, sure." Peter shrugged his wet rain jacket off and hung it on the doorknob, shivering as a chill ran down his neck. He flipped the light switch next to the door, to no avail. A hint of light revealed an empty living area and a worn path in the carpet, leading to a hallway off to the right. Should he take off his shoes?

Brice's shoes squeaked as she reached into the overhead cupboard. She pulled down four jars at once. "Some of these should still work." She half-dropped them onto the countertop between the sink and stove, and they clinked together with a sound like wineglasses and Thanksgiving dinner.

Peter reached for the lighter next to the single burning candle.

At the same moment, Brice turned and stuck a hand out for it herself. Her cold fingers brushing his. Her gaze snapping to his.

A thrill shot through him at her touch, but her cold gaze put it in check. Peter lifted his hand, standing down. "I'll get more candles." He stepped to the open cupboard over the range.

She flicked the lighter and set to work, lighting a second candle.

Peter reached in to the dark overhead cupboard, thinking of spiders, and wrapped his fingers around a mason jar. A dark hallway came off between the refrigerator and the range, a creepy shadow in his peripheral vision. "What's down the hall?"

"Basement. Garage. Laundry room." She slammed a mason jar onto the countertop. "I can't believe my mom moved without telling me."

"Yeah, that's a bum deal." Fingers tingling, he brought down two more jars and set them with the others.

Brice lit a sixth candle, pushed a dud to the back of the countertop, and moved four candles to the kitchen island. "After my sister died, she tried easing the pain with drugs."

"Antidepressants?" Peter slid four more jars to her. He'd cleared the first shelf, but the second shelf held more.

"Uh, no." Flickering candlelight reflected on blond hair matted to her forehead and on her face as she gave him a hard look. "Nothing so tame."

"Oh. Sorry."

"Yeah, not a fun time. But that's what she does. She can't handle the pressure." Brice grabbed a candle and stuffed the lighter into a front pocket of her jeans, her gaze turning to the candles flickering on the kitchen island . . . no, rather, she looked toward the dark hallway on the other side of the empty dining area.

Peter grabbed a candle too and followed her.

She shuffled across the carpet, her steps slowing as she neared the hallway. Their candles threw eerie shadows on the walls and animated four half-open doors. Sucking in a breath, Brice pushed open the first door on the left and stuck the candle through the doorway.

Peter came up behind her. A battered blind with bent and missing slats hung in the window. A closet door leaned against a wall. Smudge marks gave away where furniture had once been, the bed, a dresser, possibly a desk. "So, if your mom texted you, where do you think she is? I mean, she's obviously not here. Why would she—"

"It wasn't her. Someone wanted me to think it was her." Brice jerked from the room, making Peter jump back, and she proceeded to the second door on the left. After gazing into the room for a few seconds, she stepped inside.

Half-lowered blinds covered the window in this room too, these ones in better shape. One bi-fold closet door hung at an angle; the other was missing. Brice stood with her head down by a fist-sized hole in the wall, maybe looking at something on the floor.

"Your bedroom?" Peter envisioned furnishings in the room. Nothing frilly. Everything purposeful. But not necessarily neat.

"Yeah." She squatted, set the candle on the beige Berber carpet, and pried something from the baseboard molding. She glanced at it—a folded paper? a photograph?—and stuffed it into a back pocket of her jeans, taking care to avoid touching it to her wet jacket.

Peter watched but decided not to ask. A pain of sympathy stabbed him. He couldn't imagine going home to find his bedroom empty, his house empty, everything that was his . . . gone. Every award, picture, and toy from childhood; every project he'd labored over; every stitch of clothing that he hadn't taken with him on the last day . . . gone.

She straightened and shuffled along the perimeter of the bedroom, looking up and down the walls, maybe visualizing it the way it was before. "I-I have these nightmares." She continued pacing, her gaze unfocused now, reminding Peter of Toby when his mind shifted to a zone he alone could enter.

"These ugly hands latch onto my sister and start lifting her away from me." She sucked in a breath. "I try so hard to hold onto her, but I-I can't stop it from happening. In an instant she's gone, and I feel so . . . yucky inside. I have to try to get her back, so I go look for mom. I want her to help. I'm"—her voice cracks—"desperate for her to help, but I can't find her anywhere. I find strangers and more strangers. But not her."

A look of powerlessness rippling through her expression, she stopped pacing and slammed her palm to the wall. The candle in her other hand nearly flickered out. "Mom's always been like that. She trusts these losers, lets them into the house, with me and my sister here. And then one day, things seem like they might change. She starts seeing this man, says he's a Christian. He's different. She's different. But after my sister dies, Mom pushes him away too." Brice paused, her voice deepening with her next words. "And it's worse than before. That's when the social workers stepped in."

All his personal hopes for a relationship with her settled in a distant part of his mind, and he only wished he could erase her past and write a new one for her. One where she wouldn't have had to suffer or live in fear. One where her mom acted like an adult and she and her sister were cherished and protected. One that wouldn't have led to this pain that haunted her, that plagued her.

Brice turned from the wall and met Peter's gaze. "Not my house anymore." The flame of her candle flickering wildly, she blew from the room. Sparing no glance for the bedroom across the hallway, she strode back to the kitchen.

Peter followed at a distance and stopped in the entrance to the kitchen, his gaze resting on the dark hallway and not Brice. After a stretch of silence, not sure what to say to her but feeling like he had to say something, he said, "So who would've sent you the text? And why? Think they knew you'd come all the way out here?"

"I dunno. Maybe the same people who trashed my foster parents' house." Brice turned her back to the little countertop between the range and the dark hallway and hoisted herself up to sit on it.

"Why? What do they gain from it?"

"People are mean. Do they always need a reason?" The look in her eyes said she may have known more. "I just don't get how they got my number."

"Don't look at me. I don't even have your number."

She smiled.

"Now what?" Peter set his candle on the island counter, next to the others, and he pulled himself up to sit across from her.

"Now we wait for your friend. Are you sure he's coming?"

"Yeah, he'll be here." He'd told Roland to call if he couldn't find a ride. No call yet, so . . . "Don't worry. The rain will slow, then we can change the battery and head back home."

A distant look in her eyes, she nodded and turned her face toward the front door. Muffled rainfall created a soothing white noise. The yellow flames gave a degree of warmth. But nothing could erase the deep pain she must've felt every day.

Peter sighed and gazed at the little blue flame in a candle next to her, expecting it would soon flicker out. He couldn't erase the past, and he couldn't change her today. But he could be her friend, if she'd let him. He didn't need anything more. Didn't need her to be his girlfriend. He just wanted to be there for her.

Something stirred in his soul again, reminding him . . .

"Hey, I want you to have something." Now was the time. He reached into the neckline of his shirt and lifted the chain with the Saint Joan of Arc medal over his head.

29

STORM

DESPITE THE DRIZZLE and the cool air, Roland had worked up a sweat from having ridden his bike hard all the way over to the Brandts' house. Clammy and uncomfortable, he peeled off his black jacket and tugged his t-shirt straight. He'd found the battery and toolbox easily enough. Now he stood under the overhang of the Brandts' detached garage, out of the rain, the toolbox and battery at his feet.

He'd knocked on the Brandts' door to tell them what he was doing. Mrs. Brandt already knew, so Peter must've called her. Then Roland had called Papa. Now all he could do was wait.

Roland glanced at the time on his phone and peered down the road, in the direction Jarret would likely come from.

Would Jarret come? If he didn't, Roland would have to knock on the Brandts' door again. Maybe Peter's aunt would take him. He'd hate to have to ask her. Didn't he know anyone else?

A red car appeared in the distance. Jarret? The car cruised down Forest Road as if the driver had no intention of stopping. Drawing near, it finally slowed—Jarret's cherry-red Chrysler 300.

Roland exhaled. He wouldn't need to find someone else to drive him. Jarret had come to the rescue.

Guilt teased him. Jarret had ended his date early just to help him. Sometimes he still struggled to believe that Jarret had changed. He was really trying. He'd probably do anything Roland asked him to do. And here Roland had called Keefe first, afraid to simply ask Jarret himself. He needed to get over his fear of speaking . . . to ask a favor or before groups or to someone who might not agree with him. All of it.

The Chrysler swung into the Brandts' driveway and jerked to a stop a few feet from the garage. Two blurry figures showed through condensation and raindrops on the windshield: Jarret and his new girlfriend, Chantelle.

Not wasting a second, Roland grabbed the toolbox and battery and rushed to the trunk through a sprinkling of rain. Jarret wouldn't want him to put the battery anywhere else in the car. The trunk popped open and Roland arranged everything neatly beside a shipping box and a plastic shopping bag stuffed with garbage. He slammed the trunk and jumped into the backseat. An intense "new car smell" hit him hard, along with the hint of an underlying sour smell.

"Thanks, Jarret. I really appreciate this."

"Yeah." Jarret sounded like his old self, disgusted with the inconvenience.

"Hi, Chantelle," Roland said to Jarret's girlfriend. "Sorry to ruin your date."

Sitting in the front passenger seat, Chantelle twisted to face him, a lock of blond hair curling up on her shoulder. She flashed a smile, though her eyes remained cold.

Before long, they were on the interstate. Jarret had balked at the route Roland suggested they take, the route Peter had told him to take. It probably didn't matter. As long as they reached their destination. With a nicer attitude, one that seemed forced, Jarret then asked Roland a few questions about Peter's car and his reason for going to Rapid City.

Chantelle only seemed interested in conversation when she realized Peter had gone to Rapid City to do a girl a favor. Then she wanted to know everything. Not wanting to fuel any rumors, Roland had given the briefest answers. But Chantelle wouldn't give up until she got the girl's name. Then she responded with a few condescending comments and a cruel laugh.

Once that conversation ended, Roland watched raindrops out the window and turned to his own thoughts. Peter had wanted him to discover who had vandalized Brice's house, and he just may have figured it out. He still needed to discover the motive. He wouldn't be able to talk to Peter about it tonight, not with Brice around. He'd have to tell Peter later. Then Peter could decide whether to tell Brice. She would probably know the motive better than anyone.

The radio came on and a Christian rock song played, but Jarret switched the channel to classic rock. Then he asked Chantelle what kind of music she liked, and they got into a lengthy conversation about their favorite this and their favorite that.

Roland tried tuning them out, but he still caught bits and pieces, and he couldn't help thinking they didn't have much in common. While Jarret had always been a bit narcissistic, he still had interests and hobbies that involved others. Chantelle was very much into herself and social media.

Sudden movement in his peripheral vision made Roland snap his attention to the front of the car again. Chantelle had whipped her phone out and was trying to show Jarret a picture of something.

Roland glanced and wished he hadn't.

Jarret's head had turned too, but he jerked his attention back to the road and blurted, "I hate looking at pictures."

"But they're pictures of me," Chantelle said flirtatiously, still trying to show him a picture of herself posed seductively in a swimsuit.

Just what he needed to see while he was driving. Just what he needed to see after the type of relationship he'd had with his last girlfriend. Was he headed down the same path? Hadn't he been trying to change? Why would he put himself to the test so soon? Maybe he didn't want people to realize he'd changed because it would threaten his "cool" image. He should at least date girls who held the values he was trying to have.

Chantelle rested a hand on Jarret's shoulder and bit her bottom lip. Then she whispered in his ear.

Jarret glanced at Roland in the rearview mirror. Hoping Roland didn't hear? Wishing he wasn't there? Did he see Roland as a reminder that he should say something to her?

A combination of disappointment and disgust surged inside Roland. Jarret recently told him he'd better find his voice because he might have something to say one day. "And you wanna be able to say it," Jarret had said. And here Jarret couldn't even find his voice when it mattered.

But maybe this was Roland's test. Maybe he needed to say something to help Jarret think about the situation he was putting himself in. Did Roland want to be the kid who kept his opinion to himself when it mattered? No. He was going to be different. Today. Starting now.

"So, Chantelle, do you go to church?" Roland blurted, somewhat amazed that he actually said it.

Jarret glanced up at the rearview mirror and shot Roland a warning look.

"Me?" Chantelle flipped golden curls off her shoulder, backed away from Jarret, and twisted to face Roland. "No. I . . . mean . . . I have. But hardly ever. Why?"

"Are you a Christian?" Roland avoided Jarret's gaze in the mirror. Had Jarret asked her this question already?

"I don't know. I guess so. I mean, I celebrate Christmas. That counts, right?" She giggled and looked at Jarret.

"Hmm." Roland turned back to the window. There. He'd done it. If Jarret hadn't thought about it before, he'd think about it now and—

The engine roared. Jarret gripped the steering wheel as the car accelerated. The rain pounded harder on the windshield, the thumping wipers appearing useless. The windows provided nothing but a blurry view of the road under an occasional orangish street light.

Tensing, Roland reached for something to hold onto. Okay, so Jarret didn't appreciate his comments, but he'd still think about it. Rather than tell Jarret to slow down, Roland turned to prayer. *Please, Lord, don't let us get in an accident.*

A few minutes later, as if in answer to his prayer, a police siren blared and red and blue lights flashed behind them, adding color to the rainwater streaming down the back window.

With a headshake and a groan, Jarret gradually slowed the Chrysler and pulled onto a strip of grass alongside the road.

Roland felt a twinge of guilt as Jarret got a speeding ticket, but he thanked God anyway. An accident would've been far worse.

30

WHO'S THERE?

"WHAT WAS THAT?" Eyes open wide, Brice turned her head toward the dark hallway next to her.

Peter's senses snapped to high alert. He strained to hear something other than the muffled sounds of rain and wind. "What was *what*?"

She hopped off the countertop and stood facing the hallway, her arms tense at her sides. "I don't know. Thought I heard a scraping sound, like from the basement."

"I'm sure it was nothing. Probably rats."

She didn't budge. "Yeah, one of the basement windows was always loose. Something could've gotten in, I guess."

They'd been sitting on the countertops for like an hour, him blabbering on and on about the upcoming camping trip, past camping trips, stupid things he'd done over the years—anything to make her smile or laugh. And she'd rewarded him with a few smiles and laughs, and a few wild stories of her own. He'd even told her Saint Joan of Arc's story. She'd listened, her expression a mix of disbelief and admiration, but at the end of the story she'd put the chain on over her head and tucked the medal inside her shirt. Neither of them said another word about it.

And now, as much as he wouldn't mind sitting on countertops and talking all night, he scooted to the floor and came up beside her. He was always up for an adventure. "Wanna check it out? Too bad you don't have any flashlights lying around your old house. These candles don't give off much light."

"*You* can go down there." Her eyes twinkled. "I'll go see if the noise came from the garage."

"Yeah, maybe Roland's here." Having no intention of checking the dark basement alone, he strode to the big window in the living room. The rain had lessened but clouds still covered the sky, hiding the moon and the stars.

The door to the garage squeaked and scraped open, and then more noise . . . from the basement? Then his ringtone sounded "The Imperial March" from Star Wars.

Yes! He pumped his fist. Roland must've made it.

Peter grabbed his phone, checking the caller ID as he swung it to his ear. "Hey, man, tell me you're here."

"Yeah, we're by your car. Where are you?" The rain drumming in the background competed with Roland's low voice over the phone.

"You gotta turn up the next street." Peering out the window, he gestured with his arm as he spoke as if Roland could see him. "It kind of angles back and you'll go over a big ditch then we're in the first house you come to. It's kind of hidden behind trees and stuff, and it's dark, so don't look for a light. Just look for the dirt driveway. And there are some cars parked on the street but none directly in front of her house."

"Okay, we'll find it. See you in a minute."

As Peter shoved his phone back into his pocket, Brice came up beside him. She snatched his rain jacket from the front doorknob and tossed it to him. Then she yanked open the door.

"Find anything in the garage?" Peter set his damp jacket on a kitchen counter and came back to Brice's side.

"Naw, it's empty."

A minute later, headlights sliced through the dark as a car swung into the driveway.

Peter smiled to himself, glad that Roland came through.

The car drew near—Jarret's red Chrysler 300—crawling up the driveway, toward the attached garage. The car jerked to a stop, but no doors opened. Then the engine revved and the car turned, racing into the front yard.

Not expecting it, Peter laughed. "Man, he just totally turfed your yard."

Brice shrugged. "Not my yard."

The car stopped near the front stoop, but Roland still didn't get out. Maybe he was gathering his things.

"Think I should go out there?"

"Why?"

"Maybe he needs help—"

A back door flew open and Roland jumped out, hood up. He stood in the rain for a second, leaning into the car, probably talking to Jarret, who had twisted around in his seat. Then he slammed the car door and raced to the trunk.

Two seconds later, he slammed the trunk and jogged to the front door.

Peter opened the storm door to Roland's pale face peering out from under the hood of his jacket. "Way to come through, man. Come on in." He waved at Jarret, wanting to thank him, but Jarret turned away. He still couldn't believe Jarret had done a favor for him.

"Let me take that." Peter grabbed the toolbox and Brice grabbed the battery, leaving Roland empty handed and looking a bit awkward. "You two arguing all the way here?" Peter said with a grin.

Roland's mouth cracked open and his eyes narrowed with a look that said he didn't appreciate the comment. He glanced over his shoulder. "I'll be right back." Then he dashed back outside, and Jarret lowered his window.

"So now we just need to wait for the rain to let up." Brice set the battery on a countertop and hopped back up.

Roland dashed into the house, pushed his hood back, and took a breath, the kind a person takes when relieved to have gotten through something. Must've been the car ride with Jarret.

"Sorry, no lights." Peter closed the door and motioned for Roland to follow him to the kitchen glowing in candlelight. "And no snacks. Nothing to drink. But we've got candles."

"So why are you guys out here?" Roland followed him across the carpeted space, taking measured steps as if his eyes hadn't adjusted or maybe his leg hurt.

"Eh, we think we were pranked." Peter set the toolbox next to the battery and pulled himself up to his spot on the countertop, directly across from Brice, who sat hunched and chewed a fingernail.

"*We* weren't pranked." Brice looked up. "I was pranked. You act like we're a couple."

Peter smiled, loving her attitude. "No, I don't. But I am here with you, so I'm a victim of this prank too."

"I'm no victim," Brice said.

No longer seeming to pay attention to Brice and Peter, Roland faced the black window over the sink. The rain kicked up and pelted it with vengeance.

Roland shivered, rubbed his arms, and looked around as if studying everything, but maybe he had something on his mind.

"Are you just gonna stand around in the dark?" Peter said. "Why don't you pull up a counter?"

Roland leaned against a cabinet instead and stuffed his hands in the front pockets of his faded jeans. "I need to talk to you." He glanced at Brice, who was still worrying a fingernail. "Privately."

"What about?"

Before Roland could answer, a door behind Brice creaked open and footsteps pounded on the basement stairs.

Peter and Brice jumped off the countertops simultaneously, Brice cursing, Peter's heart bouncing out of his chest.

Kids with flashlights and flickering candles paraded into the living room, chanting, "Brice, Brice, Brice . . ." Smelling of the outdoors, they wore rain-soaked jackets and some had dripping hair, as if they'd just come in from the rain. How had they gotten into the basement? Brice did say something about a loose window. Maybe they crawled in through that. Maybe she'd come in that way too.

More and more kids stomped onto the scene, their heavy footfalls making the house shake. Must've been more than twenty of them. Most of them went to River Run High. Peter even knew a few of their names.

Everything about Brice tensed, from her posture and hands curling into fists to her face and neck, everything as tight as the string on a drawn bow. She pushed past Peter, shoved aside the nearest chanting kids, and stomped into the midst of them in the living room. She zeroed in on a girl in a black hoodie.

"These are the Empowerment kids." Roland spoke over Peter's shoulder. "That's Tessia. And I've got to tell you something."

Peter turned to Roland with half-formed questions in his mind. Before his brain could wrap around one, Brice shouted, "What's this about?" in a heated tone.

"Uh oh." Peter took off, sneakers squeaking on the kitchen floor, and dodged around a few kids until he stood where he could see Brice.

The kids formed a circle around Brice and Tessia. Some shined flashlights upward on their faces, making their chins glow and creepy shadows dance around their eyes. Others held glass candles with twisting flames that made tall humanoid shadows dance around the room. Rain pelted the window on the back wall, adding tension to the moment.

"We need to talk." Tessia motioned for everyone to stop chanting and she edged closer to Brice. While her tone held a hint of gentleness, her rigid body and the tilt of her chin showed something more aggressive. She stopped a few inches from Brice.

"You got me all the way out here on a night like this to talk?"

"You won't talk to me at school, and you don't answer my calls or texts."

"That's because we *don't* need to talk." As she spit out the word "don't" she sliced the air with her hands and moved even closer, forcing Tessia to step back.

Tessia raised her hands, looking ready to grab Brice's arms, if need be, to restrain her. "Yes, we do."

"Well, I don't want to talk to you." Brice planted her feet, one forward and the other back, like a boxer ready to throw a punch. Tension radiated from her to everyone in the room.

"You need to hear me out." Tessia did it; she touched Brice, gripping her upper arms.

Without hesitation, Brice swung her elbows out and twisted her body, breaking Tessia's grip.

Peter's heart skipped a beat and he jumped, certain that Brice's next move would cause someone physical pain. Should he try to stop her? Why didn't Tessia's entourage try to break it up? Everyone could see where this was headed.

Rather than attack, Brice stepped back and glanced at a few other faces. "So, you brought all them?"

Peter breathed again, glad she hadn't swung. But the negative charge hadn't dissipated either.

"These are your people." Tessia's expression and tone softened. "They understand you. They're on your side."

Not understanding the situation in the slightest, Peter looked at Roland.

Roland stood outside the ring of kids, in the shadows. He nodded as if he *did* understand. Was that what he wanted to tell Peter? Something about them?

"My side of what? I don't have a side." Leaning forward aggressively, Brice shoved her hands in her back pockets, maybe to keep from doing violence with them. "I just want to be left alone."

"You're trying to hide who you are, and you don't have to do that." Tessia's smile faltered.

Brice huffed, her lip curling up. Her body moved, twisting slowly from side to side. She was a ticking timebomb. "I'm not trying to hide anything. You don't know what I'm going through, so leave me alone." One hand escaped her back pocket and landed on Tessia's shoulder, shoving her back a foot.

Tessia's face contorted, transforming from concern to wild eyes and an open mouth. Then her gaze dropped to the floor, and she stooped for something. "See?" She straightened with a photograph in her hand, probably the same one Brice found in her bedroom. "This is who you are." She held it up for Brice to see.

Peter stole a glance. Four girls stood arm in arm. One was Brice and the other Tessia, but he didn't recognize the two girls between them.

Brice snatched the photo from Tessia and stuffed it back into her pocket. She shook her head. "Just leave me alone."

"I'm not leaving you alone. You need us. We're your friends. *They* aren't your friends." She swung a hand out, indicating Peter and Roland.

"Yeah, right." Peter bit his tongue to keep from saying more. He'd only make things worse. But he couldn't keep from shifting his weight from side to side and glaring. He *was* her friend and he'd do anything for her.

"You know they're Fire Starters," Tessia continued, one eyebrow climbing her forehead with a cocky expression. "They belong to the most close-minded, judgmental group there is. If they're acting friendly now, it's because they think they can change you."

Outrage ripped through Peter, so he had to bite his tongue harder to keep from saying something. Brice could handle this. She knew the truth. He didn't need to explain himself to her. Who cared what the rest of them thought?

Brice shook her head slowly, the way Roland's brother Jarret did when two seconds from exploding into a fury of rage.

"You don't think so? Do they know you? The real you?" Tessia turned one hand palm up. "Because if they did, they'd condemn you. You saw the words on your garage, what they did to your yard, and that tree—"

"Okay, now I understand." The low voice came from outside the group, from where Roland stood. Roland?

While most kids remained focused on Brice and Tessia, Peter and a few Empowerment kids turned to Roland.

"What?" Peter mouthed.

"I got it," Roland said, and Tessia's litany of hate stopped. "I know who did it. And I know why."

31

STANDING UP

THE MOMENT THE EMPOWERMENT KIDS EMERGED from the basement and stomped through the house with a noise like thunder, Roland's resolve to speak to Peter and reveal the truth he'd discovered had hightailed it out of here. And when Tessia had started trash-talking the Fire Starters to a group that seemed to agree, he'd felt like the apostle Saint Peter warming his hands by the fire, hoping no one recognized him as a follower of Jesus.

But he'd also figured things out. Tessia's false accusation made it all clear to him. "Okay, now I understand."

Marshall, who stood two feet away, turned and gave a little headshake. He looked Roland up and down as if shocked that he'd dared to speak.

The heat from the imaginary fire he stood warming himself by intensified. He hadn't meant to say it aloud. He sure didn't want to explain it to anyone. Why should he? Tessia didn't have to agree with him on anything. She didn't have to like what the Fire Starters believed. She had her own version of truth.

Flames from the imaginary fire flickered and snapped. He could almost hear Pilate saying, "What is truth?" while he gazed upon Truth in the flesh.

Peter turned toward Roland too. "What?" he mouthed from a distance. He stood just inside the circle of kids, while Roland stood outside.

Tessia continued insulting the Fire Starters. Brice stood glowering at her. Was she buying it?

Nothing, he almost said . . . like Saint Peter denying Jesus, like Pilate doubting Him, like the disciples who walked away because the teaching was too hard to accept. But no . . . he didn't want to be them.

"I understand now," Roland said, loud enough for everyone to hear. A tingling sensation ran down the back of his neck. Okay, if he had to explain it to everyone, he would. "I know who did it, and I know why."

With scrunched eyes and confusion on his face, Peter shook his head. Shadows and candlelight gave him a humorous look, distorting his features. "What are you talking about?" he mouthed to Roland. The Empowerment kid next to Peter glanced, but then Tessia said something rude to Brice, and the kid turned back to them.

Marshall even turned away.

"You don't know me. You don't know what I want." Brice inhaled a deep breath, her nostrils flaring—air compressing before combustion. Then she became a bolt of lightning or an arrow loosed, lunging forward, striking Tessia with her shoulder, ramming her back.

Roland tensed, tempted to step in and break it up. But they'd stop soon, right? And they weren't his friends. Tessia's friends had the greater responsibility to break this up.

Tessia grappled to push Brice away. One hand to Brice's face, the other to her arm, Tessia gained a bit of distance.

But Brice wasn't having it. Like a bull ready to charge, she leaned toward her opponent. And Tessia leaned toward her. A split-second later, they crashed together in a violent hug. They shuffled around the room, their arms snapping to new positions to get the upper hand. Twisting, grunting, stumbling, they dropped to the floor.

A sick this-can't-be-happening feeling overcoming him, Roland found himself rocking toward and away from them. Someone needed to do something. Someone needed to stop this.

The kids formed a tighter circle, drawing together as they watched the fight, backing up when the fighters got too close. Whispers and even chuckles rose up here and there as Tessia struggled to pin Brice to the floor. Didn't anyone care? Wasn't someone going to stop them?

Movement in the circle of kids, over where Peter stood, made Roland look. Fists clenched, Peter curled his arms and gritted his teeth. His gaze connected with Roland's, and an unspoken communication passed between them.

Shirking off the desire to have someone else step up, Roland pushed Marshall aside and rushed toward the fighters, racing with Peter. Eyes on Tessia, the wrestler on top, he slammed his good knee to the floor and snaked his arms under hers and around her shoulders.

Tessia struggled against him.

Roland heaved, using his body weight to yank her off Brice.

As if connected by a rubber band, Brice lunged toward her, stopping only as Peter's arms wrapped around her waist from behind.

Half-sitting now, Roland dragged Tessia back another foot.

"Get off me," Tessia spit over her shoulder, her fingernails digging into Roland's arms. "Let me go."

"No more fighting," Roland said, his mouth close to her ear. He'd never restrained a girl before, and the sooner he could let go, the better.

"Fine." She dug her fingernails deeper into his wrists, but her posture relaxed.

Fairly certain she wouldn't jump back into action, Roland slid his arms out from under hers and scooted back another few inches. The impression of her fingernails on his arms remained. His heart thumped hard and his leg hurt a bit, but he didn't think he'd twisted it. Suddenly aware that several kids stared at him, he wished he had something to grab onto to get back up.

Peter and Brice stood up together, him holding her upper arm. She jerked her arm free of his grip and leaned against the wall, panting.

Shifting to a better position, Roland planted a hand and prepared to pivot onto his good leg and somehow get to his feet. Then a hand appeared in front of his face.

Marshall stood before him, head tilted to one side, reaching down to help him.

Roland hesitated then he took the offered hand and let Marshall yank him up. "Thanks."

"Any time. And I mean that." He gave a squirrelly grin.

"It's time for you to go," Brice growled to Tessia.

"No."

Weariness washing over him, Roland glanced at the dark ceiling where shadows and candlelight fluctuated in strange patterns. A burst of rain pelted the back window. A waxy, smoky odor wafted through the air, carrying a hint of something stale. Hadn't they had enough?

His conscience told him now was the time, but resistance kicked in. He'd have to say things they wouldn't want to hear. Pictures from the saint book came alive in his mind. Saint Alban . . . he only had to drop a little incense to a false god and he wouldn't have been scourged and beheaded. Saint Paul of Cyprus . . . he refused to desecrate a crucifix and was burned alive. Saint Joan of Arc, steadfastly faithful to the will of God despite her young age . . . every apostle except for Saint John, who lived a long life. Groups of saints. Old saints. Young saints. Every one of them willing to die for their faith, to speak for the truth despite the difficulty.

Images of saints flashed through his mind and then stopped on Nicholas Pieck.

And a noose was thrown over the rafters inside a barn. "I would rather endure death for the honor of God than swerve even a hair's breadth from the Catholic faith."

He wore the brown Franciscan habit, the clothing of a mendicant friar.

The crowd jeered. The noose was lowered into place.

Eyes on the noose, Nicholas opened his arms and welcomed death.

In a sudden rush of thoughts, Roland's perspective switched to Nicholas' perspective. He saw what the saint saw. His eyes weren't on the noose. They were on Our Lord. He saw Jesus scourged and bloody, hands tied and head crowned with thorns. "Behold the Man." Love for Christ made him welcome the sacrifice.

Roland snapped back to the present. Tessia and two others huddled around Brice, speaking to her, trying to convince her to join them and embrace her differences. Everyone else watched.

"Listen!" Courage shot through Roland's veins. He turned and scanned faces, making eye contact with anyone who looked at him. "I've got something to say."

Tessia shot Roland a scowl. "You can stay out of it. You have no say."

Roland strode to the middle of the room, intensely aware that everyone watched him. A voice in his head told him to be quiet and return to a shadow, but a louder voice said he had to speak. "Yeah, I know. My opinion doesn't matter 'cuz I'm one of the privileged. I'm straight, white, male, and a Christian."

Marshall's shoulders slumped, and he flung his hands up with a look of defeat.

"And you're rich." Tessia propped her hands on her hips and tilted her head. "So, really . . . just shut up. This is between us and Brice. You can go home."

"I'm not ready to go home yet." One hand at his side, Roland propped the other on his hip and shifted the weight off his sore leg. "You were trashing my religion, so I've gotta say something. But before I do, leave Brice alone." He made a sweeping gaze, wanting to make eye contact with as many kids as possible, finding their eyes cold. "All of you. Why are you trying to make her do something she doesn't want to do? I mean, Empowerment is all about respecting people regardless of differences and beliefs, right?"

"You show up at two meetings . . ." Hands still on her hips, eyes dark and challenging, Tessia moved toward him. "You don't know what we're about. Some people have a hard time accepting who they really are. They need extra help. And that's where Brice is."

"That is not where I am." Brice spit out a bad name and jerked toward Tessia, but Peter grabbed her from behind again.

"Secondly," Roland continued, "leave my faith alone. Leave my Church alone."

Mumbling went around the room. Tessia huffed. "Yeah, a church with all male leaders, half of them corrupt hypocrites, the other half cowards."

The scandals he'd heard in the news made him angry too, but he wasn't about to deny his faith or leave the Church because of it. "Listen, people sin and fall short—even priests and leaders—but it doesn't mean the Church is wrong. It doesn't change the truth that's been passed down from Jesus. It just means we're all sinners, in need of a savior."

"Right," she said, her tone incredulous. "Guys like you, you're the problem. You're the reason some people feel bad about themselves. You think you're right about everything and everyone else is wrong."

"That's not true. But I believe some things are wrong. You want me to change my beliefs or at least hide them. I can't do that."

"People like you need to change your beliefs." She raised her voice. "They're wrong."

"Says who?"

"Says everyone that your belief system judges. That's who. Why do you think it's okay to tell other people how they should live?"

"I don't tell anyone how to live their life. I told you what I believe. You didn't agree so you shut me down."

"Preach it, Roland." Peter let out a laugh and pumped a fist in the air, garnering a few ugly looks.

Encouraged by Peter's support, though he was likely the only person in the house who did support him, Roland went on. "You don't like it, but the Catholic Church has been teaching the same thing for 2,000 years, and it's not going to change for you. Every generation is entitled to the full truth. And it's the Church's job to bring it to them, not to change the truth to make every generation happy."

Tessia groaned dramatically. "Everything changes. Times change. People change. Your Church needs to change too. It's outdated."

Roland shook his head, feeling an inner strength he'd never felt before. "People change and times change. But God does not change. The truth doesn't change."

Everyone fell silent. Even the rain seemed to stop.

Since they all stared at him, and some didn't appear entirely hostile, he continued. "So your group, Empowerment, you want to build a more tolerant culture that doesn't leave anyone out. I like that. I'm all for that. But you threw me out of Empowerment because you don't agree with my beliefs. Does everyone have to agree?"

More silence.

"I don't have to agree with everything you believe to treat you with respect"—he shifted his gaze to Marshall—"or to be your friend."

Marshall blinked rapidly. Then he dipped his head and smiled as if Roland had been flirting.

"People who respect diversity should also respect diversity in thought and ideas. No one should be afraid to speak their mind."

"But you judge people." Tessia's tone softened.

"No, I don't. But I do judge actions. If you're going to listen to your conscience, you have to. That's different from judging a person."

"No, it's people like you with your stereotypes and biases that—"

Roland stepped into her space. "Don't even go there. I know what you did." Now, he had to do it. He had to accuse them all. He turned away from her for a second to convict Marshall with a glance too. "You want people to believe that we're like the KKK or something. You want to create the appearance of hostility where it doesn't exist. You wanted Brice to think she needs you and that no one with the Fire Starters could possibly be her friend."

"Wait, what are you talking about?" Brice took two long strides toward Roland.

"But it's not true." Having one more thing to say before answering her question, Roland turned in a slow circle and made eye contact with everyone who looked at him. "You are all welcome with us, even if you don't believe what we believe. Even if you do things we don't agree with." Turning full circle, he locked gazes with Tessia now, ignoring the hate on her face. "But don't expect us to keep quiet about it. Because it doesn't do anyone any good to hide the truth."

Brice grabbed Roland by the neckline of his shirt.

Startled by her aggressive touch, he lost his voice and his mouth fell open.

"What are you talking about? What did they do?" The look in her eyes said she realized it now too, but she needed to hear him say it.

"No one vandalized your house because they don't like you." He lifted a hand to indicate the kids all around them. "*They* vandalized your house. They burned the tree. They wrote those words on the garage."

"What?" said a few different kids, shock in their half-whispered voices. Kids glanced at each other, then almost everyone turned toward Tessia.

Roland squirmed. Okay, maybe he was wrong, and it wasn't the entire Empowerment group.

Brice stared for two full seconds, her gaze shifting between his eyes, the gears in her mind putting it all together. Then she released his shirt and turned to Tessia. "You . . . did that?"

Stepping backwards, Tessia shook her head. "I-I don't know how to reach you, Brice. We were all so close before . . . before your sister died."

"So, you burned a tree in my yard?"

Gasps went around the room. And grumbled comments of disapproval, one of which Roland made out. "Wow, that's low."

"You needed to know the discrimination that exists," Tessia said. "People can be mean to someone who's different."

"Right. And these guys came out to my house to fix everything. None of you lifted a finger to do anything." She shot a few angry looks around the room. "In fact, you're the ones trying to label me, make me think everyone's against me, that somehow I'm a victim. I am not a victim." She turned to Peter. "Come on. Rain's stopped. Let's go change that battery."

Peter and Brice strode to the kitchen. The group broke up, several kids moving to comfort Tessia, others moving to the front window or to a friend.

Marshall approached Roland, who still stood in the middle of the room. "I respect what you said, Roland."

"Thanks."

"And I want you to know"—he dipped his head and peered up at Roland, shadows and candlelight distorting his features—"I didn't agree with what Tessia did."

Having just found his own voice, Roland sympathized but couldn't leave it at that. "You still went along with it. It was your gas can. Sometimes you have to speak up."

"I did speak up." He lifted his hands, palms up and shifted his weight rhythmically. "That's why we came up here. But even that night, I mean, I told her I didn't want any part of it and it was a bad idea. But I couldn't stop them. Then the next day, at school, I told her she needed to tell on herself, at least tell Brice and try to clean up the mess, make things right. Of course, she wouldn't, and she threatened to blame me if I told on her. I still kept trying and she finally agreed to tell Brice."

Marshall bobbed his head from side to side. "That's what this was supposed to be, but apparently Tessia changed her mind again. I don't think she would've told Brice if you hadn't . . . well, I guess it's good that you figured it out. It's all out in the open now. Better that way."

"Yeah. Sorry I judged you. I guess I figured everyone with Empowerment was in on it, but I shouldn't have jumped to that conclusion."

"I forgive you." Marshall batted his eyes.

A smile came to Roland's face. He admired Marshall's courage in standing up to Tessia. But a few loose ends bugged him. "So, hey, were Tessia and her cohorts responsible for the fish in that girl's locker and those 'outcast beware' posters?"

Marshall shook his head, his lips twisting to one side. "No way, but I think I know who did."

"Who?"

"You know Gavin Wheeler in our speech class?"

Roland nodded, not surprised.

"I saw him and one of his buddies making the signs in the bathroom. He ducked into a stall, laughing, when I came in."

"Oh, figures. So what about the rock through Caitlyn's window?"

Marshall pursed his lips then he glanced at the ceiling and sucked in a breath. "Yeah, sorry. That was Tessia's idea too. I accidentally let it slip that you found the gas can and she . . . didn't like that you were snooping around."

With a breath to push back his irritation, Roland gave him a stern look. "You guys could've hurt somebody. Caitlyn has little sisters and brothers, one's just a baby."

"Oh, crapola." His hand shot to his forehead, guilt and a hint of fear in his eyes, like maybe he regretted having admitted it. "I-I didn't want her to do it but she . . . did anyone get hurt?"

"No. But still."

"Yeah, you're right." He lifted his hands. "Never again. I'm taking what you said tonight to heart, Roland. I'm not going along with things anymore."

Letting every trace of anger pass, Roland smiled. Whether Marshall kept that promise or not, it was a start.

Marshall started to walk away. "Hey, I saw your ride drop you off and leave. Do you need a ride home?"

"Are you offering?" Roland couldn't believe it. Even after all he said, Marshall had no hard feelings.

"Yeah. I mean, I didn't drive but you can ride with us." He pointed to a tall boy who stood a few feet away from him. The boy nodded, his expression showing he also respected Roland.

"Thanks." Roland pointed to Peter. "I'll make sure Peter gets his car running, head back with him, but I appreciate the offer."

Marshall smiled and walked off with the tall boy, toward a group near the kitchen island.

The front door creaked open and the chatter lessened.

"Hey," Tessia shouted and everyone silenced and turned to look.

With battery in one hand, Brice stood by the open front door, Peter—with the toolbox—behind her. The calm outside indicated that the rain had stopped or at least lessened to a sprinkle.

Tessia stepped away from her circle of friends. "We'll stick around until you get Peter's car running. Just in case."

Her hard expression fading, Brice nodded then stepped outside.

Shifting the toolbox to his other hand, Peter gestured to Roland, indicating that he was going with her.

Roland nodded.

While the group by Tessia still carried on with a bit of emotion, the tension had gone. And no one paid any attention to Roland now.

He took a deep breath and exhaled, feeling at peace with himself. Happy to be unnoticed, but more than happy that he'd spoken up.

32

MARTYRS

RELISHING THE MOMENT, Peter inhaled a deep breath of cool campfire-scented air and gazed for a moment at the cloudless sky. The twilight had brought a few stars with it. Gaze traveling downward, he appreciated the treetops that remained motionless on this windless evening. They'd prayed for good weather, and God had delivered. It was perfect weather for camping and for the bonfire.

A firefly looped through the air, catching the attention of one of Caitlyn's little sisters, who jumped up and chased after it. She stumbled on another child who sat with his parents on a blanket behind Caitlyn's family. Groups of kids and families, sitting on blankets and lawn chairs, filled the sloped grassy area on Bonfire Hill. Most of them looked at Peter, waiting with expectation for his presentation. And the lighting of the bonfire. Always Peter's favorite part of the whole camping trip.

Peter stood before the towering pyramid that he and Dad had built for the bonfire. It looked a lot different than the one they'd built last year. Not necessarily bigger but better, more structured.

With a nod of his head, Peter signaled to Dominic. The spotlight in the grass before him popped on, a bright ball of light blinding Peter for a second. Dramatized angry voices and jeering came over the sound system, followed by the sound of a chariot and horse hooves on a stone road. The sounds faded.

Wanting the timing to be just right, Peter waited a second. Then he lifted the cordless microphone to his mouth and said, "So a rabbi, a priest, and a minister walk into a bar."

Laughter spread through the crowd. He was supposed to be giving a presentation about a martyr, so they weren't expecting that.

The group's reaction encouraging him, Peter continued, "The bartender looks up and says, 'What is this, a joke?'"

More laughter. A few groans and lighthearted comments. "You're supposed to talk about a saint," one girl shouted.

"Okay, okay." Peter held up a hand. "Lame joke, but we always picture the saints with these serious expressions, their eyes raised to heaven and their hands folded in prayer. And I'm sure they all prayed, but that doesn't mean there weren't a few saints that could make you laugh. Joy is a gift from God, right?"

A few people responded in agreement.

Peter continued, "Blessed Pier Giorgio Frassati was always playing practical jokes on his friends and family. And Saint Thomas More once said he believed the truth could be told laughing. So, I'm gonna tell you about a saint with a sense of humor: Saint Lawrence."

The sounds of early Rome, shouts and clomping horse hooves, came through the sound system again, increasing in volume just the way Peter had told Dominic to do it.

"Lawrence lived in Rome in dark times some two hundred years after Jesus died. Hostility against Christians was growing. And these early Christians, they expected suffering. The message of Christ dying on the cross spoke so loudly to them that they considered it the highest honor to accept martyrdom. And the Roman emperors were happy to oblige."

Peter pulled a lighter from his pocket and lit a little wad of kindling in a niche he'd built at shoulder level in the side of the pyramid. The flame lapped up the kindling and snapped toward the wood above and on one side of it. A single glowing flame in the dwindling light. *Perfect.*

"The Romans didn't understand these Christians. Rumor had it they took part in secret love feasts where they ate flesh and blood like cannibals. Mostly the Romans didn't get why Christians refused to sacrifice to their Roman gods. I mean, what an insult. Everyone in Rome prayed to them. There were so many, you could take your pick. And these gods and been with them for ages, you know. Ever since they created them, that is. Anyway, show some respect."

A few kids booed. Others chuckled.

"These were the times Lawrence grew up in. Shortly after the pope had been arrested, Lawrence knew his turn was about to come. He also knew that Rome was greedy. As a deacon, he was responsible for the material goods of the church and for distributing alms to the poor, so before they came for him, he sold all the sacred vessels and gave all the money to the poor, the widows, and the orphans of Rome.

"When the prefect of Rome heard rumors of gold chalices and candlesticks and silver cups, he told Lawrence to bring him the treasures of the Church—for the emperor, of course, not for himself—and if Lawrence would do this, he could live.

"Lawrence said, 'The Church is indeed rich!' and he asked for a bit of time to get everything in order." Peter moved the microphone closer to his mouth for effect and he quirked a brow. "Time to implement his plan. And over the next three days, he gathered the blind and lame, the maimed and leprous, the orphans and all the widows, and he presented them to the prefect, saying, 'These are the treasures of the Church.'"

Peter grinned with admiration for Saint Lawrence's courage. "Can you believe he did that? Well, that only ticked the prefect off, and in anger he told Lawrence he would indeed have his wish: he was going to die a martyr's death. And he prepared a big grill with nice, hot coals beneath it and placed Lawrence on top. Flames leaped up, charring his skin, roasting him like a chicken." Peter paused for effect.

"But he was no chicken. He was brave." Peter turned to the flame in the niche. It had tripled in size, looking like a fiery hand clawing its way out of the pyramid. While facing the flame he said dramatically, "The light shines in the darkness, and the darkness has not overcome it."

Then he turned back to his audience, but because he'd just looked at the flame, he could only see shadowy figures.

"We all want acceptance," Peter said, speaking low and close to the microphone. "No one wants to stand apart, to be looked upon as different, misunderstood, labeled, judged . . . condemned."

The audience came back into view, Peter's gaze falling on Roland, who sat between two empty camp chairs. Roland had taught him a thing or two last night at the house Brice used to call home. Brice had also taught him a thing or two.

"If you believe strongly in something, it shouldn't matter what others think, what they say, what they do." He paused. "What they do to you."

Roland lowered his head, as if Peter's words touched him.

For some reason that choked Peter up, so he had to really concentrate to say the next line. "Your faith is in something bigger than you, some*one* bigger than all of us and everything. And if you deny Him for your reputation or to stay out of the spotlight or to be liked and accepted by the world, you might gain the world, but you'll lose yourself in the process."

He scanned the crowd, wanting everyone to take his message to heart. In addition to the Fire Starters and their families, other kids from school had come, including several from Empowerment and . .
.

Peter blinked and did a double take. A kid with hair so light it stood out in the dim light. Brice? She was here!

Roland looked up and cleared his throat, snapping Peter's attention back to his business.

Gripping the microphone and dropping his gaze, Peter continued. "You can't just go along with things when they're wrong . . . or you . . . you become what they want you to be and not who you really are. Better to live ready to die for the truth than to live dead to the truth and to who you really are." He found Brice again in the crowd. "Or who you're called to be."

He paused again, still staring in Brice's direction, though he couldn't tell if she saw him.

"Saint Lawrence was no coward. Persecution and torture did not dim his faith. And it didn't even crush his sense of humor. After a while of burning on one side, flames searing his flesh, he said to his torturers, 'I'm done on that side. Why don't you turn me over?'"

Gentle laughter spread through the crowd.

Peter smiled, satisfied with his presentation and the effect it had on everyone. "So, let your light shine. Let the flame of truth and love burn within you and set the world on fire." With his last word, he stepped away from the pyramid and signaled to Dad.

Flames burst forth from the top of the pyramid, just the way he'd rigged it to do. People gasped and exclaimed, and applause filled the air. The bonfire would burn from the top level down, lasting well into the night. This would be the best one yet.

A feeling of contentment settling inside him, Peter handed the microphone to Dominic, who was handling lights, sound, and props, and he sat in a camp chair beside Roland.

"Nice job." Roland bumped Peter's fist.

"Thanks. You're last, right?"

Roland sucked in a breath and nodded with a look of dread.

"Eh, you'll do fine. Especially after last night. This is a less hostile audience."

"Think so?"

Peter shrugged, "Eh, don't judge them."

The expression of dread faded a bit, but Roland didn't look entirely convinced.

"If I've learned anything lately," Peter said, "it's don't judge someone because you really don't know what they got going on."

Roland faced Peter again. "Yeah, but you can judge actions."

"Well, yeah," Peter said with a nod. "You gotta do that."

Two kids from the Empowerment group ran by, one chasing the other, both laughing. Dominic spoke into the microphone, introducing the next presenter.

"So you convinced Brice to go camping, huh?" Roland said.

Peter turned to where she had been standing, but she was no longer there. "I didn't think she was coming, but I did see her a few minutes ago. I hope she stays. I wonder if she needs a tent." That was another thing he'd come to realize. He could offer her his friendship and pray for her, but—as much as he wished she'd be his girlfriend—he couldn't change her. He had to leave that to God. "What do you think she thought of my presentation?"

Roland made no reply. His gaze had drifted to—

Oh, Caitlyn just stepped onto the "stage" area in costume, ready to give her presentation. The stage was set apart with a line of luminaries—candles in white paper bags. Sheets hung behind the stage. Caitlyn and Kiara had painted trees, windows, columns, and plants on the sheets, trying to give the impression of a cloister garden. It made a nice backdrop and hid the dressing area and props. She'd been practicing her skit all week, and she looked confident under the spotlight.

A smile stretched across Roland's face, and Peter knew he'd never get an answer. Caitlyn held his attention.

She'd colored her hair brown for the occasion, and it gave her a striking look. She wore a long blue dress patterned with stylized gold lilies (the French *fleur-de-lis*) and silver "armor" around her neck and waist. She was Saint Thérèse de Lisieux—who did not die a martyr—dressed as Saint Joan of Arc, who did.

"I want to play the part of Joan of Arc," Caitlyn as Saint Thérèse said to Kiara, who was dressed as a Carmelite nun. They both stood near a microphone on a stand and their voices carried through the surround sound. "Ever since I learned about her, I've longed to accomplish the most heroic deeds."

"Silly Thérèse, you are a Carmelite nun. You cannot rally troops or fight on battlefields."

"But the spirit of the Crusader burns within me." Caitlyn pressed her hands to her chest and gazed upward at the star-filled sky. "I long to die on the field of battle in defense of Holy Church."

"Sorry, Thérèse, the best you can hope for is to die on the grass of the cloister gardens, but I doubt any of the sisters will give you cause to die defending Holy Church."

Peter laughed aloud. "What a great line. Die on the grass of the . . ." He glanced at Roland, who sat spellbound.

"Oh, but I long to anyway. Come, put on this costume." Caitlyn lifted a silver vest and *wings*. "You can be Saint Michael the Archangel." She smiled playfully.

"So . . . she's playing a saint playing a saint?" Roland blinked.

"Uh, yeah." Peter was about to make a funny comment, but then he heard a familiar voice over his shoulder, someone saying, "Hey." As he turned to look at the speaker, an audible gasp escaped him and his camp chair tilted. With a less-than-smooth move, he jerked it back in place.

Brice stood at his side, the hint of a grin on her face and the light from the bonfire reflecting off her white-blond hair. "Why are you dorking out? You knew I was here. I saw you looking at me before lighting the bonfire."

"Hey, yeah, I'm just happy you're here." Heart hammering in his chest, he stood and gestured toward an empty camp chair next to his. He wanted to tell her how glad he was that she'd come and ask if she was staying the whole weekend, but no more words came out.

"Is that her?" Not appearing interested in taking a seat, Brice looked in Caitlyn's direction. "Her," she repeated as she tugged on the chain around her neck, lifting the Saint Joan of Arc medal out of her shirt.

"Huh?" Peter glanced from Brice to Caitlyn twice before he understood. "Oh, yeah, Caitlyn's pretending to be Saint Joan of Arc, or actually, she's pretending to be Saint Thérèse pretending to be . . . uh, never mind. Yeah, that's her."

Brice stared for another moment then nodded and said, "I looked her up online. Saint Joan of Arc. She was pretty cool. And not just because she dressed like a guy." She gave Peter a crooked grin.

Stunned that she'd actually researched a saint, it took Peter two seconds before he laughed. "You looked her up, huh?"

"Yeah. She had a lot of courage. All the way to the stake. I admire that. Makes me think there must be something to what she believed."

"Uh, wow." Peter found no words. A big balloon of hope floated up inside him.

"Yeah, and I just had a talk with Tessia. You know, it's not that I hate her. It's just when I see her, I think of my sister, and I know it's not Tessia's fault that she died. The roads were icy and a semitruck crossed the midline." She shook her head, a distant look in her eyes. "Anyway, losing my sister was hard for me to deal with. Tessia's the whole reason I didn't join Empowerment. Otherwise, I would've."

"Oh so . . . are you joining Empowerment?" The balloon of hope deflated, spiraling down, down, down . . .

"What?" One eye narrowed and her head jerked back. "No. Saint Joan of Arc and all you Fire Starters got me realizing I need to think about a few things." She took a few steps backwards then she smiled and took off again.

"Wow," Peter said, breathless, astonished, amazed, and regaining an ounce of hope. Curious to know where she was headed, Peter watched her go. She disappeared behind a group of kids and reappeared a moment later near a make-shift concession stand in the distance. Not sure he could he trust his eyes, he took a step back and blinked. Was she talking to Father Carston?

Clapping started and kids stood, blocking Peter's view. He turned in time to see Caitlyn and Kiara bow and wave and stumble to gather their props.

After their skit, kids took down the backdrop and revealed the next backdrop, a stylized outdoor scene with a moody sky, craggy mountains, and a few nondescript soldiers. Dominic came out with an acoustic guitar. He wore a traditional Mexican hat and a sash of ammunition draped across his chest. In the light of a single spotlight, he sat on a cooler and told the story of Saint Jose Sanchez del Rio. Between parts of the young martyr's life, he played the verse of a song he'd made up. Not sounding too bad.

The next two presenters rapped out the story of Saint Paul, Peter finding himself mildly jealous of their skills. Dominic and Fred worked the spotlights for their presentations, bouncing them around creatively.

Finally, after all the other skits and presentations, Roland stepped out alone onto a stage empty of all props, except for a noose that hung from an overhead branch. With a solid black backdrop behind him, he stood under the spotlight with one hand in the front pocket of his black jeans and the other clutching the cordless microphone. Then in the simplest way possible—and not looking out at the audience—Roland told the story of Saint Nicholas Pieck. His voice cracked a few times, as if the saint's story really spoke to him. Then he came to the dramatic conclusion, telling how Nicholas and the other priests were offered freedom in exchange for denying their faith.

Roland finally looked out at the audience, the spotlight making his eyes stand out. "Nicholas spoke for them all when he said, 'I would rather endure death for the honor of God . . .'" He froze and then swallowed hard. "'. . . than swerve even a hair's breadth from the Catholic faith.'"

He seemed to struggle a bit through the retelling of their martyrdom. But then again, a few people in the audience seemed to struggle with it too, judging by the sniffling that came from here and there. When he finally completed the story, he lowered the mic and bowed his head.

Enthusiastic applause turned into cheers, whistles, and a standing ovation.

Roland lifted his head and peeked out, the hint of a grin on his face.

"Encore," Peter shouted, knowing there would be none. Pride for his shy, little friend welled up inside him. After just one strange night, Roland had come a long way.

For an outcast.

33

VICTORY

SAINT NICHOLAS PIECK, pray for me. Help me get through this.
Roland took a deep breath and readied himself to step through the
door of speech class.

"Hey." Jarret came up behind Roland and whacked his arm.

With an exhale and welcoming the delay, Roland turned to him.
"What's up?"

One side of his mouth curled up as he grinned. "Heard a rumor
that you found your voice." His smile continued to grow and pride
showed in his eyes. "You found your attitude."

"What'd you hear?" Roland wasn't sure he wanted to know. It
was either about his presentation at the campground, which he'd
sort of messed up but got a lot of praise for anyway, or it was about
what he'd said to the Empowerment kids, which went over a lot
better than he'd hoped.

"You never told me what happened when I dropped you off in
Rapid City, had to hear it from the rumor mill."

Foster Mason, Dominic the chief gossiper's friend, shuffled past
Roland and Jarret and into the classroom. He and Roland were the
only two left to give their first speech.

"What you did took guts." Jarret stuck a thumb in his belt loop, his posture, attitude, and even the tilt of his head exuding confidence. "I don't think I'd even have done it."

"I guess I had something to say."

"Guess so." He gave Roland another crooked grin and tapped his shoulder with his fist. Then he walked backwards a few feet and said, "Prouddya."

Roland couldn't help but smile. Jarret was proud of him. Wow! Maybe he could keep that in mind as he struggled through his talk for speech class. And maybe he could keep Saint Nicholas Pieck in mind too.

Pulling his notecards from a back pocket, Roland stepped into the room just as the bell rang. Rather than write out the entire speech, he'd jotted down a few phrases and decided to simply speak from the heart. Hopefully, his mind wouldn't draw a blank as he stared at his fairly blank notecards.

Mrs. Kauffman called on Roland to go first. Foster exhaled and slumped back in his desk, his arms flopping to his sides.

Without allowing himself to hesitate, Roland got up from his seat. *Saint Nicholas Pieck, help me now.*

"You got this, man." Peter leaned across the aisle to bump Roland's fist.

"Good luck," Marshall whispered, twisting around to face him.

"Thanks, Marshall," Roland said aloud, slapping Marshall's back as he passed by, no longer embarrassed to call the boy with pink hair his friend. Brice, in the back corner of the room, had even thrown him a nod of encouragement.

Inspired by Brice's speech, which had little to do with herself, Roland had rewritten his speech to repeat some of the things he'd said to the Empowerment kids. Somehow the average white guy had become the bad guy and everyone else the victim. Wasn't that discrimination too? That had to change. And what about diversity of thought and belief? No more silencing people who disagreed or slamming someone because of their gender, faith, or race. It was time everyone embraced their right and responsibility to speak the truth, in charity, regardless of how others welcomed it.

Even though his temperature spiked and sweat dripped down his back, somehow—miraculously—the words poured out of him and they all seemed to fall into place and make sense. A few kids even made eye contact and nodded now and then, inspiring him to keep going with confidence.

Toward the end of his speech, a bit of fire had surged through his veins and the words came out with force. "We don't have to agree, and we ought to respect each other, but don't expect me to compromise truth because it makes someone uncomfortable."

Finished, he dropped his cards to the podium. He'd meant to tap them into place, but they'd fallen from his sweaty hands in a way that looked intentional, cool like a mic drop.

Everyone clapped, the kids in the back of the room chanted, "Ro-land, Ro-land, Ro-land!" And a few people reached out to bump his fist as he strode back to his desk. Without the limp.

Roland suppressed a grin. He'd done it. He'd conquered his debilitating fear of speaking. Not that he'd offer to give a speech if he didn't have to.

But now he could focus on his next task: preparing for Confirmation. He'd never even thought about it until Keefe brought it up last night after returning from the discernment retreat. The three of them had missed receiving the sacrament. After Mama had passed away, Papa had taken a step back from faith, and now they all had to catch up.

He liked the idea of picking a Confirmation saint. For the past year, Saint Conrad of Parzham had been his favorite. Now he really liked Saint Nicholas Pieck too. But maybe he'd keep researching and find another saint he liked just as much. The saints seemed to help him in ways he'd never imagined possible. What would he conquer next?

Sometimes you can't stay silent.
No matter what others think.
No matter who hates you for speaking.
No matter the label they give you.
No matter what friends you lose.
Because the truth is important. The truth is a person.
Jesus Christ.

RESOURCES

www.truthandlove.com - a Catholic resource for anyone seeking the tools to accompany our brothers and sisters who experience same-sex attraction.

In Pursuit: Confessions of a Gay Catholic Teenager by Christina Mead - a powerful tool for you and your teens. Besides AJ's autobiography, this book includes over 20 pages of questions and answers based on his story, and on common misconceptions about the Catholic Church's teaching on sexuality, love, and marriage.

Did you enjoy this book? If so, help others enjoy it, too! Please recommend it to friends and leave a review when possible. Thank you!

I send out a newsletter regularly so that you can keep up with my newest releases and enjoy updates, contests, and more. Visit my website www.theresalinden.com to sign up. And while you're there, check out my book trailers and extras!

Facebook: https://www.facebook.com/theresalindenauthor/
Twitter: https://twitter.com/LindenTheresa

ABOUT THE AUTHOR

Theresa Linden is the author of award-winning *Roland West, Loner* and *Battle for His Soul*, from her series of Catholic teen fiction. An avid reader and writer since grade school, she grew up in a military family. Moving every few years left her with the impression that life is an adventure. Her Catholic faith inspires the belief that there is no greater adventure than the reality we can't see, the spiritual side of life. She hopes that the richness, depth, and mystery of the Catholic faith will spark her readers' imaginations, making them more aware of the invisible realities and the power of faith and grace. A member of the Catholic Writers Guild and the International Writers Association, Theresa lives in northeast Ohio with her husband, three boys, and one dog.

Printed in Great Britain
by Amazon

40848932R00169